LONDONGRAD

Reggie Nadelson, journalist and film-maker, is the author of eight novels, all but one of them featuring her New York detective Artie Cohen. Her non-fiction book about Dean Reed, *Comrade Rockstar*, is being filmed by Tom Hanks and Dreamworks. She divides her time between London and New York.

LONDONGRAD

REGGIE NADELSON

Atlantic Books

London

First published in Great Britain in
trade paperback in 2009 by Atlantic Books,
an imprint of Grove/Atlantic Ltd.

Copyright © Reggie Nadelson, 2009

1 3 5 7 9 10 8 6 4 2

A CIP catalogue record for this book is available from the British Library.

ISBN: 978 1 84354 833 1

Printed in Great Britain by the MPG Books Group

Atlantic Books
An imprint of Grove Atlantic Ltd
Ormond House
26–27 Boswell Street
London
WC1N 3JZ

www.atlantic-books.co.uk

For Alice, my best friend and sister

If I had to choose between betraying my country and betraying my friend, I hope I should have the guts to betray my country.

E. M. Forster, *Two Cheers for Democracy*

"I'm dead," says Anatoly Sverdloff, gasping for air, lungs shot. He whispers this in Russian, in English, the crazy mixture he speaks, but stumbling, gulping to get air in, trawling for oxygen, voice so small, you can hardly hear him. He can't breathe. His heart is killing him, he says, pushing the words out in short helpless bursts.

Medics, nurses, other people crowd around the bed, a whole mob of them, shaking their heads to indicate there's no hope.

Hooked up to machines, thick transparent corrugated tubes, blue, white, pushing air into him, expelling the bad stuff. IVs stuck in his arms trail up to clear plastic sacks of medicine on a metal stand. He wears a sleeveless hospital gown that's too short.

On his back, this huge man, six foot six, normally three hundred pounds, but seeming suddenly shrunken, like the carcass of a beached whale. Only the dimples in the large square face that resembles an Easter Island statue make him recognizable.

Somewhere, on a CD, schlocky music is playing, music will help, somebody says, and a voice cries out, no, not that, put on Sinatra, he loves Sinatra. Or opera. Italian. Verdi. Whose voice is crying out? Tolya's? No one is listening.

More doctors and nurses bundled up in white paper suits like spacemen come and go. But there's no reason for it, no radioactive poison in him, why are you dressed like that? the voice says. Everybody has a white mask on, and white paper hats. Party hats. Somebody is blowing a red party whistle. People wander in and out of the room, some lost, others looking for the festivities. The guy is dead, somebody says, there's no party.

1

A single shoe, yellow alligator, big gold buckle dull from dust, is near the bed, just lying there. Somebody picks it up. His massive feet sticking out from a blanket are the gray of some prehistoric mammal, as if Tolya is returning to a primitive form, the disease eating him from the inside out.

And then he's dead.

He's in a coffin, for viewing, and he turns into Stalin, the enormous head, the hair, the mustache, the large nostrils, why Stalin? Why? Or is it Yeltsin? Big men. Big Russian men.

My best friend is dying, and I can't stop it, and he says, Artie, help me, and then he's dead, and I start to cry. Stop the music, I yell. Turn it off! Suddenly I have to sit down on a chair in the hospital room because I can't breathe anymore. Somebody tries to stick a tube in my nose but I fight back. The tubes trip me, I'm tangled in clear plastic tubes, falling.

He rips off the tubes, pulls out the lifelines, the IVs, and all he says is, "I knew Sasha Litvinenko. I met him, and they killed him and nobody remembers the poor bastard anymore."

PART ONE
NEW YORK

CHAPTER ONE

From behind the bar at his club in the West Village, Tolya Sverdloff looked up and saw me.

"Artie, good morning, how are you, have something to drink, or maybe a cup of good coffee, and we'll talk, I need a little favor, maybe you can help me out?" All this came out of his mouth fast, in a single sentence, as if he couldn't cram enough good things into it if he stopped for breath.

In the streaming shafts of morning sunlight coming in through a pair of big windows, he resembled a saint in stained glass, but a very secular saint, a glass of red wine in one hand, a Havana in the other and an expression of huge pleasure on his face. He stuck his nose in the glass, he swirled it and sniffed, and drank, and saw me watching.

"Oh, man, this is it," he said. "This is everything, a reason to be alive. Come taste this," added Tolya and poured some wine into a second glass. "A fantastic Ducru. I'll give you a bottle," he said. "As a reward."

I sat on one of the padded leather stools at his bar. "What for?"

"For coming by at this hour when I call you," said Tolya, who tasted the wine again and smiled, showing the dimples big enough for a child to stick its fist in. He brushed the thick black hair from his forehead, and rolled his eyes with pleasure at the wine, this big effusive generous guy, a voluptuary. Wine and food were his redemption, he always said.

"So what do you need that you got me here at the fucking crack of dawn on my first day of vacation?" I said. "I'll take that coffee."

He held up a hand. Some opera came in over the sound system. "Maria Callas," said Tolya. "*Traviata*. My God, has there ever been a Violetta like that?"

While he listened, I looked at the framed Soviet posters on the wall, including an original Rodchenko for *The Battleship Potemkin*, and wondered how the hell he had got hold of it.

"Coffee?"

"Try the wine," he said. "You should really come into business with me, you know, Artie. We could have so much fun, you could run this place, or we could open another one, you could make a little money. Anyhow, you're too old to play cops and robbers."

"I'm a New York City detective, it's not a game," I said. "You met somebody? You sound like you're in love."

"Don't be so pompous," said Tolya and we both burst out laughing.

"Yeah, I know."

"You working anything, Artemy?" He used my Russian name.

Like me, Tolya Sverdloff grew up in Moscow. I got out when I was sixteen, got to New York, cut all my ties, dumped my past as fast as I could. He had a place over there, and one in England. Tolya was a nomad now, London, New York, Russia. He had opened clubs in all of them.

"I am on vacation as of yesterday," I said. "Off the job for ten fantastic days, no homicides pending, no crazy Russians in need of my linguistic services." I stretched and yawned, and drank some more of the wine. It wasn't even nine in the morning. Who cares, I thought. The wine was delicious.

Tolya lifted his glass. "My birthday next week," he said.

"Happy birthday."

"So you'll come to my party?"

"Sure. Where?"

"In London," he said.

"You know I worked a case there once. It left a bad taste."

"You're wrong. Is fantastic city, Artemy."

I drank some more wine.

"Best city, most civilized."

Whenever he talked about London these days, it was to tell me how wonderful it was. But he described it as a tourist might— the parks, the theaters, the pretty places. I knew that he had, along with his club there, other business. He didn't tell me about it, I didn't ask.

He put his glass down. "Oh, God, I love the smell of the Médoc in the morning, Artyom," said Tolya, switching from English to Russian.

Tolya's English depended on the occasion. As a result of an education at Moscow's language schools, he spoke it beautifully, with a British accent. Drunk, or what he sometimes called "party mood", his language was his own invention, a mix of Russian and English, low and high, the kind he figured uneducated people speak—the gangsters, the nouveau riche Russians. He taunted me constantly. He announced, once in a while, that he knew I thought all Russkis were thugs, or Neanderthals. "You think this, Artemy," he said.

His Russian, when he bothered, though, was so pure, so soft, it made me feel my soul was being stroked. Like his father spoke when he was alive, Tolya told me once. His father had been trained as an actor. Singer, too. Paul Robeson complimented his father when his father was still a student. He had the voice, my pop did, said Tolya.

"You said you need a favor?"

"Just to take some books to an old lady in Brooklyn, okay?" Tolya put a shopping bag on the bar. "You don't mind? Sure sure sure?"

He already knew I'd do what he wanted without asking. It

was his definition of a friend. He believed only in the Russian version of friends, not like Americans, he says, who call everybody friends. "My best friend, they say," he hooted mockingly.

"I would go myself," said Tolya, "but I have two people who didn't show up last night. Which a little bit annoys me because I am very nice with my staff. I pay salary also tips, unlike many clubs and restaurants."

It was one of Sverdloff's beefs that most staff at the city's restaurants were paid minimum wage and made their money on tips. "I hate this system," he said. "In Spain it is civilized, in Spain, waiters are properly paid," he added and I could see he was starting on his usual riff.

"Right," I said, feeling the wine in my veins like liquid pleasure. "Of course, Tolya. You are the nicest boss in town."

"Do not laugh at me, Artyom," he said. "I am very good socialist in capitalist drag."

Tolya had called his club Pravda2, because there was already a bar named Pravda, which the owner, very nice English guy but stubborn, Tolya said, had refused to sell him. Club named Pravda must belong to Russian guy, Tolya said. English guy won't sell me his, I open my own.

Pravda2, Artie, you get it?

You like the pun, Artie? You get it? Yeah, I get it, Tol, I'd say, Truth Too, *In Vino Veritas*, blah blah, you're the fountainhead of all that is true, you, in the wine, I get it.

Originally, he'd planned on making P2, as he called it, a champagne bar he'd run for his friends, to entertain them, and where he would only sell Krug. He added a few dishes, and got himself a line to a supplier with very good caviar, and a food broker, a pretty girl, who could get excellent foie gras, he told me.

To his surprise, it was a success. He was thrilled. He gave in to his own lust for red wine, big reds, he calls them, and only

French, the stuff that costs a bundle. And cognac. Some vodkas.

I wasn't a wine drinker. People who loved it bored the shit out of me, but sometimes Sverdloff got me over in the afternoon when the wine salesmen come around and we spent hours tasting stuff. Some of them were truly great. Like the stuff I was having for breakfast that morning.

Tolya saw himself, he had told me the other evening, as an impresario of the night. I said he was a guy with a bar.

He liked to discuss the wines, not to mention the vodka he got made for him special in Siberia that he kept in a frozen silver decanter. He went to Mali last January to visit his Tuareg silversmith. He stayed for a month. Fell in love with the music.

Sverdloff liked the idea of the rare piece of silver, the expensive wine, liked to think of himself as a connoisseur. It's just potatoes, I said. Potatoes. Vodka is a bunch of fermented spuds, I told him.

"So you'll take the books for me?" Tolya said.

"Give me the address." I finished the wine in my glass.

"They're for Olga Dimitriovna, you remember, you took some books before, the older lady in Starrett City? She likes you, she always says, please say hello to your friend. I got them special from our mutual friend, Dubi, in Brighton Beach, very good editions, Russian novels, a whole set of Turgenev," he added, and picked up his half-pound of solid gold Dunhill lighter with the cigar engraved, a ruby for the glowing tip. He flicked it and relit his Cohiba.

"Of course."

"Thank you for this, Artie, honest. It is only these books, and some wine, but this lady depends, you know?" He put his hand into the pocket of his custom-made black jeans, and extracted a wad of bills held together with a jeweled money clip. "Look, put this inside one of the books. She won't take money, but I know she needs."

I took the dough.

"I would go myself if I could," he said.

"Yeah, yeah, and how would you ever find Brooklyn anyhow?" I picked up the bottle and poured a little more wine in my glass.

"So you'll go now, I mean, you're waiting for what, *MooDllo*?" he said, his term of affectionate abuse, a word that doesn't translate into English but comes from "modal" that once meant a castrated ram but moved on to mean a stupendously stupid person. An asshole was maybe the right word, but in Russian much more affectionate, much dirtier. He glanced at his watch.

"What's the hurry?"

My elbows on the bar, I was slowly winding down into a vacation mode, thinking of things I'd do, sleep late, listen to music, some fishing off of Montauk, maybe ride my bike over the George Washington Bridge, see a few movies, take in a ball game, dinner out with some pals, maybe dinner with Valentina though I didn't mention it to Tolya. He was crazy about his daughter, Val, and so was I. If Tolya knew how much, he'd rip my arms out. She was his kid, she was half my age.

"Pour me a little more of that wine, will you?" I said.

"Just go."

"I hear you. I'm going."

"You'll come by tonight?" said Tolya.

"Sure."

"Good."

I was halfway out the door, when I heard Tolya behind me.

"Artemy?" He stood on the sidewalk in front of Pravda2, and held his face up to the hot sun. He waved at a delivery guy, he smiled at a couple of kids on skateboards. He was lord of this little domain, he owned it, it was his community. I envied him.

"What's that?"

He hesitated.

"You used to know a guy named Roy Pettus?"

"Sure. Ex-Feeb. Worked the New York FBI office back when, I knew him some, worked a case, a dozen years, more maybe, around the time we met, you and me."

"I don't remember," said Tolya. "Anyhow, he was in here, asking about you."

"When?"

"Last night after you left."

"Pettus? What did he want?"

Tolya shrugged. "Came in wearing a suit, said he wanted a glass of wine, didn't drink it, didn't look like a guy who knows his Pauillac from his Dr Pepper. Made a little conversation with me. Asked about you."

"What about?"

"How you were, were you still working Russian jobs," said Tolya, "How's your facility with the lingo. Doesn't ask straight out, but kind of hangs around. Tells me we met at your wedding, knows you got divorced. Pretends he is just making conversation, but what the fuck is a guy in a suit like that doing in my club? I got the feeling it was why he dropped by, wanting to ask about you."

"Why didn't he just call me?"

"What do I know? Maybe he's just some old spook who likes playing the game, what do they call it, tradecraft?" said Tolya laughing and making spooky noises and laughing some more. "Well, as my daughter says, whatevs, right?'

"Yeah, right. Last I heard Roy Pettus retired home to Wyoming."

I headed for my car at the curb. I had gotten it washed in time for vacation, and it looked beautiful, gleaming and red, the ancient Caddy convertible. I climbed in, put the Erroll Garner disc into the slot, and turned the key.

"Think about coming into the business with me, okay?" Tolya called out.

Already I was listening to the joyous music of *Concert by*

the Sea, but I took in what Tolya said. Every month or so, when he asked me again, more and more I thought: why not go in with Sverdloff? Why not take him up on it, a trip to London, a chance for a new life, stop chasing fuckwits who murder people? Maybe it was time.

"Don't get lost in Brooklyn," Tolya called out, grinned and waved me away.

CHAPTER TWO

If I had gone straight to Brooklyn from Tolya's, if I had not stopped at home to grab some swim shorts and call Valentina, maybe I could have avoided the whole damn thing, maybe I would have avoided the little kid, yelling and waving, mouth open in an O with a howl coming out.

By the time I saw her, as she darted into the street, I was a second away from running her down, from killing her. Sweat covered my face, ran down the back of my neck. The bag on the seat next to me fell on the floor, books tumbled out, the books I was taking to the old lady for Tolya.

I slammed on the brakes. I got out of my car in the middle of the street. There wasn't much traffic out here in this dismal corner of the city, but a few cars were honking now, and I yelled at them and grabbed her up, the kid who was yelling, and sat her down on the curb. It was a warm dry day, gusts of wind coming off the water half a mile away. Balls of newspaper and dust rolled along the nearly empty street. It was a holiday. July 4.

On the broken sidewalk out here at the edge of Brooklyn, where it butts up against Queens, I put my arm around the kid in the dirty pink t-shirt and tried to get her to talk to me.

After a while, she calmed down some, and started talking in a tiny voice and I realized she was a Russian kid. I asked her name. Dina, she mumbled, and pulled at me, and I followed her across the street, which was lined with ramshackle houses, some of the windows broken and covered with plywood and plastic. In one of the yards weeds had grown up over the skeleton of an old Mercedes. There was garbage everywhere. A desolate place, fifteen miles from the middle of Manhattan.

Dina ducked under some rough bushes. In front of us was a gate to an old playground surrounded by chain-link fencing. There was a padlock on the gate. A piece of the fence was missing and Dina got on her belly and crawled under it. I followed her into a wasteland of overgrown weeds and grass, used needles, empty bottles. It was silent, a thick, dead silence, except for something creaking, a low raw sound I couldn't identify.

The jungle gym was broken. The sandbox was empty, no sand to play in. Dina was silent now, too, she had stopped babbling, stopped talking. Then she lifted one skinny arm and pointed and I followed her gaze and saw it, a figure on a swing. It was the source of the noise, the raw creak, the metal chains grinding against the poles where the swing hung.

Wrapped in silver duct tape that glinted dully in the morning light, the figure – probably a woman – was sitting on the swing, arms tied to the chains with rope, a harsh wind moving her back and forth. Or maybe it was her own weight that propelled her as she went to and fro, back and forth, on the swing in the deserted playground in Brooklyn.

"When did you find this?" I said in Russian as softly as I could, though there was nobody else here.

"Is she dead? She is dead?" said Dina, and then suddenly broke away from me, and ran out of the playground, head down, too fast for me to catch her, a blur of skinny legs and arms and pink shirt.

I called it in, and went back to the swings.

I caught the body and held her still. She was heavy. She seemed to lean against me. I stumbled and tripped and fell on my knees. A broken bottle cut me and blood stained my ankle.

The feel of the greasy duct tape dank from humidity made me want to gag. I could feel this was flesh under the tape, that this had been a woman.

I've been a cop a long time, twenty years, more, but this was so surreal, for a second I thought I was hallucinating. I didn't know what to do, not when the body against me seemed to breathe in and out of its own accord.

Was she still alive?

From above came the sound of a solitary plane; piercing the blue sky over the city, it came in low over the Jamaica Wetlands on its way into JFK.

I had to know what was under the tape.

Holding the body still with one arm, I lifted a small section of tape off the face. The tape rasped against the skin. It had been crudely done. The tape came away easily. I touched the skin near the nose lightly, and I saw one of her eyes and thought I felt it flutter, as if it might suddenly open.

She was dead. I never was an expert on physical death but she had been on the swing a long time, far as I could tell.

Wrapped up first? Dead first?

I wanted to beat it, get out, go back on vacation, but I had to wait for help. I didn't want some other kid like Dina stumbling in here and seeing this.

Listening for sirens. Wishing I had a cigarette. Sweating in the hot sun, all I could do now was wait.

I didn't know what else to do so I sat on the swing next to her. Together, the dead woman and me, we swung back and forth, to and fro, like kids early in the morning with nobody else to see them.

Behind me was the sound of sirens, of voices, of footsteps. I got up off the swing, turned and saw them coming, a small army trooping onto the playground.

Somebody had removed the gate so the ambulance people

could get through. Uniforms, detectives, forensics people, all of them streamed in. It was like a tribal ceremony, the woman wrapped in silver tape on the ground now, everyone else moving around her in a ritual dance.

I spotted Bobo Leven, a young detective who was Russian-born. I went over and told him what I knew and then I started out of the playground. Bobo tried to follow me. I told him it wasn't my case. I happened to be around, but I was leaving. He wanted my help, but I said I was sorry, I had to go, I was on vacation.

"Good luck with the case," I said finally, shaking loose of Bobo Leven, hurrying away now as a couple of photographers from forensics brushed past me to take more pictures of the corpse like the paparazzi of the dead.

CHAPTER THREE

On the wall of Olga Dimitriovna's place were three photographs, black and white pictures of children staring straight at the camera, and she saw me look at them as soon as I entered the apartment.

"Yes, you imagine these were taken by Valentina Sverdloff, isn't that right?"

I nodded.

"Please, come in, Artemy Maximovich," she said, a wiry woman about eighty, sharp as a bird, with a humorous face who was crazy about reading, especially novels. I placed the bag Tolya had given me on a table, and she took one out and admired it.

"So, tea? Coffee? A sandwich also? You are hungry, Artemy Maximovich?" She went into the tiny kitchen to prepare food.

I put my head through the kitchen door and said I'd have a sandwich with my coffee. I wasn't hungry, but I knew she was a solitary old lady who wanted me to stay a while and talk. I didn't remember the photographs.

"Valentina gave them to me, a month ago, I think."

"You know Val?"

"Of course. For a time she comes to me for her Russian lessons. But not lately. The photographs are of children at her orphanage in Moscow."

"What orphanage?"

"Where she gives money," said Olga. "I think perhaps not an orphanage but a shelter for girls. Please say hello. Please, sit down," she added.

The apartment was small, the furniture old. Olga still gave Russian lessons, she had told me, but the money wasn't much. From a radio came a Beethoven sonata.

Out of the window here on the sixteenth floor, I could almost see the playground where I'd just been. In the other direction were the nineteen brick buildings of the Boulevard Public Housing project. I could see the vast Linden Houses, too, tens of thousands of people stacked up in scores of towers and below them the tangle of urban outlands and inner suburbia, bagel stores and storefront churches, squat low synagogues, C-Town supermarkets, Chinese restaurants with bulletproof windows, makeshift mosques, Indian takeouts. And the water, the Jamaica Wetlands, the network of wild islands where water-birds congregate and the dirty strip of beach where gulls pick over garbage for their breakfast.

I love the water. I used to go out on the party boats from Sheepshead Bay and fish for stripers and blues. A few miles away from where I stood is a secret place I go sometimes, a nice tavern at the edge of the wildlife sanctuary, where you meet other cops and fire guys, Irish mostly; you drink some beers or Guinness and there's a breeze and it smells unbelievably sweet.

My phone was ringing, but I turned it off and sat with Olga Dimitriovna and ate my fried-egg sandwich and chatted in Russian. She told me there had been three muggings in her building. I told her to keep her door locked at night and the chain on, and I gave her my cell number.

"Anatoly Anatolyevich Sverdloff is a good man," she said. "He gives to everybody. Please say thank you." Olga pushed her wire-rim spectacles on top of her head, thanked me again, and offered me a glass of brandy. I refused.

"Please, come back, Artemy," she said. "And tell Valentina

to come." She kissed my cheek, papery lips against my skin, and handed me a box of chocolates, which she had wrapped carefully with fancy gold paper and a red ribbon. "For Mr Sverdloff who sends me the books. You'll give this to him?"

"Yes, of course," I said.

"Tell Valentina I miss her, please."

"Is there anything else I can do for you?"

She shook her head. "But maybe I will call you for help with some of my neighbors. They are afraid."

"Of the muggings?"

"Of everything, crime, black people, of the new kind of Russians, of anything different, of a feeling that they may have to move again, or leave America. Most are legal, but they are afraid. They pull down their blinds and pray to God," she added. "Except God isn't listening. So some of us fight instead. We fight landlords. We remember how to fight. Goodbye, again, Artemy."

As I walked along the corridor of Dimitriovna's floor, I could hear classical music from behind the doors. Doors opened a crack, mostly old people looking out to see who it was, and if it was safe, and seeing other tenants looking out of their apartments, greeted each other in Russian, and fixed social arrangements for cards and tea. One elderly man held the door open long enough to take a good look at me.

"Who are you?" he said in English with a thick accent. "What do you want?" He was angry, I could see he felt I was some kind of interloper, somebody without any real business up here. Maybe he figured me for a developer.

Decades back, these high-rise towers had been built to house immigrants, forty bucks per room back then. They were almost trashed in the 1980s by gangs and guns, and people bolted their doors and rarely went out.

Now the crack dealer creeps had gone the place was threatened instead by Trump, or some other feral developer: take it over, raise the rents, blow it up, co-op it. Looked like by fall the deal would be done.

But Olga Dimitriovna and her friends weren't going to budge easy, not without a fight, not after they'd made a life, a village up on the sixteenth floor, the old-timers helping the new ones, everybody in and out of each other's apartments, sitting out on nice days on green and yellow plastic deckchairs, as if the sidewalk in front was a front porch; or making trips over to Brighton Beach to shop or eat on special occasions or maybe to the 92nd Street Y in Manhattan for music once a year.

They would resist. They would organize. If necessary, they would fight. They had survived everything else. Stalin, Hitler. Coming to America.

But even here, thousands of miles from Moscow, people were paranoid. Russia was hot as hell, in several senses, and now Putin was rattling his nukes, and people were secretly thinking: will America bend to these people? Will they cut off the stream of Russian immigrants? Will they listen to Lou Dobbs, the asshole on CNN who rants about immigrants every night? Even Russians with American passports, think: will I have to move again? Where will I go?

Near the elevator, I turned on my cellphone.

"Who is it?" I said, but the signal was dead.

I banged on the elevator door. Where was it?

Some of the tenants reappeared in the hall and watched until the elevator came and I went away. Ingrained in them was a deep suspicion, even hatred, of cops. Somehow they knew I was a cop, or suspected it. I realized I was still carrying the fancy box of chocolates and in the heat, I could smell them. I got into the elevator, feeling somebody was on my back. I opened the chocolates. I ate one. It had a nut in it.

CHAPTER FOUR

I was still holding the chocolates when I left the building, and as I got to my car, I thought I saw the kid, the Russian girl, Dina.

"Hey!"

I ran after her. Maybe I was wrong. Maybe it was the hot sun in my eyes. I ran until my lungs burned. I caught her near a wire fence that divided the street from a water-plant facility, and a stretch of filthy beach.

When she saw me, she stopped. She hadn't been running away from me.

"Why were you running?"

"I was looking for somebody," she said in Russian.

"Who?"

"Nobody."

We were outside a broken-down housing project. Some of the little yellow tiles had fallen off the façade, like scabs off a half-healed wound.

"You live here?"

She shrugged.

"You want to tell me something?"

"Yes."

I looked at her. "You're hungry?"

She nodded and I took her into a bodega on the other side of the street and bought her a ham sandwich and a Coke and a bag of Fritos and watched her eat all of it without stopping. I wondered when she had her last meal. All the time I was with her, she stared at the box of chocolate. I gave it to her. She shoved the candy into her mouth.

"Where do you live? Will you show me?"

"I have something," said Dina, clutching her fist shut.

"Show me."

When she opened her hand, she had a thin silver chain with a blue ceramic evil-eye charm in light blue and white.

"Where did you get this?"

"In the playground," she said.

I waited.

"Will you give me money for it?" She looked up at me and her eyes were like a desperate little animal.

"Why should I?"

"I got it from the playground. I got it near the swing."

"You took it from her?"

"No. I picked it up."

"How much?"

"One hundred."

"No way," I said in Russian. "No deal."

"Fifty." She was tiny and hungry and scared and an easy mark. The necklace wasn't worth five bucks.

"I'll give you twenty-five," I said and she lit up like somebody had turned a switch.

I gave her some bills with one hand while I called a friend, a good female cop I know who would come and help me get the kid to a safe place.

"I want to go home," she said.

I held on to her as best I could, but as soon as she felt me loosen my grip—I couldn't handcuff her or anything—she broke away, same as earlier, just broke free and ran like hell and disappeared among the broken buildings.

*

"Artie?" It was Bobo Leven, the detective who had answered the call on the playground case. He was leaning against the jungle gym smoking. I looked at the swings. The body was gone.

"Yeah, hi, Bobo."

"You got my message?"

"I got it. I'm in a hurry, so what do you need?"

"Thanks for coming."

"Yeah, sure," I said. Bobo looked anxious. "You'll do the case fine, Bobo, you'll make your name with it."

His real name was Boris Borisovich Leven, but everyone called him Bobo. He was twenty-eight and smart as hell, having finished Brooklyn College in three years instead of four, followed by his MA at John Jay in criminology. He was still living at home these days, out on Brighton Beach with his parents.

And he knew the Russkis out there as well as anyone in the city, including me. Also, his mother, who ran a little export-import business from the house—Russian embroidery, varnished boxes, cheap porcelain, that kind of shit—went back and forth a lot, so he had a handle on what was doing over there. Bobo had cousins every place: LA, London, Miami, Los Angeles, Moscow, Tel Aviv.

At six four, with the kind of long springy muscles you get if you work out right, he played good basketball. He had an accent, but he was a handsome kid with nice manners, and when I needed a favor, he was always ready.

I had worked with Bobo Leven a few times. And once, I took him out drinking with a couple of the guys, and he loved the tribal aspect of it, the fact you could say things you couldn't say to anyone else in language you could never divulge to civilians. He knew there were things that only other guys on the job understood. They liked him okay. But one of my oldest friends said to me, "He looks nice, he acts respectful, but I don't trust him much."

*

A couple of hazmat guys, white paper suits, yellow rubber boots, showed up and started working over the playground, taking samples of dirt, looking at their Geiger counters, whispering to each other through their masks, and Bobo, seeing them, looked nervous.

"What are they here for?"

One of the guys removed his mask and I recognized him from a job I did once. Couldn't remember his name, and he was older and heavier, but the face was the same. I went over and talked to him out of Bobo's hearing. I didn't want him getting in the way. The wind puffed out the papery white hazmat suit.

"What's going on?"

"Somebody thought the scene could be hot," said Tom Alvin, name on his badge. "They always think a scene is hot, you know, man, I mean, it's an obsession, they find a case, they send us in, and what the fuck difference does it make, you know? They're consumed, man, with the idea of a dirty bomb. They read too much shit in the papers, you know, like that spy thing over in England, what was his name, the Russian dude that got poisoned? You heard about that? Some kind of radiation shit, but it was like a couple of years ago. Man, we better all pray McCain gets elected, he's like a regular fucking war hero and if we get trouble, he's the guy." He paused. "You wanna know what they should do?"

"What's that?"

"They should stop seeing movies that got nothing to do with what's going on, all them big thrillers with nuclear shit in them, and worth nothing, nada, zero. They should spend some money inspecting container ships, and the baggage holds of all those aircraft from crazy places, how about hospital waste, how about them nuke plants that got no controls? But we don't got no money for that, right, man? It's coming, but not like this in some fucking playground, or in somebody's sushi like the guy in London. One day, it'll just come outta the sky, bang, like the

24

Trade Center, bing bang boom!" He snorted, threw his smoke on the ground, crushed it with his foot and put his mask back on. "Artie, right?"

"Yeah."

"You working this?"

"No, just passing by."

"Didn't you work a nuke case way back in the day, out by Brighton Beach? You tracked some nuke mule who carried stuff out of Russia in his suitcase? I remember that. With some of those fucking Russkis, right?"

"Yeah," I said.

"So you think you got something here?" I gestured at the swing.

"I'm not sure. You want me to give you a call?"

I nodded in Bobo's direction. "Call him, if you want."

"What did the hazmat guy say?" Bobo asked.

"Give him your number, he'll call you."

"So would you work this with me, Artie?"

I told him I was seriously on vacation.

"I can call you for some advice?" He was polite, but I didn't feel comfortable with this guy. Maybe all he wanted was to do the case right, but there was something I couldn't explain. I wanted to get away.

"Or maybe we could have a beer together once in a while and I could talk through it with you?"

"Sure," I said, and headed for the street, Bobo following me, scribbling in his notebook fast as he could write.

Outside the playground, I leaned against Bobo's red Audi TT and wondered how he could afford it.

"Nice car," I said.

"Thanks."

"So what do you think?" said Bobo, dragging in smoke the way only a Russian guy can do it.

"I don't know," I said.

"Me either. I mean, Artie, you been on the job all this time, and who the fuck tapes up some poor girl and leaves her to suffocate in this shitty place?"

"I don't know, Bobo, I don't know who likes making people feel pain."

"You're wondering if they taped her up before she was dead?" said Bobo.

"I have to go," I said. "Keep in touch."

"A guy once told me once you get close to a case, you can't let go, isn't that right? Artie?"

"He was probably drunk," I said. "You don't know anything about me."

CHAPTER FIVE

Stacks of pink cold cuts lay on trays, little mountains of cubed cheese, orange, yellow, white, carrot sticks, candy bars, bagels, rolls, pastries that glistened, shiny under the lights, were arranged on platters, and NYPD guys in uniform were gobbling up food as fast as they could, as if they didn't know where their next meal was coming from, shoving food into their mouths, piling it high on paper plates. The long tables were set up outside the sound stage.

"Craft Services, they call it," said Sonny Lippert, my ex-boss, when I found him at the Steiner Movie Studios where the old Brooklyn Shipyards had been.

He picked up his plate and sauntered out into the courtyard, and I followed him. He sat on a canvas directors' chair and gestured to another one. I sat next to him.

I wanted his advice before I saw Bobo Leven again. The dead girl wasn't my case, it was Leven's, but I couldn't let it go. The image of the girl on the swing stayed with me like floaters that stick in your eye, float on the surface of your brain, clog your vision. Some guy had told Leven when I got close to a case I couldn't let it go, but that was crap. I was happy to turn it over to Leven. I was curious was all. I had seen the girl on the swing first and I was curious.

Or was I fooling myself? Had I become some kind of obsessive, one of those cops who can't get the smell of a homicide out of his nose?

It wasn't that I planned to work the case, I only wanted advice. Any information I got I'd pass on. Anyhow, I owed Sonny Lippert a visit. I hadn't seen much of him lately.

"So, Artie, good to see you, it's been a while," said Sonny, who was wearing a captain's uniform, the kind of dress blues guys wore to funerals. I had never in my life seen Lippert dressed as a cop. Almost all the years I'd known him, it was after he left the police force to work as a US attorney.

"What's with the outfit?" I said to Lippert who had been my boss on and off for years until he retired.

"Nifty, right," said Sonny, smoothing his navy blue jacket. "Fits me nice, right? I sucked up to the wardrobe lady, man. These people are cool. Listen, man, you want to go hear Ahmad Jamal with me in the fall, one of the last of the greats, man?" he said.

Long ago Sonny and me had started listening to music together. He still calls everyone "man", a leftover from his younger years when he hung out with jazz guys. He still listened to the music with real love.

When I was still a rookie and broke, he sometimes invited me to concerts at Carnegie Hall and sometimes to the Vanguard. It was with Sonny I first heard Miles Davis in person, and Stan Getz, and Ella.

"What the hell are you supposed to be?" I said, smiling because I suddenly felt affectionate towards Sonny.

"I'm a police captain, man," he said, buttering a roll he had on the plate on his lap. "I'm an extra. The movie I'm working. I'm a consultant. I told you. Didn't I?"

All around us real cops and fake movie cops, both, smoked and ate. One guy bit off half of an enormous sesame bagel stuffed with cream cheese and lox, tossed the other half in a garbage can and began kicking a soccer ball around the huge yard of Steiner Studios. Beyond the yard that was surrounded by a high chain-link fence, twelve, fourteen feet, was the old waterfront. With the staggering view of Manhattan and the river, once all this had been the Brooklyn Navy Yards where World War II ships were built.

"What do you know, you haven't been a cop since Shaft was in action," I kidded him, drinking my root beer.

"I sit around all day and actors come by and we shoot the shit about being a detective, and I tell them how to walk and talk, make it look real."

"How the fuck do you know how cops walk and talk?"

"It's not brain science, you know, Artie, man. One of the producers, so-called, said to me, you have that authority thing, Sonny. You got it. Teach them." He laughed. "I tell them how it is, then they go and put the girls in low-cut tops and tight pants. I mean, what female detective is going to fucking dress like that in real life? Or maybe they do now. Maybe the real ones get how they dress from the TV cops," said Sonny, heading into one of his riffs. "Truth is nobody knows what's real anymore," he added. "A lot of actual cops I know have stopped using the old lingo. Once civilians started picking up stuff from *Law and Order*, you know, bus for ambulance or on the job for being a cop, guys started dropping it. Hard to tell the difference, right, man? Reality and fiction, man, who can tell?"

"Jesus, Sonny."

"So you came by to chew the fat, shoot the breeze, what, Artie?"

Sonny sat back on his canvas chair and looked me over.

Small and tightly wound as clockwork doll, his hair is still black and I have to figure he dyes it because Sonny must be pushing seventy. He seems a lot younger, doesn't look much different from when he recruited me out of the academy back when. Over the years, I had worked for him on and off, usually on Russian cases. He likes to remind me how green I was when he first spotted me. I talent-spotted you, man, he'd say, like he invented me. Used to make me nuts.

Growing up in Moscow like I did, I thought I was pretty streetwise. Moscow kids, we figured ourselves at the center of the universe, the center of a vast country that was always centralized. Moscow was the place where everything happened, politics, literature, science, movies, music, everything.

We thought we were hot shit. In fact, we were so cut off from the world, we didn't know how provincial we really were until word began to trickle through. Back then, all I had from outside, the only evidence there was better, something that reminded me of my dreams, was the music, Willie Conover's Jazz Hour on Voice of America, and a few illegal Beatles tapes.

Anyhow, when I met Lippert, I was new in New York, young, willing. Lippert saw he could use me. I spoke languages, I knew which fork to use, more or less, and Lippert told me he could use me on certain special jobs. I was plenty available for flattery, which Lippert doled out in just the right doses.

For years I didn't trust him. I knew he used me when it was convenient, but, retired or not, he was still the most connected guy I knew in the whole city.

The cop actors vied for Lippert's attention, asking him if they looked okay, if they walked okay, if they resembled the real thing. For a while, he passed out advice, and they sucked it up gratefully.

"You should get in on this consulting thing, man," said Sonny. "It's very competitive, I mean every ex-cop wants in, and some still on the job would love it, and I could help you get a gig if you want, you could be a movie cop, if you wanted, maybe even go on screen, like an extra or something, man. You're still pretty good-looking. I could introduce you." He glanced over at the fence that surrounded the studio, "Jesus, look at that," he added.

Beyond the fence was a group of Hassidic men, with long black curls and big black hats, white shirts, black pants. They had been kicking a soccer ball around. Now they came to the fence, and stared, incredulous, hostile, at the fake cops. Maybe they figured them for the real thing.

A black actor was sitting on a canvas chair, reading, his back against the chain-link fence. He heard somebody rattle the fence and looked up. A Hassidic guy said something disdainful about blacks. The actor got up, body tense. Other actors crowded around him.

Insults were exchanged. You could feel the anger rise. Everyone started yelling. Only the fence kept them from fighting.

It was as if the Crown Heights riots were starting all over.

"Just fucking cut it out," a crew member yelled. "Everybody, just back off," he said, and then it stopped. On our side it was only make-believe, and there was the chain-link fence.

"Can we talk, please?" I said to Sonny again. "And not about make-believe, okay? Now?"

"Don't get your hair in a braid, man," he said and walked me across the cement courtyard, away from the crowd.

We sat on a cement block and he asked what was eating me, what I'd been up to.

I told him what I knew about the dead woman – or maybe she was a girl – on the swing, and about Dina, the kid who found her.

"You went there how? How come?"

"I was taking some books to an old lady in Brooklyn, that part doesn't fucking matter, and I saw Dina running around in the street. I want you to tell me about duct tape, and about who does this kind of murder, does it ring any bells with you, anything you ever heard of? Sonny?"

"I heard about some, Albanian, maybe even Russkis, they get these girls, they prostitute them, the girls refuse, they try to run away, the creeps who own them do this kind of stuff. The duct tape, killing them this way, it's a warning, keep still, don't do anything, keep your mouth shut. It could be Mexicans, but I don't think so, not around here." He looked at his watch. "I can get out of here for an hour, if you want, I can take a look at the scene," he said. "You have your car? I'll follow you."

I didn't want Sonny at the scene, it wasn't my case, it would complicate things, but he was already on his way to the parking lot. I saw he was eager, glad somebody had asked him about the real world.

"Murder Inc.," were the first words out of Sonny Lippert's mouth when he climbed out of his dark green Jag near Fountain Avenue.

I walked him over to the playground where I'd seen the body. It had been taken away, but forensic crews were still picking over the site. Lippert followed my gaze.

"She was there," I said. "On the swing. Tied to it. Posed."

"Go on."

"Somebody was making a point," I said. "Right?"

"Anybody look good for it?"

"I don't know."

"Weird, man, this is exactly where the mob used to dump the bodies times I was a kid," said Sonny. "Murder Inc., Jesus Christ, it was famous, man, I mean we used to come over here and look for them. The bodies. You remember a song called 'When My Bobby Gets Home'? We kids used to sing 'When the Body Gets Cold'. All of us kids, all we wanted was to play ball for the Dodgers or join up with Murder Inc., maybe get to kill someone. Sometimes we did a cat, you know, strung it up from a light bulb, dumped the body out here. You don't think it's funny? Come on, Artie, man."

"Listen to me, Sonny, try to think."

"Yeah, yeah, okay, there were real Jewish gangsters then, big time. Jews and Italians got along, man, you know why?"

"Yeah, what's that, Sonny?" I said.

"We were all short," he laughed. "You know, we called this part of Brooklyn the Land of the Lost," he added.

When Sonny Lippert set out on one of his riffs, when he rambled, you had to wait. Tangled in his past, he had to climb out of the web. It took him longer and longer these days. I sometimes felt he'd just disappear into his own past and never return.

"The Land of the Lost, used to be wild dogs, packs of them, around here because of the garbage dump close by."

"Right."

"I'll make some calls, if you want," Sonny said.

"Sure, Sonny, thank you. I should probably get going." I knew there was no point keeping him here.

"You know you can call on me anytime, man, you know that."

"Thanks." I put my hand on his shoulder and he smiled slightly. "Thank you."

"She was naked?"

"I don't know."

"Look for her clothes, man. I'm telling you, look for the clothes. You always find it in the clothes. They looked? Your girl on the swing, girl on a red velvet swing."

"What?"

"Nothing, man. Just something out of a story," said Sonny, then looked up as Bobo Leven appeared at the edge of the playground.

He greeted Sonny formally. He was polite, he showed deference. He asked him some questions about the case, what did Sonny think, did he have any insights? He was attentive.

"I have to go," Sonny said.

"I'll walk you," I said, and went with Sonny back to his car.

"What is he?" said Lippert glancing towards the playground and Bobo Leven. "What is he, Artie, your Sundance?"

*

"He have anything interesting to say, Mr Lippert, I mean?" said Bobo when I got back to the playground.

"Anybody find the girl's clothes?" I said.

"We didn't find anything, not yet," Bobo said.

"Put a few uniforms to work on it, Bobo, get some of the beat cops to look everywhere for the clothes," I said and shoved the necklace with the blue charm on it in my pocket, and didn't know why.

All the way to Brighton Beach the presence of the charm in my pocket, reminded me of the dead girl. I was going to meet Valentina Sverdloff. By the time I got there, I wished I'd unloaded the charm on Bobo Leven.

CHAPTER SIX

"Hello, darling Artie," said Val as soon as I saw her at Dubi Petrovsky's bookshop. She kissed me like a big sloppy puppy on the cheek, not having to reach up because she was as tall as me, just met me head on and kissed me. "Did you get my message?"

I'd come from the playground. By the time I got to Dubi's, on Brighton Beach Avenue, people were out strolling in the late afternoon, a holiday afternoon, buying fruit, eating hot dogs, heading for the beach.

The bookshop was next to a juice bar. Dubi sold books in Russian, other Sov languages, English books on Russia, his own books on the Beatles in the former Soviet Union, other stuff too, CDs, DVDs, said you had to do it to stay afloat. He had added photographic equipment, old-style cameras, antique lenses, dusty packages of printing paper. From someplace in back "Penny Lane" was playing. I didn't mention the girl in the playground to Dubi, or to Val; I didn't want to think about it. I didn't want it in my life.

"I got your message," I said to Val. "Do you want to go swimming?"

"I need a favor," she said.

"Anything."

"Thank you."

For a while Val had worn her hair chopped into a platinum crew cut, but she had started growing it and letting it go back to her natural red color. I liked it better. She wore a little white t-shirt and cut-off jeans.

"I was going to call you," said Petrovsky, emerging from the back of the shop. "You thirsty?" he asked, then, without waiting, disappeared and returned, carrying a trio of cold Baltikas for us. "Good to see you, Artyom. You want this beer, young Valentina?"

She thanked him and asked about his own work, claiming his attention, his affection, like she always did. She was the most instinctively generous person I knew, curious about everyone. She rarely talked about herself, except to a few close friends, never dropped names; in spite of her height and beauty, she was a modest girl.

"What are you looking at?" She grinned at me, and went back to the books.

I drank some beer. "Go on, Dubi. You said you were going to call me?"

"This was a peculiar visit yesterday," said Dubi, rubbing his hand over the high forehead, the large hawk-like nose. "This skinny guy in western boots comes by to look at books, he says, and makes conversation about you, tries to make it casual, like how good is your Russian, do you buy Russian books? I get this impression this is why he comes."

"He gave you a name?"

"He used a credit card to pay for some stuff. R. Pettus," Dubi said.

"Yeah, he's nobody, Dube. Just a guy, an FBI agent I knew around 9/11, we worked some stuff together. He retired."

"He buys a Russian–English dictionary, and says give Detective Artie Cohen my regards, if you see him."

"Right." I wondered, for the second time that day, what the hell Roy Pettus wanted. "It was probably nothing," I said, but

I didn't believe it. A cold hand seemed to brush my shoulder, like a ghost. Except I don't believe in ghosts.

"I'm just going outside to make a call," I said. "Val? You okay?"

She put her head up over the boxes. "Happy as a pig in shit," she said. "Dubi has the most wonderful photographic books. I'll be a little while longer."

Nobody except a security guard at the desk in the FBI office answered when I called. It was a holiday. I called a number I had in Wyoming. All I got was a machine. I remembered Pettus had a daughter somewhere, New Jersey, maybe it was. There was a Cheryl Pettus listed in South Orange. A man who answered said she had moved. Finally I got her.

Cheryl told me sure, she was Roy Petttus' daughter, and as it happened her dad was in town for her wedding. I told her who I was and she was okay with it, but said she had to go over to Seton Hall, the Catholic college where she was teaching a summer course. She said she'd get her dad to give me a call. Said she didn't want to give out his cellphone. I said congratulations on the wedding, but it was urgent, and we hung up.

A few minutes later, Pettus phoned me back. Wanted to see me, he said, know how I was doing. I said fine, come on over, and he said I can't tonight, rehearsal dinner, wedding tomorrow. What about Sunday, and I said, fine, what's up, Roy, I thought you retired. He said, can you meet me Sunday morning?

There was nothing out of the ordinary in his voice, and I didn't mention that I was pissed off the way he'd been going around asking my friends about me. That could wait until we met. Instead, I made a couple jokes. I said, so what's with you, Roy, you back in the spook business?

CHAPTER SEVEN

"So what's the favor?" I said to Val.

"Tell my dad not to go to London. Will you tell him? You will, right?"

"Why?"

"It's not good for him, just trust me, okay?" She had come out of Dubi's shop, her arms full of packages. "Artie? He's going over to London. Soon."

"Yeah, he told me he was going, but so what?"

"When did he tell you?"

"This morning. How come you're so edgy?" I took her packages

"I worry about him, he's such a big baby sometimes, he's so like unbelievably ready to believe people." She kissed my cheek. "You'll talk to him tonight, okay? I'm sorry to keep nagging, but thank you, Uncle Artie," she said, half mocking. "Well, you're like an uncle. My dad and you, you're like brothers, right? He always says. He'll do what you tell him, he will."

"You won't go for his birthday?"

"No."

"What's up with London? You used to go a lot, you used to spend weeks and weeks there," I was surprised by how urgent she sounded.

"I hate what London does to him, my dad, ever since he opened his club there. He behaves like one of those dumb-ass oligarchs, you know? He buys big-time art. You know the joke about the oligarch who says I just got a tie that cost four hundred bucks and the other oligarch says, I paid six hundred for the same thing. Daddy buys and buys and buys. It's like he's addicted, like he wants to be one of them."

"He always bought a ton of stuff, he loves it."

"Just listen to me, okay? I'm telling you, this is different. He hangs out with ugly people. Greedy, bad people. Russians. Crooks. They think they're respectable, they put on this front, but they're crooks. When it comes to money, they'll do anything it takes."

"So you're telling me you don't like London anymore."

"It's not a joke, okay?" she said, sounding bitter. "I don't want to ever go back."

"There's something you're not telling me." We walked up onto the boardwalk.

"Just please trust me, okay, and don't ask. You have to love me and my dad enough not to ask," said Val. "Tell him I need him here. Lie if you have to. Promise me? If you love me, do this."

I promised her. I would have promised her anything, much more than she knew.

"You still want to swim?" I said to Val a few minutes later when we were on the beach, sand warm underfoot. I put her packages on the ground.

She shook her head. "Too many rip tides this summer, Artie, too many people going under. I'll wait for you. Go on. I'll watch," she said, and held up her camera. She watched while I took off my shirt and jeans. I felt shy.

"You look cute in those swim shorts," said Val, and held up her camera. "Smile for me, Artie, darling. I'll take your picture."

The water off Brighton Beach was cold as hell, and I swam hard as I could, and it ran over me, waking me up, the sun deliciously hot on my head even late in the day.

I dove back in, tasted salt, spat out the icy water. I turned over on my back and felt the water slide over me, and buoy me up; I squinted into the sun and blue sky.

For a while I floated on my way back, then swam towards the toy-size ships on the horizon as far as I could. When I turned around, I saw Val on the beach, watching me, waving. As I ran towards her, she pulled a towel from my bag.

Around us families were picking up babies and plastic buckets, shaking out their towels, getting ready to go home. A pretty girl in a little yellow halter-neck top and a bikini bottom was sunbathing on the beach near me and she glanced over and smiled. I smiled back. I'm not dead yet, I thought.

We walked up to a restaurant on the boardwalk where the owner let me change my clothes in the bathroom. When I came out, Val was sitting at a table and we sat and drank and the day seemed to have spilled golden light over Brighton Beach, turning it into an Impressionist painting. Two elderly women, arms linked, held green and lavender nylon umbrellas over their heads, like parasols; a red-headed girl in pink sweats pushed an old lady in a wheelchair, while a dachshund, tied to the chair, trotted behind them; two old Russians sat on a bench in checkered caps playing chess.

People were settling into the cafes along the boardwalk. "Castles In The Sand", an old Stevie Wonder number from an album called *Stevie at the Beach*, was playing somewhere, and then came the Temptations' "Under The Boardwalk", as if somebody had compiled summer music to go with the glorious weather.

I watched Val. So intent was she on what she was doing, she didn't see me. She took a picture of three old men in wheelchairs playing cards. She snapped them just as one guy won the game with a triumphant slap of the cards on the fold-up table where they played.

"Why don't you get a new camera?" I said, gesturing at the camera that was always around her neck.

"It may look like a junk-store relic to you, but it's a Stradivarius to me, my darling," she said. "I love my Leica M3—it puts me in the frame with all the greats, the guys from Magnum who invented photojournalism. Cartier-Bresson always said it opened his eyes and allowed him to grab those, you know what he called them, Artie? The decisive moments. I read he thought the silky noise of the shutter was like a Rolls-Royce door closing. Silky noise, wow. And it let him get close to things, this funny camera. Robert Capa took it to war, Eve Arnold took it around the world and into Marilyn Monroe's secret life," she added. "Okay, so I'm a fool for it, so I read too much about these people, but they're my heroes. I love the feel of it—it's like, I don't know, like a part of me." She picked up the camera again, and took my picture. "Anyway, it belonged to my grandfather in Russia. Am I boring the shit out of you? I bore all my friends with this camera shit."

"You never bore me," I said. "You want me to take you back to the city?"

"You have any gum?" said Val.

I put my hand in my pocket, digging for some chewing gum, and found the chain with the charm.

"Val?"

"Yes, Artie, darling?"

I took the necklace with the little blue and white charm out of my pocket.

"You ever see something like this?"

"Sure."

"Where?"

"Anywhere that there's crazy, superstitious people. Or fashionista babes, same thing. Rich Russian girlies like them with diamonds. Some believe this shit, remember the Kabbala stuff, Madonna's red strings she was pushing? They buy into anything, even Landmark."

"What's that?"

"It's the East Coast version of Scientology. No matter how many get degrees at NYU, the Russkis still believe hair grows on billiard boards. My best friend's grandmother—she's Ukrainian—is so superstitious, she thinks if you touch a Jew, you're going to die from some Christ-killer disease. I once saw her staring at another friend of mine's hair. I asked how come, she said she was wondering if this girl, who's Jewish, had horns. She was serious."

"What about this charm?"

"It's just fashion. Artie. Where did you get it?"

I told Val and as soon as I told her I was sorry.

She turned it over. "Look, see, there's this D on the back, it's a party favor from a club named Dacha. Over in Sheepshead Bay."

"You go there?"

"Once in a while," she said. "People think Heaven is a cooler club, but Dacha has more action and also people eat pickles with their vodka like the old country and everyone dances like crazy. You want me to walk you over?"

"Yes," I said, and suddenly there was a crack in the sky, a noise that split my ears. Boom. I started. Val jumped. She grabbed my hand and we ran up on the boardwalk as another rumble, like thunder, like war, and then we all looked up.

Fireworks exploded over Coney Island, red, white, blue, gold, Roman fountains, pinwheels, flowers, flags, somewhere the sound of a band, live, from loudspeakers, and everybody along the boardwalk, a solid wall of people almost a mile long, yelled and cheered.

"Happy July 4, Artie, darling," Val said, kissing me on the mouth where the smell of her perfume and lipstick and suntan lotion stayed for hours.

CHAPTER EIGHT

Val, Val, Val, the girls cried out when they saw her, all those young girls, eighteen, nineteen, long legs, long hair, faces already flushed with anticipation and now with recognition, as if a celebrity had suddenly appeared. She smiled and hugged them, and exchanged kisses, a big sister to these girls waiting outside the club. Wound around Val's wrist was the chain with the blue ceramic bead.

Overlooking the water in Sheepshead Bay, a mile along the Brooklyn coast from Brighton Beach, was Dacha. A free-standing building painted to resemble a Russian country house, it was dark green, with silver birch trees stenciled on the side. Dressed up in a puffy shirt, his pants stuffed into high black boots, a large guy with a shaved head the size of a basketball barred the outside door, and manned the velvet rope.

"You're coming," I said to Val, and she shook her head.

"Oh, Val, come have just one drink," a girl with carrot hair said, and Val said, "Take care of my friend Artie, okay, girls? Whatever he needs," she said and gave me back the chain with the bead. "Artie?" She took her packages—the books from Dibi's shop—from me.

"What, honey?"

"You'll talk to him tonight? My dad? okay? See you later."

"Disco night," said a kid, a Russian boy, not more than twenty, with contempt as I went into the club where the Bee Gees were wailing their stuff. He had a thick accent, slicked-down hair, sharp suit, no tie. He fondled a wad of bills.

The multi-level club was filling up, as more and more people poured in, talking English, Russian, the boys on the make eyeing the spectacular girls with long legs, cheekbones to cut glass, perfect tits, tiny skirts, glittering jewels, stilettos. The air was thick, heavy with perfume and hormones, and the music, the Bee Gees, Village People, Donna Summer, Gloria Gaynor.

I looked at my watch. It was still early, just after nine, and there were people eating dinner, families, some of them getting up to dance, kids, older people. And could they dance! The middle-aged dancers knew all the songs and they could cut it, singing along, Marvin Gaye, James Brown, Abba.

I went looking for the manager, up a spiral staircase that led to a bar and a roof garden. At a corner table, Val's girls had gathered, and they waved at me, and smiled, and beckoned me to their table. I waved back and went out on the roof so I could use my phone.

People were sitting around tables up here smoking, drinking cocktails, watching the last fireworks over the ocean. I walked to the edge of the roof and looked out over the canals, the fishing boats, the low-lying houses that ran right up to the beach and the ocean. I called my old pal Gloria Lopez and I got lucky. She was working the night shift.

Gloria had been on the job, a young detective in Red Hook when I met her, but after she had her baby and dumped the creep she married, she did some forensic courses and went to work in a lab. Mainly she worked on fibers. But could network better than anyone I ever met, not counting Sonny Lippert, and she was a great girl with a low humorous voice.

We went out to dinner once in a while, we caught a movie, a couple times I stayed over at her place. If I wasn't hung up on Valentina, I could have gone for Gloria but I'd already screwed up enough lives, and we kept it light.

I told her about the dead girl in the playground. She had already heard. Had seen it on TV, had heard from colleagues asking for forensic help on duct tape. She asked what I wanted and I said could she get a picture. A couple of minutes later Gloria called back. She was sending a picture of the girl to my phone.

"Thanks. You have anything on the time of death?"

"They're saying maybe around one, two in the morning, something like that, I could get some more on it, if you want," said Gloria.

"Thanks again."

"That Russian cop, Bobo Leven, you know him, right, Artie? He's been sniffing around me."

"Yeah?"

"I don't get him. Somehow he got one of the guys here to send him a picture of the dead woman, he said he needed it right away, said he was on the job, the primary. He's very ambitious, yeah, he hangs here whenever, he's always looking into microscopes and asking about fibers and shit, he was here today, so I did what I do, I humored him, but I didn't tell him nada. That right?"

"You always do it right," I said, and she gave a dirty sexy laugh into the phone and we agreed to go for Dominican food later that week in uptown Manhattan where Gloria lived with her kid and her mother.

Before I put my phone away, I looked at the dead woman in the picture Gloria had sent me. She was on a metal table in the morgue. Marks on her face where the duct tape had been peeled away. She was very young. She was pretty.

The bar was solid with human flesh now, and I leaned on the bar itself, a slick blue glass surface, ordered a beer, showed the bartender my badge and asked if the manager was around.

A squat guy, square shoulders, bad skin, came alongside

me and I could smell his heavy cologne. Said he was the manager, name was Tito. Tito Dravic, he added, then gestured to the bartender with some kind of authority. My beer arrived pronto, a fat short bottle of Duvel, great Belgian stuff with a big head.

"Anything wrong?" Tito Dravic was nervous. Plenty of people under twenty-one were drinking, and there were kids trading E, too.

I pushed the silver necklace with the blue bead along the slick glass surface of the bar. Wary but not hostile, Tito had an accent I couldn't figure. He picked up the silver chain. "Yeah, we gave these away as favors, sure."

"When?"

"You want exactly when?"

"Yeah."

I held back on the picture Gloria had sent to my phone. It felt obscene, as if the dead girl was trapped in it the way she had been trapped inside the duct-tape shroud.

If I was getting squeamish, I was getting too old for the job. Death needed respecting, but if you were on the job, you did whatever it took. Otherwise, you got out.

What I wanted right now was out of here. The music, the heat, the crowd were driving me a little nuts, maybe because I was sober. You can't do clubs sober. You need the high from booze or pills. I was thinking of beating it, but I followed Dravic into a little office behind the bar, where the walls were covered with framed clippings.

One of the clippings caught my eye, a picture of three girls in a local newspaper, including one with short blonde hair, big smile, long legs, tiny skirt. Jesus, I thought. The girl in the picture on the wall was the same girl in the picture in my phone. The dead girl from the playground.

I pointed to the picture. "You know this girl?"

"Sure, why?"

"What's her name?"

"Masha," Dravic said.

I showed him the photograph in my phone.

Instinctively he put his hand over his mouth as if to keep from crying out. "How?"

"You knew her well?"

"I knew her. How did it happen?"

"You have a name besides Masha?"

"He real name was Maria, everybody called her Masha." He sat down on the edge of the desk, color draining from his face, the skin suddenly gray, drab.

"Masha what?" I said.

"Panchuk. Her husband's name, I think. I never knew her own."

"There was a husband?"

"Yeah, for a while. I don't think she liked him much. I'm not even sure if he was still around the last few months."

"What else did you know about her?"

"I thought you wanted to know about the blue charm. They're connected, the charm, Masha?"

"Go on."

"We give out favors when business is slow, during the week, usually. The girls like these things, evil eyes, they call them."

"Okay, so tell me some more about Masha."

"Tall. Blonde. Pretty. Short hair. Crew cut almost. You want the picture?" He reached up to the wall and took the framed clipping down.

"You have one of her alone?"

From a folder on the desk, he got a picture, a color snap, a bad photograph but it was her, and she was tall and skinny, long-legged, wearing a skirt slit to her thighs, big earrings, smiling and posing. She looked very young.

"Can I keep it?"

"Sure."

"So you knew her pretty well, but you didn't fucking know she was dead, even though the story's been on TV already?" I kept my tone even, but I was feeling pissed off with this guy.

"I was upstate at my mother's in Kingston for a couple days, I did three shifts straight here and then I went up to her place to sleep."

"Your mother doesn't have a TV?"

"It was broken," he said. "Yeah, it's true. I only got here an hour ago, so I didn't know anything."

"Nobody here mentioned it?"

"You're telling me you people already made her identity public?" asked Dravic. "So how come you asked me for her name? If I knew earlier, I would have called somebody. How did it happen?" His eyes welled up.

I told him.

"My God," he said, then grabbed his phone, made a call, talked fast, hung up.

"The guy that was on duty before, he said another cop was nosing around earlier."

"Listen, please, man, I'm sorry I came on so heavy." I said. "Just please tell me whatever you can." I had almost lost him by sounding aggressive, and now I changed my tone. You get a lot more that way, and now Dravic offered me the chair, and switched on a fan. It was a tight fit, me, him, the little office piled with crates of booze.

"Masha was here a lot," he said. "A few weeks ago, she starts pestering me for a job, says she has some fucking bartending certificate, I tell her, it's not for a kid serving hundreds of crazy people at midnight when they're already soused and high, you have to scrape teenagers off the floor when they OD on Midori shots and E."

"She stopped bugging you?"

"I told her I'd give her a tryout. I tried her out, a couple of weeks ago, Tuesday night, easy crowd. She wasn't bad, but I didn't like it, I wasn't sure she was even twenty-one, I wasn't sure she was eighteen, tell you the truth, she dressed up older and wore a lot of make-up and she had a real grown-up body, but I thought she was a kid, something about her, so I told her, you have to get some real ID if I'm gonna keep you. She was using fake stuff, driver's license, social security card, but crap, the kind you can buy for sixty bucks. She left. I didn't hear back."

"Any rough stuff in the club?"

"We get mostly Russians, but the kind with money, they come to party, show off their moves. No fights. Some tension once in a while, especially when there's a Ukrainian bunch."

"Masha got involved?"

"She could work both crowds, she was very good-looking, and sweet. She was a great dancer. I probably have a video someplace from a dance contest."

"Where?"

"The main office is on the next block over, there's a house where they keep most of the stuff. I put it there. I might have something else for you."

"What's that?"

"She had this little résumé, you know, not much but a couple places she had worked, a few bars, I put it in a file, that any use to you?"

"Plenty."

"Can you stop back Sunday? It's quiet Sunday. I could go over to the office and get you the stuff."

"What's wrong now?" I said.

"I have to do this when nobody else is around."

"I need it."

"Look, please, man, if I try to get anything out of there now, it'll be a problem, trust me, okay, please?"

He looked frightened. Dravic glanced at the door of the little office. I figured if I pushed him too hard, he'd balk, or somebody else would get in the way, so I pulled back.

"Right," I said. So, you were pretty nice to her, you gave her a tryout as a bartender, even if she was underage—you had something with her?"

"No," he said, hesitating just a split second. "She was just a nice girl."

"And the husband?"

"I didn't get the feeling he would be happy if she was even talking to other guys, it was like he owned her, she had a tat with his name on it."

"You saw it?"

"She told me. It was not, you know, visible exactly."

"You're Russian?"

"Serbian dad, Russian grandma on his side. My Mom's a hippie from upstate New York."

"You speak Russian?"

"My grandmother taught me some."

"Right. So what else?"

"The Russian girls, they look great, but they can be really chilly, peevish, you know, petulant, like they'd rather be doing some other thing really important, you know, like smoking cigarettes, you know that look? It's the same everywhere, I met some of them in England when I worked there, just the same fucking thing. Masha was different. She was nice to everyone."

"How nice? You think Masha was hooking?"

"I don't know."

"She wore expensive clothes?"

"Yeah, so what?"

His face tightened up. I wondered if he had been in love with Masha.

I started to go. He put a hand on my sleeve, put it there too hard, clutched the fabric too tight. He was furious, pissed off at me for asking if the girl was a hooker. He kept hold of my arm, and he was solid, muscled, built like a bull.

"Let go of me, man," I said. "Fucking let go."

"Yeah, sorry," said Dravic. "There's guys, I don't know,

Rumanians, Albanians, whatever, they come in with these girls who are really frightened and you can see the bastard owns them."

"Serbs?" I wanted to get him riled up, I wanted him to hit me if he had to. It would tell me something about him and the dead girl. He didn't. He lowered his voice. He understood that I was now a threat to him.

"What else?" I said.

"I mean they keep the girls' passports. The girls are like slaves. Man, if I have kids and they're girls, I'm sending them someplace else."

"Where's that?"

"Yeah, where?" said Dravic. "Where on earth?"

CHAPTER NINE

After I let Tito Dravic go back to work, I called Gloria and told her the dead girl's name, I told her about the tattoo, and then I started for the street. I'd had enough of the club, the drunks, the heated-up flesh, the bad music. I was going back into the city, but there was something I had to do first.

As I passed the girls who had greeted Valentina on the street, one of them followed me. Her name was Janna, she said, she had carrot hair and a clinging little blue silk dress that was tight on her ripe burnished body. She was maybe twenty.

"Can we go out for a smoke?" she said. "Would you mind, Mr Cohen?" She was polite, and we went out to the street and over to the canal where the fishing boats were. Crowds of people sauntered up and down, cars honked, people waved American flags. The fourth of July.

Janna offered me her pack of cigarettes, and I took one. I figured if we smoked together she'd relax. She was tense, coiled up.

"You were in because of the girl that died, right?" she said.

"You knew that?"

"Oh, in these clubs talk goes around faster than the ecstasy goes down," she said. "And Tito has a big mouth. He retails gossip as a way to hang out with us."

"You don't like him?"

"He's okay. He's just kind of low-class, you know?"

I showed her the picture.

"Masha Panchuk," she said. "We liked her. We tried to help her."

"Help how?" I said, and I saw this girl, this Janna, wanted in on the case, that she was curious, nosey maybe. Maybe like Dravic, she wanted to retail the story.

"We knew she needed a job. She didn't have any family, only a grandma someplace in, I don't know, Kiev, or somewhere," said Janna. "There was a guy, a husband? She wanted out. She was just a good kid."

"You Russian?"

Janna said she had grown up in London, and her parents were both Russian. Her friends in the club had Russian parents, but had been born in Brooklyn. They were at NYU, studying business.

"I don't want the others to know about this, they're American girls, they don't know how anything works, and I don't want to scare them. You know, I said to one of them, Don't you long to travel, and she said, well, yes, but I couldn't go anywhere I don't feel safe. They're frightened."

"Listen, you want to help?"

"Yes."

"You need to go back in the club?"

She couldn't tell what I was after. I could see it in her unformed pretty little face.

"I don't know. Why?"

"Where did Masha buy her clothes, where do girls out here get stuff? Show me."

"There's shops around Brighton Beach. Masha liked a lot of glitz."

"Okay, you want to help, show me. My car's around the corner."

She hesitated, and then, rising to the challenge, to what she saw as a dare, she put her smokes in the little purse that dangled from a sparkly chain on her shoulder.

"Sure," she said and she followed me to my car and got in, and jabbered while I drove back to Brighton Beach, jabbered half frightened, half excited. I could smell the excitement, especially when I hit the gas hard. She lit up another cigarette.

"I knew something was wrong," said Janna. "She tried so hard to get it right, to dress right, she told me she had lived outside London, as if it gave her some kind of qualification, some kind of status is the word I want. Maybe because my accent is sort of English." Janna looked up at me. "Everybody loved this girl, boys, girls, everybody, I don't just mean in a friends way, I mean loved as in wanted, but also liked. She slept with a lot of people."

"Was she hooking?"

"Probably. But there was this air about her that drew you in," said Janna. "She said she was twenty-two, I think she was a lot younger, I mean like seventeen, and I'm pretty sure she was illegal. I saw her in the city at some club. You could talk to my dad."

"You said your dad's Russian?"

"Yes. Should I call you Detective? I'm sorry, I don't know what to call you." She pointed at a side street in Brighton Beach and I pulled into it, and she got out and I followed her to a shop. Even at this hour it was open, but it was a holiday and people shopped late.

"Here," said Janna. "I know Masha had a dress that she got here." She pointed at the rack of shiny clothes. The woman who ran the place glared at us. She figured me for Janna's sugar daddy. Janna pushed the clothes along the rack. When she came to a short dress, pink with some kind of glitter on it, she stopped.

"It's what I saw her in the last time. One, maybe two nights ago," she said. "You want me to put it on?"

"It's okay," I said, but she had already disappeared into a dressing room.

She reappeared in the dress, plucked a platinum blonde wig

off a rack of cheap wigs, the kind you get for Halloween. Imitating girls on a catwalk, in her high-heeled sandals and the wig and the pink dress, Janna strode up and down the room, admiring herself in a mirror.

"So she looked like this," she said, as if she had cracked a big case. I realized now she was pretty wasted. I should have seen it earlier.

"It's enough," I said. "I have to go."

"I could go with you."

"Just get your clothes back on, and I'll take you to the club," I said and while she changed again, I saw the owner stare at me some more before she picked up her cellphone, dialed and began talking about me to someone at the other end. She was talking Russian. She probably figured me for a guy who came out to the Beach from the city to pick up little girls.

CHAPTER TEN

All the way back to the club, I felt somebody on my tail, somebody watching, following. I didn't know who the owner of the clothing shop had called, didn't know if she called local cops, or security people, to say there's a creep from the city hanging around.

"Why can't I stay with you?" said Janna. "It's fun playing detective."

I thanked her and told her to go back to her friends, realizing that I'd created a loose cannon. I didn't know the girl. I didn't know what she'd tell her friends, her parents.

I pulled up near the club, and got out with Janna and walked her back to Dacha where there was a long line at the velvet rope, the guy dressed as a Cossack standing at it.

"Thanks," I said, and watched her go into the club, then come out again.

"Listen," she said. "There's this young guy, a cop, he's here tonight, he comes a lot. He knew Masha, he could maybe help you."

Dressed up, black linen shirt, cuffs turned back, white jeans, expensive loafers, hair freshly cut, a gold watch, bright against his tanned arm, Bobo Leven was greeting people everywhere in the club. He shook hands. He thumped them on the back, he gave guys hugs, he kissed girls. Then he saw me.

I cornered him, made him go into the bar.

"I thought you were working the case," I said.

"I am working it, Artie, it's okay, I know what I'm doing." He greeted the bartender who brought him a Coke.

"So you're a regular here, you must have known the dead girl."

"I saw her a few times."

"You already knew her name?"

"I wasn't sure if it was Masha, not at first," he said.

"You didn't tell me?"

"You said you didn't want to be bothered with this, so I didn't bother you. You said you were on vacation."

"That's bullshit, Bobo."

"You want to hear what I have?"

"Sure."

"Masha had a husband named Zim Panchuk. From Lvov. Ukraine."

"I know where it is."

"They maybe met in London where they were both working, him as a truck driver, her as a maid. He took her to Alaska. He was legal. He had a job on the pipeline. Soon as they got there, and she was in America, she dumped him and probably came to New York right away."

"Yeah, and the husband?"

"I called. He left his job two days ago. He went back to Russia."

"You got a lot of stuff pretty fast."

"I called around."

"You didn't think to call me?"

"I'm sorry, Artie. If you want I'll keep you in the loop, I just thought you didn't want in. But from now on, you'll be my first call, man."

"Yeah, well, I have to get back to the city. One more thing, Bobo."

"What's that?" he said.

"Where were you last night?"

CHAPTER ELEVEN

A girl I knew slightly was coming out of the building with her dog, a dachshund, and we exchanged views on the noise in the street the night before and cracked some jokes about the tourists. She was going up on the roof one night and shoot at them with a beebee gun, she said, and I laughed. We agreed to get coffee some day and I felt better. Coming home here to my place off Broadway where I'd lived for fifteen years made everything okay. I was home.

Upstairs in my loft, I switched on the news and got scores from the game last night—the Yankees were so lousy this summer only a faithful dog of a fan like me would care. I was thinking of switching to the Dodgers. At least they had Joe Torre.

Already there was a report on the girl on the swing. Speculation had begun on Masha Panchuk. It was a holiday weekend and the news cycle was hungry and everybody had an opinion: it was drug-related; the work of some nutjob seeking attention; a crazed terrorist. There was even an item about a Brooklyn artist who made human forms out of duct tape he had purchased after 9/11 when the city bought the stuff in bulk so we could all tape up our windows against some future nuke attack. I turned the TV off.

With Clifford Brown on my stereo, and listening to the incredible "Joy Spring" solo, I got into the shower, let it pour hot and hard over me, then switched to ice cold. When I got out I looked in the mirror.

I was looking okay. I'd been sleeping, I had quit smoking for the most part, I lost a few pounds.

Clean clothes on, I fixed some espresso. My place was looking good. I'd bought it cheap years earlier when nobody wanted a place down here, and I had scraped down the old wood floors myself until they shone. Got some nice mid-50s furniture. Put up shelves.

On the walls were framed photographs of the musicians I love—Stan Getz, Ella, Duke, Lester Young, Dizzy, Miles. Maybe I'd retire and take lessons. My father had loved the music. Even in Moscow, he had loved it.

I checked my messages. Tolya had called twice, reminding me I was due at his club to sample new wines. Another friend wanted to know if I'd go fishing the following day. It was okay. Everything was fine. I was okay.

On that night when I drove over to Tolya's place, Manhattan felt like a cruise ship, an overcrowded pleasure boat, getting ready to sink, but full of people having a ball as it sailed through the lit-up streets. Any minute, though, it would hit bedrock and start to go down, too loaded up with ambition, real estate, money, talent, sex, drugs booze, work, and always money. It was ready. It was ripe. Something had to explode.

In the summer, New York lived in the streets. Restaurants and bars spilled their customers out onto the streets, along the big avenues, on the grid of streets running river to river, and in the winding alleys downtown.

The streets were jammed with tourists gorging on the city, the dollar cheap. Everywhere you heard foreign voices, Japanese, French, Brit, all of them frenzied, rushing the bars, restaurants, even stores that were open late to service them, to sell them stuff, any stuff, sneakers, computers, sheets, like they were expecting disaster, their last best chance, as if they, too, somehow knew a crash was coming. The streets seemed to shudder from so many pounding feet, I felt I could feel them move, judder, throb, under my own feet.

Every transaction took place over food, booze, coffee, drugs as people hurried, hurry, hurry, to get some whatever it was while the stock market went up four hundred points, then down four hundred points. Oil skyrocketed, money was made out of smoke and mirrors and fraud, and there were more homeless out on the streets than I had seen for years.

Already one or two TV pundits were predicting recession, depression, the end of the world. George Bush said everything would be just fine and dandy, but nobody believed him about anything anymore.

A money guy I sometimes ran into at Tolya's bar had told me the end was coming, that there really was something rotten in the financial world, something bad, that we were all going down, even the big banks, the brokerage houses, all of it. The end is coming, man, he'd say, and everybody would laugh. You're like one of those preachers in the street, they'd say, and laugh at him, and then order another bottle of wine that cost a thousand bucks.

In a month or two or three, this guy insisted late one night, it will tumble, collapse, fall into a depression unlike anything since 1929 and there would be bodies falling from skyscrapers on Wall Street, they way they had fallen from the Twin Towers.

I only half listened. I didn't have any money anyway.

The West Village had changed since I first got to New York when, for a while, I lived in a crummy walk-up on Horatio Street and hung around the Village Vanguard to hear the music. Bums pissed on my front steps, but writers still went to the White Horse Tavern, and gay men haunted the Hudson piers where you could take some sun and smell the stink of pollution in the river.

All gone.

Brownstones on tree-lined streets housed movie stars, limos idled at the curb outside pubs where painters used to go back in the day, and nobody, not the writers or artists or jazz guys, gave a rat's ass for money. Manhattan's Old Bohemia had disappeared.

My head felt thick. I couldn't stop thinking about Masha, the duct tape, the way she died. I parked in front of Pravda2, and went in, and then I knew what had been bothering me, making my head thick, making me edgy, unnerved by the noise and the night.

CHAPTER TWELVE

A wall of sheer noise rose up at me when I went through the door of Pravda2. The rosy light made the faces beautiful. Among them I looked for Val, but she wasn't there.

"You'll ask him, you promise, you won't let him go to London, right?" I remembered her words. I didn't understand her obsession, her urgency, the fear I had seen in her face. I'd tell Tolya, but later.

Over the sound system came Sinatra on an album he recorded in Paris, maybe his best. "They Can't Take That Away From Me", sang Frank.

I made my way to the bar. At the far end, Tolya was talking intently to a chubby guy in black, the two of them sipping red wine.

For a while I sat and drank a Scotch and watched the crowd, looking for Valentina. I asked the bartender if he'd seen her.

"She was in earlier."

"Is she coming back?"

"I don't know."

Waiters slipped through the spaces between tables with finesse, the usual ballet, hefting plates, depositing platters of oysters and langoustines. I got a steak sandwich, very rare, on fresh French bread.

For Tolya food was not just fuel or even simply a nice thing. I once had to track him to the Bronx where he was examining some baby lamb at the uptown meat market. Food was central to life, he said, you could not exist without it, and what he wanted, he had to have.

Fresh mozzarella had to come from Joe's Dairy on Sullivan Street the same day he ate it. A tongue sandwich on rye bread, he wanted sliced very thin, and the bread had to be rye, so fresh it was almost moist, with those little seeds and the mustard German and brown. He once described this to me for about ten minutes and then he said he had to get to the Carnegie deli because talking about the tongue made him hungry for it.

Sinatra sang "Night And Day".

I waited until the club began to empty out, until there was only a couple at a little table, touching each other's faces, and a small group of men still talking wine with Tolya.

There were times now I got the feeling he was playing a part, that he spent more than he had on his clubs, that he flew to London and Moscow all the time for show, that he was surrounded by people who clamored for his attention, but why, why these people, rich, but pompous, a lot of them, people who dropped brands and names? These days, Tolya fell for the kind of flattery that he would have laughed at once. Among them were Russian names, and I'd say, oh, come on, Tol, these people are creeps, these oligarchs you love so much, your Olegs and Romans.

"Don't be an ass, Artemy," was all he ever said.

At four the last customer left, Tolya came out from behind the bar, and rubbed his face.

"I'm just going to lock up," Tolya called up. "Then we can drink serious wine."

"How come you tend bar yourself?"

"This is for fun," said Tolya, locked the front door, came back, took a cigar out of a box on the bar, put it in his mouth and lit it, puffed at it for a few seconds.

"Everything's okay?"

"Sure."

"You're going to London?"

"You decided to come. Fantastic."

"Why don't you stay in New York instead? The weather's better," I said because I couldn't think of anything else.

"Valentina told you to say this?"

"Yes."

He laughed. "You're not exactly subtle, Artyom."

"Is she coming tonight?"

He shrugged. "I don't know. She didn't say." He stared at me. "There's something going on with you and her?"

"Don't be stupid," I said, and finished my drink.

"You talk to her behind my back?"

"Fuck off."

"Let's go upstairs and have a drink," he said, and held up a bottle of red.

"Not that stuff," I said, gesturing at the single malt he always poured for me. "Just regular Scotch, okay?"

The wine in one hand, he picked up a bottle of Johnnie Walker Blue, his idea of regular Scotch, led me to the back room, then up four flights of narrow stairs and out onto the roof. He was pretty nimble for a big guy.

"Sit," he said, gesturing to a pair of overstuffed armchairs arranged on a worn red and blue Persian rug.

On a table between the chairs was a bottle of vodka in an ice bucket. Tolya put the Scotch and the red wine next to it. There was a short-wave radio. A small CD player with speakers.

We sat, he poured, he puffed his cigar, we admired the city lights. The late-night buzz was fainter now, the city turning quiet. I didn't mention the girl on the swing. I didn't want Tolya involved. He got involved, he brought in his guys, as he called them. They poked around, they screwed up my case. It had happened before. I didn't need Russian muscle on this thing. It wasn't even my case.

"So you like my nice roof here?" he said, and told me he'd finally bought the whole brownstone.

"I thought no more real estate," I said, drinking the Scotch, which was delicious.

"Artyom, is teeny tiny little building, not real estate," said Tolya in his fake Russki accent. "Times are not so good, Wall Street goes down the toilet, economy is shit, so I like to buy real estate for my kids, you know? I buy them little bit in New York, what can ever happen with real estate, right? Also, they like America. They are Americans," he said. He chuckled, a big man's laugh. "America, all is money, all is shopping malls and consuming," he said, and when I mentioned his eighteen pairs of bespoke Gucci loafers, some in rare skins, all with eighteen-carat gold buckles, he only shrugged. "Shoes are Italian," he said, and broke up laughing.

Tolya Sverdloff didn't like America much. He didn't like the politics, he didn't like what he figured was the land of George W. Bush. He kept a place in the city, he did business here, bought and sold real estate—the huge penthouse near Sutton Place, the SoHo loft, another one in the Meat Market district. He claimed most of it was for the kids, for Val who loved the city and considered herself an American, and her sister at med school in Boston.

In the Soviet Union, Sverdloff's parents had been stars among the Communist Party faithful, and well rewarded for it, his mother a movie star, his father a director. He grew up with access most kids like me had never dreamed of, and I didn't have it bad as most.

The parents idolized certain American writers like Arthur Miller and Clifford Odets, actors like John Garfield in his day, and Bogart and Brando and musicians like Paul Robeson and

Pete Seeger, but they had the Russian intellectuals' prejudice against American culture.

To Tolya they said rock and roll was redneck music. He didn't listen. Rock and roll was what got him through the Soviet years, he always told me, though it was the British stuff he loved most. The Beatles were his redemption and his rebellion as a teenager in the USSR, his line in the sand. "We didn't rebel politically, there wasn't any point, but we went into internal exile with the forbidden music," he said. "It was different country then, this US of A," he told me. "Music was incredible then."

We argued. He pulled my strings. We drank. I told him, when I had had plenty of Scotch, that he was a sell-out, a rock and roll hero who became a businessman. He beamed whenever I said it. Money was his art now, the richer he was, the greater an artist. He was my best friend and he had saved my ass more times than I could count.

"You really love him, don't you?" Val had said to me once, and she was right, of course, but we didn't talk like that, we talked like guys.

That night, sitting on the roof, we drank too much and suddenly, sometime very late, Tolya said, "I'm going to London on Sunday, Artemy."

"Already?" I thought about Valentina.

"Like I told you, I will spend my birthday there in my lovely city, this beautiful green place," he said, pushing the graying black hair back from his huge forehead. "London!" he said, as if it were a woman he was crazy for. "This is so beautiful a city, you should come. Come next week. My birthday is next week. We'll have a party. I'll take you to my place in the country also, which is eighteenth century, and so beautiful and was previously owned by very famous politician."

"What's the big deal with London?"

"It is sympathetic to good food and great wine, and also to

Russians, and it is a civilized country, a civil society, a place of laws and culture."

"Enough about bloody London," a voice said, as Val came through the door, walked across the roof, kissed me on the cheek, sat on the arm of Tolya's chair and flung her arm around her father. "You're obsessed," she said.

"Hello, darling," said Tolya. "What would you like?"

"I'd like for you not to go to London."

"I won't stay too long. I promise."

"But we could have a nice summer here, we could go out to the house in East Hampton, we could go fishing together in Alaska, like we said, wherever you want. Please, Daddy?"

"Afterwards. I promise you." He looked up at her, surveyed the floaty green summer dress she wore, and smiled. "You look nice."

"Thank you."

He loved his daughter better than anything on earth. They were connected in the most elemental way, father and daughter. I was jealous, not because I wanted her—which I did—but because of the way they were together. I have no kids. It makes me sad.

"Artie, the club, was it okay?" said Valentina. "You found what you needed?"

"What club?" said Tolya.

Again I held off telling him about the dead girl. It wasn't just that he'd set up his own guys to investigate it. Maybe I didn't want Val upset.

"It's nothing. I was helping out a guy on a case in Brooklyn."

"It's Bobo Leven?" he said.

"Yes, but it doesn't matter."

"It doesn't but whenever he comes in the club, I watch him, he's like, what do you call it, grapevining all over you, listening to you, trying to pick your brains out," said Tolya who was pretty drunk now.

"You'll go swimming with me tomorrow?" said Valentina.

"Sure," I said. "I'll call you in the morning."

"Not too early. I'm going to a party."

"Now?" Tolya said, glancing at his watch.

"I'm a big girl, Daddy," she said. "Daddy?" She got up and then squatted near her father, and took his hands. "Don't go. Please."

"What's bothering you?"

"I don't know. I just have this bad feeling, like I ate something off. They do bad stuff to Russians in London."

"But I'm very small potatoes, my darling, nobody is going to bother me," said Tolya. "I'm not Boris Berezovsky, after all."

"Please?"

"I'll think," he said. "Don't nag."

She kissed him and got up to go. Tolya called after her.

"What is it?"

He took an envelope out of his pocket, and handed it to her. She looked inside and smiled. "Thanks, Daddy. That's nice." She kissed the top of his head. "You're turning gray. You'll have to start dyeing your hair," she giggled. "See you both tomorrow, okay? Love you."

When Val had gone, Tolya asked me again if I wanted to come to London with him. I said I couldn't. What I didn't tell him was that I wanted to stay in New York where Val was, that I wanted to go swimming with her and take her to dinner.

"How come Val's so worried?" I said.

"She thinks they're killing Russians, some silly shit, Artyom, in London." For a split second he looked uncomfortable, then he said, "But this is just small, little part of things, and who except English would give asylum to so many people, and protect against bad guys? Also, me I am not in that league of oligarchs. I'm little guy, Artyom," he said, dropping his articles everywhere, making himself sound like a peasant, as if he didn't know better.

"But you'd like to be, wouldn't you? A big guy," I said, and saw that it bothered him, that his eyes shifted inwards. He wanted it. He wanted the whole thing. It gave me the creeps. It turned him into a man I didn't really recognize. Then it passed. He laughed, and we had some more to drink, then he stretched out his legs, inspected his cigar, looked out at the Hudson River, then back at me and said, "It's just business."

"What kind of business? In London?"

"Restaurants. Wine. All my life I know that without good food, life is nothing, so now I am in the good-food business. In Europe they understand this. In Russia they understand. You have no idea, Artemy, these Russians, these guys, Dellos, Navikov, they get big respect, they are considered true food guys and they are Russians, not French or Italian, and they understand restaurants, they are changing Moscow, they spend money, they buy great chefs, and now they open up in London, London has become wonderful Russian province along with food center of the universe now." He reached over and turned on the CD player, and put his head back and closed his eyes. "Tito Gobbi," he said. "*Don Carlos*. Gorgeous, yes?"

For a while we listened, then Tolya suddenly said to me, "You know what is my favorite book, Artyom?"

"*Nineteen Eighty-four*," I said, recalling how he had for years carried a tattered Penguin copy. He put it in his pocket and took it out once in a while to read a passage to me. I always told him *Brave New World* was much closer to the way things had been in the USSR, but Tolya loved Orwell very much.

"But also *Slaughterhouse 5*. Recently I reread this. I am also a pilgrim, like Billy Pilgrim, also unstuck in time, also tumbling in the ridiculous. This writer, Kurt Vonnegut, I love this man. I feel like that, London, Moscow, New York, planes in between, other places, nothing fixed, nothing regular, like many people these days, just falling free here to there. Even as a boy, I always feel I am in contact with creatures from another planet."

He smiled. "Not like UFOs, asshole, you know what I mean," he said.

Glass in hand, Tolya got up and leaned on the parapet, looking out at the city. Suddenly, as he turned to look at me, I saw a look of pain cross his face, of sudden sharp physical pain held in. He put his hand to his left arm.

"What's the matter with you?" I said. "Tolya?"

"Nothing."

"Tell me."

"I drank too much," he said.

"What? Talk to me. Sit down, for chrissake."

Sitting in the chair, he pulled up his pink silk socks.

"Come with me. You can be part of it, you know what is happening in London, how much money, how this lovely adorable government takes just teeny little taxes, and how they are civil and have good courts. Money, you can scoop off trees. This is stupid, still being a cop, Artemy, what for? Big stupid people are cops. You know what they call them in London? Detective Plod."

"Pick," I said.

"Pick what?"

"Pick money off the trees. Not scoop."

"Ha ha. So your English is better than mine, I am younger than you. You'll be fifty before me. You won't come, will you? So you'll watch out for Val, yes?"

"She's not going to turn into a pumpkin, she's twenty-four."

"You'll take care of her, won't you? Artie? This is not some joke."

"Yes."

We drank and watched the sun come up.

"Good." He got up. He held the bottle of Scotch out. I took a glass and poured a shot for myself. "Mr Pettus will ask you to watch me. This is why he came to my club, Artemy."

"Why would he want me to watch you? Tolya?"

But he didn't answer, just watched the sun coming up over Manhattan, and then fell asleep.

At six, Sverdloff dozing in his chair on the roof, I went home through the glorious New York dawn. I'd been up all night. I was exhausted, but edgy, the girl on the swing, Tolya going to London, Val trying to keep him here.

At home, I thought about the case, I made notes, I went out for a walk to clear my head. I wasn't sure at all how long I walked along the East River, trying to get a fix on things. That evening when I got home, I got into bed and fell dead asleep.

Some time after dark—I leaned on one elbow trying to see a clock—the buzzer rang. It was Valentina. I let her in. Without a word, she took off her jeans and shirt, and slipped into my bed, and it was early in the morning before she left.

CHAPTER THIRTEEN

Sunday morning, Tolya left New York. He called early. He was waiting for me outside the yellow brick loft building where he lived in the old Meat Market. His black hair still wet from the shower, he looked sober.

"Why do I feel you have a case, that you're working on something and you don't tell me, Artemy? In Brooklyn? Val asked you about it at my club. You ignored her."

"It's a homicide Bobo Leven is working. I gave him the benefit of my wisdom," I said.

"You don't want to tell me?"

"It's fucking grim, a young girl murdered. Just enjoy your trip, okay?"

"Take care of Valentina. I trust you with her only in public places."

We laughed, but I felt sad and I couldn't say why. Maybe it was the early morning, the soft balmy summer dawn, the kind when we had so often staggered home from parties together.

"I'll try," I said. "What airline are you on?" I added, making stupid small talk to change the subject.

"You think I am flying commercial? Please."

He smiled. He seemed okay. He said that Valentina was still asleep at home and he had checked on her, and in her sleep, she had smiled at him. I didn't say she had been with me.

Somehow, I would redeem myself with him, one day, some day.

"You have keys for my place? In case," said Tolya.

"Yes."

"And all my phone numbers?"

"Yeah."

"You'll think about coming with me in business, in restaurants? You promise?" He looked at his big gold Rolex. "What's the date, Artyom?"

"July 6. You okay?"

"Please, I just want to set my watch, you think I'm getting senile?" He adjusted his watch. "We'll have some fun before it's too late, Artyom. Okay? Before we die. Thought we'd die before we got old, like they say back in the day, right, when I was rock and roll god, but now we have to hurry up."

For a second it occurred to me that—I'd thought it before—Tolya's clubs were some kind of cover, but cover for what? I didn't know. I didn't want to know.

"One other thing, Artyom," he said.

"Sure."

"This Roy Pettus, stay away from him."

"Don't worry. I'm seeing him later, I'm going to tell him to fuck off, you know?"

"Don't see him at all. Just don't. These guys, Artyom, these spook people they are the same, they work together, they exchange information, it's capital for them, like cash," said Tolya. "I have to go now."

He climbed into the black Range Rover that was waiting for him at the curb. He shut the door. He pressed his face against the window, pushed his hair back from his forehead. It was already gray at the roots. In the face against the window, I could see how he would be as an old man.

Don't go, I wanted to say.

"Take care of her," he mouthed through the car window.

Tolya put his hand, big, like a pale pink ham, flat on the

window, a sort of farewell gesture, and I remember thinking, not knowing why I thought it, that I'd never see him again. Then the car pulled away.

CHAPTER FOURTEEN

It was quiet downtown when I went to meet Roy Pettus, the Sunday of a holiday weekend. No lawyers cluttered the monumental steps of the courthouses, or leaned against the columns of this imperial New York, no supplicants or secretaries or jurors fed up with endless waiting, nobody except a few tourists heading for Ground Zero, and homeless men stretched out on benches in the shade of the trees. And pigeons. And pigeon shit.

It was sultry. I tried not to think about Valentina and couldn't think about anything else. A few minutes later, I saw Pettus.

He crossed the street near City Hall, stopped to light up a cigarette, and then he continued towards me. He put up his hand in greeting. Then he held it out.

"Artie, good to see you."

"You too, Roy." I kept it cool.

He looked around, maybe from habit and said, "Can we walk?"

"Sure."

We set off towards the Brooklyn Bridge. Pettus looked a lot older than I recalled but it was more than a decade. The sandy hair was white, cut short. The sunburned face was lined, the pale eyes watery. He walked straight, though, and he was dressed square as any FBI man: pressed chinos, white button-down shirt tucked in, cellphone attached to his belt. Only a pair of worn cowboy boots marked him as off duty.

I asked Pettus how Chugwater was. He said okay. I'd known him when he was an agent at the New York FBI office, must be fifteen years, and we both worked the nukes case on Brighton Beach together. Afterwards, he retired to Chugwater, Wyoming where he was born.

I drove through it once on a trip out west, but I didn't know Roy's address and I didn't look him up. Wasn't much there, just an old railroad siding, a grain silo, a couple shops and a place that made chili. And the endless empty spaces of prairie in all directions. I had wondered what it would be like, living in all that emptiness.

"Congratulations on your daughter," I said. "The marriage. Cheryl, right?"

"Thanks," he said.

I waited for him to give something away, tell me why he'd been bugging my friends. We walked. He smoked. In front of us the great gothic arches of the bridge rose in the early sky. The sun through clouds that had moved in turned the river to a stream of hot tin.

"So how come you've been talking to my friends, Roy?" I said finally. "You could have just called me up."

"Yeah," he said. "I'm sorry for that." He didn't explain.

"Tell me what you need," I said pleasantly, and I could see he was confused. He had wanted me off my guard, angry maybe, pissed off at least. Figured he'd get more out of me, make me say something I didn't want to say.

My father, when he was with the KGB all those years back, knew how to get information out of people better than anyone I ever met. In the 1960s and early 1970s, he was a star, enough of a star that they let him travel. He had been to New York.

Always be quiet, my dad had said. Always wait. Getting information is a sort of seduction. Be cool was his message, though he would not have used the word.

The blowhards, the guys quick on the draw with clever retorts, the furious, the overly confident, never learned anything worth knowing.

"So you're here to celebrate?" I said. "You want a soda, a coffee Roy?" I spotted a guy with a cart a few feet away.

"Thanks," he said, and I got a couple of Cokes and gave him a can. "You want to walk across the bridge?"

"Sure. You like the guy she's marrying?"

"What?"

"Your kid."

"Yeah, yeah, he's fine. Nice boy, nice enough." He was distracted.

"I'm sorry you didn't call earlier, we could have grabbed some lunch," I said. "I could have taken you by my pal Sverdloff's new club, he serves nice wine."

He nodded.

"You're back on the job?" I said.

"You knew?"

"I was guessing. Lot of guys went back, you were pretty much always a patriot," I said.

"Since after 9/11," he said. "Had to do it." Pettus added, leaning against the brick structure at the center of the Brooklyn Bridge and looking out at the river. "Mostly I work out west, out of Denver, closest place to where I live where there's a big office."

"I'm guessing you get here to the city, though, some of the time, that so, Roy?"

"Yeah, sometimes I do some stuff here."

"Who with?"

"Liaison stuff. Your guys. Ours. Joint Force on Terrorism. This city is the only place they do it right. You didn't just wait on Washington."

"Right," I said.

"Critical," he said. "Without them, we'd be screwed."

Pettus put the Coke can to his lips and swallowed the rest of his Coke. He walked to a trash basket and deposited the Coke can, walked back, lit a cigarette and offered me one. I didn't want it.

"You're good with languages, aren't you?" said Pettus. "You've lived different places. You have friends."

"I'm just a homicide detective, Roy, that's it, and I'm on vacation."

"You're better than that."

"There is nothing better," I said, and he smiled.

"Your old boss, Mr Lippert, I mean, he used to say you were sharp and smart and you knew your way around. Worldly, was the word I think he used," Roy said.

In silence, we walked down the slope of the bridge towards the Brooklyn end, and I turned and started back again. Pettus had trouble keeping up and I stopped for a minute and let him catch his breath.

"Artie, there's no vacation from the terrorists. No vacation. And it's coming again, Artie, we just don't see it, it's coming in a nuke in a container on a ship into Jersey, it's coming over the Mexican border, it's coming in some kind of financial meltdown."

"We'll be okay," I said, as we walked to the Manhattan side of the bridge. "In New York we got really good guys, we get good intel on terrorists now, we even send our people to Tel Aviv, London, Pakistan, as soon as there's an incident, we get our own people on it."

"That's what I mean," said Roy.

"What do you mean?" I said. It was hard keeping cool. I was angry at Pettus for going to Dubi, and to Tolya. "What's on your mind, Roy?"

For a while he talked some more about terrorism and patriotism, and then he said, "We need you. We need your skills.

We need you in places where you can learn what's going on.

And then I understood.

"You're saying you want me to be a spook, a spy, a curtain-twitcher, as my mother called them? You want me as a creature—for what, for who? Your people? The CIA? Listen, Roy, man it's not me, I'm sorry, but I don't do that stuff. I do cases here in New York. We fight our own kind of terror, homicides, rapes, like always. Maybe Sonny Lippert's been reading too many spy novels."

"There are no local cases anymore, Artie. Everybody's caught up in a spider web of shit, it encircles the globe like the ozone, you follow up something, it takes you somewhere else, borders are fluid, easy to get across, nothing is local." It was the longest speech I could remember him making.

"This was your idea? Talking to me?"

He nodded.

"Your idea to go to my friends, too, to ask around about me?"

"I'm sorry about that."

"You knew they'd tell me."

"I'm sorry about that. People say you still speak good Russian, no accent."

"You went to see Dubi Petrovsky for this? This is why you saw him?"

"Yes."

"You asked him how good my Russian is?"

At first I had thought it was my Arabic Roy was interested in, and I didn't get it because the Arabic I learned in Israel was pretty basic stuff. Now it was clear, the reason for him asking how good my Russian was, I put it all together. I'd been stupid not to see exactly what he was after. But I made him spell it out even while I watched the river, the skyline, the city. My city. Mine. I wasn't going anywhere else.

"I'm not leaving the city or my job, so you can forget about it," I said.

"This is another Cold War we're in, Artie. Things are moving fast. The FSB—what they're calling the KGB now—run the whole show. They run Russia."

"I know what the FSB is."

"Everyone thinks they just got some kind of Russian-style capitalism, maybe a little light authoritarian stuff till they get the economy fixed, but that somehow they're okay, and they're our pals. Bush says he looked in Vladimir Putin's eyes and saw his soul. What's he think, it's some kind of prayer meeting? And John McCain he looks at him and sees KGB on his forehead, and he says so, and he thinks this is the way you deal with them?" This was a blaspheming kind of thing for somebody like Pettus who had always been a good Catholic, not pious, but devout, and also a staunch Republican who thought Ronald Reagan was a dead god, and who would walk over broken glass for a guy like McCain. Pettus had been in the Marines in Vietnam.

"I work homicides, it's all I do, okay? I'm speaking loud enough?" I said. "So I speak Russian, so what? What the hell do you want with me being a, whatever it is, some kind of spy bullshit? I mean they have all that lingo, they talk about tradecraft and curtain-twitchers, and moles and shit. I guess I could study up, read the books." I kept my tone light. "Why didn't you just call me for fuck's sake, Roy?"

"I'm sorry. It was stupid. I don't know. I get used to doing things a certain way. If it will help, I apologize. I'll apologize again."

"Right."

"This Russian thing's serious. We get calls for help from the Brits, especially, who are in bad shape. They didn't see it coming, they were obsessed with the Islamic stuff. Ever since Litvinenko, that Russian that died from polonium in London, everyone's going nuts. Artie, the Russians poisoned one of their own, he got out of line, they killed him on British soil."

"I heard nobody was exactly sure what happened."

"I'm telling you the truth. The Brits, they're paying big time for their government that opened the door, they got greedy, they let rich Russians into London, tax free, and the money came and the crime followed. It's coming here."

I'd had no plans to leave New York before last night, and after, after Val stayed with me, I was never going away. We didn't say anything. We hardly spoke. After I left Pettus, I'd call her. I wouldn't push her. I'd buy her breakfast was all. Or lunch.

"I have to go," I said, and we walked to the Manhattan side, and off the bridge. "You think I live in some bizarro alternative spook universe? Honest to god, Roy, how in the fuck would I ever know anything about being a spy in a foreign place? What do I know about London?"

"You worked a case there once."

I smiled. "You've been in my files."

"I'm just talking, right? You can relax," said Pettus, tossing his cigarette on the sidewalk and putting it out with the worn toe of his brown cowboy boot. "I'm just here to shoot the breeze with you, just passing through. Get your view of things is all. I always got an interesting angle off of you, Artie. Always valued it. Like running things through a different prism."

I accepted what Pettus said but deep down I felt it was bullshit. He had a job in mind for me, and I wasn't going anywhere, I wasn't leaving New York.

"Right," I said. "You're pretty interested in helping the Brits."

"We owe them. My dad was Canadian. He was in the Air Force. He went over in 1940 and flew in the Battle of Britain. The Brits did it for us then and they're doing it for us now."

"It's a long time ago." I put out my hand. "Roy, keep in touch."

"You know these people, Artie. You come from there. You

speak the language. You understand the territory. You got it in the blood."

"What the hell is that? I was sixteen when we left Moscow."

"You got a feel for it, though."

"Who says?"

"I'm not going to talk patriotism to you. Like I said, I just wanted to chat, honest to God."

"There's a load of Russians, very patriotic, very devoted to the USA and right here in New York. You probably got a few in Wyoming."

"What about your friend, Sverdloff? He devoted? I heard he doesn't love America."

"What about him?"

"He spends time over in London. Got himself a club here, a club there, another one in Moscow, he has houses everywhere, hangs out with the real money. Isn't that the truth, Artie? You're pals with him, with his kid, too?"

"How the fuck do you know that?"

"Why? It's a secret?"

"Is that what this is about, about Sverdloff? You want me to spy on my friend? Go fuck yourself."

"Come on, Artie, man, you know Sverdloff is one of theirs."

"What the hell do you mean?"

"I mean Russian."

"Sverdloff isn't a spy."

"Don't be a horse's ass, Artie. Sverdloff will do whatever he has to do."

"You don't know what you're talking about."

"We're in trouble, Artie. The whole damn free world."

"I haven't heard that line for a long time."

Pettus got out his smokes again, lit one and offered me the pack.

"Can we talk again?"

"It won't make any difference."

The phone rang while we were talking. I looked at the number. It was Valentina. I didn't want Petttus watching me when I talked to her.

Have breakfast with me, she had said earlier before she left my place. Let's have breakfast.

"You're in a hurry?" said Pettus.

"I'm in a hurry," I said. "I have to go," I added, left him in front of City Hall and called Val back.

"I'm looking at the ocean," she said. "It's such a gorgeous day."

For a moment I thought she had gone away. I felt panicky.

"Where are you?" I said. "Val?"

PART TWO

CHAPTER FIFTEEN

Doing ninety, I was in my car heading for Brooklyn to see Valentina. I had left Roy Pettus, broke away from him and his terrorist fables about the Russians. I wasn't leaving New York for London. I wasn't going into the spook business.

Alongside the Belt Parkway was the water, the harbor, the sunlight on the Statue of Liberty making it glisten. I had driven this road a thousand times, past Red Hook and the ancient warehouses, past the new cruise-ship port, the parks and garbage dumps. I knew every landmark, but I hardly saw them now, just drove as fast as I could and listened to Louis Armstrong's *Hot Fives and Sevens,* "Potato Head Blues" making me even happier than I already felt.

Hearing Val's voice, I felt happy. And anxious. I wasn't sure how to behave. For her it hadn't been—I didn't know what it had been for her. For me, something else, something like hearing Armstrong for the first time. I was forty-nine years old and I felt like a kid.

I went back over every word of the brief conversation we'd had half an hour earlier, when I was leaving Pettus.

"Come on out. I'll buy you breakfast," said Val. "And we can swim, if you want," she said.

"Where are you?"

"Brooklyn."

I was so relieved she was only in Brooklyn, I started laughing.

"What's the matter?" said Val.

"Nothing. Where in Brooklyn?"

"You remember that apartment my dad bought for his mother, my grandma, Lara, when she came to America, before she died? Did you ever see it?"

I remembered.

"I'm on my way."

"Good, I want to see you. Coffee's on," she said, and laughed, the throaty, dark laugh that was like an older woman. "If you're good, I'll buy you blintzes," she added. "Strawberry."

"I could meet you someplace, we could eat someplace," I said, nervous now.

"Come to the apartment first."

I had planned to go to Dacha, the club in Sheepshead Bay. Tito Dravic, the manager had promised me a video and some paperwork on Masha Panchuk, the dead girl on the swing. It was still early.

In Brighton Beach near the boardwalk overlooking the ocean was a condo built half a dozen years ago for Russians who had made some dough in America but didn't want to leave the neighborhood. Old people, mostly. Others who had moved up and out, Long Island or New Jersey, kept an apartment for the ocean view, the shopping, sentiment, an investment.

Tolya Sverdloff had bought a condo for his mother the time she was in America. I didn't know that after she died, he had kept it.

A doorman with gold braid on his shoulders was reading the *News* in the lobby and when he saw me, he faked a smile and buzzed the Sverdloff apartment, and I went up in the elevator with an elderly couple, their arms piled high with bags of food. I could smell the lox.

*

"Come on in," her voice called. The door was open. I went into the apartment and saw her.

Behind a makeshift desk near the window, talking into the phone, reading some papers, doodling in a notebook, her face was scrubbed, no make-up, a pencil stuck behind her ear, she wore a red blouse with long sleeves and a white cotton skirt that fell below her knees. Her feet were stuck in a pair of yellow flip-flops. From somewhere—her iPod, maybe—came the sound of a lovely bossa nova track.

"Hey, Artie." She looked up, pointed at the phone, at a chair. "I won't be long, okay? There's coffee on in the kitchen, honey, and you could grab me a mug, too," she added.

I remembered the place. When Tolya bought it for his mother, he had furnished it with a black leather couch and some easy chairs, which were still here but piled with files and folders and books. On the wall was a bulletin board with the names and addresses of orphanage facilities and shelters in Russian. Tacked to the cork board were also six of Val's photographs of Russian children. Staring into the camera, the kids looked bruised, tired, hopeless.

Most of the bedroom furniture was gone—the old lady, Tolya's mother, Lara Sverdlova—had had a taste for frilly covers and gilt mirrors. All that remained was a bed covered with a plain white linen spread. That, and a large movie poster with Lara as a young star in an old Soviet picture. In it, she was dressed as a farm girl riding a tractor, and it made me smile. Sverdlova had always been glamorous and even in a babushka, and on the tractor, she was perfectly made up, and her hands mani-cured. My dad had adored her.

In the small kitchen coffee was dripping into a glass. The smell was intense, and I poured it into a couple of mugs and went back to Val.

She beamed, got up, kissed me on the cheek. "You like my disguise?" she said indicating the blouse and skirt.

I gave her the coffee. "I like it," I said.

"I deal with a lot of poor ex-Soviets now, some from the Stans, Uzbeks, Tajiks, those people, and the Bukharians, I always think it sounds romantic, the region is called the Silk Road, you know? Tashkent, Dushanbe, really, really isolated and strange, and suddenly they're in America. People just hanging on. Some of them are religious, I don't go around in shorts or tight stuff, it makes my job easier if I look okay to them. But the ones who don't make it out are in real shit," she added.

"How come?"

"They live in these backwaters. I went once, it's incredible, like something out of prehistory, and there's no money, and no work, so they go to Moscow and eventually some of the girls end up working the streets, or the train stations, or worse. The people here get the news, family members get in touch, I try to put my people in Moscow in contact. Sometimes it's the girls themselves," she said.

"How come I didn't know about all this?"

"I only started not so long ago. You didn't convince my dad to stay, I guess," she added.

"I'm really sorry. I tried."

She shrugged. "It's okay. I saw him before he left. He said he'd make the London trip short. I hope he will."

"What was in the envelope he gave you at his club?"

"You're a nosey bastard," she said, and grinned. "He gave me a big fat check for my little foundation."

"I could give you a check."

"You're adorable, Artie, let's not talk about depressing stuff, let's go eat and maybe have a swim, or sit in the sun."

"I want to hear more about your work," I said. "I do."

"I'll tell you while we eat,"she said.

"I don't know why you're not fat, you eat all the time."

"Maybe it's genetic." She picked up a copy of the *Post* from a chair. "You know about this, Artie?" Val showed me the picture of Masha Panchuk in the paper.

"Yeah, I heard."

"When did you hear?"

"Why do you ask?"

"I knew her," said Valentina. "Masha, right?"

When we were settled at a cafe on the boardwalk, and Val had ordered smoked fish, having changed her mind about the blintzes, and we were both drinking Bloody Marys, she asked me again what I knew about the dead girl.

"What do you mean you knew her?"

"That club out in Sheepshead Bay, the one I walked over to with you Friday night, Dacha, or maybe someplace in the city. It didn't snap into place until I saw the paper. I recognized her from the picture, not the taped-up one, Jesus, Artie. Sometimes I wonder."

I was surprised by Val's cool, her composure. Most people, unless they're on the job, pull back when the talk turns to dead people, to the cases filled with bare-knuckle ugliness.

"It doesn't bother you, talking about it?"

"Of course it bothers me, but not the way people think," said Val. "The stuff I see in Moscow is pretty shitty, so at least it makes me less of a pussy crybaby than most of my friends."

"What kind of stuff?"

While I was asking, the food arrived, and Val dug into the huge platters of smoked salmon, whitefish, sable, sturgeon. She put butter on her bread, and piled it high with fish.

"What kind?" she said. "Little girls put out to work as prostitutes, parents who slash them, I mean on their faces, with rusty razor blades, if they refuse. This is big business in Moscow and no one does anything."

"Tell me about Masha Panchuk. How well did you know her?"

"Was that her last name? I didn't even know. I knew she was Masha, I got that, I remember, but I hardly knew her at all," said Val. "Some of my friends told me she was illegal and I tried to figure out what to do for her, but I couldn't, so I would give her little presents, stupid shit that girls like, a little purse, some make-up, I don't know, some money or something, and I asked my dad about her, but he didn't like me going out to the clubs, and anyhow, I'm always shoving my giant feet into things, so I just let it be this time." She waved at the waitress, called her by name, asked Tanya how the kids were, and asked for more coffee. "Maybe I should have stayed with it, I mean helped Masha out, but I didn't. Also, I pretty much stopped going to clubs last winter, you know, I mean I'm too old."

"You're twenty-four," I said

"Yeah, but old for my years." She laughed and ate more fish, and more bread, and thought about cheesecake. Val leaned back and looked at people on the boardwalk. "You want to swim?"

"I'd sink if I swam after all this food," I said.

"What are you doing for dinner tonight? You could buy me an early birthday dinner if you want. Weird that my pop and I have the same birthday, isn't it?"

I was flustered. I tried my usual line of joking with her.

"You're supposed to think of me as your uncle or something," I said. "Anyway, your father would not just kill me but do it slowly in little pieces, like the worst stuff he ever learned from his not-so-nice-nik friends. You know how they killed people in old Russia? You want me to tell you how they did it, Val? You're thinking Pugachev, the bandit outlaw, from old times, right? I read the Pushkin story. They really did nasty stuff." Val picked up her fork. The middle finger on her left hand was missing. She saw me looking at it.

"I know, my dad worries because he thinks this is his fault."

*

When she was ten, Val was snatched from the Sverdloffs' apartment in Moscow. It was the 1990s, the gangster years in Russia, and Tolya was in real-estate deals with bad people.

Tolya had been at home when they took Val, but he was dead drunk, fast asleep. He never got over it. It was his fault and he knew it, that they took his little girl, kept her for three days, cut off her finger and sent it to him. He left Moscow after that, and took his family to Florida to live in a gated community.

He offered Val plastic surgery. The best, he said. He urged it on her. You'll be like new, he said. She refused. She wore her stump like a badge of honor, the way she wore everything— her beauty, her height.

She was a passionate, funny girl, but there were times when her eyes turned inward and she seemed far away. Maybe it was to do with the kids she helped in Moscow, the things she had learned that made her want to cut out, to stop the world. There were times I thought of her as a girl in a garden, dreaming, planning, a book on her lap, her eyes shut, listening to the crickets and the wind.

"I'm a mutant, Artie, darling," she said. "I'm too tall and too weird. I take pictures because I'm obsessed with looking at people. Sometimes I find myself staring at them in restaurants or on the train. I want to know everything. It's just how I am. I once ate a little piece of film, a piece of the negative, to see what it was like, see if I could make it get inside of me—Jesus, Artie, why does my dad have to be in London?"

"He likes London."

"I know, and I'm a grown woman and I should let him live his life." She gulped her coffee and added, "I just like it better when he's here." She got up.

"Where are you going?"

"What, my dad put you on my tail? I have to go pick up some stuff so I can pack it up."

"What stuff? Where are you going?"

"For the kids, clothes, meds, stuff. I send it ahead of me to Moscow. I'll probably go over in a couple or three weeks, and then only for four, five days, it's just I need to get things ready." She sounded defensive.

"Tolya knows?"

"Maybe. Butt out, darling. Look, I'm just going to Moscow to do a few things and spend a few days with my mom who's on vacation."

"I thought she lived in Boca."

"Yes, so what?" Val was exasperated by all my questions. "She does live in Florida, but she can afford to travel now, so she travels, my dad gives her whatever she wants, even though they're divorced, he says, she is the mother of my children, you know? In that pompous voice he puts when he's on a roll? My mom has a great big dacha near Barvika, outside Moscow, okay, everything she dreamed of when she was a girl and she married my dad, and they lived in a one-room apartment in Moscow, back in the day. But her tastes she developed in Boca, right?" Val smiled at the idea of her mother's tastes. "So she has the condo in Boca, and a place in London, and a great big dacha in Barvika, I mean huge, with a fabulous pool with faux Impressionists painted on the bottom.

"She was just this provincial Russian girl when they got married, and he was like this big rock guru in Moscow, and he performs and she lies down on the stage one night and licks his boots. She was gorgeous. What a crazy time, I wish I was there, the 80s sound so fabulous in Moscow. Well, whatevs. Anyhow, my mom's new dacha has marble and gold taps, and there's a tennis court, and a pool, one indoors, one out."

"What about her boyfriend?"

"He loves it. You remember him? The one who wears the yachting cap and the real gold buttons on his blazer? He has money, but now he feels he has class. I mean he's global now. I think he comes from New Jersey. So, you see, I'll be in safe hands. You should come visit. Moscow is wild. Daddy's club is hot, he's a star, he'll be going on celebrity chef or something, or celebrity wine master, whatever." She leaned over the table. "I love him a lot, Artie. I love my dad, you know, more than anyone? I won't do anything to make him worry, I promise. Or you."

"But you're careful, right? I mean you don't get crazy when you talk to officials over there, about the kids you help and stuff."

"Of course not. But it's fine, it's all really official, we get help from NGOs, we get help from the US ambassador. You think I want to get involved with anything weird over there? Forget about it. I'm an American. I'm a perfect American girl, right?" She pursed her lips and made a rueful noise.

"You have a Russian passport?"

"Yes. Also."

"You travel a lot, you, Tolya."

"We like to travel," she said, half sardonic. "Movement is everything. My mom remembers when she was my age, the only place she was ever allowed to go outside the Soviet Union was once to Bulgaria." She put her hand up to her head. "God, my head hurts," she said.

"You okay?"

"I've been feeling kind of weird lately, I don't know, my stomach, my head. I've been using some new chemical in my darkroom, I think the smell makes me feel bad."

"What kind of stuff?" Tell me, I wanted to say. Tell me and I'll make you feel better whatever it is.

I wanted to put my arms around her, but I just drank my coffee.

"Oh, Artie, it's nothing. Listen, did my dad ask you to work for him again?"

"Yeah, every other day. I think he feels sorry for me because I'm always broke."

"Don't go into business with my dad. You wouldn't like it."

"Why not?"

"That would mean the end of your love affair."

For a moment I thought she meant us, her and me, and I was startled.

"What love affair?"

"You and my dad, of course," said Val. "Not like that, you idiot, I mean, never mind. It's about the best kind, about friendship. But if you went into business, you'd have to do things you wouldn't like. It would offend your moral code," said Valentina.

"I don't have a moral code. You make me sound like some guy with a poker up his ass. What moral code?"

She sat down again, this time on the edge of a chair, put her elbows on the table and her face close to mine. "Well, not that kind," she said and kissed me lightly on the lips. "For sure not that kind, Artie. We got past that last night, didn't we? That kind of crap that says I'm too young for you, you hear me?"

I nodded.

"I'll tell you everything tonight, I will, I promise."

"Yes."

"And you don't remind me of my uncles one bit," she added, leaned over the table again and put her hands on either side of my head, and I thought to myself: don't do this. I thought to myself: don't feel like this. Stop. I was besotted, but it was temporary, it was a fantasy, it was like falling for a girl in a movie. Wasn't it?

The hours she had spent in my bed weren't casual for her, I knew, but it wasn't for the long term. I was too old. I was her father's best friend. I wanted her so bad I could hardly look at her, but I had to, I had to pretend we were still just friends, just family, the way we always had been. I felt, in the far distance, a little door closing.

"Tonight?" I said.

"You're going to take me to dinner," she said. "Don't look so serious," she added.

"I'm fine."

"You look gloomy as hell," she said, then leaned over, kissed me three times on the cheek and the little gold cross she wore on a thin chain dangled against my forehead, as if she were a priest making the sign of the cross so I'd be safe. "I have to go," she added. "I'll meet you. Dinner. Around nine. Ten? And we could go to a late movie after? Or dancing?"

"Dinner," I said. "Yes. Where?"

"My friend Beatrice's, over in the East Village, you know the place? She cooks that fantastic spaghetti carbonara, my dad loves it, we go and he eats like everything on the menu."

"On East 2nd Street, right? Ten."

"Around ten," she said.

I kissed the top of her head and said, casually as I could, "See you tonight."

"Darling, I always show up for you, you know that, sooner or later. Sometimes later, I know, it's my vice, bad time-keeping, but for you, I always show up."

"Promise?"

"Artie, I do love you."

All I could do was scramble in my jacket pocket for some money to pay the check. I couldn't look at her, I couldn't say what I wanted to.

"Artie?"

"What?"

"People worry about me, I say, listen, I was named for Valentina Tereshkova, the first woman in space, and she came back, so I always come back, too. I'll definitely be there." She kissed me on the cheek once more, stuffed the last piece of cake into her mouth. "You are stuck with me, Artie, darling. So I'll be there, or as we used to say when we were little kids, cross my heart and hope to die."

CHAPTER SIXTEEN

The club on Sheepshead Bay was shut up. Closed on Sunday, a sign said. Tito Dravic had told me there was a house on the next block that the club owners used as an office, and I walked around the corner. A row of small ramshackle houses was on the narrow side street. The trees cast shadows on the sidewalk. Nobody was around except a tiny kid riding a tricycle up and down the street.

On the porch of one of the houses was a stack of beer cases, a crate of wine, another of vodka. I figured it was the right place. Next to the door was a piece of paper taped on the wall, a message scribbled on it: 'Deliveries for Dacha', and below it a cell number. I called the number. Nobody answered.

The door was locked from the inside. I called Dravic's name. It was quiet. Too quiet. I was sweating in the heat, and unnerved. Dravic had said he'd be there, but when I knocked and then called out again, nobody answered.

At the back of the house was a patch of yard with scabby dry grass, a plastic table and chairs. The back door was shut but not locked and I went into the kitchen where crates of booze and glasses were piled everywhere. On a table was a package wrapped in brown paper. On top was an invoice from a local printer. Inside were flyers for the club. I was in the right place. The office, Dravic had said.

It was too quiet. No noise. Nothing. Somewhere outside, a car revved up, pulled away. I ran outside, but it had gone.

In the house again, I went through the kitchen into a room where computers and phones sat on two large tables, there were three scratched filing cabinets, a big flatscreen TV, more crates of liquor, a yellow fake leather couch, a few chairs.

I looked everywhere. There was something wrong, somebody had left in a hurry. Dravic maybe.

The drawer of a filing cabinet was open, paper spilled out. There was paper on the white shag rug. The couch was rumpled, the pillows tossed around as if somebody had been digging around, looking for something. When I pushed aside the dirty drapes at the window, I saw an envelope half-hidden on the sill. It had my name on it.

Did he leave in a hurry? Had he hidden the envelope on purpose? Did somebody come looking for it?

I didn't wait. I took it and left, same way I'd come, through the back door and the yard and around to the street where my car was parked.

Somewhere I heard a door open. I looked down the row of houses. I didn't see anyone. Then it banged shut and I got into my car, tossed the envelope on the seat next to me, and turned the key. As soon as I pulled away from the curb I stepped on the gas.

I was a couple blocks away from the house when my phone rang and it was Bobo. He said he had an address for Masha, that he was headed for her apartment.

"You want to come with me? I mean, could you come? I'm getting fucked up on this case, Artie, I'd appreciate it."

"Sure," I said. "Give me the address. Where is it?"

"Near Neptune Avenue," he said. "Where the Paks live."

*

"Everybody here likes Masha," said the guy at the video store who introduced himself as Mohammed Najib. "Nicest girl anywhere," added Najib, a tall reedy guy with a little white cap on his gray hair and the stoop of a man who reads too much.

Music from some Pakistani film came from one of the sets in the video store. Teenagers browsed the racks, giggling and making cracks.

Najib, who said everybody called him Moe, said he would show me the apartment where Masha had lived above his store.

"Of course, Officer Leven has already seen it," added Moe. I couldn't judge the tone. The guy—Moe—was polite, but I could see Bobo made him nervous. When he offered tea, Bobo barely thanked him, and I thought: what the hell is wrong with him? Just say thank you, Bobo, I mumbled to myself. Moe excused himself to wait on a customer.

"You were here?" I said to Bobo out of Moe's hearing. "You were already here?"

"Yeah, so what? I figured I'd take a look, other guys on the case had already been, I didn't want to bother you. Now I need your help."

"Never mind." I was impatient. I wanted to look at the stuff in the envelope Dravic had left for me. Soon, I thought to myself, I'm going out to take my vacation days and go sit in the sun. I said it over and over, like a mantra. I hated the idea of myself as a guy who never took a break, who couldn't let go. I said it, but I didn't believe it.

Little Pakistan is how it was known, this large chunk of Coney Island Avenue, not far from Brighton Beach. Ever since the 1980s when some Russians began moving up and out, Pakistanis—out here they called themselves Paks—moved in. Before 9/11 it was a bustling crowded community where people got along. Once the planes fell on the towers, once the backlash began, some of them fled. A cop I knew had called me about the tension, he was worried, he had said. Told me there were FBI guys snooping around, Homeland Security assholes, police brass wanting to look good, look patriotic.

In the end, maybe 15,000 residents had gone, some of them deported, others who just left temporarily out of fear. It was a shitty deal. But people came back. The community rebuilt. Some of the Pakistanis were doing well enough they could move on. Turks coming in now, take up the space.

It was dusk. The avenue was lit up bright, video stores, restaurants, insurance brokers, car parts. There were a couple twenty-four-hour joints where cabbies ate. Last few years when I was working around Brighton Beach, I sometimes went by for a meal.

Outside the video store, Bobo lit up a cigarette, and listened to music from the video store.

"Man, sounds like somebody stepped on the cat," he said. "I can't believe Masha lived upstairs. How could she live in a dump like this?"

A couple of women, their heads covered with scarves, strolled by, chatting and laughing. Bobo stared at them.

"What's with you?" I said.

"Okay, I don't like them. Okay? Say I have prejudice, I mean after 9/11, Artie, come on."

"Stop fucking staring, Bobo."

"I'm sorry, but I don't like it, okay? I just don't, so I'm not PC, you should think about it, Artie, you're also Jewish."

"What difference does that make?" I had never been in a synagogue in my life except for a bar mitzvah once when a friend's kid turned thirteen.

Moe reappeared.

"Can I help you?" he said, and I realized he had a British accent. On his t-shirt was an *Obama For President* button.

"Masha Panchuk's apartment?" I said.

"Yes, of course, I'm sorry. I was distracted. Come up, please."

"You from England?" asked Bobo.

"Yes, as a matter of fact," said Moe. "I was born and grew up in a place called Bradford. Man, I would never go back. Too wet and cold, rains all the time. I'm so sorry about Masha."

"You knew about her? That she was murdered?"

"You told me," he said. "You called the store and asked if she had lived here."

"Right," said Bobo. "You didn't think to call when you knew she was missing?"

"I didn't know until I heard from you," Moe said. "She came and went. Often I didn't see her for several days. In fact, I saw her Saturday, she was going out to shop."

"Who else had extra keys, besides you?"

"I don't know, maybe she made extras. I can't say," said Moe. "I keep spares because I own the building," he added.

We followed him into the doorway next to his store and up three flights of stairs. "I'll be downstairs if you need me," he said, not looking at Bobo.

"What the hell is wrong with you?" I said to Bobo. "You think you get anything by talking to people who help you like that?"

"I don't like them, okay?" We stood on the landing. The apartment was sealed. Bobo carefully removed the tape and opened the door.

"Who got it sealed?"

"I did," he said. "Soon as I found out where it was. I didn't want anyone except guys working the case going in."

"It's not okay," I said. "How come it took you so long to tell me where she lived?"

"You didn't seem interested."

Inside the tiny studio apartment was a bed, a dresser, a table, a tiny kitchen behind a curtain, a bathroom. It was a furnished room, and all Masha had added were a couple of posters of boy groups she must have liked.

In the closet were her clothes, jumbled together, some on the floor, some stuffed into shelves or on cheap wire hangers. Hard to tell if she'd been messy like a kid or somebody had come here to look through her things.

"Look for her clothes," Sonny Lippert had said.

"You still didn't find her clothes, right? The stuff she had on when they killed her?"

"I have four guys working on it," said Bobo Leven. "I told them to leave the stuff here until we looked at everything."

I pulled out some shoes, a bag, a jacket. There were expensive things in the girl's closet. The kind of things I expected Val to wear, or her friends. There was no pink dress, no pink party dress with sparkles on it.

"What was she wearing when she was murdered?"

"Nothing," said Bobo. "At least nothing when the tape was removed."

"You think they killed her in the playground, taped her up there?"

"Probably not. Too risky."

"So what happened to her clothes?"

"We're looking, like I said. You have some thoughts?" he said.

"Yeah, look for a pink party dress. Let me know."

Between us we worked over every inch of the place, her clothes, the make-up in the bathroom, a few paperback books, her iPod, a tiny pink address book. I scanned it, there were names of a few friends, city agencies, bars. Bobo said he had seen it, had it copied, put it back. Send me a copy, I said. Nothing in it, he said.

I wanted to get to the envelope Tito Dravic had left me, wanted the résumé he had promised me, and the tape, Masha Panchuk dancing.

"What about this?" Bobo held up a small roll of duct tape

he'd found in the bathroom.

"Probably somebody used it for sealing the window when it was cold. Anyhow, it's black."

"Yeah, right, this is a fucking waste of time," he said.

"Get somebody from your station house to go over the place again, okay? In detail."

"Yes, Artie, of course."

On the street, Bobo on his phone, I went in to thank Moe and give him my number in case anything came up.

The weather had turned sultry. Humidity clung to my skin. It had been a long day, and now I felt I was fighting the air that was like syrup on my skin, heavy, thick, cloying. Music played out of car windows as guys rolled along Coney Island Avenue. Rap. Rappers call it music. I call it shit.

"I have to go," I said.

"You don't get it, do you? You don't know anything." He snapped his phone shut.

"What about?"

"These people, Artie." Bobo was looking to pick a fight with me. I let him talk. "My cousin Viktor was fighting in Chechnya against these assholes. You have any idea what that was like for a Jewish boy from Moscow? If all young soldiers get beat up, all new Jewish soldiers get double beating, one for being Jewish, one for being from Moscow."

"What's it got to do with the Chechens?"

"You don't know shit some of the time, pardon me, Artemy. Over there in the former USSR, they would like to kill all the Jews, except maybe one for each province. You remember that old saying about how every Russian governor always had one Jew for show. A Show Jew, Artie. But you don't remember," said Bobo. "You think the guys at my station house feel different?"

"Well, then, fuck them, too. Get over it. I'm not having you alienate half of Brooklyn because you hate Muslims, okay? You zip it up, Bobo."

"I'm Russian. I'm also Jew. You have a lot of towel-head friends, Artie?" His tone was mild but the words were aggressive.

At the center of this string bean of a kid with his shambling walk, his punk haircut, was a determined, ambitious cop. And angry. He was learning fast. Before long he'd stop taking shit from anybody, including me.

"So, Artie. Here," he said handing me a card. "I also found this in the apartment. In the medicine cabinet."

Natasha Club, it said. The best in Russian Women.

"What is it?"

"Mail-order brides, you say, I think. Or whores."

"There's something else?" I said to Bobo.

"Yeah, something else. I want to tell you what it was like at home, okay? Caucasians from down there from the Caucasus, they come to Moscow, they take over most of the market stalls, they're dirty people, and they blow up stuff in Moscow. Apartment buildings. Subway stations. What the fuck are they in Moscow for? And here, now they're here, in Brooklyn, and how come they make their women wear those bags over their heads?"

I ignored him. He was baiting me and I had no intention of fueling his rage. He could get over it or he could fuck off for all I cared.

"How well did you know the dead girl?" I said.

"I knew Masha a little. She was great dancer. Always twelve guys hanging around for her."

"Fine. I'm not going to ask how come you didn't tell me you knew her in the first place or what shit you know about Dacha, the club, just find out who they were, the twelve guys, also the girls she knew. Get me some hard information."

"Not twelve exactly."

"I get it. I get it's not exactly twelve, but however many." I was impatient. "What else?"

"Once we eat on the boardwalk on Saturday night, a group, seven, eight friends, we just sit out and watch the ocean and talk. Masha was there."

"Write it down. Send me an e-mail."

"Artie?"

"Yes?"

"You ever wonder about the m on Masha, the one somebody made with a knife?"

"The lab's been looking at it all along."

"You wonder what it stands for? You think it stands for Masha?"

"Yeah, maybe."

"What about Mohammed, what about this guy Moe?"

"Don't be ridiculous," I said, but he'd planted the seed of doubt into my head where it could take root.

Bobo's car was at the curb. He unlocked the door.

"I'm on it," he said, his voice turning chilly. "You don't have to bust my balls."

"Very nice car," I said. "You got it where?"

"My parents."

"Your parents are doing so well?"

"Fuck you."

"Give it a break, Bobo. Relax."

"No, I don't want to fucking give it a break. My pop opened another dry-cleaning place. Why? You think because my parents are living in Brighton Beach, they're crooked? Because I'm living at home I'm in on some game, too? I stay there to help out with my mom who has arthritis bad, right? The car was a present, right? It was my birthday present."

"Forget it."

"No. Let's discuss. I take a lot of shit from you, okay, so I learn this way. But some stuff it's not okay. Not okay that you think I take money in some way unclean, you know? Not all Russians are corrupted bastards," he said in English and then switched to Russian, his voice very cold and very low. "You think that all of us are just creeps, I know that, Artemy, I know how you think, you always show it to me, one way or the other. You've turned into an American, so for you Russians are gangsters or religious nuts, you've forgotten your country, and I don't care about that, but get off my fucking back. I'm not your kid."

"Calm down," I said.

"Sure."

"One more thing, Bobo."

"Yeah?"

"You slept with her? You slept with Masha? You had something going on?"

CHAPTER SEVENTEEN

Standing near my car, I opened the package I had taken from the house in Brighton Beach and found a videotape, and a few sheets of paper. I scanned them, and then yelled for Bobo Leven who was climbing into his car. He shut the door and jogged over to me. I held out a piece of paper. He took it, read it, grunted.

"Jesus, Art."

"Yeah." I felt sick.

"Masha Panchuk waited tables for your pal, Anatoly Sverdloff," he said.

"Give me a cigarette."

Bobo handed me the pack along with his lighter.

"Fuck it, Artie, didn't Sverdloff mention this?" said Bobo. "He didn't tell you one of his girls was missing?"

"Why would he? Maybe he didn't know. Maybe she was a temp."

"Don't be so defensive, but you have to figure by now someone maybe called him about it, Sverdloff, I mean. Right? Or you want to do that?"

"He's on his way to London. He didn't have anything to do with Masha Panchuk's murder."

"You want to hang onto that raft, like they say, Artemy?"

"Fine. I'll call him," I said.

"You trust him, right?"

I lit the cigarette and handed him back his smokes and the lighter.

I worked my phone, I made some calls, nothing. I turned to Bobo.

"Find Dravic, if you can," I said. "He was supposed to meet me at the house the club uses as an office, he wasn't there, I just tried him on the phone, there's no answer. I called the club, nothing. Now I'm thinking he was scared, but of what? Scared because he promised to give me some stuff on Masha Panchuk? Did someone overhear us talking at the club?"

"Sure," said Bobo. "I will work everything," he said formally, his English sounding as if he had learned it in school, his Russian accent more pronounced now. "I will be taking everything into consideration, of course, Artemy."

I knew that Bobo Leven would get into everything, he was tenacious, relentless, one of those cops, even at his age, who never let go. At two in the morning, he'd still be at his desk doing the paperwork. Before the other guys got into his station house, he'd be combing his computer, and then when they arrived, he'd bug them for scraps of information. The phone would be permanently attached to his ear, he would be calling, asking, bribing if he had to. I had known a few cops like Bobo. It wasn't just that he wanted to make a name for himself, it was who he was, what he lived for. Everything would come under scrutiny, he would talk to everybody, Albanians, Jamaicans, Mexies, Serbs, Russians, and he would go through every detective report on crazy people, on thugs who sliced people up, on the kinds of knives they used, and if they also used guns, and he would read medical reports, and reports on duct tape, fibers and feathers, anything he could get his hands on.

Every single homicide pattern that was anything like the case would be worked by Bobo; so would cold cases he kept in a bottom drawer.

Moving around, he would get to Starrett City, Brighton Beach, looking at how people had been mugged, sliced, killed. He wanted this case, and he would go without sleep, night after night, until fatigue made him crazy.

"I'm going back to the city," I said, but Bobo didn't answer; he was already on the phone, already tracking Tito Dravic.

In my car, I studied the picture of Masha I had with me, I stared at it hard as if it would give up some secret, and without warning a faint finger of panic crawled up my neck. The thing I hadn't seen, the thing I didn't want to see.

But I had to look. And I looked, and the face stared back at me.

If some creep had snatched Masha Panchuk, and Masha had worked at Tolya's bar, was it Masha the creep really wanted? Was it a mistake? Were they looking for someone else? Somebody connected to me? Somebody who scared Tito Dravic bad?

Masha Panchuk, in the picture I held, was tall with short platinum hair. It had been taken the month before.

The face looked back at me, and in it, there was the resemblance. To Val. She looked like Val. Val's hair had been short and blonde, too. Only recently had she let it grow out; only recently had she let it go back to her dark red.

Had I missed this? How? Did I fail to see it because I didn't want to see it?

I started the car, I drove like crazy back to Brighton Beach, to Val's office, and when I got there she was gone. I called her. Val? Val? Answer the phone!

CHAPTER EIGHTEEN

Val?

All the way home, I called, I put my phone on redial, and when I got to my block I barely noticed that Roy Pettus was leaning against the wall of the Korean grocery on the corner. Holding a bottle of Coke, he saw me pull up. I put my phone away.

"Hello, Art."

"Roy. You following me?"

He looked at his watch.

"Nope, just hoping you might be coming home before I have to go back to New Jersey," Roy said who was wearing a suit, the jacket too big, the collar of his shirt too tight. "You give my offer some thought?" he said. "You okay, Artie? You look shook up."

"What offer?"

"Coming in with us."

"No thanks. I'm helping out on a homicide. I'm busy."

"The Russian girl, right? I could give you some stuff on this, help you finish it up."

"What kind?"

Leaning forward, his head jutting out of his tight shirt collar, he reacted fast, and said, voice low, "This personal with you at all, Artie? You have a stake in this case?" He stuck his finger into his collar like he was suffocating. "God, I feel like a horse's ass, suit and tie, haven't been in a get-up like this for years since I left the city." He adjusted the jacket. "It's too damn hot for this."

"You want to come up to my place?" All the time we were talking, I strained to hear my cellphone. Call, I thought. Val?

"Thanks. That would be fine," Pettus said. "I won't stay long. Just need to cool off."

Upstairs at my place, Pettus removed his jacket carefully, folded it neatly on a kitchen stool, sat down on another one and asked if he could smoke. I said sure and got him a cold Coke, which he asked for, confessing he was addicted to the stuff.

I put a glass and an ashtray in front of him, then checked my messages and my e-mails, while he watched me, guessing how frantic I was, that I was waiting to hear from somebody.

He concentrated on his drink, but I knew he was looking around, watching me, taking a good look, appraising my place, me, how I lived. It was what he had wanted, maybe even why he had been waiting for me on the street in front of my building.

"Nice place," he said.

I got a beer from the fridge, sat opposite him and said, "Thank you." And waited.

"Tough living in the city these days. Expensive."

"Roy, let's skip the small talk."

"Just wanting to help."

"Spit it out, Roy, you're still wanting me to go to London, spy on the Russians there, get involved, is that it? If so, please don't follow me around and bug my friends, it doesn't make me feel comfortable at all."

"Like I said, I'm sorry about that," said Roy. "We're in trouble," he said, as the phone rang, and I bolted from the kitchen to answer it. It wasn't Val.

"Not the call you've been waiting for?" Pettus added mildly.

I didn't answer, just said, "What makes you so sure I'd be good at this stuff, this whatever you call it? Intelligence. Isn't that the polite term, Roy? Isn't that what Bush calls it every time he wants some more money to bug our phones? It's all just bluster, it's just the fucking Russians rattling their missiles and stamping their feet."

Pettus crushed out his smoke, got up, loped across my loft, admired some photographs on the wall, looked at my books, picked one out and examined it. I couldn't see the title. From one of the big industrial windows that faced the street, he looked at the building opposite mine. He turned to me.

"I am really sorry for not coming to you straight," he said. "I don't know what got hold of me. I need your help. We need you bad. It's that simple. I can't think of anyone else I can ask, or trust."

Climbing back on the stool, he put his elbows on the counter, asked if he could have another Coke and smiled, as if at his own pathetic addiction to the soda.

"You'd be attached to Scotland Yard along with a few other NYPD detectives."

"For real? Or as a cover?"

"You'd be working normal terrorism stuff, of course, but it's obvious you'd hang out with some of the new Russians, being a Russian yourself."

"You're figuring if I'm in London I'm spending time at Tolya Sverdloff's London club. With Russians."

"It's where they go."

"I can't do that. I'd be lousy at it."

"You've been undercover from time to time in New York, right? Even doing your homicide cases, you specialize in getting people to tell you things. Right? This isn't any different." Roy turned the pale brown eyes on me. "You have the gift," he added.

"What makes you think that?"

"Your dad, wasn't he an agent? Didn't he work for the KGB back when? I read he was the best, subtle, he could charm anything out of anybody."

"How the hell do you know?"

"When the Soviet Union collapsed, for a time we were on good terms with their people, they let us read a lot of their stuff."

"A long time ago, Roy. It's not genetic."

"People tell us it's like a family, KGB, FSB as it's become. They only trust their own. Your family was in the business, you're part of it, it's dynastic."

I saw now what Pettus wanted. He wanted somebody ex-KGB guys would trust, maybe even current FSB guys.

I didn't answer.

"Your job here, I could clear you on that. There's plenty of detectives could take your place for a while."

"You already checked?"

"Yes."

"Look, there's a whole lot of Russians in New York, cops, too, I'm sure you can buy a couple. People who speak the lingo better than me."

"We want somebody who looks and sounds American."

"Well, you could always pay somebody."

"We don't want people we can buy. We need people who do it for America. Don't you owe this country?" said Pettus softly. He didn't harangue, he didn't yell, just asked. "Isn't that what your father did in his day, for his country?"

Putting his jacket on, Pettus fished in the pocket, put a card on the counter.

"I've put all my numbers on this," said Pettus. "I'll be in the New York area for three more days. Please call me, Artie."

*

114

Rattled by Pettus. I drank a shot of Scotch. Then I called Sonny Lippert.

"Go on, man."

"He told me we owe our friends in London, Pettus said they need to watch out for the Russkis?"

"He's right, man, about that, at least. I'm guessing he wants you to move into some kind of intel work, and why not? You got the brains, man. I mean, like you could be a spy man, James Bond, George Smiley, whatever," said Sonny. "Joseph Conrad."

"But why the snooping around?"

"Fuck knows, man. Obviously he wanted you to know he was at it, maybe put you off guard, maybe let you know he knows where your friends are, what do I know, maybe Roy Pettus has turned into J. Edgar Hoover in his old age, or maybe he just likes spying on people."

"You know him at all?"

"Some. Years ago. Always seemed like a straight arrow, far as it goes. You want me to ask around?"

"Yeah. Could you, Sonny?"

"You told him to work it up his ass, man?"

"I was polite."

"Good. Cause these days they can snatch anyone they feel like, and they say it's under the roof of Homeland Security which we all know is a pile of doggy do, man, right, to mix a couple metaphors, right?" Sonny laughed, but it was a bleak cackle.

Val?

From the yellow envelope I got at the house in Brighton Beach, the envelope I figured Tito Dravic had left me, I took the DVD. I put it in the machine.

On the screen a bunch of kids in their twenties were dancing at Dacha. People around the floor watched, yelling, singing.

The picture zoomed in on Masha Panchuk's back, and she

was wearing a silky pink dress. She danced like a pro. Her partner was older. A rough older man, stubble on his face, coarse black hair. After a second or two, she was gone, disappeared into the crowd.

Crouched on the floor, I put my face up against the screen, close as I could, played it again. Even from the back, Masha looked enough like Val for somebody to get it wrong. A thug for hire, who didn't ask for ID, could have confused them.

Slung around Masha was a tiny purse, a small golden envelope on a long silk cord, best I could see. It looked expensive. So did her shoes. High-heeled sandals made of some skin, something silver.

I called Val again but there was no answer. I got in the shower, got out, sat in front of the TV, wrapped in a towel, waited for Val to call. I watched the news again without seeing it. Put on some music I didn't hear. Pettus had left his cigarettes behind and I lit up.

If Pettus wanted me bad enough, he'd fix it. If he could make a case for me working the Russians out of London, it would happen. The department would agree. You said the words Homeland Security these days, and it trumped everything else. If you didn't salute back and say, yessir, they could figure out a way. If you were a cop, like me, they could transfer you wherever they wanted.

Could they? Could Roy Pettus lean on them hard enough? I'd quit. I could hook up with Tolya Sverdloff, I could become a businessman, or a bartender. All I knew was New York City. It was all I ever cared about.

I got up and put on Ella Fitzgerald and listened to some Rodgers and Hart tracks, including "Manhattan". For once, it didn't divert me. Didn't make me happy. I shut off my stereo.

I was feeling messed up, waiting for Val, worrying about the connection between her and the dead girl, Masha and Tito Dravic, and Masha and Val. What was Masha doing with a bag that looked like one of Val's, and expensive shoes?

After a few minutes, I got dressed, put on a new linen shirt. I felt like a fool dressing up for dinner with Val as if it were a date, as if I were in love with her, and got the hell out, and as I was getting in my car, she called me back.

"Ten is what I said, Artie, I said I'd meet you at ten, at Beatrice's, okay, at the wine bar, it's only nine, right? I gave you the address? Look, I'll be there, I promise."

"You said nine or ten."

"God, you're so literal," she said. "Between you and my dad I'm going nuts, you call, he calls, you leave messages, what's going on? I'm fine. Daddy's fine, he's in Scotland or someplace playing golf, he stopped off, I mean, please, Artie, darling, go solve a crime or something, and I'll see you in an hour. Honest to God, I'm fine!"

At nine-thirty, I was on East 2nd Street, sitting at the bar of Il Posto Acconto, drinking a glass of red, watching a game on the TV, and waiting for Valentina.

At ten she hadn't arrived. Half an hour later I was on the street, leaning against the side of the building, watching a guy with tattoos tinker with a Harley. At the curb was Beatrice's vintage yellow Caddy. I had parked my own car just behind it.

People were out, drinking wine, strolling, calling out, happy, and I tried not to let it get to me. Val was always late. Maybe she'd stayed in the office in Brooklyn. I was making myself crazy.

Beatrice, who owned the Caddy and wine bar, pushed back her streaky blonde hair, pinned it up with a pink plastic hair clip, adjusted her tomato-red skirt, poured me a shot of tequila which she considered a cure-all, and went and got me a bowl of spaghetti carbonara. She asked about Tolya. They had a special thing going and there were times they sat together and discussed the merits of a tomato or a white truffle or some herb from Puglia you couldn't get anywhere else.

I wasn't hungry. The kind of dread you get on a bad case had enveloped me. Across the street, an argument started, there was the sound of somebody falling on the sidewalk. I didn't go over. I was glued to the seat where I sat.

By midnight, I knew Val wasn't coming. She had forgotten. She had gone dancing. She was with somebody who called at the last minute.

"I'm a bad girl," she always says, laughing at me.

"Honey, don't drive like that," said Beatrice, offering to take me home, drop me off. "You shouldn't do that, okay? *Senti*, please, my little adorable Artie?"

I said I'd be fine. I got my car. I drove around for a while, my phone on redial. When it finally rang, it was a wrong number.

I was tired. The heaviness that crept up behind my teeth, the kind that seemed to infect my jaw, came over me. I went home, took a cold shower, changed my clothes, and made instant espresso.

If I called it in to the cops and Val was only out on a date, she'd kill me. She'd say I was a jealous old man.

I'd give it a couple more hours. I drove around. I went back to the playground in Brooklyn, I talked to a uniform watching the place. I was going nuts.

Outside was a sad little shrine, a few votive candles in glass jars, a bunch of roses from a bodega, already wilting, a photo-copy of Masha, a little icon next to it.

"Dravic's alibi checks out," said Bobo out of breath as he arrived at the playground in Brooklyn. I had called him and he came as fast as he could, he said.

"Go on."

"I called Dravic's mother up in Kingston to check he was there when he said he was, when Masha died, and she confirmed, and she gave me the name of a couple of people who also saw him at a bar up there. I asked where he is now, and she said he'd left."

"For where?"

"Relatives in Belgrade, the mother said. She said he had planned it, but I could tell she was scared, Artie. He didn't kill Masha, but he got scared by someone. Maybe like you said, because he promised you Masha's resume."

"When did he leave?"

"This morning."

"Belgrade, Jesus."

"I'm working on it."

"What about the clothes?" I said, looking around the playground where I found Masha on the swing. It was dark and empty except for a couple of patrolmen.

"What about the clothes, Bobo?"

"I'm on it. I got people picking over every leaf in a ten block area around here."

"Good."

My phone rang and I answered it. Wrong number. I tried Val and I knew Bobo was listening, but I didn't care.

"I'm going to need you," I said, and stared out over the playground.

"Of course. Anything. Should I come with you now?"

"Not now. I'm going back to the city, just keep your cell phone on, okay?"

"Yes, Artemy," he said. I got out my car keys, dove into my car, and drove like crazy to my apartment, got the keys to Tolya's place – I remembered he had given me spares – in the Meat Market district.

You don't smell blood anymore around the Meat Market. There are only fancy restaurants now.

On my way to the yellow brick building where Tolya had his loft and Val had her apartment, I went past loading docks where once, in the morning, huge carcasses had been rolled into storage facilities, cold dark spaces that smelled of meat and bone. All gone now.

CHAPTER NINETEEN

"Val? Val, darling? Are you there?" I unlocked the door to the Sverdloff place. "Val?" My voice echoed, cheerful, brittle, too loud as I went inside.

It was dawn, Monday morning, the sun coming up, the light coming in through fourteen windows, each ten feet high.

"Val?"

From the top floor—Tolya owned the building and lived on the top floor—you could see the city in every direction, the river, the Empire State, the downtown skyline.

I went through the living room to the door of Valentina's apartment which Tolya had created for her. It had its own entrance to the hall where the elevator and stairs were, but I had come in through her father's place.

Once, she had planned to get an apartment of her own in the East Village, but Tolya said, don't, please, darling, I don't like this area in East Village, I'll make you an apartment here. Don't go yet. She gave in.

Her door was locked. I went back into the hallway and tried the other door to her apartment. I banged on it and began yelling and when I heard heavy footsteps on the stairs, instinctively I put my hand on my gun. It was only Bobo.

We didn't speak. Bobo had heard me on the phone earlier, trying to reach Val, had seen how frantic I was and he had come here without my asking.

I gestured for him to come up, and he followed me. I had to ask him to unlock Val's door. I didn't want Val thinking I had smashed into her place in case she suddenly appeared. I just hoped he was better at picking locks than me. I was half out of my mind. I didn't want to go inside.

"I should go inside first," said Bobo Leven who put his hand lightly on my arm. "It's okay like that?" He reached for the antique brass doorknob Valentina had found in a thrift shop on Madison Avenue.

"Sure."

"Probably it is nothing," said Bobo. "Probably she is just maybe out to the beach or something."

"Yes."

He opened the door and went in. I waited. I could hear him walking over the hardboard floor, first in the living room, then the bedroom. I waited. Bobo reappeared.

"Nobody is home here," he said. "Is okay."

"Thanks."

"Probably you don't want people knowing about this or somebody will tell her father and he will go crazy?"

I nodded. He got out a pack of smokes. We both lit up.

"You want me to look at where she goes, who she knows, but quiet, right, Artemy?"

"That would be good. Yes. Tell people you're on the Panchuk case, and nobody at your station house will ask you questions, right?"

"Exactly," said Bobo. "I say just like that."

"I want you to find Valentina Sverdloff. Nobody has to think she's missing, maybe she's just out with some guy, or someplace taking photographs, or like you said, at the beach. I don't want her father going crazy and calling in the thugs he uses for body-guards. I don't want her going crazy at me because she thinks I'm pestering her. I need you to promise."

"Yes, you said already, I understand." He spoke Russian

now, as if to convince me he was serious.

"I'm sure Val is just at the beach on the island," I said again. "She forgot we were having dinner. She just forgot, right? Isn't that how girls are? They forget? Girls, boys, the mood just kind of takes you, you stay out all night?" I could hear myself running on, desperate.

"Yes," he said softly. "It is like that."

"Daddy? You there? It's me, Val, listen I'll be home in the morning. Don't go insane, I mean, I'm fine. I'm at a friend's. A girlfriend's place. See you."

When I turned on Tolya's answering machine for a second I thought the message was from the night before. Any time now, Val would come walking into the apartment.

But it was an old message, I realized.

I looked at my phone, then turned it off.

Tolya had been calling me. Sending me e-mails. It was nine in the morning, July 7. Tolya's birthday coming up, what was it, two, three days? He had asked me again to come to London, big party, he had said. I'd have to take the calls soon. In the messages he asked about Valentina.

I went out on the terrace that was planted thick with flowers, pink and violet geraniums, low shrubs nearly trimmed. A glass still half full of orange juice was on the redwood table. Next to it was the *Post*. I picked it up. It was open to the story about Masha Panchuk. MUMMY GIRL, the headline read.

For a girl her age, twenty-four, her birthday the same day as her father's, Val was neat as hell. I'd forgotten. Her laptop wasn't there but she often took it with her, in a bag slung over her shoulder.

One wall was covered in books, paperbacks, textbooks, novels, cookbooks, and hundreds, maybe thousands of CDs and DVDs. There was a good Bose sound system, and I turned it on. *Spring is Here*, a Stan Getz album I'd given her, came on. The last thing she'd listened to before she went out.

It was a faintly anonymous room as if she alighted here from time to time, but was always on her way somewhere else.

In her darkroom on the work table was a single print, a picture of Tolya with a bottle of wine in his hand, head thrown back, laughing. He filled the frame.

A few negatives lay on the table, too, and a box of brushes for cleaning them. Staticmaster, the brushes were called. Something about the box caught my attention. I picked it up and looked at it, then put it back. I was wasting time on stupid details.

On the dresser in her bedroom were framed photos: her twin sister, her mother. A picture of me she had taken over by one of the Hudson piers.

Squinting into the sun, I was smiling at her, a dumb smile. I recognized the green shirt I was wearing in the picture. And one of Tolya and me, on his terrace, arms around each other, laughing. And a picture of a young guy I didn't know, a handsome guy, maybe thirty, dark hair, blue eyes.

More pictures of the same man were in a drawer, some taken in London, some in Moscow. I didn't know who the hell he was and I was jealous.

In the pictures, the way he looked at Val behind her camera, you knew he was in love with her. And she with him. Maybe she had another life. I was a fool.

Val?

In my head I saw Val like Masha Panchuk, suffocating inside the hot sticky tape, dying slowly somewhere on the fringes of the city, in a desolate park surrounded by dirty needles, or out by the water where gulls picked over garbage for their breakfast.

Did the killer who murdered Masha Panchuk take Val?

I was paralyzed. If I called her friends, there would be questions and Tolya would hear. By now I would have settled for almost anything, even a call from some creep to say she had been kidnapped. How much? Money was easy. If it was only money, it would be okay.

I called her and called her until I was hoarse.

Val?

"I saw her."

It was later that morning when Bobo called. "It was Valentina," he said. "It was her."

"Where?"

"Artie, I saw her. I saw Valentina, I really see her, it's okay, everything is okay."

"Where?"

"I see her from my car window on 52nd Street, way over near Eleventh Avenue, Hell's Kitchen, she goes around the corner on this red Vespa, she has a red scooter, right? Artie?"

My knees seemed to buckle. I didn't care about anything else. I didn't care about any of it, except that Val was okay. He had seen her. Bobo had seen her. I got out my phone and called Tolya.

"Jesus Christ, Artyom, what's all the excitement?"

"Nothing. Nothing. I just saw Val on a red Vespa. You should make her wear a fucking helmet, or something. It's dangerous." I was out of my mind, I hardly knew what I was saying.

"Listen, I know this, asshole, but they wouldn't leave off until I bought it, an early birthday present."

I left the apartment, went out, and started to walk. I walked to the river. Had Bobo really seen Val? Was it her? I started to worry. I needed to see her myself, so I walked. How many hours did I walk around the city after that? I went up to Hell's Kitchen, I went everywhere I knew Val went. As far as I knew. How much did I know about her? I didn't know she had a red scooter.

Maybe it hadn't been her at all? Bobo had only glimpsed her. Why didn't she answer my calls? It was after midnight now and I was feeling crazy.

CHAPTER TWENTY

Tuesday 2 a.m.

Even at two in the morning, Sonny Lippert was awake. Maybe Lippert could help. I could trust him.

He had opened the door to his apartment in Battery Park City. Rhonda Fisher, his wife, was asleep, but as always, Lippert was awake reading, listening to music. Out of his sound system, the real thing, turntable, tubes, came "Somethin' Else", a great Miles track with Cannonball Adderley and Art Blakey. Sonny was in sweatpants and a t-shirt. In his hand was a glass of single malt.

"Can I get you one?" he said. I shook my head. "But you didn't come here for a drink."

"Valentina Sverdloff disappeared, no calls, no nothing. I was supposed to meet her on Sunday night. I can't reach her."

Lippert turned off the music. He put his drink down. He was brisk.

"Who else knows? Please, sit down." Sonny sat on the edge of the leather sofa, and I sat on a chair.

"Bobo Leven."

He shrugged.

"You didn't bother to tell me this before now?"

"I didn't want the media."

"You think that's all I do, I call the fucking media, man?"

"You like the publicity, Sonny." I said. "I'm sorry."

"Any connection with the dead girl, what was her name, on

the swing? Panchuk?" Suddenly Lippert was sharp as ever.

"The dead girl, Maria Panchuk worked at Sverdloff's club, Pravda2, over on Horatio."

"I know where it is."

"Panchuk looked like Val. Somewhat like," I said.

"You think they did Panchuk by mistake?"

"I don't know. Maybe they wanted both. Maybe Panchuk was an early warning."

"Because of Valentina's father?"

"I think she was into stuff she shouldn't have been."

"What kind?"

"Kids."

"You're crazy, man," said Lippert.

"Christ, Sonny, no, but Val helped out at women's shelters in Russia, and with little kids, orphans, abused girls, she sends stuff over, she goes there, she gets in their face, the officials. I've seen the letters," I said, thinking of the files in Val's closet.

"A big mouth like her father."

"Sonny, listen, I've never said this to you before, I'm desperate. This girl is like my own family. I know you don't like Sverdloff, but that doesn't matter. I have to find her before Tolya Sverdloff finds out and sends in his guys who will fuck it up worse and get her killed. I've been everywhere, and I have not one fucking idea what I'm doing. I'm running on empty here, and you have to help me."

"Calm down, man," he said, and put his hand on my arm. I grabbed hold of his shirtsleeve. "Please, Sonny," I said.

"I'll help you."

"Thank you. I need a smoke."

Lippert fished a pack out of his jacket pocket, and passed them over. "I was supposed to quit. I can't."

"I've never been so lost before, Sonny. I keep turning up stuff that has nothing to do with Valentina, or even with Panchuk, the dead girl. I got a Serb club manager scared off bad enough after I talked to him that he left for his mother upstate and maybe to Belgrade. This guy knew Masha, better than he let on, I think, but his alibi checks out."

"Where's Sverdloff?"

"In Scotland."

"Jesus! What for?"

"Golf. I don't know. He left for London Sunday morning, and now he's playing fucking golf."

"Let's just focus on the Sverdloff girl, okay? Let's just work that, Artie, man, you with me? Forget the rest for now, leave the rest to the others. Take me through everything," Sonny said, and I told him everything.

"I was in London a couple times," he said.

"What?"

"Yeah, London, you said Sverdloff was in a hurry to get back to London."

"Sonny, Jesus, man, a girl is missing and you're going to give me a travelogue."

"It's related. I'm thinking Sverdloff goes to London where his daughter doesn't want him going, and Roy Pettus wants you in bloody London. To keep an eye on Sverdloff, maybe? Maybe that's the part he didn't mention.

"It's a weird country, man, really weird," said Sonny. "They major in spy shit. Your pal Sverdloff is not the most fucking transparent guy I ever met. I gotta think this thing with his kid is all about what he's been doing, making money in London, stealing money, doing stuff with people he shouldn't be doing it with."

"And this is a way of getting to him, through Val? But why here? And who the fuck is they?"

"I'm just trying to think about the Russkis all living over there in London, all the secret stuff, state killings. Man, Lenin would be jumping up out of his grave and clapping his blood-soaked hands. I know, man, I remember. My parents were devoted. They believed."

I grabbed his arm. I was panicky.

"I'm telling you something here," said Lippert. "I'm thinking this out. If they got to Valentina, they're after her father. She's an American. She lives in New York. They're not coming this far for a girl who likes helping out with orphans. I think she's alive," said Lippert. "Listen to me. I don't think she's dead. I think they want something out of her. You need something to drink?"

"No."

"Artie, man, I'm going to make some very discreet phone calls to guys who retired and don't have an ax, and who owe me. Okay? You listening?"

I nodded.

"You've been to her apartment."

"Yes."

"So you have keys, right? She lives with her old man, doesn't she? Go wait for her. Wait for a call. I'll work this, I swear to you, I know how it is with you and Sverdloff."

"Thanks," I said.

"What's the thank you bullshit?" said Sonny. "I'm on it. It will be okay." For Lippert this passed as extreme optimism.

"Art, man?"

"What?"

"If Roy Pettus wants something from you, make a trade for information about Valentina. He has connections even I can't touch. Tell him you'll do whatever, if he gets Valentina Sverdloff back. Call him and go wait for her. She'll turn up there, or the creeps who took her will call looking for her old man, I know it. Give me a couple hours," he said. "You want me to go with you?"

I shook my head.

"Then go."

CHAPTER TWENTY-ONE

When I got to Sverdloff's building, there was light in the sky, and already people were coming out of the elevator with their dogs, two little rat dogs, a big Lab, somebody with a suitcase holding the door open, and I couldn't wait, I just bolted up the stairs, the endless-seeming flights of stairs, running faster and faster, until my legs burned and I couldn't breathe, and all I could think about was Valentina and Tolya and how I had failed, I could see them in my mind's eye, could see the girl Masha Panchuk too, the blue eyes staring up out of her duct-tape shroud, and when I slammed into the apartment, Bobo Leven had just arrived, had just got to the place, and was waiting there in the living room, to tell me that Valentina Sverdloff was dead.

"Where is she?"

Bobo nodded towards her room.

I was already moving towards Val's apartment, towards her room, but Bobo put out a hand to stop me. Wait, he said. Wait for me.

"Tell me."

"One of my guys found some of Masha Panchuk's stuff, it had been buried near the playground, behind a derelict gas station. I was looking for you when Lippert called and said you were on your way here."

"And?"

130

"There was a part of a pink dress, a high-heeled sandal, and a little gold purse with Masha's clothes, there was a card inside." He gave it to me. It was Valentina's card. "I think they killed Masha because she had this card, and she looked like Valentina. They killed the wrong girl the first time. Somebody figured it out," Bobo said.

"I came here, and the door was unlocked, Artie, and inside is Valentina Anatolyevich Sverdloff, this lovely girl, she is there." He lapsed into bad English, and switched to Russian. "I am so sorry."

"When did you get here?"

"Few minutes," he said.

I started for her room.

"Please, do not go in that room alone. Please."

I told Bobo to wait. I looked at the card he had given me, and then I went into Val's place, through her living room into her bedroom.

On her bed, Val looked asleep. Unharmed. Her feet were bare. There were no marks on her face or legs or arms so far as I could see. She was pale, composed, expressionless.

On the floor near the bed were wrappers from the Antistatic brushes I'd seen earlier in her darkroom, but I couldn't deal with anything now, all I could do was look at her. I sat down beside her on the bed.

Her hands were crossed on her chest. Her eyes were shut. The thin gold chain with the cross was around her neck. I tried her pulse. I put my fingers on her neck. I leaned close to her mouth. There was no breath.

I picked up one of the hands, and it was still soft, still pliant and soft and smooth, a young girl's hand except for the missing finger. She hadn't been dead long, as far as I could tell. Maybe I got to the apartment an hour too late. I had left my watch at home. I was going crazy.

How long did I sit in there? Eventually Bobo came into the bedroom and leaned over and took her hand out of mine. I rubbed my hand across my face.

"What should I do, Artie? Tell me how I can help," he said.

"What time is it?"

"Four minutes after nine in the morning," said Bobo, and I asked him to check flights to London.

I couldn't tell Tolya about Valentina by phone. I had to go. I had to be there. It would kill him, but if it didn't, at least he could hit me. He could blame me for failing, for not taking care of her, he could at least take it out on me, if he wanted.

"Artie?"

"Just stay here, okay? I want you to stay here until I leave."

He looked up from his BlackBerry.

"You can get a non-stop, JFK, get you into London around six tomorrow morning."

"Do it." I tossed him a credit card. I figured there was enough for a cheap ticket on it.

"If Sverdloff calls?"

"By the time I get on the plane, it will be night-time in London. I hope to God he's still playing golf in Scotland, or at some fucking party. Try to fend him off. Tell him I'll be in touch. Tell him I'm calling any minute. Just give me a little time, can you do that? Try to stay here with her, don't call anyone."

"Of course."

"After I go, just do what you have to, Bobo. It's your case now. This is yours. You work this like you were hanging onto a twenty-storey building by one fingernail, you get me? Find him."

"I don't know how to work this without you."

"You know plenty. You'll solve the thing, you'll find out who killed Panchuk, and you'll find out who killed Val. I have to go. The same creep killed them both. He killed Masha thinking she was Valentina, then he killed her."

"I don't know."

"I'll call you? I have to get my passport, some other stuff." I felt very calm and cold. "Lippert will help you, he'll do it for me."

Before I left, I looked at Valentina again, and I understood.

Somebody who had loved her had killed her. The killer had suffocated her and then put her on her bed, hands crossed to make it look as if she was only asleep.

Standing next to me, Bobo put out his hand to shake mine, and this formal unlikely gesture moved me, and I choked up before I ran down the stairs and out to my car.

CHAPTER TWENTY-TWO

On the way to the airport, I made one stop.

Roy Pettus was at a hotel on Lex, a Radisson so new you could smell the carpets. A girl at the desk gave me his room number after I badgered her and I went up to the ninth floor and banged on his door.

"It's open," Pettus called out, and I went in.

It was a nondescript room. The furniture was new and ugly. There was no sign Roy Pettus had been here except for the leather suitcase he was packing and the smell of Camels.

He snapped shut his bag, sat in one of a pair of small armchairs and gestured to the other one.

Pettus crossed one leg over the other. He wore pressed jeans, a white shirt and the cowboy boots.

I couldn't sit. I started for the door, then turned around. I hated the idea of being in hock to Pettus.

"I can trust you?"

"Yes," he said.

"You have to keep your mouth shut. I need you to help me keep the media off this. I need time. I need ten hours of time. I don't know who else can call in that kind of favor."

"Go on."

"Valentina Sverdloff is dead."

"Tolya Sverdloff's daughter?"

"Yes."

"When?"

"Somebody left her in her own bed. Last few hours. I was there earlier, she wasn't there, I went back, she was there." I stared at him.

"How?"

"She was probably suffocated. Somebody put a pillow over her face."

"While she was asleep? Somebody who had access to her place?"

"I think so."

"I am sorry," he said. "I offer you my condolences, and also to Mr Sverdloff," he added in that peculiar old-fashioned way.

"Tolya doesn't know."

"Where is he?"

"London," I said.

"What else can I do for you?"

He got up, went to the bathroom, returned with a glass of water and handed it to me. He looked at the bag I had put on the floor.

"You're going to London to tell her father?"

"Just the media, please. Just make sure it's kept quiet until I tell Tolya. That's all. If that's possible. Is it possible? Roy?"

"I can try."

"Thank you."

"You think somebody went after her to get at her father?"

"Yes. Maybe. If they did, then he's in trouble. I have to go over. I have to tell him first, I have to do it in person. You understand that?"

"Of course." He put out his hand. "I'll see what I can do, Artie. I'll try to help you. How old was she?"

"Twenty-four this week."

"Same as my girl," he said. "When are you leaving?"

"Soon."

"I'll be in touch," said Roy Pettus.

"Thank you," I said.

He shook my hand, walked me to the door, watched me go down the hall towards the elevator.

After I left, I realized Pettus had not asked me for anything in exchange. He didn't ask me for favors, he didn't propose I go to work on some Joint Force or attach myself to the Brits, get him intelligence, or spy on Sverdloff, he didn't ask anything at all, just patted me on the shoulder and shook my hand.

But in Pettus' mind, I was now his, I was in his play, maybe only with a walk-on part. He had wanted me in London, and he was getting what he wanted, I thought as I boarded the plane that evening. He never asked, never said a word, it was enough for Roy Pettus that I needed him. In some way, he'd ask for a payback, in some way, some time, and by the time the plane took off it felt like a threat.

PART THREE
LONDON

CHAPTER TWENTY-THREE

I stood in front of Tolya Sverdloff's house in London, trying to figure out how to tell him his daughter, his Val, the only thing in the world he completely loved, was dead. Murdered. Suffocated with a pillow, lying on her own bed, as if she had just gone for a nap. And that it was my fault for not taking care of her. I felt like somebody had ripped my guts out.

It was early. Heavy green trees lined the long street. Overhead the sun was flushing out the early London mist, pearly light skimming the tall white houses. Milk bottles rattled as a delivery guy placed a couple of quarts on the stoop next door. A woman in tight red shorts jogged by, a tiny dog like a mouse on a leash behind her.

Notting Hill. London. July. This was Tolya's Eden, his paradise, the shining city on a hill where he had believed no bad thing could ever happen.

I'd been up most of the night, crammed in a plane seat, my head hurt now, jaws, teeth, neck, too little sleep, too much Scotch. Most of the way across the Atlantic, I'd stared into the darkness, thinking about Tolya, thinking about Valentina. If I dozed off, I dreamed about her as she had been the other night at my place, alive, laughing, beautiful, curious, or at breakfast on the boardwalk, eating lox, cracking jokes, snapping pictures. Asleep it was much worse. I forced myself to stay awake.

From the other direction a second woman appeared, this one in sky blue, also jogging, and smoking, and the two woman, both young, not more than thirty, stopped a few feet from me and kissed three times, and greeted each other in Russian. I strained to hear them.

Was this what Roy Pettus wanted from me? Check out the Russians in London? Eavesdrop?

So far as I could find out, he had kept the media in New York at bay, Val's death had not been reported and I knew he'd want something in return soon.

How long did I stand outside Tolya Sverdloff's house? Time seemed to collapse. I stared at the doorbell. I put my bag down on the steps.

Mercedes, Audis, Range Rovers lined the street, punctuated by Smart cars and Minis and VWs in red and racing green and yellow and blue, little colored buttons of cars, shiny in the early light like M&Ms on this rich, gorgeous street.

From a door opposite where I stood, a man emerged with a little girl in a straw hat. I could hear them laughing softly as they climbed into a red Range Rover and the girl tossed her school books onto the back seat.

A man in a black linen jacket and pressed jeans, a guy talking softly into his collar, suddenly moved into the frame. He had been standing a few doors down. He was, I figured, somebody's guy, some kind of muscle who kept a lookout on behalf of the inhabitants in one of the pretty houses.

Tolya never got up early. I would ring the doorbell and he'd come out, grumpy about the time, grinning because I was there.

"You came for my birthday," Tolya Sverdloff would say, seeing me in front of his door. "You just arrived? You flew overnight?

I'm so happy, my friend. Come in, Artemy," he would say, and I would have to tell him the truth.

Past sleeping houses, doors gleaming with fresh paint, red, black, past pink, white, purple flowers tumbling from window boxes, I walked toward the church at the end of the street, light glistening on it, turning the stone gold.

A few blocks away near Portobello Road, I found a coffee joint. The smell of fresh coffee hit me. A young guy in back was grinding beans and packing them into silver bags. He made me some espresso to go and I asked him if I could leave my bag for a while. He just yawned, dumped more beans into the grinder and said sure.

I walked. I told myself Tolya was still asleep. Why wake him? I thought. I made excuses. I tried not to think about Valentina's death, and who killed her.

Was it the same thug who murdered Masha first, by mistake, and left her on the swing? I couldn't think about anything else. Somebody had killed her to get at her father, to warn him.

Tolya had been messing with bad people, maybe in New York or here in London, and he got out of line, made too much money, told too many jokes; Valentina's murder was a warning. I would kill him.

This was the real consequence of murder. The horror was for the people left alive, unspeakable if they were the parents. It would go on and on for them. Their friends, not knowing how to respond, not wanting to know the ugly things, would look the other way. And it would never ever stop until they were dead themselves years later—of natural causes, the obits might say, though there would never be anything natural in their world again.

This knowledge, that he, Tolya, was a target, that Val's murder was a threat, a warning, would make news of her death even worse for him.

Trucks delivering vegetables edged past me on the crowded

road. The color of strawberries already on a stall was an intense, other-wordly red.

In the next street a guy unloaded flowers off a van for an outdoor flower store. Pink, green, red, yellow, purple all in tight bunches. Next door was a public toilet in a building made out of pale green tiles. The whole place had the quality of a fairy tale, or an article in a glossy travel magazine.

On the front page of a newspaper I bought was a picture of Litvinenko, late fall '06. Scanning the story I saw that British officials had now confirmed it was the Russians who killed him. A two-year investigation had revealed that it was state terrorism. As of this morning, it was official. I bought a bunch of white tulips for Tolya.

At Tolya's house, my suitcase on the polished stone step, I finally rang the bell. My pulse pounded in my neck, I tried to form up some words before he opened the door. Then, from inside, I heard the heavy steps, steps coming down a flight of stairs, coming towards the door, his cheerful voice calling out in mock irritation: "Okay, okay, I'm coming."

"What time is it?" said Tolya.

Pulling a huge black silk bathrobe around him, feet bare, hair a mess, eyes clogged with sleep, he said, "Jesus, Artyom, Christ, you wake me at this crazy hour, but I forgive you. You came for my birthday. I'm happy. Come in."

Taking my suitcase, he set it down inside, closed the door, hugged me and kissed me three times on both cheeks, Russian style, and let out a stream of insult and affection.

"You came for my birthday? You came for my party? You are a good friend, I knew you would come, I have surprise for you, in your room. Come," he said, leading me to the staircase with the curving banister.

"And Val?" he said. "When's she coming? She's not going to

forget my birthday, is she, I'm giving a big party, she says she is coming, she texts me, come upstairs," he said, chattering at me in Russian, in English, joking around, telling me about the party, what he was serving, what vintages, which caviar.

I felt like a fraud.

I followed him up the staircase, its ancient stone steps salvaged from some palace, some chateau, smoothed thin by centuries of wear, polished to a high gloss. At the top, Tolya put down my bag. "Welcome!"

Double doors led into a large room with high ceilings and curly plaster moldings. The tall windows looked out onto a green square. On an antique wood table in front of the windows were boxes wrapped in fancy paper and tied with ribbons. Famous labels. Designer stuff. Next to the packages was a large photograph of Valentina in a silver frame. I tried not to look at it.

"Presents," said Tolya, glancing at the packages and smiling. "I have very very nice friends, so many presents come. Don't look like that, so gloomy," he added, glancing at me. "It is not a big birthday, I will be forty-six in one day, and I am younger than you." He laughed, and found a half-smoked Havana in his bathrobe pocket, put it in his mouth, and said, "What's the matter, Artyom? You didn't curse at me as usual on my birthday because you're almost four years older? You didn't bring a present? No, look you brought for me these wonderful flowers," he said, and took them out of my hand and with them the newspaper still held.

Glancing at the front page, he made his way to the kitchen with me in his wake. "Come," he said. "We'll eat. You'll feel better."

Even while he made coffee in a red and chrome espresso machine, he talked, exuberant, fully awake now, glad to see me, full of news, and plans for my visit. And I listened and tried to find a space where I could tell him why I was in London. He put on the radio, listened briefly to the news about the Litvinenko case. Turned it off, talked some more about his birthday party.

He felt bad about Sasha Litvinenko, he said, the story had haunted him a long time, but he had worried enough, and he had tried to help find the killers. The thing was not to mourn but to celebrate life.

"I mean I offered what I knew about Sasha himself to someone I know who could use it. I didn't do anything stupid, Artemy. I didn't. Don't worry. You always think I'm going to get in some kind of trouble."

I couldn't speak. I drank a glass of water, but my throat closed up. Tolya chattered on.

"But we don't need to talk about serious stuff, you're here on vacation, unless Roy Pettus persuaded you to become a spy." He laughed his escalating laugh which, as it reached its peak, made him shake. "Listen, it's okay, right?" said Tolya. "You don't have to worry. Now let's talk about where we will have lunch today, and then we'll go buy presents for Valentina. Her birthday too, you knew that?"

I nodded.

"Also, I said to myself finally: Anatoly Anatolyevich, stop this crap with your kid. She's a grown-up. Leave her some space. Give her some peace. She's a young woman now. Let her find her way. This comes to me in the middle of the night recently when I wake up and I think, I have to let go of Valentina, I say to myself, Artemy is right, I can't watch over her forever, and it is you who has always said this, and you approve, right?"

He pulled the espresso and handed me a dark green cup, then looked out of the window into the green communal garden. "I am so happy you're here in London," he said. "I've found my Zen place, my Brigadoon, you remember this disgusting musical they loved so much in Russia? I remember one production in Moscow where the fantasy Scottish never-never land becomes socialist paradise. You ever saw this?" He drank some espresso.

"It was so awful people had to bite their lip to stop from laughing. My father directed it, it almost killed him. They put my mother in this plaid dress and she had to sing some schlock, which almost killed her, this was a woman who preferred Wagner." Tolya turned from the espresso machine and belted out a song. "Go home, go home, go home with Bonnie Jean," he sang. "I could have been musical star." He laughed, and added, "So who the hell was this Bonnie Jean? And what's with the glen?"

Tolya still laughing, I went to the glass doors and out onto a balcony. In the lush square below, four tiny girls with pale hair were hanging like pretty little monkeys from a jungle gym. Others chased each other, while their mothers and nannies watched and baked in the sun.

When I went back to the kitchen, Tolya was looking at some newspapers, drinking coffee, and chatting to somebody in his phone. He hung up.

"You can smoke in here if you want, Artyom, you don't have to go onto the balcony. What's with you? You haven't said a word, not even when I sing. What's wrong?"

I reached for the water glass.

"Artie? What's going on? Maybe you should go take some sleep, and later I'll take you for lunch," he said, his voice sober, faintly concerned now, but for me.

It was me he was thinking about. He had no idea. "You don't feel good? What's the matter, Artyom?" he said again.

CHAPTER TWENTY-FOUR

When I told him Val was dead, Tolya stayed at the kitchen table where he was, not moving, his hands wrapped around a coffee cup, his cigar in an ashtray, the morning sun coming in from the window on the white tulips in a blue glass vase, the sounds of little children from the green gardens outside, the smell of coffee.

The ash on his cigar grew and tipped over into the ashtray. Fried eggs, untouched, on a yellow plate were on the table like a still life. The phone rang. In another room a TV played, or a radio. Tolya didn't move. It was as if his soul had already left the room, leaving only his body. No motion, no expression, no sound at all.

Then, suddenly, he bent over, his head bowed, his arms wrapped around himself. Like an immense turtle, a creature from prehistoric times, he seemed to pull himself inside his shell, make a shield, protect himself from this body blow.

"I'm sorry."

"How?"

"Somebody put a pillow over her face while she was asleep," I said. I didn't know this for sure, that she had been asleep, but I thought it would help him if he thought she had been sleeping.

"I wish they killed me instead."

For a minute, he stayed where he was, head on his knees, breathing too hard, gasping for oxygen, his right hand on his

146

left arm, as if he expected a heart attack. What he finally sat up, I thought he might hit me.

Instead, he simply said in Russian, very formally, "It is not your fault, Artemy."

He picked up his phone, got up from the chair, went to the kitchen counter, found a second cellphone lying on the stretch of dark marble, began making calls on both of them and only turned back to me to say, "How is it I didn't hear this on the news?" he asked.

Roy Pettus had kept his promise. Nobody had reported the story. If he could keep it quiet, Pettus had real clout.

"You fixed this?" Tolya said to me.

"Yes."

"Good," said Tolya. "Artemy, they tested her? They did tests?"

"For what?"

"Radiation, they have antidotes, I understand this, I know about this, my God, get her tested," he said as if Val were still alive. He was going crazy while I watched, helpless.

From the kitchen I followed him to the living room, but he moved away to a window where he pressed his face against the glass, his back to me as if he couldn't stand to hear anything else I had to say. And then, without knocking, the man I had seen in the street came in. He went quickly across the room to Tolya and seemed to make a little bow.

With a square head and brown crew-cut hair, he was about five ten and compact and ordinary. When he removed his black linen jacket, there was a gun in his waistband, and his white shirt was tight across the muscled chest. His face was expressionless. The only odd thing about him was that a piece of one ear was missing.

Without saying anything, the man watched Tolya attentively, like a soldier waiting for orders.

Tolya picked up a pack of cigarettes lying on the white

marble mantelpiece and lit it with a match. I had never seen
Tolya smoke anything except the big cigars or light up without
the solid gold Dunhill as big as a brick. When he looked at me,
his eyes dull, face sagging, there was nothing left of my old friend.

Suddenly exhausted, I went to the room next door, glimpsed
my haggard face in a long gilt mirror, slumped on a chair, called
Bobo Leven in New York and left a message. Wake up, I said.
Test her, I said. Test the apartment. Test for anything, alpha
gamma, cesium, red mercury, polonium-210.

It was what Tolya wanted. I didn't believe Val had been
poisoned, but he had asked me. At least he would know I had
done something.

When Bobo called me back, he argued about the testing, and
I started yelling, "Do it. Just do it."

"I am going to New York now," said Tolya, coming into the
room, sitting on a chair next to mine. "Please tell me everything."

"I'll tell you on the way."

"Tell me now."

So I told him. I told him about the dead girl, Masha Panchuk.
When I showed him her picture, he remembered she had worked
at his club in New York a few times and wanted to tend bar,
but she was too young and didn't know anything about wine.
I told him about Tito Dravic, the nightclub guy in Brooklyn
who had disappeared.

"Talk about Valentina," he said.

"We were going to have dinner. She never showed up. I looked
for her, I went crazy, then somebody said they saw her on a red
Vespa. It wasn't her. By the time I got back to her place, she
was there, on the bed, like I told you," I said.

From somewhere deep inside him I heard a faint noise, as if
of pain, an animal whimper.

I thought he might implode, that he might collapse inside
himself like one of the Twin Towers.

I put out my hand.

"Did the creep who killed Masha kill Val?" he said.

"We can talk on the plane."

Tolya got to his feet.

"I need you to stay here in London for me," he said. "Somebody reached out to her from this side, I have to go to New York to collect her body, to make sure nobody touches her. I can't be in both places. Will you stay here for me?"

"Tolya?" I reached out to touch his arm.

"Yes?"

"I'm coming with you. I know what went on in New York, I can show you, I have leads, I have people working this, please. I need to be there, with you, and for Valentina."

There would be a funeral, I thought to myself. I had to be there. I had to say goodbye or it would never ever leave me, the feeling that she was still alive, that I could call her and hear her voice.

He glanced at me. "You loved her," he said. "She was your family, too."

"Of course." I saw he didn't know the rest of it, about Val and me. "Of course," I said again. "Like you."

"Ride with me to the airport," he said. "I'll try to explain."

Tolya was half out of his mind. Voice calm, manner determined, but in his eyes I could see it. He started out of the room. I followed him.

"Please, stay here," he said. "You don't understand, do you?"

"I'm not sure."

"For Russians, London is the bank, the offshore island, the money, and where is money is killing, where people are rich, criminals come, more and more and more," said Tolya. "I did some bad deals, Artemy. I took too much."

"You want to tell me?"

"I'll try. Five minutes," he said, and left me alone in the beautiful room with curly plaster ceilings, a fancy fireplace and on the mantel, red orchids in black and gold porcelain pots.

We left the house ten minutes later. Tolya was wearing a plain dark suit, no tie, and carrying a tan raincoat. In his hand was a small canvas suitcase and a plastic bag. No gold Rolex, no Guccis. On his feet were plain cheap black shoes with laces, the kind an accountant or a teacher might wear.

He climbed into a black Range Rover and gestured for me to follow him into the back. The guy in the linen jacket was in the driver's seat. He turned his head, and looked at Tolya who nodded. For a surreal second or two, I thought the driver was going to kill me.

"I have arranged a plane," said Tolya as we set off.

Biggin Hill, he said, private airport, a Gulf Five would be waiting. He had borrowed it, had called friends who could make a plane available.

London passed outside the window in a blur. We got on some motorway. At the edge of it nondescript houses, big box stores, anonymous malls passed. I barely looked out. I waited for Tolya to speak. I didn't ask about the plane or its owner.

"Again," he said. "Tell me."

I took him through it all again, especially Val's disappearance, her death, what I saw, heard, thought, knew. I told him who had been working the case, what kind of people were on the job, how high up I had taken it, everything. I recited the details as if I were officially on the job, reporting to a superior. It was what Tolya wanted. I described the playground, the silvery duct tape, the girl on the swing—Masha Panchuk—her blue eyes, her hair, her resemblance to Valentina.

He didn't speak, just nodded, making me go on and on, stopping me only for the detail. I thought it would choke me, getting the words out to tell him how Val looked on the bed, the little gold cross, the green summer dress neatly arranged. There were pictures of her Bobo had taken for me with his phone but Tolya didn't ask and I didn't offer.

For most of the trip he spoke Russian to me. He talked fast. He was jumpy.

"Did you know I met Sasha Litvinenko?" said Tolya suddenly.

"I think you probably said."

"Poor bastard, they killed him with polonium-210, fucking poured it in his tea and it ate him up from inside. He was a decent guy. And I went on believing I was safe, that anyone could be safe."

Ivan, the driver, from the shift of his shoulders, his head, the way he positioned his body, it was as if he was trying to hear what Tolya was telling me. It was only a feeling I got, but it made me uneasy. If somebody killed Val to get at Tolya, who could he trust now? Who could I trust? Maybe Tolya was right. Maybe whoever killed Valentina, it was set up out of London.

Trees hung down over the road. The sky, low, dark, filled with scudding black clouds, seemed to lie across the countryside like a dirt blanket. We were someplace in the countryside now, winding roads, low-lying houses, an old pub with a thatched roof, planes overhead, rain.

"Let me go on," said Tolya.

"Yes."

"I tried to believe Litvinenko only had bad luck, bad karma. I wanted to believe in London, in British justice, in a civil society. I was happy here," he said softly. "And the theater. I was raised with this idea of great theater by my parents, Artyom, and they loved this language, this English, as beautiful as Russian and bigger, a big language, flexible, opulent, dirty, poetic. What writers! What actors! I consider language reveals the soul of a place, that it is the soul. I was entranced. I even become big-time member of these great theaters, I become Olivier Circle

Member of Royal National, imagine, and I go and I meet actors and I see everything," he added as if in a daze. "What the fuck am I talking about?" Tolya sat up. He put his cigarette in the ashtray, rubbed his face. "I thought I'd stay here for good." He raised his shoulders, a kind of shrug of despair.

"You know when it first hit me?" Tolya went on. "That there was no place safe, no place good for me?"

"When?"

"I discovered that the guy who killed Litvinenko was on British Airways flights between Moscow and London. That same month, he took many flights. He left a radioactive trail. People were tested, the planes were cleaned up, they said. They said it was clean. I didn't believe it. Artemy?"

"Go on."

"I was on two of those flights, and Valentina was with me."

Did Tolya think he had been poisoned? That Val got a dose of polonium on those flights between Moscow and London? It was nearly two years back. And I thought that, knowing she was dead, he had lost his mind.

CHAPTER TWENTY-FIVE

For a few more minutes, we rode in silence.

"Talk to me," I said, while Ivan manoeuvered over country lanes and I saw a sign for the airport. "If I'm staying in London, tell me who, who doesn't like you, who did you do bad business with, who do you owe? If you think somebody killed Val to get at you, I have to know." I put out the cigarette in the car's ashtray and waited.

"So many," said Tolya. "I was trying to tell you, there was the polonium on the planes, there were people who wanted me on those planes, and still I didn't believe it. You think I'm crazy? So I'm crazy. But people said Sasha Litvinenko was crazy."

"It was a long time ago."

"Yes, but other things. Little things I ignore, I say, no big deal, and then you arrive and tell me they killed Valentina," he said. "Now I believe it. All of it." Tears filled his eyes and ran down his big cheeks. Tolya made no noise, but his face was wet. "Now, just like that, this morning, like I wake up from a dream, I see it. London is only like a Potemkin Village, a façade, the more beautiful it is, the more corrupt, the more great art inside mansions, the more brutal the people. It has a rotten heart of money." He stopped, winded. I put out my hand to touch his sleeve. Gently, he pushed it away.

"You're saying they hurt Val because of London?"

"They can reach out any place. Not hurt, Artemy, we do not

153

need these euphemisms. They killed her. Murdered her. Slaughtered my girl. I never talk to you about business. You don't question me. We're like *goluboy* in the military, you and me: don't ask, don't tell."

"I'm sorry."

"It's not your fault."

"You can tell me anything."

"I don't like to upset this balance," he said.

"What balance?"

"I know you keep a balance between friendship for me and not being involved with all my shit, so you can be proper policeman, and I honor this in you, Artemy, this moral code." He pulled another fresh cigarette from the pack, lit up with a throwaway orange Bic.

"That's what Val said."

"What did she say?"

"Something about a moral code."

"You and Valentina were close?"

I didn't answer.

"I'm asking you a question," he said.

"Sure, she said I was her Uncle Artie." I looked straight ahead. I asked him for another cigarette. He passed me the pack and the Bic lighter. I lit up, I drew in the smoke, and blew it out hard, as if it would make a screen between us.

"Where's your gold lighter?" I said.

"I left all my things, jewelry, everything in the apartment. You take what you need, what you want. You see? You understand?"

He didn't want anything on him that would identify him, not his wallet or lighter or his fancy shoes. It didn't make sense because people everywhere knew Tolya, but it made sense to him now. He figured if somebody killed him, he didn't want them taking trophies.

"Artie?" He put his hand on my arm. Tolya almost never used

my American name. I didn't know why he used it now. "Tell me," he said, and for a second I thought he meant Val, I thought he meant about Val and me, and I didn't know what to say.

"This girl, Masha Panchuk, I saw her picture on TV," said Tolya. "I should have said something. I recognized her only afterwards, the next night, I was already in bed, and I thought, should I call Artie, and then I fell asleep. So what, I said to myself. So she worked for me only two days last winter. I didn't want trouble."

"It wouldn't have changed things."

"Guys like me can always change things," he said. "I could have helped her. I could have called you when she was dead and said I knew this girl. Maybe it would have made a difference for Valentina." He closed his eyes. "I always worried about her. Not just for silly stuff, like she stays out late, but more deeply, you understand?"

"Can you tell me about it?" I said.

"For Val's sister, I never worry. Her sister is in medical school, she will be a great doctor. Val is different. She wants to save the world, I want to help her, I build a nice legitimate business for her, I pay tax, I join community groups, I pay much more than minimum wage, I do not ever hire illegals in the kitchen, which is perhaps the only place serving food in New York City which has not one illegal, not because I approve of the American stupid obsession with foreigners, but because I want everything perfect for Val." He leaned back. "For first time everything is nice and in order, I am in New York, I have one little club, my Pravda2, I try to be content, and then I see how much money I can make in London."

"Money?"

He smiled bitterly. "Yes. Money. You're so naïve, Artyom. British government makes this tax haven for people like me, for rich Russians. London is like an offshore island."

"You said that. What shore?"

"European shore, American shore, shore of paradise, who cares? For Russians, like a, what do you say, day at the beach."

"No rules."

"No rules. And for Russians this is the godsend," he said. "Maybe already five, ten years, some even more, so I come in very late, but there is always more. They can hide money, they can spend, they can invest in real estate, shares, anything, all this money they make from buying whole pieces of the earth. These are people who buy and sell oil, nickel, aluminum, sugar, oil, gas, diamonds, everything, the earth itself, people who use sugar and soy and turn it into money, who make fortunes on orange juice, who manipulate whole countries. Russians floating on oil, all the money in the world." Tolya paused. "While it lasts."

"Go on."

"It's not your fault. You think you failed me, you didn't watch over Valentina, but it was me. I wanted too much. I got so greedy. My God, what did I do?"

"No, Tolya. It wasn't you. It was some bastard who killed her, not you."

"It was me," said Tolya. "Such a simple beginning, you know? People say, why not brand your club, why not do this style of luxury in London, Moscow, Dubai, Tokyo? It seemed like a good game, so much fun."

"People kill for this?"

"For anything. You want an example?" said Tolya. "Right. It's very hard to get good caviar, Russians, we shat into the Caspian for years, we killed all the fish. The Iranian side is better, expensive, but first class. But of course there are Russian fishermen who do business with Iranian fishermen. With money nobody cares. I heard from somebody is always same, even in military, did you know Russian generals and Chechen rebels pump their gas at the same hole? Literally. Caviar is the same. Together these guys find a little place to fish sturgeon that make eggs so pure, so delicious. Deluxe, premium, melt-in-your-mouth big gray pearls. And I have a little connection. And sometimes I cheat."

"You're saying someone killed Val because of a caviar deal?"

"Also wine, wheat, you can buy Russian wheat fields now, anything. But even when I get my club in London and my club in Moscow, I don't know how to play this game, and so I joke around like always. I joke about Putin. I joke about the money he stashes in Swiss banks. And some creep, the kind you can visualize FSB written on his forehead, tells me shut the fuck up, and I laugh at him. He's in my club every night for a week. Just watching. I realize it's like the Cold War, they're still here, no matter what you call them, KGB, FSB, whatever you call them. They watch me, and still I don't shut up, or stop, I think: I can do what I like, this is London, and so they kill Val."

"Why New York?"

"Because she is there. These people go where they want, this is killing by the state, Artyom, like old days. They move very freely. And it comes from the top."

"I can help you better in New York, I can do more if I'm with you."

"Please. For me," he said. "And for Valentina."

"What about you?"

"I will be fine in New York. I have people," said Tolya, and then I understood. He wanted me in London to work the case. He also wanted me out of New York so he could use his own people, he could do things I couldn't do as a cop. Things he didn't want me to know.

"Who knows you're here?" Tolya asked. "What about this Roy Pettus? This FBI schmuck who came to my club in New York?"

"He helped me keep the media out of this."

"Don't go further with him, please, Artyom. We keep this in the family, unofficial, you tell one person, everyone knows. We do not trust officials, FBI, CIA, MI5, 6, KGB, FSB. All the same."

"Pettus is on our side."

"There is no side."

"Tolya?"

"Yes, Artemy?"

"Who asked you to get the books to Olga, the old lady in Brooklyn?"

"I don't know," said Tolya. "It was through Val. A lady in London asks her to do this." He looked at me as the car finally pulled into the airport and stopped.

We got out. As if he had a chill, Tolya held his tan raincoat close to his body.

I reached in my pocket and pulled out the photograph of Val and the good-looking boy.

"You know this guy?"

"Yes. I don't like him," he said.

"Why?"

"Val brings him over once and I don't like him, no reason, just a feeling. Too eager, too slick, too polite with me, as if he wants something but never says. I think he was in love with her, though," he added grudgingly. "I didn't want to believe it. She says to me, Daddy, you are jealous of every boy since I'm twelve years old."

"He has a name?"

"Greg. It's all I know."

We walked to the terminal building.

"If you go to New York, and you make noise, they'll kill you," I said.

"I have to take Valentina's body before they cut her up," said Tolya.

I didn't tell him that the medical examiners were already at work. I didn't have the guts to tell him. Deep down, he knew, of course.

"Will you stay, Artie? Please? Stay in London a few days.

There will be no funeral without you. I promise this. I will not bury my Val without you."

I nodded.

"I'll call whenever I think of more things for you," he said. "Please, do your work as a cop. You're a good detective, Artie, sometimes great. You will know what to do," he said and now he sounded calm. As soon as he saw I would stay in London, he seemed to calm down.

"Tolya?"

"Yes?"

"You won't do anything stupid in New York? You won't employ your guys in any stupid way? You won't run some kind of war by yourself?"

He didn't answer, but reaching into his canvas carry-on, Tolya pulled out a plastic bag wrapped around something. On the bag it said Mr Christian's Delicatessen. Inside was a gun.

"Here," said Tolya. "Take this, be careful. There's no license for you to carry it. Be careful. In the house in Notting Hill there is money if you need it. My guy will be there for you."

He called out softly and Ivan hurried over. He made a little bow. "Ivan will drive you back." said Tolya.

"What's his other name?"

"Danilov."

From a few feet away, I looked sideways at Ivan Danilov and saw that he was staring straight ahead. I didn't like him, but I had never liked Tolya's "guys".

"Everybody loved Valentina," I said.

For a split second Tolya opened his mouth as if to howl, but no sound came out.

"I got my wings burned off, Artemy," he said finally, face swamped with tears now. "I got greedy and I got burned, and I fell down, it's my fault, I fell and crushed my little girl."

CHAPTER TWENTY-SIX

That night, after Tolya left for New York, I was on the roof of Pravda22, his London club. For each club, he had announced, he would add a 2. The buzz of excitement mixed with the whoosh of girls' silky skirts in the breeze of an early summer evening, the sounds of voices, the buzz of traffic.

Below were the streets, low houses, deep gardens. People were sitting out on balconies, on the street, spilling onto the sidewalk from pubs and cafes. A kid whizzed by on a skateboard. From nearby, a motorbike roared.

I felt somebody watching, as if from the houses, behind the lights, up in the trees, as if there were people looking at me from all around, the way you might in a forest, the birds, the monkeys staring at you. Or ghosts. Ghosts in the green summer trees. The air was heavy on my skin, humid, and somewhere a streak of thunder rumbled.

Downstairs inside the club I wondered if he was in New York yet. I looked at my phone. Nothing.

It was jammed, the air full of Russian voices. The waiters glided among the tables, with huge buckets of champagne on ice and platters of sushi. I introduced myself to the bartender.

"Yeah, mate, good to meet you," said the bartender when I introduced myself. "Mr Sverdloff said you'd be in, said to give you whatever, you know?"

Roland was his name, he said, and I remembered Tolya saying

I could trust this guy if I needed somebody. Trust him, more or less, Tolya had said.

Roland was his name, he said again, and I nodded, "Yeah, thanks," I said, and he said, "They call me Rolly. Australian. Read Russian at uni. Everyone calls me Rolly. Anything you need, mate." He was a skinny guy, striped shirt, long humorous face. Mate. Matey. Like a sailor doing a jig.

At the far end of the bar was a guy in his fifties, long hair, straggly beard, sloping shoulders, paunch, cheap gray shoes. A second-hand book was propped on the bar. *Crime and Punishment* the guy was reading in Russian.

"Mr Sverdloff's poet, like his Pindar, mate," said Rolly. I looked again.

What kind of poet? I wondered did he write odes to Tolya? Was he some kind of praise singer in Tolya's pay? Before I could get away, he detained me, and started talking at me in Russian, about Russians in London, about the true believers, the communists, the democrats, the nationalists, on and on and on, Putin, the anti-Putinistas, the Kasparovites, who believed Gary Kasparov wasn't a chess player but a god. Decried money, pissed on capitalism. I tossed some money on the bar. Finally he left.

From behind the bar, Rolly held up a glass to make sure it was clean. He beckoned me back to his end, and said, "Mr Sverdloff tells me to serve him, give him drinks and food, don't charge him. Says he can be our conscience. I think he's our pain in the royal, you know?" He put the glass down and reached for a bottle of vodka. "He comes in early, I keep him at the end of the bar so he doesn't bother the others with his bullshit, but he leaves early, knows a good thing, mate, so he doesn't make a fuss much," said Rolly. "He's been in London a while. Teaches, I think." He was making a martini while we talked.

"You ever meet Valentina Sverdloff, Sverdloff's daughter?"
He hesitated.
"What is it?"

"You're Mr Sverdloff's friend, right?"

"Yes."

"It's tough to say exactly."

"Try."

"She was a knockout," he said.

"That's not what you were thinking."

"You mean because I'm gay? I can see what a girl looks like can't I?"

"You were thinking something you didn't want to tell me. You want to walk outside for a minute? Grab a smoke?"

"Sure," said Rolly, talked to another bartender, and went out onto the street with me where he lit up a smoke and sighed.

"Valentina," I said. "You knew her. How well? Listen, level with me. Tell me what you thought about her, don't fucking hold back, okay?"

Drinking his beer, he looked surprised.

"You sure, mate? I mean, you're her dad's pal, right?"

"Just fucking please tell me."

"Men were crazy for her, and she was drop-dead gorgeous when she bothered, I'm saying sometimes she came by, no make-up, old pair of jeans, she was okay, but when she was done up, it was like Jesus H. fucking Christ. She was fantastic, I might be gay but I know sex on a stick." He glanced at me. "I'm sorry."

"She had friends?"

"Sure. Girlfriends. Men. Men came round like bees to honey, though she was bloody demanding."

"One guy in particular?"

"Oh, yeah, baby," said Rolly with emphasis, while he took big sucks on his smoke. "Now he was very cool."

"Did he pay for the drinks?"

"Of course not. It was her daddy's club, they didn't pay though I got the impression he wasn't absolutely rolling in it, the boy I mean."

"Was he after her father's money?"

"Who can tell? You want to know the actual truth about her, Valentina, the way I saw it?"

I nodded.

"She was a scary girl. Intense, you know?" said Rolly. "She'd talk about orphanages in Russia, the bloody politics of the place, I could see some of the customers look at her as if she was mad."

"Anything else you can think of about the boyfriend?"

"Just he looked amazing, crazy about her, a lot of fucking charm, mate. Perfect manners. Never said a thing when she started in on one of her rants, but I could see it made him uncomfortable when she talked about how corrupt officials in Moscow are, I mean it's not fucking brilliant in a club like this to say Putin has billions stashed in a Swiss bank, is it?"

"And she liked him?"

"Crazy about him. I think she was one of those girls who everybody wants, but she had never really fallen for anybody, and this time, it was very big, very hot."

"He was Russian, wasn't he?"

"I didn't notice. Yes, I think so. He only spoke English to me. Said his name was Greg."

"Nothing else?"

"Not with me," said Rolly. "But I was just the help. I better go back in. You coming?"

There wasn't much more I could get at the club so I went back to the house which was a few blocks away and sat in a canvas chair on Tolya's patio. It was back of the house and joined up with the communal gardens just beyond. Fireflies spat their glitter onto the thick dark summer night, and I sat, drank some Scotch and watched people go in and out of their houses.

They carried trays and bottles, they sat around outdoor tables and yakked and laughed. Kids ran on the grass.

For a while I tried to figure how to look for a man who had killed Sverdloff's daughter as a warning.

From my cell I called Bobo Leven in New York, told him to get me anything he had on Tito Dravic, the Brooklyn club manager. Told him to keep working everything, including the initial m carved on Masha. I wasn't convinced it was her own initial, I was guessing the killer left it because he liked to sign his work. Then I went into Tolya's house through the garden door.

Sleepless, I wandered through the house. On the marble mantel in the living room was a stack of invitations, heavy white cards. I picked them up. Balls. Parties. Picnics. Races. One was for Saving Girls, a charity ball. Host: Anatoly Sverdloff. It was Val's charity. I looked at the date. The night after the next. I'd be there. I wanted to know what these people had heard, how much they knew. Russians.

From the room where I crawled into bed finally, but still restless, I leaned on one arm and looked out the side street window. Tolya's SUV was there, and his guy, Ivan, was leaning against it, smoking. I could see the burning red tip of his smoke.

A minute or two later, another car drove slowly up the street, slowly maybe just to avoid the speed bumps, maybe because the driver was looking for something.

I changed rooms. I went to bed in a room away from the street. I put the gun Tolya had given me on the bedside table. The clock, an alarm clock in a blue leather case, was next to it. The illuminated green dial read 3.04.

Couldn't sleep. Got up one more time, smoked a while, standing at the window, saw black shapes outside, something in the gardens, maybe just teenagers, maybe something else. I felt trapped between the two sides of the house.

Exhausted, jet-lagged, so heavy I felt like I was carrying

somebody else, another whole body, on my back, I dozed. Except for a few miserable hours sucking in stale air on the plane, I hadn't slept for a couple of nights.

Only now, in my half-sleep, then in my dreams, did I finally grasp that Valentina was really gone. I pushed my face into the pillow.

CHAPTER TWENTY-SEVEN

Bray was the name of the little town where Tito Dravic had worked. Bobo Leven got me the information same as he got me the information that Dravic had turned up in Belgrade and refused to talk to anyone. I was guessing he was scared by Masha's murder, by offering to help me. Scared him so bad he'd left New York.

The town was an hour out of London, and the River Inn where Dravic had been a waiter sat in a plush green grove of trees on the banks of the river Thames. Yellow-green willows brushed their feathery branches against the water.

A lovely sweet smell came up as I got out of the cab from the train station, green, fresh, light years from the crappy playground where Masha had been tied up to the swing.

Another part of Tolya's make-believe paradise was the English countryside. I knew Tolya had a country mansion someplace. His Eden.

"Ten pounds," said the irritable cab driver when I gave him dollars by mistake.

Even before I got to the front door of the hotel, it hit me that Dravic had known Masha Panchuk better than he said, and that he knew her long before she got to New York.

How bad did it hurt when he found out she had a husband, that she was probably going out with other guys, maybe working as a hooker? Did he watch her with men at the club in Brooklyn and want to kill her?

As I left the parking lot at the inn I noticed the same Mercedes SUV I had seen from the window the night before, the SUV that rolled slowly over the speed bumps on Tolya's street; or maybe I was just going nuts.

"Can I help you?"

The hotel smelled of polish and fresh flowers. In the bar off the lobby, a young guy was setting up for lunch. Chilling bottles of white wine in a tub of ice as delicately as if they were tiny missiles, he clocked my presence and asked for the second time if he could help.

"Can I help you, sir?" I wasn't sure why I did it at first, but I twisted my wrist to glance at the gold Rolex I had taken from Tolya's place because I'd left my watch in New York. I made my accent slightly foreign, faintly Russian. I realized he had seen the watch, had taken note of my accent.

The Rolex sat on my wrist, big as a quarter pounder, gold, diamonds surrounding the dial.

"I'd like some coffee, please," I said.

"Of course," said the waiter attentively. "Would you like some breakfast, sir?"

I said I'd be out on the terrace where tables were set for lunch. As I sat down, I asked for some cigarettes, took Tolya's lighter out of my pocket, flicked it in the sun, examined the familiar design—a cigar engraved on the surface with a large ruby for the burning tip. Tolya always carried it. The waiter who had seated me rushed away to get my coffee and a newspaper. He obviously figured me for somebody with dough, maybe a rich Russian.

From where I sat I could watch boats drift along the water, the beautiful houses on the other side, a few kids scrambling down the bank, and then, without me really noticing at first, a man emerged from the hotel and sat at the table farthest from mine, next to a large terracotta pot of red geraniums.

He wore jeans and a white t-shirt. He spoke Russian softly into his phone. He saw me look. Nodded politely like well-bred strangers in some period movie, then closed his phone and opened his copy of the *Financial Times*.

When the waiter brought my coffee, I peeled a ten off the wad of Tolya's notes I had in my pocket and said, "You have a minute?"

He nodded. I asked him about Tito Dravic. He said he knew Dravic before he left for the States. I showed him the picture of Masha Panchuk.

"Oh, sure, Masha worked as a maid here for a few weeks," he said. "She was a sad girl. Pretty, but so sad she wore it like a coat."

"She was close with Dravic?"

"I don't know. I heard something," he said. "Hang on a minute." He disappeared into the hotel, and a few minutes later a stocky woman in a white skirt and dark blue blouse came out and hovered. She introduced herself as the assistant manager. I didn't identify myself as a cop, but I implied this was some kind of official visit. The woman looked tense. Easy to intimidate.

"Sit down, please." I said. "You knew Masha Panchuk, and Tito Dravic?"

"Why do you ask?"

"Miss Panchuk worked for a friend of mine," I said. "In New York. I said I'd ask about her when I got here. They were close?"

"Yes," said the woman who didn't tell me her name, just her title. Yes, she said again and told me that Tito was upset when Masha went away. That Masha took up with a fellow, name of Zim something. "She told me she was going to Alaska with him. I told her she was mad, she had a good job here, but she didn't take any notice."

"Did Dravic know?"

"I imagine he knew, and not long after Masha left, he said he was going home to New York."

"When was this?"

She shrugged. "Last winter perhaps?"

"You knew she was dead?"

"We heard. I am so sorry."

"Is there anything else you can tell me?"

She got up. "Do you speak Russian?"

"Yes."

"Come with me, if you would."

I took a gulp of my coffee, glanced again at the middle-aged man in jeans—good-looking, expensive haircut, unlined face—and I followed her into the hotel and upstairs to a small office. She picked up the phone. A minute later, a young woman appeared. She wore a maid's uniform, she was very young and pale and serious.

The manager spoke to her in bad Russian and gave her permission to answer my questions.

"You knew Masha Panchuk?" I said.

She nodded.

"And Dravic?"

"Yes."

"They were close?"

"Yes," she said, not volunteering more than she was asked for.

"Masha went away without him?"

"She gets married with Zim. Tito is unhappy. After a while he returns to the United States."

"How unhappy?"

"Very unhappy and angry. I didn't like to be near him," the girl said. "One time I found him punching the wall with his fist until it is covered in blood."

"And Masha?"

"I never saw her again."

*

Masha was dead. Dravic was in Belgrade, refusing to talk to anyone, which was as good as dead.

Had Masha first gone to the Brooklyn club to get help from him? To tell him it was over with Zim? That she only used Zim to get to America?

It was a dead end. What I wanted was the son of a bitch who killed Valentina.

The manager told the Russian girl to go back to her work, then said to me, "Is your friend looking for someone to replace Masha Panchuk?"

"It's for me," I said. "I'm going to be living in London for a while and I need someone good."

"You'd like a Russian girl?"

"Yes."

She didn't ask why, just made a phone call, wrote on a piece of paper and handed it to me.

"This is the agency we used for Masha. They have good workers. They supply many of the important Russian families living here."

"But you're not Russian?"

"No, just plain English," she said.

"A lot of Russians come to the hotel?"

"Yes," she said. "We have a marvelous chef, two stars in Lyons before he came to us, absolute genius, and a very fine wine cellar and the Russians want only the best. Many come here to stay which is why we hire quite a few Russians as maids and waiters. Many of the wealthiest Russians have country estates quite close by. We cater parties for them, and the houses are marvelous, and the best art."

"So it's okay? You're happy about it?"

"Of course we're happy," she said. "The Russians come and they are wonderful tippers. As long as it lasts," she said.

"What do you mean?"

"One of these days the whole thing will come crashing down."

She shifted her glance from me to the wall and back, and I realized she was not just uneasy, but on edge and maybe a little bit nuts.

Was she afraid of her world crashing? Of the Russians fleeing? Of the wave of money receding and leaving her stranded on some imaginary beach?

"How do you know?"

She looked up at the ceiling.

"I hear things," she said, and I didn't know if the woman meant God talked to her or she got messages through the fillings in her teeth or she eavesdropped on the Russians in the hotel.

"Can I trouble you for a light?" said the man in jeans when I got back to the terrace.

"Sure." I handed him the gold lighter I had borrowed from Tolya. He shook a cigarette out of a pack and lit up, then handed the lighter back.

"Nice," he said. "I noticed it earlier."

"Right."

"I was just wondering where you got it."

"Why?"

"I've only seen one other lighter just like it. It belongs to Tolya Sverdloff."

CHAPTER TWENTY-EIGHT

"I'm Laurence Sverdloff," he said, "Tolya's cousin. It's his lighter, isn't it?"

"Yes," I said, and told him my name.

"You have another name, Mr Cohen?"

"Artie," I said.

"In Russian you are Artemy Maximovich?"

"I'm not Russian," I said. "But, yeah, once it was my name."

"Good, yes, like Tolya told me," he said. "Then it really is you. I'm sorry to make a fuss, but this horrible thing with Valentina. It makes you look in the rear-view mirror twice, you know?" His accent was neutral, stranded somewhere between America and England.

He was in his mid-forties, tall, wiry, and comfortable in his jeans and t-shirt, though I was guessing he was the kind of business guy who went everywhere first class as if he owned it. When he smiled, I saw the resemblance with Tolya.

"My real name is Laurence Sverdloff Antonovich" he said. "In America, they called me Larry," he said. "Somebody picked this ridiculous name when I went to grad school at Stanford. God, I loved California. Name stuck. Whatever, but then Artie's not much better," he said, smiling, making his charm work hard for him. "Have you heard from my cousin?"

I didn't answer. I wanted this Larry to fill the silence, tell me something.

"I bloody worry about what he'll do to find out who killed Valentina. Nothing matters to him anymore except that. I wish you were with him."

"He wanted me here."

"He thinks it's all about London," said Larry.

"Is it? You could go to New York," I said.

"It would make things worse. People watch where I go."

"What people?"

He didn't answer the question, just said, "Tolya and me, we grew up together, his father and mine were brothers. Both dead now," said Larry, picking up his own lighter from the table as he reached for a cigarette. I'm afraid I only use my old Zippo." He lit up. "I'm scared for him, when we were kids all I wanted was to be like him, my cousin Tolya, my idol, this daring guy. He had every illicit book under his bed, he was very rock and roll and for real. I wanted to call myself Ringo, but my father threatened to send me to the military academy, he said, we named you for the great British actor, and you want to call yourself for a what? A Beatle? So I gave in. I didn't have Tolya's balls."

"I asked who's watching you."

"People who I offend," he said, and went on to recount how his father had been a director, like Tolya's.

"How'd you make the money?"

"You assume I have money?"

"Come on."

"I went to Stanford, my English was already pretty good, made some money in Silicon Valley," he said. "I played the game in Moscow. Made more. Back to California. So I go all the way to America, which I love, to marry an English girl who's a doctor and wants to come home to work in the National Health Service here."

I tapped my fingers. I wanted the meat and this guy was giving me the empty bun.

"I married a socialist." He laughed. "What comes around, eh? You know my grandfather went to high school with Trotsky," he added. "Seems like they were always fighting because grandpa's pop was in the fur biz. Sable."

"You're not here by accident, are you?" I said to Larry.

"No," he said. "I knew you were coming to London, Tolya told me, and before he left, he called and said I should keep an eye on you. I'm sorry for all the cloak and dagger stuff, but my driver saw you leave Tolya's and head this way and he called me. Apologies, Artie."

"How come you're telling me all this?"

"So you'll trust me," he said. "What are you looking at?"

Just behind Larry, a guy with the square jaw and sloping shoulders of a piece of Russian muscle was hovering. Wanting to get into Larry's eye line, to signal him, tell him it was time to get out of here, I figured. I mentioned it. Larry turned around, then got up from his chair and put some money on the table.

He held up the newspaper. "You saw the story?" He gestured to a piece on Litvinenko. "The Brits are saying what everybody already knows, that this was an act of state terrorism. Now it's official. I should go. Why don't you ride with me, come have some lunch, if you want, or else my guy will take you back to London. His name is Pavel. He's a good man, by the way."

Half an hour later, we arrived at Larry Sverdloff's house. There was a high black wrought-iron gate which opened as if somebody had been watching for us. Larry's driver, Pavel, went through it, up a circular drive and parked in front of a long low-slung stone mansion. The sun had come out and it gave the stones a golden color.

We had come in the Merc—the Brits loved their cars, and gave them nicknames—with a Range Rover behind and in front. Through the narrow country lanes we had come like a military convoy. These Russians, Tolya, his cousin, others, used their drivers, their guys, like little armies. They used them as advance parties to protect them, spies to watch out for them, servants to do their bidding. Other things, too. Under his jacket, Pavel carried a gun.

I had a vision of them constantly in motion, driving around the countryside, through the London streets, the drivers reporting back to headquarters. England was a crowded little country, too many cars, too many drivers, too many cameras hanging from buildings and trees, like strange fruit.

From the front door of the house, a woman appeared. Larry greeted her in Russian, introduced me, we shook hands. Basha was her name, she said, and smiled. I saw in the way Larry Sverdloff talked to her, the way she used his first name, he played at being a benign laid-back guy. He was still in charge. The people who worked for him were modern-day serfs. Most were Russian. I was betting plenty of them were illegal. If they left him, where would they go?

Around the huge house were gardens planted thick with flowers, neon blue hydrangeas, purple iris, creamy roses. Ancient trees spread green shade over lawns. Beyond them I could see huge vistas of green, more trees, a lake glittering in the distance. I could see how jealous Tolya would have been. His cousin was a player with a castle and the courtiers to go with it.

"Shall we swim?" said Larry.

He lent me a suit, I changed in a pool house, and for a while we swam silently.

A powerful swimmer, Larry was clearly a guy who worked out, wiry, compact, big shoulders, no fat at all. Without agreeing, we raced the length of the pool and back, and I knew he expected to win. I let him win. A happy opponent was useful, though there was no reason to figure Larry Sverdloff for the opposition.

Afterwards, he tossed me a thick blue towel, and used another one to dry his hair. Basha, the housekeeper appeared with a tray of sandwiches and drinks. Larry took a can of Diet Coke, popped the top and drank it. Somewhere a bird tweeted in a tree.

"You think this is all nuts, somebody like me riding around in that tank of an SUV? Living in this place?" said Larry.

"Is it?"

"Fuck knows," said Larry, smiling suddenly like a regular guy who found himself in an unexpected, almost ridiculous situation.

"You've seen a lot of Tolya the last few years?"

"Yes," he said. "He never mentions me?"

"No."

"He probably doesn't want to involve you," said Larry.

"What in?"

"His business. My business."

"He told you that?" I took a beer.

"He doesn't have to. He talks about you a lot, I know how he feels."

"What's his business?"

"Whatever he can get."

I drank from the bottle. "What's that mean?" I said.

"Look, when we were kids in Moscow, he could always get books, or jeans, or go up to Tallinn to a flea market and come back with Pierre Cardin sunglasses. He would wear those sunglasses and imagine he was somewhere else. The glasses invested him with his own kind of power. They were magic glasses, he always told me. I believed him. "

"And now?"

"He thinks he's still a rock and roll hero except now his music is the money."

"So?"

"He shoots his mouth off," Larry said. "People think he's a wild man."

"Do you?"

"What?"

"Think he's a loose cannon?"

Larry looked up. Clouds, ominous fat purple clouds scrambled across the sky and thunder rumbled through the humid afternoon. I followed his gaze, and saw him glance in the direction of the house.

"Ten years ago I was living in a nice little suburban place outside Palo Alto," he said.

"Yeah, so what made you give it up, I mean other than your wife wanted to live in England?"

"Greed," he said. "At first."

"And second?"

"You probably want to know about Valentina. I loved Val," he said, "I was her uncle and her godfather."

"What about the boyfriend? Greg."

"I met him at a party. He seemed fine. Val was crazy about him."

"I want to talk to him."

"I'll try to help."

Larry's phone rang. He picked it up, listened, got up, a towel still around his neck.

"I want to get back to London," I said.

"What's the hurry?"

"I don't like the country."

"Right," he said. "I'll try to get hold of Greg for you. Meanwhile I'll give you a phone number. You might need help, right?" He said it straight, it wasn't ironic, not sarcastic, just a statement of fact. "Come up to the house," Larry added. "You can shower and change. I have an office out here, I do a lot of my business instead of my main office in London," he said. "It's easier, safer, and I've discovered most people are willing to make the trip."

"I bet."

He shrugged. "If they want something, they come. I might be able to give you something that will help. My driver can take you back to London later," said Larry, who didn't wait for my answer.

CHAPTER TWENTY-NINE

Larry Sverdloff's office was in a free-standing building in back of the house, out of view of the gardens, or the beautiful rooms I had glimpsed on my way to shower and change.

In a room next to the office were two sofas and an armchair and in them sat five men, leaning forward, waiting, a little anxious.

A couple of them were Russians in open-necked shirts. The three Brits sat straight, they were tense, they looked like supplicants, like people who wanted something, needed something from Larry Sverdloff.

When I came in, they looked up expectantly, then went back to staring at their hands. A woman who said she was Larry's assistant came out of his office, greeted me and asked me to wait.

"He'll only be a minute," she said.

Through the window I could see cars in a parking area, could see one leave, another arrive. I got the sense Larry wanted me to see all this, wanted me to understand his power, his authority.

After a few minutes, Larry came out and said, "Hi, Art, God, I'm sorry I was late. Come in."

We started for his office, the men who were waiting got up and greeted him. He shook their hands. There was no trace of irony on his face, no glimpse at all of the guy I had been swimming with an hour earlier.

He was comfortable with the power he had over the men in his outer office.

On the wall in Larry's own office was a huge Matisse, a thing so beautiful, I couldn't stop looking. Larry followed my gaze, but he didn't speak, and then from his pocket he got a scrap of paper with a number. "This is somebody you could call if you want help, use my name, okay? It's a good contact, and safe," he said.

I was impatient with all of it suddenly. I stayed on my feet.

"Don't you want to sit, Artie?"

"I'm fine. What's so fucking hush-hush?"

"Yeah, okay, I was holding back, but I realized if you're going to find who killed Val and who wants Tolya dead, there are things you should know. Please sit down, it will take a while," said Larry, glancing out of the window.

"Sure," I said, sitting on a worn leather chair. "You keep looking around, you ride in an armored car, I don't get it."

"You don't believe it's necessary?"

"This is England. They don't even carry guns here. It feels like a lot's going on for show."

"You mean you think it's posturing, that I do all this stuff to show people I have power?"

"You want an answer?"

"Sure."

"Yes. I mean, what's it for? You think you're in so much danger? Come on," I said.

"They killed Valentina."

"In New York."

"They killed Litvinenko. There have been others. I've had threats. Even my kids. I try to keep it normal for them, I don't want them going to school with guys carrying loaded AKs, like some people."

"Jesus."

"No matter where I go, I can't get away, here, California, vacation, it doesn't matter."

"Because you owe somebody?"

He smiled just slightly. "Because of who I am."

"I don't get it."

"I'm a Russian. Like Tolya, like you."

"No fucking chance," I said under my breath.

Larry got up and looked out of the window, turned back to me but didn't sit down.

"You can't escape from it," he said. "The religion, the politics, the KGB, FSB, the Kremlin, the power, the paranoia, the fear, the fact that until a century ago most of us were serfs, slaves, really, we didn't even have last names, all surreal, the fact that thirty-seven per cent of the population can't see the need for indoor plumbing, that men are dying younger and younger, that we've produced the most sophisticated music and literature and graphics in the past, and we're living in the Middle Ages, and we shoot journalists who tell the truth. It's getting worse." In Larry's face was something I hadn't seen before, a kind of passion, or was it obsession?

"I thought you were a businessman, I thought you were in it for the dough."

"There will be a lot of shit coming," Larry said. "Soon. Soon, Artie, they want Georgia, they want Ukraine, I'm betting before the end of the summer, there will be tanks in Tblisi, Art, and nobody will know if it's a response to the Georgians or if the Georgians wanted it, provoked it. People will take sides, they'll rattle nukes. There's only one power and it takes in the whole damn place, the whole former USSR, you get it? You want me to spell it out, you want me to write the name?"

"Sure. I'm only a New York cop, help me out."

He lowered his voice to a whisper, and said, "Everything comes from the Kremlin," he said. "Everything goes back to Putin."

"What does it have to do with Val?"

"Tolya," he said. "Maybe me. A warning."

"You have people on it?"

"I have official friends. The number I gave you is one of them, somebody who can help you with Valentina. Use it."

"Official?"

"I don't operate like my cousin, I do this stuff inside the system. It works better. And we'll find them, whoever killed her, the way we found out who killed Sasha Litvinenko."

"Who?"

"Name is Lugovoi. Maybe you read about it. He's in Russia, no extradition. They'll protect him, but nothing is forever."

"Who's we? I don't believe the bullshit about it all being official. There's other people."

"You don't need them," he said.

"Can you fix for me to meet this guy, Greg?"

"There's a party tomorrow night. Maybe he'll be there. Charity thing Tolya cooked up. It would have been for Val, now it will be in her honor," he said, and his eyes filled up. I couldn't tell if he was acting or not. "Call me anytime. But be careful."

"What of?"

"There are people like me here who want things to change in Russia, you know their names, these are people who are in much worse danger, they go on TV, they give interviews, they never travel without whole armies of security." Larry sat close to me now, and leaned forward. "This is where we put our money, this is what we work for, to make it better in Russia, to stop all this. This is why it's dangerous."

"What the fuck are you talking about?" I said, impatient now.

Larry got up. "The next revolution, Art. I have to go now. See you at the party tomorrow night."

CHAPTER THIRTY

"Watch it, mate," said a fat man who pushed past me on the street in London.

Fuck off, mate, I wanted to say, but I kept my mouth shut. By the time I got back to London from Larry Sverdloff's place, it was a dripping day, wet, warm. I looked at the number on the door of a Greek grocery store on Moscow Road. I was looking for the agency where Masha Panchuk had been hired to work at the country hotel.

People looked pissed off, they snapped if you bumped into the them, in the stores they were surly. London had become a mean place since I'd been here a dozen years ago. Maybe it always was.

"Bloody London," I said half aloud. It was what I had felt even then. It was a city that got to me, made me half fall in love with it, then shoved me away, snarling.

In a row of little stores, electrical appliances, laundromat, coffee place, I found the building and rang the bell. Somebody buzzed me in, and I climbed three flights.

"Maids, Butlers, Chauffeurs" the printed sign read in English. Under it, on a piece of cardboard, the same sign was written out by hand in Russian. The door was open.

A middle-aged woman with a kindly face and a hairy wart on her cheek was singing a Russian lullaby to the plants she was watering on the windowsill. Turned when I entered, said her name was Ilana. On the other side of the room was a second door. I figured it led to a bathroom.

"Please, sit down," said Ilana, taking the chair behind a desk that held only a calendar and an old desktop computer.

I repeated what I'd said at the hotel in the countryside that I was looking for somebody to take care of me in London. I didn't mention Masha Panchuk, not at first, and I didn't know if the hotel had called Ilana. She pulled her computer screen towards me so we could both see it and then scrolled through pictures.

I made conversation. On a hunch, I switched to Russian. She smiled. I reflected on the humor in the street where the agency was being called Moscow Road. There was some history here, she added. Aristocrats had lived here; just around the corner in St Petersburg Mews, too. Russian businesses had opened over the years, she said, because it was close to Paddington Station where the train from the airport came in, and close to the Russian Embassy if you needed visas for your workers; and so people clustered around it, and after a while it had become a little joke.

Where do you go when you get to London? Moscow Road, they would say to each other.

Flashing my gold watch, I looked at the pictures she showed me on the computer, photographs of the girls who could clean. All good girls, she said. Hard workers. Nice-looking.

Did she think I wanted something else? I had implied I was a rich Russian and she believed it, the way the woman at the hotel had believed it. I felt I was in disguise.

More girls were displayed on the screen. Was this a front? Were they offering hookers? I pointed to a girl who looked about fifteen.

"I like this one. How old is she?"

"Twenty-one," said Ilana. "Very nice girl."

"She looks younger," I said.

I offered Ilana a cigarette and we both lit up, and I let her know what my tastes were. I said, of course, I really did want somebody to clean. It was just I liked attractive people in my house, I liked girls with good manners who could double as waitresses and knew how to greet people at the door, and wear a nice uniform.

"Of course," she said, "what else?"

We looked at more pictures, then I returned to the little girl I had chosen first.

From my pocket, I took some money out, and slid it under the calendar on the desk. She didn't look, but she smiled faintly.

"Can I confide in you?" she said.

"Of course," I said, adding we were both Russians and people of the world and we understood each other.

"This little one, she is young, but we try to help everybody. It's tough for these girls. Very young, which means very good at taking instructions, like schoolgirl, yes? Very fresh, very hard-working. Shall I send her to you? We want to give our girls a chance for some kind of life."

I hesitated.

"You would like somebody older?"

"What about younger?"

"I don't know," she said nervously, peeking at the money I'd put on the desk. "I shall ask." She handed me her card.

"Expensive?"

"Yes, but these girls are good," she said, and then picked up the money I'd given her and returned it. "Thank you," she said. "But we only accept a fee once you've hired the girl."

I was surprised. She wasn't on the take after all, or did she want something else, something bigger?

Thanking her, I got up. I suggested that she put the girl she had in mind on standby and that I would call as soon as I was settled in my new house.

"Where is it?" she asked.

I told her it was in the countryside, an old mansion I had recently purchased. Near Bray in the county of Berkshire, I said, and she seemed satisfied. I said again that I would call, she said she would send the girl as soon as I needed her. I started for the door.

"For a sleep-in maid, yes?" said Ilana, but I was halfway out the door. I waited in the hall.

I heard Ilana get up, heard the scrape of her chair, heard her move around the office. When I went back in, she was coming out of the door I thought was a bathroom. A scrabbling noise.

"Is somebody here?" I said.

"No, certainly not," said Ilana, looking at me confused, unsure what I wanted, eager to supply it.

I asked about Masha Panchuk again, and there was too much hesitation before she told me she had never met the girl. She said she had an appointment and looked nervously at her watch.

From Moscow Road, I walked a few blocks to Queensway, a wide street packed with Russians, Arabs, Chinese. The air was thick with languages. Some guys were trading whatever they had in their pants pockets. Drugs? Nickel bags? Gold watches?

People like this were always out for crumbs. You could read it in their faces and their clothes. They inhabited the fringes of crime. They hung around waiting for something to happen. They bought and sold drugs or information or little girls or boys, anything they could.

I listened in. I got the Russian, the exchanges and promises and threats. Some of the Arabic I also got.

This was a shabby world of people who live off the books. You found them in every big city. One guy turned suddenly. He had a pale face and pallid sweaty skin and a missing front tooth and he stared at me. He knew I had been listening. He offered me girls. Cheap, he said. I told him to fuck off. In a back alley a hundred yards away, I found stalls selling wooden dolls, Soviet army watches, the usual garbage that had begun to appear almost twenty years ago now, the fallout from the old Soviet Empire.

As soon as I turned myself into a Russian—I talked the language even in my head—I tuned in to people around me. I caught what they said, I asked questions, I got plenty of offers: currency, girls, drugs, whatever I wanted I could get here.

A place like this, I knew, you could find out who did certain kinds of jobs and how much they cost. This was where I could find out how it worked in London now, maybe the kind of people paid to deal with Tolya, deal with his daughter. Maybe I could get a fix on Greg, the boy in Val's pictures. Maybe I was jealous, and I couldn't get it out of my head that she'd had somebody.

Here too, you could find out who would run errands. If you hung around enough, if you let on you had enough cash, you could probably find out who would kill.

Maybe this was what Roy Pettus had wanted me for. Maybe without meaning to, I was doing his business.

I bought the newspapers, British, Russian, I stopped for coffee and read some of them. I began to see that London wasn't only the banker for Russians, but a marketplace for money, for people, for information, a crazy quilt of greed, ambition, fear. There were listings for real estate, for country houses, for apartments in Russia, for furniture and gold and diamonds. In the want-ads were listings for people to service the rich: maids, escorts, butlers, chauffeurs, interpreters, wives. You read between the lines carefully enough, you spotted girls for sale.

At the other end of the street, near Hyde Park, was an ice-skating rink, and I leaned against the wall and watched for a while. Kids went in and came out, some with skates over their shoulders, others idled in the doorway.

This was a London of foreigners. Languages I couldn't even make out ate up the air space around me so that my head hurt.

So Masha had used a seedy employment agency that might or might not be a front for hookers? What difference did it make? She had been killed in Valentina's place because of a resemblance, because she had Val's gold purse. Somebody realized the mistake and went for Val.

Nothing here, I thought. Not today.

I gave one guy a few bucks, though. He was a small Russian with a sweaty face and a taste for Middle Eastern sweet things. He talked and fed his mouth with Turkish delight that left powdered sugar on his face.

I'd found him selling Russian tablecloths at a tiny stall, and he was eager and smart. Of the people I saw on the street, in stores, restaurant, stalls, this one was alert and up for business. He held out the box of candy.

"Try pistachio," he said. "Or rose water." He had a peasant accent, his Russian was crude, but on a hunch, I showed him Greg's pictures, and told him it was worth quite a bit to me to find him. By the time I left, the little man was already on his phone.

CHAPTER THIRTY-ONE

"You let them cut her up," said Tolya over the phone late that night. I was sitting in Tolya's library, the TV tuned to some Euro sports channel, the sound muted, when he called.

"They sliced her open, Artemy."

"I couldn't stop that."

He didn't speak, but I could hear him breathing hard.

"Tolya? You there? I'm coming home," I said.

"No. I want you to go to my party tomorrow night, I want you to see who comes, who doesn't come, who cries real tears for Valentina. Many people will not know you, which is good."

"Of course."

"But my cousin Larry will know you. He'll know who you are. You'll meet him at the party."

"I met him."

"I see. He sent his guy to follow you around?"

"Yes. What's with him?"

"He thinks he's going to change the world, Artemy, he thinks he's going to fix things in Russia, him and a bunch of other guys. He's okay, but anything you want to tell him, anything he asks, call me first."

"Sure."

"I left something for you in the closet. In the guest room," he said, his voice dry and affectless, his language formal, no

189

swearing, no affectionate barbs, nothing at all that reminded me of my friend.

Valentina's room was on the top floor, I climbed the stairs and stood outside the door. I didn't want to go in. The house was silent. There was only the noise of a party out in the garden, but in here it was silent.

I opened the door gently. The room smelled of Val, it smelled of her perfume, her shampoo. It was an empty space. The bed and the rest of the furniture remained. The drawers and closets were empty, as if she had barely used them, as if she had left this room long ago.

I hate what London does to him, my dad, ever since he opened his club there. Valentina had said this to me at Dubi's bookshop. *I don't want to ever go back.*

What did I expect to find?

I looked through the desk drawers, in the bathroom. Nothing. I got down on the floor and felt I wanted to stay there, wanted to just lie down on the soft rug and sleep for a while.

Under the bed was a long flat box, probably something that had been forgotten by Val, by Tolya, by the people who cleaned. I pulled it out, sat up and opened it.

Inside were freshly laundered sheets wrapped in tissue paper that smelled of sandalwood, nothing else as far as I could see at first.

Again, I searched the room. I tried to look with the eye of a cop, of a guy who had come in fresh, not knowing anything, not the place or the people who had inhabited it. Eventually I found the box on a shelf in the bathroom.

Inside were a few pieces of jewelry Val had obviously forgotten. There was a thin gold chain with a Victorian locket on it, a pair of small diamond earrings, and an antique bracelet made out of amber. There was also an envelope where somebody—Val, somebody else—had placed some stray beads, a single earring that had no mate, a gold charm resembling a Russian Easter egg. Nothing else.

I took out the envelope. Val's name was on the front. On the back was a return address. Wimbledon, it said. Wimbledon, I thought. They play tennis there.

It didn't mean anything, but I put the envelope in my pocket. What else did Val say about London?

I sat on the edge of her bed now, and tried to remember. We had talked a little about it the night she stayed with me. I had tried not to think about her. It was all I wanted to think about.

It was about one in the morning, and we were in my bed and Val leaned on her elbow and said, "I'm starving," and giggled, though she almost never giggled. Her laugh, the low husky rising chuckle that exploded at the end, belonged to a grown-up. But now she giggled, and said, I'm hungry, and I said I'd make her a sandwich, and we both got out of bed, and she saw me looking at her.

"Stop staring," she said.

"Why stop?"

"I don't know, I just feel suddenly shy," she said, and loped into the kitchen, me in some pajama bottoms I found; her wearing a ratty old bathrobe I had hanging on the bathroom door.

In the kitchen, I put bread and some cheese and a spicy sopressata on the counter. I got a bottle of red wine out of the cupboard, and poured it out. Val sliced up the sausage and ate a piece, and I made sandwiches.

"Are you happy, Artie, darling?"

"Yes."

"Do we need to talk about anything?"

"Only if you want to," I said.

"I don't want to, I want you to put on some music and I want to eat and then I want to go back to bed," she said.

I put Ella on the stereo. Ella singing Gershwin, and Val put her elbows on the kitchen counter, drank the wine and listened.

"I love this stuff," she said. "I love this music. It makes me think of New York, even when I'm here, you know?"

"I know."

"I don't want to leave, Artie."

"New York, you mean?"

"Yes."

"Me either."

"I can feel good here," said Val, pouring more wine in her glass while Ella sang "Someone To Watch Over Me". "That's you, isn't it, you'll watch out for me?"

"Yes." I held her hand.

I didn't know how the hell I'd tell Tolya but I wasn't giving her up, not unless she wanted me to give her up. Most of me knew it wouldn't go on, couldn't, I was too old, she was Tolya's kid, but a little part believed.

"Let's go back to bed," she said, and smiled a smile both wicked and sweet. And we did.

In Val's room in London now nothing was left of her except her smell.

In the kitchen I found a bottle of Scotch and did something I almost never did anymore: I drank too much of the stuff, I carried the glass through the house, I drank three, four, five shots, and I kept on drinking.

In the guest room, I opened the closet. On a wooden hanger was a garment bag and inside a tux. My size. A box on the shelf contained shirts and ties. Beside it were fancy shoes.

I tried on the clothes, and they fit beautifully. Tolya must have swiped one of my jackets to get the measurements. He had planned it all, he must have planned it before I got to London, long ago, hoping I'd come for his birthday party. Before Val was murdered, he had planned it.

In the tux and the shoes, with Tolya's watch, I looked in the mirror. Looking back was a well-heeled guy, a rich Russian, maybe, with an expensive glass of whisky in his hand, a big gold watch and plenty of dough. Nobody except Larry Sverdloff would make me for a New York cop at the party, for sure not Greg, the boyfriend.

Was I obsessed because he had been with Val? If he didn't kill her, why didn't he show up or get in touch with Tolya? He was Valentina's guy, what was stopping him? The part of me that was functioning like a cop knew the other part was jealous as hell and it was clouding my judgement and making me stupid.

CHAPTER THIRTY-TWO

Even from the entrance to Kensington Gardens, just as I entered the park, in the near distance, I could see the palace all lit up like Christmas, aglitter on the near horizon, and I could hear the Stones. A cover band was playing 'Jumpin' Jack Flash'.

As I got closer, the palace turned into a blaze of lights, lights in windows, lights in trees, little gold lights, silk lanterns with lights inside, chandeliers with candles set on tables you could see through the tall windows, real torches lining the drive. Tolya's party, Valentina's party, a party in honour of Val's charity, a party where they both should have been. In my hand was the invitation I had taken from Tolya's mantelpiece.

The band shifted to 'Wild Horses'. Security was everywhere, guys in uniform, others in plain clothes, Russian muscle speaking into the collar of their evening clothes that were too tight, others in costume.

Near the entrance where people were streaming in, was a bunch of gorgeous girls in period ball-gowns, diamonds on every part, wrists, ears, necks, greeted me. Slavic cheekbones, legs up to their armpits, the Russian babes were working the door.

All suited up in the tux and new shoes, I passed in without much trouble.

"Devil?"

"What?"

"A mask?" One of the babes was holding up a red devil mask with sequins on it.

"I don't think so."

"Cat?"

"What?"

"I think there's others," she said worriedly, sorting through the basket.

"I'll take the devil."

Kensington Palace, where Lady Diana had lived – somebody dropped this into conversation as soon as I got in the door – was close to the Russian Embassy. Maybe in the next Revolution, the new Russians could set up shop here.

London had always been a good place to operate out of. My mother used to tell me about it, late at night when Moscow was asleep. She told me how Lenin, Trotsky and Stalin had been in London: Lenin and his wife had stayed in a nice place in Kensington; Stalin, who was broke, in a flea pit. She liked spinning stories about the so-called Soviet heroes. It made her feel better. It was her form of sedition, these late-night sessions.

From the look of the guests streaming into the palace, many courtiers, Tsars, more than one King Louis, a couple of Rasputins, and the others in regular clothes, jewels glittering, they already knew the next Revolution would not take place during Marxism-Leninism class, or folk-dancing.

"Jumpin' Jack Flash is a gas gas" went the lyrics you could never get out of your head. This band was almost as good as the original, the beat, the strut, the bluesy heart.

I had always secretly preferred the Stones to the Beatles, even as a kid in Moscow, when the Beatles were like God, and everyone prayed at their altar; and though I loved them for a long time, after a while I couldn't stand the reverence. And now, at the entrance to Kensington Palace, the noise was like a drug. It picked me up and carried me into the place, where I saw, in what felt like a druggy hallucination, Marie Antoinette, or maybe it was Catherine the Great, wobbling towards me, the heels of her large blue silk pumps going tippy-tap on the marble floor.

This Marie had very big feet, she was six feet tall plus a yard of powdered wig on her head, thick corkscrew curls hanging down her neck. Shoulders of an Olympic swimmer, big boobs pushed up most of the way so that when she bent over you could see her nipples. Until I saw them, and even then, I thought it was a guy in drag.

Her blue dress, weighed down with lace and sequins, was so wide that people scuttled away to avoid getting hit as if by a bumper car in an arcade. Unlike the ladies of the eighteenth century, she had a deep hard tan, and a voice that, when she shouted out to friends who passed, could crack Coke bottles. Overhead chandeliers hanging with crystals, and lit up with real candles, made her diamonds glitter hard as the tan.

I pushed the devil mask up on top of my head. Maybe I should have come as Lenin, I thought, and it was then, near the door, me adjusting my red mask, that the Marie Antoinette or whoever she was held out her hand as if she expected me to kiss it. I gave it a shake.

"Alexandra Arkadina Romanov," said Marie through puffy lips thick with implants and gloss. "And you are?"

The band moved on to "Mother's Little Helper".

I said hi to Marie. She said this was her party, or at least she was on the committee, and that she had been Valentina Sverdloff's best friend. In mourning for her, she said, we are all in mourning, but one must carry on.

I'm looking for a guy named Greg, I said to her, but she wasn't interested. She asked where I was from and I said New York, and she said, no, originally, and I said I was original, and it went on like that for a minute or so, until she spotted better prey, a fat guy in a red frock coat with lace dribbling down his front.

"Artie." It was Larry Sverdloff. He was not the kind of guy to put on a costume, and he was wearing tails and white tie and he looked good, the stuff was custom-made. He shook my hand. "I'm glad you're here."

"Yeah, sorry I'm late."

"It's fine."

"How come Tolya got this place for a party?"

"They rent it out," he said. "You can rent pretty much any place you want. Can I get you a drink?" He signaled a waiter who swerved in and out between people, carrying aloft trays of champagne and other booze as the crowd grew, and you could feel the heat. There must have been five hundred people. I scanned the room, looking for Greg.

"You've heard from Tolya?"

"Only a message to deliver when I make the speech. I'm playing host for him. You okay? You have everything you want?"

"What about Greg?"

"I put out lines. I'm sure you'll meet him. Excuse me," said Larry. "I'm going to make a speech soon, then we can talk. There's somebody I want you to meet here. "

"Yeah, who's that?" I was getting sick of Larry's games, if they were games.

"Somebody else. She'll be somewhere, probably out on the terrace smoking."

"Who?"

"I'll explain."

"Fine, so what's her name?"

"Fiona," he said. "Excuse me."

The band was on "Brown Sugar". I looked around for the musicians, I went through one gilded room after the other, all of them packed, five hundred rich people giving off heat and ambition, and a band playing Stones numbers. I realized the music was coming from outside, from a big white tent out on the lawn.

Everywhere I went, people swarmed around me, shook my hand and bowed, and asked who I was, but didn't care.

I met a guy who had made a fortune installing bulletproof glass, I met art dealers who could get you a Francis Bacon or a Monet, depending on your taste, and people who would protect your art collection because there had already been killings on that front, they said, and I didn't know if they meant in the financial sense or the other kind that made you literally dead.

Actors, famous actors I'd seen in the movies, were around, dotted across the room like decorative objects. Brits with braying nasal voices in white tie and tails bragged about their agencies where you could hire butlers with pedigree, realtors who told me Russians liked living in houses near famous people, Belgravia was good, any place near Sean Connery a top choice. Or people with titles, God how the Russkis loved it, they'd say, oh, do meet the Earl of Fuckwit or whatever, and you could see them creaming their pants.

And there were Russians I recognized from news magazines, the big ones, the ones with the fleets of yachts. These were men who had swiped chunks of the old USSR, oil, gas, airlines, aluminum, the works. Faces as famous now as Lenin and Stalin and the other ghouls.

I went into a room with painted ceilings, looking for a drink. The bar was massive, twenty feet long, covered in bouquets of white flowers, white roses, white peonies, and along the rest of the surface, gold-colored tubs filled with ice and champagne bottles. Magnums of champagne, Krug, the really good stuff I knew about from Tolya's club, and ranks of glittering crystal.

Tons of caviar was heaped on ice in gold and silver bowls, glistening black and gray and pearly and golden. I thought about Tolya's caviar deals, and wondered if this was part of it.

Waiters, dressed in black knee pants and tailcoats and those stupid white wigs, served it up on gold plates, and I was betting they were real.

As a child, I'd seen a news item on TV about a dinner at Buckingham Palace attended by the Soviet ambassador where all the plates were made of gold. It was intended to show us how decadent the West was, but my mother and her pals turned down the sound of propaganda and peered at the pictures to work out if there really were gold plates in London.

Drink in hand, mask on my face, I went out to the terrace, scanning the crowd for Greg. I had his picture in my pocket.

The night was warm and damp. The band was playing "You Can't Always Get What You Want" with what seemed to me an epic sense of irony. Somewhere close by I could hear a helicopter. On the walls of the tent, I could see the outlines of people dancing, like a puppet show.

"Are you Artie Cohen?" a warm low voice said.

She was tall, slim, brown hair, cut so it fell to her chin, bangs to her eyebrows. She lit a cigarette without any fuss, her hands long, thin, her gestures small and efficient. With her other hand, she pushed the cat mask that covered her eyes and nose onto the top of her head. Her eyes were gray.

"I'm Fiona Colquhoun," she said.

In spite of a serious expression and not much make-up, or maybe because of it, she was pretty sexy. Plain long black dress, three strands of pearls around her long neck. No wedding ring.

"*Le tout Londongrad*, eh? I shouldn't smoke." She tossed the cigarette into an urn on the terrace and said, "Let's walk a bit, shall we?" She led me towards a separate building out on the lawns, a huge barn of a place, but beautiful and mostly made of glass.

"What do they call this?"

"The Orangery," she said.

"You know about this stuff?"

"I was always a history nut, old houses, my grandmother used to take me. This one was a greenhouse."

"Some greenhouse."

"Yup, you want to go in? There's carvings by a guy called Grinling Gibbons, it was so beautiful they probably used it for supper in the summer, and entertaining their pals. Or shall we sit out here?" Gracefully she sat on a marble bench and I sat next to her.

"I needed some air," she said. "Russian sentimentality makes me gag."

"You knew my name?"

"I took a flyer on it being you."

She didn't offer any other information, so I played along.

From a little silver purse she took a fresh pack and lit up again.

"You smoke a lot."

"Indeed."

"It will kill you."

"Give me a bloody break. My God, look at that," she added, starting to laugh.

The guy passing, probably an old Russian thug from the 90s, had been recycled for respectability, and was stuffed into his tails and white tie.

Like a penguin looking for his mate, he waddled across the terrace. I was drinking too much. I thought I saw Gorbachev. The real one. Not a guy in costume. Fiona followed my glance.

"You know who all these people are?"

"Some," she said.

Fiona sat quietly beside me, and when I asked, she pointed

them out, relaying names, the football players, fashion designers, wives, mistresses belonging to oligarchs, the businessmen and members of various factions and feuds, British politicians in hock to Russian money. Politics inside politics, she said, like Russian wooden dolls, people who had been allies in Russia, were enemies in London.

"Feuds?"

"Of course. Some of them are creatures of the Kremlin and owe it like they were vassals, others want to overturn it. You've heard of Berezovsky, Abramovich, Deripaska. I think your country just refused Mr Deripaska a visa."

The band moved onto "Ruby Tuesday".

"You're wondering how I knew your name?" said Fiona Colquhoun.

"I guessed." I looked around for Larry Sverdloff.

"Right," she said, as if she understood. "Good. Then we know what we're about."

"These people, at this party, you know them?"

"It's my job. You're looking for somebody?"

"Could be," I said. Suddenly the band stopped. People poured out of the tent towards the house.

"What's going on?"

"A speech, I imagine," said Fiona.

"You knew Valentina Sverdloff?"

"I met her once or twice. Let's go inside."

In a long room lined with windows, hung with chandeliers, lit with candles, over it all was an immense screen, widescreen, like a movie theater with images of Valentina projected on it. I didn't want to look. There wasn't any choice, it hung there over everything, lit up by thousands of candles and dozens of chandeliers. A thousand people looked up.

Then the slide show stopped. A picture of Val was frozen on the screen. In a silver gown, diamonds in her ears, face made up, hair done, she barely looked like herself.

But she knew how to pose. She had earned some money modeling when she was in high school, she had hated it. In that picture, ten feet high, behind the eyes, I could see the self-mockery. The whole crowd was looking at her like she was an icon. And then she spoke. I thought my heart would crack.

"Hello, everybody," said Valentina. "I'm sorry I can't be with you. But I want to say hi and thank you for coming and for giving to my foundation."

From the screen she talked about the girls she tried to rescue in Russia, the little ones, the older ones, girls who worked train stations as prostitutes, some as young as ten or eleven. She asked her friends to give what they could, she smiled and smiled, and then she thanked everyone in that husky voice. She thanked her father and her uncle and blew them kisses. For a few minutes she talked, and when she stopped all that remained was her image on the screen.

She had made the video because even before she was murdered, she knew she wasn't coming for the party, though Tolya had gone on believing she'd show up. There was something in London that Val hated more, or that scared her more than she had said.

Next to me stood Fiona Colquhoun, not watching the screen, watching me instead. Around us, people began to weep. One woman with a long face cried uncontrollably.

There followed more speeches, by Larry Sverdloff, by friends of Valentina, people sobbing, talking English, Russian. A choir in Russian peasant outfits got up and sang some old folk songs and it was corny but haunting, and I felt I had to get away but I couldn't. And I remembered something.

One night, when was it? Last year? On a cold fall night we had been walking by the river, me and Val. She was wearing a heavy green sweater and jeans, and she started singing in Russian.

She had been learning, she said. She wanted to surprise Tolya. And she sang the old Russian songs, revolutionary anthems, other stuff, and we walked and I had been glad it was dark and she couldn't see me crying.

"I think you wanted to meet Greg," said Fiona whispering into my ear while the speeches finished and people began to leave the room.

Where?"

"I saw him go out towards the band," she said, and took my hand and led me to a white tent where inside the band started up again and people took to the floor.

Scores of people started to dance, then more, all moving to the music. Russians, Brits.

Fiona gestured with her head, and I saw him, Greg, a tall guy in a tux and a mask with a girl in a milkmaid outfit, blonde hair to her waist. She wore a cat mask. Greg had Pushkin's face on his own mask.

Anybody who grew up in Russia would know it, Pushkin, our national hero, the most admired man in Russia even though he died in 1837. We kids all knew Pushkin, the face, the poems, by heart. Maybe this guy, this Greg, figured himself for a hero.

I was sure he knew I was watching him. He knew who I was. Maybe Val had told him about me, her dad's friend, her "Uncle Artie". And then, for a split second I was distracted by the band which was going crazy on "Satisfaction".

On the stage, Mick Jagger did his stuff, strutting, twirling, smirking. I'd figured it for a tribute band, a good one. It wasn't. It was the Stones. It was the real thing.

"Jesus," I said under my breath. I had lost sight of Greg.

"The big Russians hire bands privately," said Fiona. "A perk of my job, Artie. My kid goes to a party, the parents fly in

Britney Spears. I've seen McCartney, they pay anything, millions, sometimes two, three bands, once I saw the whole bloody Royal Ballet." She followed my gaze, I was staring at the Pushkin mask. "You want to talk to him. You want me to insist?"

"What makes you so sure you can force him?"

"I'm pretty persuasive," she said.

I didn't wait for Fiona, I got myself close to Greg, close enough so he could hear me, close enough he could see me. In the seconds between numbers, as the band stopped playing, I called his name out.

He turned his face, the Pushkin mask, towards me. The hair was cut short, almost black, the mouth smiling—all I could see of his face was part of his mouth and the blue eyes through the eye holes in the mask.

For a second he was so close I could feel his breath, this pretend Pushkin, I could feel it, and I leaned into him, my mouth next to his ear. "You killed her, didn't you?" I said. "You did it, isn't that right? You killed Valentina and I'm coming for you," I said. I was pretty drunk.

He didn't say anything at all, just smiled slightly and then moved away and slipped into the crowd.

On the ground, over the lawns, pathways, skirting the Orangery, the gardens, the huge trees, the torches, I was running, looking for him, swerving between people watching the sky. My lungs hurt from running, my head was full of booze, but I ran, looking for him.

The Stones had finished. An orchestra was playing the 1812, and now fireworks threw up huge gold flowers into the sky, red white and blue waterfalls, Russian flags, Union Jack, more flowers, and in the light of it, I thought I saw him again. He saw me. He raised the mask and showed his face. The handsome face stared at me, the intense blue eyes seemed to be smiling or laughing, and then I realized what the message was—it was a threat. He wasn't scared of me. He was coming after me.

He replaced the mask, and again I lost him. He was too good at it; had he been trained? This was a guy who could have slipped in and out of New York and killed her.

"What's the matter with you?" said Larry Sverdloff. It was ten, fifteen minutes after I'd seen Greg, and I was still looking, in the parking lot now, among the big cars, among the waiting drivers, and the drunken partygoers.

"I saw him."

"I know," said Larry Sverdloff, looking pissed off. "He told me."

"Fucking told you what?"

"That you accused him of being involved in Val's murder."

"I said I wanted you to find him for me," I said. "You didn't make much effort."

"I was going to get you together later, I thought you wanted to talk to him, not accuse him."

"Yeah, well, it's what I think. Unless you know different."

"That's crazy," said Larry. "I loved her and I loved him, too, for chrissake."

"What are you talking about?"

"He was a good kid, they were the real thing," said Larry. "My crazy cousin Tolya didn't approve of him. Val told me she loved him. I thought you wanted his help. Jesus, Artie, what the fuck are you doing?" said Larry. "I'm going to take you to my place, and tomorrow I'm putting you on a plane. Let's go."

"Where is he?"

"I don't know."

"Val stopped seeing him?"

"Yes."

"What else?"

"They broke up, so what? She wouldn't talk about it. Let's

go, I want you out of here and out of London," said Larry. "You tell people you think they killed somebody, they don't like it." He looked at the crowds, some climbing into cars, others going back for more to eat and drink. "I hate it. I hate this. I hate what it did to my cousin and to Val."

"Who? What the fuck are you talking about?"

"All of them, Russians," he said. "Bastards."

Fiona was standing close by. Unruffled, smoking, listening, she had been close by me most of the evening and she still was and I wondered what her business was, and how come Larry Sverdloff had told her about me. Was she his official contact, one of the officials he said he worked with? Something else?

CHAPTER THIRTY-THREE

I didn't go with Larry Sverdloff, I left the party, and walked out of the park, along the avenue next to it, turned right, looking for a place I'd spotted earlier, figuring that on Queensway, a bar would still be open. Found myself near an all-night cafe, no booze, kept moving.

From behind me there were steps on the sidewalk again, the scuffle of feet, the raucous hoot of young men, a low mean whistle. The crummy street where I found myself was lined with shuttered shops. The sidewalk was crumbling. A few teenagers drinking out of paper bags wandered into a late-night game arcade. A shitty chicken takeout was empty except for the counter man asleep on a table. Some Arab-looking boys glared at me from the doorway of a kebab place.

I kept walking. I heard a car coming slowly along the dark road. It slowed to keep pace with me, and then I heard her voice.

"Artie, please, get in the car," called Fiona. "I'll give you a lift."

"I want to walk," I said.

"Then at least buy me a drink," she said, and parked her Mini and got out. "Sverdloff's club will still be open," she added.

I need a drink, I thought.

"I'll walk with you," said Fiona.

"If you want."

"You'll come to Sverdloff's club?"

"Maybe."

Overhead, clouds scudded away, revealing a piece of white moon that cast a strange light over the empty streets where we walked.

Fiona had a big stride like an athlete and she talked very softly, had a way of projecting her voice just far enough so I could hear clearly but keeping it low. Nice voice. English, husky.

For a while we walked silently, Fiona smoking, and then I realized we were in Moscow Road.

"Something about this road strikes a chord?" she said.

"I don't know."

Then the shabby streets of cheap hotels and small shops gave way to tree-lined roads, pretty houses, foreign cars parked in front, trees thick and green.

Finally, I said, "What are you?"

"I'm sorry?"

"What are you? What's your job? How come you know all the Russians? How come you knew my name? Spell it out for me."

"You didn't know?"

"How the fuck would I know? I figured you were something official," I said. "But what?"

"Didn't Agent Pettus tell you?"

"Roy Pettus?"

"Yes. I've been waiting for you to ring for several days, Pettus told me you were coming across."

"Jesus."

"What did you think?"

"Tell me what you are."

Lighting one smoke from another, she told me she was a special liaison, coordinated projects between Scotland Yard and MI5.

"Your FBI," she said.

"Right."

She went on talking, told me she had studied Russian at university along with Polish and Swedish, and had done graduate work in Warsaw. Her grandmother was Polish and a scientist, and Fiona had a background in physics and chemistry because of it.

"My grandmother raised me," she said. "She thought girls should learn." Colquhoun's looks suggested an ice queen but she was open, warm, surprising. "She left me the house in Highgate where I live," she added. "A lot of Russians there, the new, the last wave, we've got them all, white, red, dead, rich, oligarchs, we've even got Karl Marx. Did you know he's buried in the cemetery at Highgate?"

"Yes."

"Unusual for an American to know, but you aren't entirely American, are you, Artie?"

"Yeah."

How much did Fiona know about me? Why was she making small talk? I wondered, and then she said, "Will you let me help?"

I didn't answer, not then. Maybe she was connected to both Pettus and to Larry Sverdloff, and it didn't make me happy, but I needed Colquhoun's help. In the street light her face was pale, the expression on her lips wry.

"I'm also a cop, Artie, if that makes you feel better," she said.

Pravda22 was almost empty, but the bartender, Rolly, saw me and beckoned us in. A few people sat at tables in the back. He knew Fiona's name.

"I've been here before," she said by way of explanation. I asked for Scotch, Fiona for a small brandy. We sat at the bar.

"You're a cop?"

"Yes, as I said. I moved in and out of the police, I went to higher education and back, took a graduate degree, worked for a while designing gender-related studies for the police college. I was a homicide detective, British style, you know, like Morse?" She smiled. "Then I shifted to one of the joint forces."

She had done the business, I realized, though she looked younger, she was probably my age, even a couple years older.

"You speak Russian?"

She nodded.

"You work with Roy Pettus?"

"I work with a good number of people," she said. "We've had to gear up quite quickly."

"On the Russians?"

"Yes, and not long ago we had good relations with them. Just after the attacks on New York, and then on London, we had marvelous relationships, your people, even the bloody Russians."

"But not now?"

"I wouldn't say we're exactly friends. The Litvinenko thing has triggered a little Cold War, we accuse them of killing him, they retaliate by persecuting Brits in Russia, the ambassador, anyone they can. Did you know there are as many Russian agents here as during the real Cold War?"

"So you work with them?"

"Not if I can help it. I prefer you Americans," she said.

Perched beside me at the bar, Fiona had great legs, a witty curious face, beautiful when she smiled. Another time, place, I would have been interested, but not now. Now there was only Val.

"I believe you worked quite a big case here in London once," said Fiona. It wasn't a question.

"How did you know?"

"It's a small country. I worked once with a detective who knew you."

"Who's that?"

"Chap called Jack Cotton."

"Christ."

"That's pretty much how Jack thinks of himself now. He's one of our top cops. He's Sir Jack now."

"No shit, so he's a top dog?"

"One of the biggest, and when Sir Jack barks, all the little puppies sit up and beg," said Fiona. "Shall I send your regards? He'll give us some help on this if I ask, if I say you asked."

"Not now." I wanted to operate on my own for now, I didn't want red tape.

"He said you were very good and rather unreliable," said Fiona Colquhoun. "That you did what you liked, and people put up with it because you get results. Good taste in music, Artie had, he said. He says you had mixed feelings about this place, always called it bloody London."

"You asked him if you could trust me?"

"Yes."

"Because he's one of yours?"

"Of course. And Sir Jack said you liked carrying a gun even in London. Is that right, Artie?"

"If I have to."

"Please don't do that," she said. "I can't help you if you do."

"Listen, I'm here because of Valentina Sverdloff's murder," I said. "I'm guessing you knew that. I'll do what I have to do," I said, and tossed back the Scotch.

In the gilded mirror over the bar, I saw a familiar figure moving in behind me, coming at me, the woman who had cried like crazy at the party, long sad face, pointed nose. I ordered another drink.

"I understand, Artie, I'm still a cop in my bones, and I know how good your people, how good they were to me, when I worked in New York," said Fiona, tapping me lightly on the arm.

"When?"

"Nine-eleven. There were Brits who died in the Towers, and a few of us volunteered to go over, our tragedy, too. Your people, police, firemen, were extraordinary. When I got back, I asked to move over to an anti-terrorism squad," she said softly. "I would like to have stayed."

"But?"

"I have a daughter, Gracie, she's twelve."

I was moved and pissed off. She meant what she said but she knew, like a great detective, if only instinctively, how to seduce. Telling me about her part after 9/11, how she had taken part in the now holy events, got to me.

"I met Valentina Sverdloff once," said Fiona.

"Where?"

"At her uncle's house. My daughter is friends with one of Larry's girls."

"Larry Sverdloff?"

Yes."

"You get around."

"He's the father of my daughter's friend, or do you think I use my daughter to spy on Russian oligarchs?"

"You tell me."

"You think because I know Agent Roy Pettus and Larry Sverdloff, I'm working both sides? Did Larry give you my name, too, is that it?" She looked at me. "I see."

"Are you? What sides?"

She knocked back her drink and got off the bar stool. I put out my hand to keep her from going.

"You met Val when?"

"About a year ago at Larry Sverdloff's house in London, one of his daughters was playing piano, Val was sitting near her, I had never seen anyone so alive, so incredibly vivid. I'm so sorry. I know you and her father are great friends."

"Was she alone?"

"Greg was there. I think he had a Russian name as well, which I didn't catch, and frankly until the other day when this case came up, I didn't think about him again. I told him I spoke the language and I loved the literature and he just opened up. Bit of a bloody nationalist, I thought, just a fraction too zealous, but he was a good-looking young man, charming, and deeply in love with Valentina. Greg told me how he and Valentina were working for the fatherland, explained to me how Putin was turning things around. Very persuasive, but he waited until Valentina was out of his hearing. "

"What else?"

"They couldn't keep their hands off each other. She was besotted. They were an astonishing couple, wonderful to look at, whispering to one another as if they had all the secrets to being alive."

I didn't answer.

"When Valentina was murdered, Larry Sverdloff called me," she said. "He thinks whoever killed her did it to warn his cousin, Tolya. Is that what you think?"

"Yes."

"I've been doing a little asking around privately," she said.

"Can you find this Greg?"

"You really do think he's a suspect?" Fiona said. "You're going to need a lot more than thinking, Artie, you need a little bit of evidence," and then we were interrupted by the long-faced woman I'd seen in the mirror.

"Elena Gagarin," she said, and held out her hand to me, ignoring Fiona. "We met at the ball." Sloshed, she had been crying, mascara streaked her face. "I was Valentina's friend," she added. "She showed me a photograph of you. She said, this is my Uncle Artie, my dad's best friend. Also at her daddy's house, there is a picture of you. So I see you, I try to say this at the party, I think, God, is this Valentina's Artie?"

She had a mild Russian accent. "I know you loved her," she went on in the naked way Russians sometimes do, especially women, as if they could peel back your skin, help themselves to your emotions. No embarrassment, nothing coy, she just said, again, "You loved her. Now she is dead. I am very drunk."

"Let's get you home," said Fiona, but Gagarin shoved her away and went on bawling.

"As soon as I heard about Val," she said, "I cried for one whole day without cease. Val was so good, she helps orphans." Gagarin looked at the ceiling. "Perhaps she is in better place now?"

"You met these girls Val helped?"

"Some, yes, surely. A few she helped particularly to come from Russia to England."

"Was one of them named Masha Panchuk? She worked as a maid."

I saw the hesitation; I saw the eyes twirl like dark saucers, then dart inward. I was sure Gagarin had met Masha, but she wasn't saying.

"I don't know this person that worked as maid."

"Think about it."

"I am glad you are in London and living close to me, I feel more secure, I am living on same square with Tolya Sverdloff, this is how we all meet."

And then without warning, Gagarin threw her glass at the wall of bottles behind the bar. The bartender Rolly took her by the arm.

"Go home," he said.

"No."

"You don't feel safe in London?" I said to her.

"No, I think first this Masha is killed, then Valentina, and next, next is me."

Somehow Rolly bundled Gagarin out into a taxi, came back.

"She comes here a lot?"

He shrugged.

"Some of the time," he said. "She was friendly with the Sverdloffs. She's done this before, she gets drunk and breaks things."

"I must go," said Fiona, looking at the tiny gold watch on her slim wrist.

"You left your car."

"I'll get a cab, I've had too much drink to drive. Shall I drop you, Artie?"

"No," I said, and watched her go.

I liked Fiona Colquhoun, but I didn't trust her. Her brief wasn't dead girls in New York. For all her talk about 9/11, she wasn't a cop anymore. She worked with Roy Pettus and she was some kind of spook, a security liaison between Scotland Yard and MI5, whatever that meant.

Most people in the spy business are so impressed with their own theatrics, the stuff they've read or seen, I never really believed them. I didn't buy the act.

Truth was, I didn't give a fuck who was running Russia or if another revolution was coming, or for Larry Sverdloff's feverish fantasies. All I wanted was the creep who had killed Valentina. I wanted something hard, sure, pure, evidence like diamonds that I could give to Tolya to make up for not saving his daughter. Then I wanted to go home.

"You asked me about Valentina Sverdloff?" said Rolly, wiping down the bar. "I didn't tell you everything."

"Yes."

"Once or twice she asked me to post some packages for her. She always asked nicely, but there was this imperious quality, and also she seemed bloody obsessive about it."

"What was in the packages?"

"I didn't ask. Best not to. Always to Moscow."

"You know where the boyfriend lived?"

"Valentina's fellow?"

"Yeah. Somewhere in south London. He asked me if I knew anybody who wanted to rent a room. Fuck me, it was somewhere, Putney, I think, or maybe Wimbledon."

"You have any more thoughts about him?"

"Maybe, but not anything I can swear to."

"Go on."

"Yeah. You know, no reason, when I heard somebody killed Valentina, it just came to me that it was him."

"How come? You said he was charming."

"Don't know. When I heard, it came into my head. You want a last drink?"

I didn't. I left. Into the dark empty London night where it was raining, rain dripping down my collar, I walked to Tolya's house. Bloody London, I thought.

CHAPTER THIRTY-FOUR

"What?"

It was four in the morning. It was raining. Water sluiced down the windows, and I was awake and still dressed, but in no mood for drunks at the door and I yelled at the intercom, fuck off. It buzzed again. Out of habit, I grabbed the gun Tolya gave me, went down, yanked open the front door. What? What!

Still in her party dress, Elena Gagarin stood on the steps. She looked scared. Her face was streaked from the rain, make-up smeared over it.

"I want to stay here tonight," she said. "I am sorry for breaking glass at club."

"No."

"Please."

"I'm sorry," I said. "Come in if you want, I'll make coffee, and I'll walk you home."

"I saw him."

"Who?"

"Friend of Valentina."

"Which friend?"

"This guy, he was at the party. Greg, he calls himself. I'm going in my house, he calls to me, and I say, go away, go away."

"What else?"

I wasn't sure if this woman, Gagarin, had picked up on what

217

I'd been telling Fiona. Being with her felt like having napalm sprayed on you.

"Greg threatened me once. Said I shouldn't listen to what Val tells me. I don't understand. I could sleep in your bed, but we don't do anything."

"How do you know Greg?"

"I told you. I am friend of Valentina, of Tolya, best friend, BFF, you say."

"I'll walk you home," I said. "Now."

"I'll go, I don't beg," she said suddenly, turned her back to me and marched to the door.

"Let me walk you," I called.

She didn't answer. Just went out into the rain, back hunched over, heading for her place. She told me it was just around the corner, and I went upstairs and and sat down in front of the TV, waiting for late calls from New York. I must have dozed, and I was still in the big leather chair, watching reruns of the Canadian women's curling team, when sirens woke me. I looked at my watch.

It was five in the morning, and by the time I got to the window, only the faint screams of the sirens were left behind, like a bad, bad hangover.

CHAPTER THIRTY-FIVE

"Is she dead?" I said to the medic at the hospital where they had taken Elena Gagarin.

"No," he said. "Bad, though."

"You got hold of me how?"

"In her pocket. Your name and number were in her pocket when the police found her. You're a relation?"

I nodded. You got more out of hospitals if they thought you were blood.

"Come," he said, and I followed him down the corridor to a room where Gagarin was attached to a tangle of IVs.

Most of her face was bandaged; one arm that lay outside the thin sheet was black and yellow. She had been beat up pretty good. A cop hovered close by.

"What happened?" I said.

"I found her," said the cop.

"How come?"

"I was passing. I'd been round to a pub with some friends, and then to somebody's flat for coffee and I was on my way back to the tube at Notting Hill Gate, and I cut around through an alleyway behind the shops, you wouldn't know it, over by where the Marks food place is, and I found her. She could barely speak. They beat her up, one used a knife, left her on a building site. Nobody noticed." He snorted. "Not even in an area where the bloody houses go for ten million quid. You're related to her. I am sorry," he said, and I thanked him and went back into the room.

The doctor told me Gagarin had been in a coma since they admitted her, and we stood by the bed, and watched her for a while, keeping watch, I thought, somebody to bear witness for this pathetic woman. A few hours before she had stood in my doorway, drenched by the rain, asking for help.

We watched her, the cop, the doctor, technician and me, watched the lines on the machines go flat. She was dead.

Thinking I was her relative, they gave me her bag to see if I could make an ID. There was a little book, and the address of a building around the corner from Tolya's where she had told me she lived.

The bag was made of fancy white and gray snakeskin with a silver buckle which when I looked closely I saw was a fake, a knock-off, a cheap version of the real thing, jammed with make-up, underwear, sweater, a few photographs, a wallet with a couple of pounds in it.

I put the photographs in my pocket and gave the bag back to the policeman, handed over my cell number, and left Gagarin to the cops and medics, and other people who tended the dead and dying.

Dead, with no ID, and only a fake bag, Gagarin seemed to have ceased to exist.

Around eight in the morning, I left the hospital, found a Starbucks—they had spread like a stain all over London—got some coffee, and went over to Gagarin's place.

A slim pretty woman, half asleep from the look of it, opened the door. She wore jeans, a shirt tied at the waist, and yellow flip-flops.

"Yes?"

I apologized for banging on the front door. I said I was looking for Elena Gagarin's flat, pretending I expected to find her in the house.

"I'm sorry," said the woman. "The police have already been. They said she was attacked not far from here. They've seen what there is, and it isn't much. They told me Elena was taken to hospital very early this morning."

I said I was her cousin and I'd come to get some things for her, to take to the hospital.

"I'll help if I can," said the woman. "But she hasn't lived here for some months. Is she all right?"

I explained what had happened. I dug a scrap of paper out of my pocket. "Is this the right address?"

"Yes, number twelve, that's right, but it belongs to us, my husband and me."

"You don't know her?"

"Look, come in," she said. "Can I make you a cup of coffee? Tea? I'm Janet Milo, by the way."

I went into the hallway. Inside what had once been a private house and was now divided into apartments was a beautiful winding staircase. I followed the woman in yellow flip-flops to the top floor where there were two doors. One was ajar.

"This is ours," she said, gesturing at the apartment with the open door where I could hear a radio playing news. She unlocked the other door. "Up top here, there's a minute little room, I suppose it was once for a servant," she said. "Elena did rent it from us for a time, oh, six months back, she said she adored the area and she was looking for a place of her own, but she could never quite pay the rent and eventually we asked her to go. We've redecorated and there's a new girl coming to live here."

"You haven't seen her, yesterday, recently?"

"No, but she did stop by, asked if we had changed the locks," she said. "The police asked to see the room where she had lived." She was pretty cool about it, but maybe it was her style. "I assume that's why you're here?"

"Yes, and she's dead," I said.

I realized now that I had never seen Gagarin go into the house. She had lied about the apartment.

"I'd like to take a look."

"I don't see why not. Coffee?"

"Do you know where she worked? You must have asked."

"I got the impression Elena was always looking for a job. She said she had prospects at one of the big banks, but I think she survived doing translations. Working at a bookshop. Possibly a club that catered to Russians, a bit of, forgive me, sponging off her friends. Quite a few of them have settled around here, sadly. She left early and came home late, and she was quiet. You're American?"

"Yes."

"It was so nice when we had Americans. I adore Americans. Not too many now," she said. "The dollar, I suppose. For that matter, there aren't too many English people, either, not round here, anyway," she added, a wry expression on her handsome English face. "Do go in. Let me know if you need anything." I thanked Mrs Milo and she said please call me Janet.

The little studio at the top of the house was the kind a student might use. It was freshly painted. Striped curtains hung at the windows, which were open and through one I could see Tolya's house on the other side of the green square.

A bed, desk, old-fashioned dresser, some lamps, a chair and a little TV completed the furnishings. The bathroom was pristine, and there was no sign anyone had been here.

Where did she live? Where did she keep her clothes?

I went and asked Mrs Milo for the coffee, and followed her into her apartment.

"Elena wasn't here last night at all?" I said casually.

"No, and we changed the locks when we redecorated. We've got a new tenant coming in this week, as I said."

"So you haven't seen her."

"I told the police that she was round several times asking if she could have the room back, that she had some money. But I told her it was already let."

"Please try to think, did Elena mention anything, did she maybe leave something?"

Janet Milo paused, and something seemed to click, and then she said, "Oh my God, I'm so sorry. You're right of course."

"Go on."

"It was a while back, and she asked if she could store an old suitcase in our storage room in the basement. I completely forgot."

"You showed it to the cops?"

"I only just remembered. I'll phone them straight away."

"Could you show it to me first?" I smiled reassuringly.

In the underground storage room, I crouched down and opened the huge battered green suitcase that had belonged to Elena Gagarin.

Clothes, shoes, underwear were stuffed into the suitcase. There were also envelopes filled with clippings, letters, snapshots. I shuffled through them, including one of Elena herself posed alongside a car that had belonged to Yuri Gagarin, the cosmonaut. Another of a middle-aged couple, weary-looking people, working-class Russians I figured for her parents. Pictures of Valentina. A picture of Greg.

I began to sweat. I'd been an idiot not to see it before: Elena and "Greg" were related. You looked at them together in the pictures and you could see it. Brother and sister? Cousins? I had been insane not to see it.

Rooting around in the suitcase, I found applications for British citizenship, credit card slips, a small notebook with telephone numbers. I tried ringing a few, including the bank where Gagarin claimed to have worked. Nobody had heard of her. There was an ID card. Her name really was Yelena Gagarin, but it was a common enough name.

This had made it easy for her to imply the connection with the famous cosmonaut, the Soviet hero, Yuri, whose daughter was known as Lena, the diminutive form of Yelena, or Elena of course. This Gagarin had a different middle name, different patronymic, which she had changed to make her game work.

It was a smart move. Elena knew the current generation of young Russians at home and abroad idolized Yuri Gagarin, that he had become a hero to them as he had to their parents and grandparents: the first big modern hero in Russia, even if he did die flying a plane drunk.

It didn't matter. He got to space first, he beat the Americans, he was young and handsome and a true Russian hero. Elena had borrowed a little piece of him, just the reputation, which was easy since she already had the name. It made her very popular. It made it easy for her to make her way, first in Moscow, then in London. In a small notebook, she had scribbled notes about her childhood obsession with Yuri Gagarin, and how she had visited the town of Gagarin where she posed with his car. In Moscow she went to his statue every year. This stainless steel cosmonaut was said to fly annually and grant you your wish.

From the suitcase diary and notebook and scraps, the postcards and letters in the box—what I could put together—she had arrived in London a couple of years earlier from Moscow, though she had grown up in St Petersburg. She already spoke good English and had worked as a cleaner for a while in a hotel near Heathrow Airport.

She got to know a few people, guests at the hotel, and then she made her move. She set herself up as a banker. She made friends with Val. Even after she left the apartment in this building on Tolya's square, she went on pretending she lived here.

A couple of letters from her mother revealed that Gagarin came from a working-class family still living in one of the crappy housing projects on the fringe of St Petersburg, near the cemeteries, where the mud made your feet sink on a damp day.

Elena wasn't related to Yuri Gagarin, she didn't work in a fancy bank or hedge fund, she didn't live on Stanley Gardens in Notting Hill, she couldn't even afford the attic room.

Who the hell was she? A girl on the make in London? A girl who had come over looking for a life, or a husband? She had managed to fake it with Tolya, Val, even me. Her lying about almost everything was her way of surviving.

I pocketed an address book I found in the suitcase. Now I was sure Greg had been involved in Elena's death. And Valentina's. The three were connected.

Heart pounding, sweating, in a small wooden box in the suitcase pocket, I found a portrait of Val in a green sweater I recognized.

But Val was dead. And even Yuri Gagarin couldn't grant me my wish.

PART FOUR

CHAPTER THIRTY-SIX

The return address on the envelope I had found in Gagarin's suitcase was the same as the address I'd found in Val's bathroom. Wimbledon.

It was Saturday. I was hungover from the party the night before. Worse, I felt messed up by Elena Gagarin's death. I didn't get any sleep, but the adrenalin shot through my body, it made me jumpy, on edge, the tension made me wired. I could smell him. I could smell this Greg.

If I could stay cool, if I kept the gun in my pocket, if I didn't lose it the way I had when I saw him at the party on the dance floor, I'd get him.

It was raining when I got to Wimbledon. Tennis, I thought. They play tennis in Wimbledon. When did they play? I thought. June? July? I took the subway.

There was a loud, harsh wail of sirens that hit me as soon as I came up the subway stairs. Outside most of the street was blocked off. Rain came down hard. Next to the subway entrance, a small crowd had gathered against a three-storey building. On the ground floor was a fruit and vegetable store.

"Move them away," said a uniform standing a few feet away. "Fucking sightseers," he said to his partner.

I went over and asked what was going on, he looked at the

gold watch on my wrist, a mixture of envy and contempt on his face. He didn't answer, as if to say, what's your bloody need to know, mate? He gestured to me to get back against the building.

It was as if I was on the other side, a civilian. Gun in my pocket, I kept my mouth shut and moved closer into the shadow of the fruit store.

Among the onlookers was the low rustle of fearful talk. Talk of bombs, guns, murder, knives. Talk of rising crime. Of terrorism. Islamists, they mumbled. Make bombs out of hair dye. They don't fucking want to live by our rules then they should fuck off home. An old man said this. A woman nodded in agreement.

Nukes somebody said, radioactive poison. Like the Russian guy.

Polonium, right? Didn't they say it jumps out of a box and climbs the walls?

Anger and fear ran through the little crowd for a few seconds, then fatigue set into their voices.

What can you do? What's there to do?

Most sounded weary but a crude rough English voice suddenly shrieked louder than the others. "They'll fucking get us!" the man said and the fear turned to hate, and I wanted out. The crowd was beginning to get ugly. I beat it, rain soaking through my clothes.

The address I was looking for was three blocks away. In the window was a handwritten card announcing a room for rent. I leaned on the bell, a woman appeared, I said I had found some mail, return address in Wimbledon, mistakenly sent to my place.

Brown skirt, beige blouse, sweater buttoned up the front, the woman at the door looked like one of my teachers at school. She had a weary, pretty face. She was about sixty, her hair was white, fine as tufts of cotton.

I repeated my story. She looked blank.

Rolly, the bartender at Pravda22, said Greg had told him there was a room for rent someplace in south London. I took the shot. "I am also a friend of Greg," I said.

"He left this morning," she said.

I asked again if she had a room to rent. I told her my name, and she nodded and said, "I am Deborah Curtis."

I introduced myself.

Without letting me inside, Mrs Curtis told me she owned the house and lived on the ground floor that connected to a garden out back. Yes, she rented out a few rooms. The house was too big for her.

I smiled and was charming. All I wanted was to get inside. I had gambled, and this time I was right.

Sizing me up, she told me that in fact Greg's room itself was available, and looked sorry that she had said it. "Can you come back later?" she asked.

"Could I just come in and dry off?" I said, smiling, pointing to my dripping hair.

She opened the door wider, showed me a bathroom, I toweled off best I could, and then she led me into a small apartment that had been built onto the back of the house. At the same time the doorbell rang.

Mrs Curtis went away to answer the door, came back to tell me a man had come to clean her carpets. "I'll be fine," I said, and she left, looking uneasy.

The apartment was empty, stripped bare of anything personal, except for a beautiful handmade patchwork quilt on the double bed. The only book on the shelf was a Bible. I began to feel London was a city of empty rooms for rent.

For a while I sat on the bed, thinking about Val and the gold cross she had started wearing a year earlier. Often, she had touched it as if touching it would bring luck. She told me once that she had started going to church.

"Don't look at me as if I've turned into some kind of religious freak, Artie, darling," she said once when we were eating tacos on a warm day in Washington Square Park. "I'm not going to join a convent or something. I'm just going to celebrate my name day, which will be February 23, for St Valentina the Martyr, and I'd like you to be there with me. Will you?"

"Do you like the room?" said Mrs Curtis, standing in the door. In her voice I heard the faintest hint of a Russian accent, the way you can make out the presence of a flavor you can't quite identify in a certain dish. From behind the glasses with clear rims, her eyes darted from me to the room, as if she was worried she had left something that didn't belong. She walked a few steps into the room.

In Russian, I said, "What's the matter?"

She was rattled, but she answered in English.

"Would you like a cup of tea?" she said.

I reached for the door and closed it so she couldn't leave.

"Tell me about Greg," I said.

"You said he was your friend."

"An acquaintance."

"Actually, there's nothing to tell," she said. "He was a nice young man, he was here for a year or so."

"And his girlfriend?"

"I didn't meet his girlfriend," she said, but her eyelids fluttered too fast. "Did he have a girlfriend? I was never certain, you see, it wasn't my business after all. I really don't actually know how I can help you." Her hand shaking, she opened the door, looked over her shoulder at me as if daring me to stop her.

I followed her to the living room.

I could hear a clock ticking.

"Who else lives here?"

"I did say. I generally have a few students in the two spare rooms but it's summer now and there's nobody. I did mention it, didn't I?"

"Well, say again."

"No one, as I said. Tea?" She moved into the living room, a small crowded room, stuffed with mementos.

On the tables were laquered boxes. On shelves that were crammed with books, Russian dolls, the heavily painted *matrioshka* porcelain statues. No family pictures though. It was as if they had been banished. Plants in the windows kept the light out.

"When did Greg leave?"

"A few days ago, I think. I'm not sure I remember actually."

"I'd like that tea, please."

"Of course," she said and went into the kitchen, then returned a few minutes later with a tray. On it were a teapot, cups, a plate with cookies. She set it on a low table, and gestured for me to sit down.

"You've lived here a long time?"

"Yes," Mrs Curtis said. "A very long time, one way or another."

"Things have changed around here?"

"Indeed," she said.

"Lots of Russians moving in."

"I suppose. Yes. Why not?"

"You have some connection with them?"

"I'm not sure what you mean. I meet the odd Russian in the shops. Some are quite charming. Very well read."

"And was Greg Russian?"

"As I told you, he seemed very nice, though I rarely saw him, he worked in the City, he was quiet."

"How old was he?"

"I really don't know, Mr Cohen. I imagine he was about thirty."

"But his business was legitimate?"

"What? Of course, Grisha would never do anything wrong." She was angry.

"Grisha?"

I had caught her off guard. My gut tightened up with anticipation. I had been right about this. I tried to keep my hands clasped politely. I tried not to fumble for some smokes. I leaned forward to pick up a teacup. My jacket fell open.

Did she see the gun?

"He sometimes called himself Grisha," she said. "I believe it was his Russian nickname."

"So he was Russian."

"Yes."

"You would want to know if something happened to this Grisha, I guess."

She took off her glasses, rubbed her eyes. Her body almost imperceptibly tensed up.

"Has something happened to him?" she said.

"Has it?"

Her effort to stay calm didn't work, her hands were in constant motion, clasping each other, unbuttoning and buttoning her sweater, prodding the table as if looking for something lost.

Putting on my jacket, I went to the window, looked out, saw the rain was letting up, got ready to leave. Behind me I could hear the rustle of paper, as Mrs Curtis knocked newspapers off a table.

"Please tell me if something has happened to him," she said. "I have to know."

"Why does it matter? If you don't tell me, I can't help you."

"He's my son."

"Where is he?"

"I don't know," said Mrs Curtis who took a cigarette from a box on the table, but didn't light it.

"When did he leave?"

"He left this morning, he came home from a party, he had been out all night, I said, Grisha, darling where are you going?"

"What time did you see him?"

"I slept in until eight this morning. He was just leaving. I don't know when he came in, I don't know anything, he was away for several days, then I saw him leaving this morning. He was out of his mind. A few days ago he told me that Valentina, a girl he knew, was dead." Hands shaking, she lit her cigarette. "He said I would see it in the papers. He had to find her killer, he said. I thought he was going to America. He was in a terrible way. He was out of his mind," she said. "With grief."

"You knew Valentina?"

"Yes, of course."

"And?"

"She was a beautiful girl."

"You knew her father?"

"He's the gangster. He's one of these new Russians who come to London, I heard he put bad wine on the market that made people ill and then sold them his own."

"Who told you?"

"Grisha said it. You didn't come for the room, did you?"

"No."

"What for?"

"I'm from New York. I'm a friend of Valentina Sverdloff," I said. "Your English is very good."

"My mother was English. She married my father and stayed in Moscow. She admired the Soviets," she said with disgust. "She came as a student from London and she met him, and that was it."

"What about Grisha?"

"He was a late child. I was already thirty-three, I wasn't married, so I slept with someone I met as a tour guide. I thought if I made a child with an Englishman, even if nobody knew— I would have lost my job—he would have English genes. Where are you from originally?"

I didn't answer.

"From your accent when you speak Russian, I would say Moscow. Is that true?"

I nodded.

"Then you understand. Many people here don't understand how we managed things. We managed."

"When did you come to London?"

"Almost twenty years now, I came with Grisha when it became possible, after Gorbachev came into power. I thought I'd be free. When I was a girl, I once told my father I was going to defect. He said he would denounce me to the KGB." She smoked without inhaling, puffing at the cigarette. "London was my dream city. My mother told me about it, the parks, the red buses. It was her fairy tale when I was a child, and later, she taught me the language, and got me books, and showed me pictures.

"I wanted it the way other young women wanted to get married. Wanted sex. It was a physical thing," she said, speaking in her educated Russian. "I saved everything, maps, books, I got a job at Intourist, and when I met English people, I asked them for stamps or even if they tipped me, to tip me in English money. I would sit at my little desk at home, and stack them up, you understand?"

"Yes."

"And I come here and it is beautiful. I teach, I send Grisha to school, he goes to America, to Harvard University to take his business degree."

"He was a banker in London?"

"Yes."

"What else?"

"What else, he makes money, he has a nice car, he travels."

"Where?"

"Often to Moscow."

"Go on."

"Two years ago he says to me he wants to go back to Russia, to study there, to work, to be part of his homeland. I said to him, darling, this is your home, but he says, no, I'm Russian. It's like a nightmare. I had escaped once. His going back was my punishment. It was fine for a while, when he first met Valentina, and they talked about helping people. She was lovely. He became serious. Soon he says he feels patriotic. He loves the soul of his country."

"Does he have a sister, or a cousin? Elena? Yelena? Lena?"

"No, of course not. What sister?"

I told her about Elena Gagarin. I showed her the picture.

"I see a bit of a resemblance," she said. "I don't know her," added Mrs Curtis and gave a short mirthless snort. "Gagarin? Yuri? A peasant. Certainly, everybody was in love with him in the old days, but now we know he was a drunk from the provinces. Who is this girl? Did she claim a relationship with my Grisha?"

"She's dead. She's in some photographs of him and Valentina. Somebody beat her up so bad last night, she died. You said Grisha's hand was bruised." I gave her a picture of the three of them.

"It wasn't him." Mrs Curtis put out her cigarette. She peered at the picture.

"Valentina was so beautiful," she said, beginning to weep. "She became my daughter."

"What?"

"You didn't know?"

"Know what?"

"They were both modern children, but they became religious. They wanted to make things normal."

My head was swimming in it. How much I hated Russia. How much I hated the religion, the obsession, the sentimentality. Valentina had been sucked in. Sucked in. By a blue-eyed Russian boy who kept a Bible in his room.

"I don't understand."

"They were married last year."

CHAPTER THIRTY-SEVEN

And then Deborah Curtis was out of the door as if she'd heard a shot. As if, like a dog might, she'd heard something inaudible to anybody else. I followed her.

"I need air," she said, and put an umbrella up, walking fast. I kept pace with her. The rain had turned to a thin drizzle.

We got to a shopping street, she turned into a cafe, I followed. She gestured at the empty chair next to hers.

"Please," she said in English, and then ordered tea for herself in Russian from a dumpy waitress, who looked harassed, dyed red hair a mess, face weary. I asked for coffee.

On the table Mrs Curtis placed a picture. In it, Val was wearing a plain white dress with long sleeves, and a little wreath of white flowers on her hair. Grisha, tall, handsome, young, smiling, was in a dark blue suit with a white flower in the lapel, and a red silk tie, and his mother, no glasses, standing straight, looked ten years younger than she did now. Val married. Did Tolya know?

"The food here is nice," said Mrs Curtis. "In case you're hungry," she added in formal English. "You carry a gun, Mr Cohen? You are a policeman?"

Around us in the half-full cafe, almost everyone was speaking Russian.

I drank coffee, she had her tea. Come on, I thought. Tell me what I need to know.

"Please tell me where Grisha is," I said.

"Why?"

"I'd like to meet him," I said. "He was Valentina's husband. I have something for him from her. She put his name on it. From before she died," I added, the lies pouring out of my mouth easily.

"What kind of things?" she said softly but reluctant now.

"Photographs. Souvenirs."

"I can take these things for him," she said. "I must do a few errands," she added abruptly, fidgeting, unable to sit still.

"Where is he?"

"I don't know."

"Call him. He has a cellphone?"

"A mobile? Yes, of course. He doesn't always answer."

There were things she couldn't or wouldn't tell me. I pushed my phone across the table. She dialed, and looked up. "He doesn't answer. It says he's out of range."

"I think your Grisha is in trouble. I can help him. He will be an obvious suspect in Valentina's murder. He was her husband, they'll look at him first. He's in Russia?"

She avoided the question. I waited. Suddenly she said, "They were distant cousins, you were right, Grisha and this Elena Gagarin. She claimed him as a cousin, and she came round once or twice, and I never knew what she wanted. They were always whispering and making plans on some business deal. I heard them mention Mr Sverdloff. Once my Grisha said Mr Sverdloff, Valentina's father, got in the way of his business. He cared too much, my Grisha, about money, I would say, Grishinka, darling, this man is your father-in-law."

"I want to help him," I said. "Please continue."

"Other young people came to the house, and afterwards

he would talk garbage to me about his feelings of nationalist pride with Mr Putin in charge. He supported it all and I said, Grishinka, darling, you talk like a fascist. And he told me to stop. We never came to blows, of course, he was always respectful."

"And Val?"

"The more he said these things, the less she came to the house. She went back to America more often and stayed longer."

"Did he go to New York after that?"

"Yes. He went to convince her to come home with him. She wrote to me a few times to say she was sorry not to see me, and I had asked her to take some books to a distant relation of mine."

"Olga Dimitriovna?"

Mrs Curtis looked at me. "Yes. You know her?"

I nodded. "Why are you telling me this?"

"Because you were Valentina's friend, and you will find my Grisha."

"Is he missing?"

"I don't know."

"You haven't heard from him?"

"Not for a few days. Except as I told you, for a minute this morning I saw him. He kissed me and left."

"Can you tell me anything else?"

"I think he had a little office up in town where he did his own work. He mentioned this. I asked to see it. He said no. It struck me as odd."

"Where?"

"I don't know."

"Think."

"Paddington area, I know because he once took me to the train station and then said he'd walk to his office."

"Was he here with you at the beginning of last week? On July 7?" I said, thinking of the night Val had died.

"No. Yes." she said. "I don't remember."

"If you want to see him, you might want to tell me the truth," I said. "Last week, was he here in London?"

"He wasn't here."

CHAPTER THIRTY-EIGHT

By the time we got back to the Curtis house, a couple of patrolman and some guys who I made for detectives were on the other side of the street. So was Fiona Colquhoun. I had sent her a text from the cafe.

"What's going on?" I said to her.

"I got your text. I had somebody at my office type in the address you gave me, and a red flag went up."

"What red flag?"

"I'll explain. Just wait," said Fiona, turning to take Mrs Curtis' arm and escort her to a police car, make sure she got inside.

"What is it?" I asked, and Fiona told me Mrs Curtis' house was one of the addresses where there had been traces of radiation. You put an address into the computer, at least the computer at Fiona's office, if it was one of the houses that had been listed, the flag went up.

"Fuck," I said.

"This house has been looked at before," said Fiona.

"Christ."

"You know it was never reported, the amount of polonium that came into London. It left a long trail, hotels, houses, restaurants, and we didn't have protective suits and escape hoods enough for our own investigators," she said. "There have been people too ill to report. Bloody Litvinenko," she added, and I was surprised. "You thought he was heroic? Did you know one of his friends called a photographer when he was dying? But I

242

don't blame him either. There was no firm ground, poor bastard."

I looked at the car where Mrs Curtis sat, the door partially open, a patrolman next to it.

"What's she doing there?" I said.

"She can't go back in."

"What?"

"There are still traces of radiation in the house. They'll have to check her as well. Were you inside the house?"

"Where are they taking her?"

"They'll give her a medical check. After that, she says, she can stay with her rich cousin in Eaton Square," said Fiona.

Before she could stop me, I broke away. There was something on my mind. I pushed past the cop, I crouched beside the open car door.

"Mrs Curtis?"

"Yes?"

"Will you be okay?"

She nodded. "I'll be with my cousin."

"Will you keep in touch with me?" I gave her my number on a scrap of paper.

"Yes. Thank you. Will you call me if you find my Grisha? Whatever should happen, I would want to know. Please? Promise this?"

"Yes," I said. "Tell me one other thing."

"Of course."

"What did your Grisha think about Litvinenko's murder, about his death?"

"He said he got what he deserved because he was a traitor."

"It's Grisha Curtis," I said to Fiona, who was sitting beside me on a low stone wall opposite the Curtis house.

Mrs Curtis had been driven away. It was raining again and Fiona held a large black umbrella over us. "Grisha killed Gagarin and I'm betting he killed Valentina. You can pick him up, if you can find him. I'm betting he's gone to Moscow. Get your people on it."

"I want you checked out, Artie. I'll take you myself. Come on, get in my car. Please?"

There was nothing else I could do in Wimbledon, so I followed Fiona into her car. We sat there, her hand on the key.

"The radiation leaves traces," she said. "You were in the house. Did you eat or drink?"

"Tea."

"Hold on," she said. "I want to read you something," added Fiona, and pulled a notebook out of her bag.

For a moment, imagining it was another life, I enjoyed sitting in the car with her, the light rain coming down, the two of us smoking. In another life, I thought again.

"Litvinenko was as good as the first victim of nuclear terrorism, did you know that?"

"Go on."

"Do you know about polonium-210, Artie? It's both completely passive and astonishingly active. It can't move through even the thinnest piece of paper, not even skin. But once it's been ingested, it moves through one's body like the proverbial knife through butter. A trace on a table or a teapot and it crackles into life, it moves about, I've read it described as devious, sneaky, elusive . . . I wrote it down," she looked at her notebook. "I try to remind myself not to be sloppy. Listen to this article from the New York Times: 'Its sheer energy punched out atoms that could attach to a mote of dust—spreading, settling on surfaces, absorbed in lungs, on lips, invisible.' The writer calls it 'a braggart, a substance whose whereabouts were blindingly evident to those who knew where and how to look. It leaped free from any attempt to contain it, spreading, and smearing traces of its presence everywhere I had been, on table-tops, door handles, clothes, light switches, faucets.' They say it crawls the walls."

"What else?"

"We see those red flags all over London. But are they for real? A trail left by Litvinenko? Caused by rumor? The myth of finger-prints? You understand the power of these legends, these myths?"

"Yes."

"All the Russians have to do is play on the myth. It's so terri-fying, fear itself is radioactive. The Cold War nuts are back in business," she added. "This is like Pandora out of the box. Irène Joliot-Curie, Mme Curie's daughter, died of leukemia for her work with polonium. My grandmother who worked with her died of cancer. I suppose it's become a kind of obsession with me. If the Russians feel it was worth the effort to export this sort of poison, they'll do anything. And even where it's non-existent, just a rumor as provocation, or intel gossip, we spend time chasing it down. Great urban myths, Artie, are hard to beat." She stopped to catch her breath.

I had worked a nuke case long ago. Red mercury, the legendary Soviet radioactive material, had turned out to be the biggest hoax of all.

"I know," I said. "What else is it used for?"

"It used to be an element in the trigger for a nuclear weapon still employed in a few Russian weapons plants. Hard to get, hard to detect. And, Artie?"

"What?"

"We don't know anything. All the cops and spooks and bureau-crats, nobody knows anything." Fiona took a pad out of her bag and scribbled something on it, then handed it to me. "Go see these people, it's a good clinic, private, just let them check you out, okay? You will, won't you? Radiation isn't a joke. I'll drive you if you like."

I said I'd make my own way there, knowing I wouldn't bother, that there wasn't time. I told Fiona I needed a favor. I said I was sure Greg Curtis had beat up Gagarin. From the house in Wimbledon I had managed to steal his Bible. I asked Colquhoun if she could get somebody to take prints off it and then match them up with Gagarin or the area where she had been mugged. I was a lousy spy, but I was still a good enough cop.

I asked Fiona to drop me at the subway. I had to do this by myself.

After I got to the station, I threw away the piece of paper with the clinic address. I wasn't going to a clinic where they'd ask me questions I didn't want to answer.

Valentina had married Grisha Curtis. She was married and she never told me. On the subway platform after I left Fiona, I was trapped by hordes of people.

I tried to avoid contact with other passengers because the gun was in my waistband and it was illegal as hell. If someone bumped me and felt it and made a stink—and there was plenty of rage in this city—I'd end up at some station house wasting time explaining things to a local cop.

Now people milled around and waited for a train, and some of them talked about the weather and what a washout the summer was, and others leaned against the wall and read their papers. I couldn't see around the mob that pushed at me as I got on a train.

At the first stop, I tried to get off the train, but the crowds pushed me back. I kept my back close to the door.

Then the train stalled between stations. You could feel a ripple of tension. The memory of 7/7 was still fresh, the memory of people slaughtered on a subway train, a bus ripped open like a sardine can.

The grind and shunt of the train starting made people relax. A girl next to me smiled, a wry kind of smile, and returned to her copy of *Harry Potter*. A man next to her in a Lenin-style cap pulled down over his forehead was reading a Russian-language newspaper, while his tiny pale wife leaned against him and talked steadily. He never put his paper down.

I closed my eyes. I was betting Mrs Curtis was already on the phone to her son wherever he was and that he would come after me.

"Come on," I thought. "Come and get me."

All I wanted was Grisha Curtis, who had killed my Valentina.

CHAPTER THIRTY-NINE

Deborah Curtis, Grisha's mother, was dead by the time I met Fiona Colquhoun the next morning at the Tate Gallery down near the river. It was early, mist hanging over the Thames, the lonely hoot coming from an invisible boat. When Colquhoun told me, at first I thought Mrs Curtis had somehow died from radiation poisoning in her house.

"No," said Fiona. "No, Artie, and the radiation scare, this time anyway, was a false alarm," she said, adding that Mrs Curtis had been found at her rich cousin's house, sitting on the terrace, dead. The official line was she'd had a stroke, said Colquhoun.

"Did Grisha Curtis show up to see his mother? Did he kill her?"

"No", said Fiona. "No evidence."

I was sorry about Mrs Curtis. I wondered if my appearance at the Curtis house set off the events that had killed her. I had more questions for her, so I was sorry about that, too.

Fiona got it, didn't think I was a bastard for saying it. She had been a real cop, even if now she was in some other game.

We walked along the river and she pointed out the spy palace across the river, an ugly modern building, letting me know she knew her way around, I thought. I had called her early that morning hoping I could play her, knowing there was plenty she hadn't told me. But she was too sharp.

Drinking out of a coffee container, she told me she had run Grisha Curtis through her computers, and, unless he was using a different name, he was still in Britain. There was no record of him leaving the country.

"We matched fingerprints on the Bible you took from the Curtis house with some on Elena Gagarin's handbag," Fiona said. "They were a perfect match. The bank where he worked confirmed he was an employee and they had prints on him from a file. He taught school in Boston while he did his MBA, and the school system printed him," she added. "He had a UK passport, and a Russian passport," she said. "I had looked at Curtis before, but it was only when Valentina died, and when you came here, Artie, that I really focused on him. This Russian stuff really is like one of those mythical many-headed monsters, you look at something, it disappears, then shows up again. For a time, on the surface, he was pretty much what he claimed. I don't know where the marriage license was filed, but I couldn't find it. Perhaps someone made it disappear."

"Yeah, what doesn't show up is that he's a murderous bastard. Thanks about the prints," I added.

We sat on the steps of the museum. I knew Fiona was killing time while she thought about something.

"I met Grigory Curtis a second time, after I saw him at Larry Sverdloff's, quite a bit later," she said.

"Where?"

"It doesn't matter."

"Recently?"

"Quite."

"You're not comfortable with telling me?"

"I'm telling you what matters. I'm sorry it took this long. I'm telling you now, if you want the truth, because I think you can help me. Before I tell you, I'd like to know that you will share whatever you find with me, and that isn't only about your friend's daughter."

"Go on."

"Is that a yes?" The chilly formality, the way Fiona's expression changed, the adjustment of her posture reminded me this was her real business with me.

"Sure."

"I think Curtis did errands for the KGB," said Fiona. "The FSB as it's now called."

"I know what the FSB is, for chrissake."

"Curtis told me, and yes, quite recently, that he thought that it was not Putin's people who killed Litvinenko, that it was the British, that we did it as a provocation, and that in any case Litvinenko was a traitor," said Fiona, who went on to tell me that she understood from what he had said that Curtis worked for the Kremlin or the FSB—the same things, she said—and they had seen in him an opportunity. "A young man taken up with a zealous Russian patriotism, and who had two passports? Quite a coup, don't you think?"

"And an American wife. You knew they were married?"

"Only when I met the mother yesterday," said Fiona. "It's when I realized I was right about him. It gave Curtis, and anyone he serviced, access to the US. I think that was the real ambition."

"He used Val?"

"Hard to say. They were certainly in love when I saw them, I can't know if he used her from the beginning or if he saw an opportunity he could retail, or if his masters exploited it. I haven't got the whole answer."

"And Val turned on him when she discovered what he was up to."

"Or when she simply discovered he was a zealot who was in love with the whole 'Russia first', thing. Bloody fascists."

"What about Larry Sverdloff?"

"I think he's on our side. I think he understands all of it, and that we can trust him. Up to a point. He wants to change

Russia, but he wants the money, like all of them. He's scared. He should be scared. There have been plenty of death threats. I told him to leave England for a few days. I think you should go, too."

"He went?"

"I don't know." Fiona got up. "It's clear Curtis beat up Elena Gagarin. I can have him picked up if we can find him."

What I didn't say, though I was sure Fiona knew, was I wasn't going anywhere until I had Curtis in my sights, until I had a way to get him for Valentina's death.

"Your bosses want to know all about me?"

"They think you're here working for Roy Pettus," Fiona said.

"And you let them think it?"

"I told you, I like you. And I really want these people, I've worked nearly two years on this. I want them, I want to put a lid on Russian terrorism before it explodes here, and I think Curtis might lead me to them, because for now there's just a wall of Russians in London, and nobody is quite what he seems, and it's very hard to break through it. I want them, Artie, I want the people who bring their poison into my country. Or spread its myth and make people terrified, the fear of fear is something your country suffers from, and we've caught it. I want all this badly enough to accommodate anyone, including you. Please be careful. I'll pick you up tonight, if you like, I'll take you to meet someone who will help you. Say, it's my boss. Just wait for me."

"A real spy?"

She smiled. "Ah, but there are no real spies anymore," she said. "Only people like me."

"How come you're doing all this?"

"I don't know. Because it's the right thing to do. And I like you," she said and blushed. "I'll find you later."

"Where?"

"I'll find you. Artie?"

"Yes?"

"It's Sunday. I was wondering if you'd like to come round for lunch."

"When it's all over, I'd like that. Lunch. Even dinner."

"Thanks."

"Wait for me."

"Of course," I said. "Thank you."

Fiona put out her hand and I shook it, and then she walked away, along the river, shrouded in the strange mist that had settled on everything.

CHAPTER FORTY

Taking the gun with me that night was a bad idea, but I didn't care. I took it when I left Tolya's around ten. It was three days since I had been to the agency on Moscow Road where Masha Panchuk got her job. When I had called during business hours, a machine picked up. Something about the place had been bugging me since I first saw it. And I was furious, crazy with anger.

The fury had built up over the time I'd been in London. And dread. I was scared of what I'd do if I was right about Grisha Curtis, if I found him and I was right. Dread of being wrong.

I ran along the sidewalk. A car splashed water on me. I yelled at the driver to go fuck himself.

On Moscow Road, the Greek grocery was shut, metal gates pulled down. Outside the church a homeless guy was stretched out, wet newspaper for a blanket.

In the building where the agency was, the windows were dark, except on the top floor. As I watched, the light there went off. The shade came down. Somebody had seen me looking.

What did I expect to find here late at night? The agency would be shut. I was operating on instinct and adrenalin and the fury.

I was surprised that the front door wasn't locked. I pushed it, then went into the vestibule. The inner door was easy. I jimmied it with my pocketknife, and went up the first flight.

Shoulder tight against the wall, I edged my way up quiet as I could, feeling the peeling paint with one hand, the other on the gun. A stink of cigarettes was everywhere. Overhead bulbs were out. From inside a couple of the doors, I could hear voices, a TV.

The agency was on the third floor. I tapped very lightly on the frosted glass with the name on it. I waited. Listened for noise. The door was padlocked and I used the butt of my gun to break it.

The room was the same as it had been, desk, a couple of chairs, a framed poster, well-watered plants along the windowsill.

But Ilana was gone, her computer was covered with a plastic sheet, and I wondered if she had been covering for someone. Was it really an agency for maids and chauffeurs? Was it a front? Both? Impossible to tell, but I sensed right away that there was something strange.

Mrs Curtis had said that Grisha kept an office close to Paddington station, and this place, on Moscow Road, was close enough. I had come on the kind of instinct that you need as a cop, something that went off in my head like a smoke alarm.

I left the lights off. Went to the window and looked out at the street where a couple gazed up at the church, then walked away, putting up an umbrella.

At the back of the office was a second door. In the desk drawer was a set of keys. I found the right one and went in.

It was nondescript, nothing on the walls, only a small conference table in the middle of the room, a pair of filing cabinets in a corner. On the table was a brand new desktop computer, and on a shelf was a row of books, Russian history mostly. I grabbed a couple at random to take with me. I'd look at them later.

I went to the computer. Somebody leaving in a hurry had failed to shut it down completely, there was no request for a password. I thought about the light in the top-floor window.

From upstairs, while I was bent over the computer, came the noise I'd been waiting for. There were footsteps. Somebody walking, then running.

And then whoever it was kept going, didn't stop at the third floor, just kept going faster, down the stairs, out of the front door and into the street.

At the window again I watched. A dark figure emerged from the building, crossed the street and slid into an alleyway on the other side. He was waiting for me.

I grabbed envelopes out of the two filing cabinets, printed off what I could from the computer, and went out. He was out there, in the dark, playing chicken with me. It didn't matter now. What I'd glimpsed in the files told me all I needed: I'd found Grisha Curtis' office.

In the street, files under my jacket, I kept close to the buildings. All the time, ever since I arrived in London, he had been out there, watching, following, but always hidden from me.

Then, something, some sixth sense, made me swerve to the right, some clammy fear. It was late Sunday night, nothing open, no cafe, no pub, just the dark wet streets, and the cold, more like November than July. How did they stand it here?

And then a hotel, light still on in the lobby. I ducked in. Asked the guy at the front desk if the bar was open, could I get a beer, a sandwich. Everything shut, he said. I asked for a room. I put cash and my passport on the desk, and while he copied the information, I looked over my shoulder, pushed some extra dough in his direction, said if anybody came or called, he'd never seen me.

"Right?" I said.

He shrugged. Figured me for a drunk wanting to sober up before I went home. I let on I didn't want my wife knowing where I was, exchanged some ugly jokes about women and booze to get his confidence, took the key, went up and unlocked the door.

My clothes were soaked. I took them off, dried my head with the stingy bathroom towel, wrapped myself in the bedspread because it was freezing. On a dusty shelf in a scratched wardrobe, I found a miniature bottle of Scotch and two cans of warm beer. The Scotch I drank in a single gulp.

There was a single bed, a TV on a table, a chair. I spread the papers I'd stolen on the table, so I could read and watch the street at the same time. It was surreal, but what else could I do? I used only a small desk light and kept it out of sight from the window.

I've been a cop long enough, done enough homicides and fraud cases, so I can work my way through paper evidence fast.

In the files were e-mails from Grigory Curtis, and faxes to him from Russia. There were notes and e-mails between him and Valentina. Records of phone calls, expense-account submissions, airline ticket stubs, the dreary detritus of a guy on the make.

Surprisingly, Curtis was a novice. He was a guy who didn't know what the hell he was doing. He didn't know how to conceal his dealings. Fragments, scribbles in Russian and English in a Moleskine diary, a few magazine articles on oligarchs in London; names underlined included Larry Sverdloff.

I took the envelopes onto the bed. One contained an address book, a diary, some Russian military medals. I drank one of the beers. I was thirsty. Fear made my mouth and throat dry.

From the material in front of me, I tracked Curtis' movements over the last eighteen months from the time he had met Valentina. At first he fell for her. Afterwards it became clear she was a good opportunity, especially when she started writing to him about her efforts to save young girls in Russia. She was fierce in her descriptions of Russian bureaucrats who got in her way, and said she intended going to the press.

At some point he persuaded her to marry him.

Some of Curtis' efforts at encoding messages to the FSB made me laugh. He didn't know how to do it, even I could decipher the material, much of it on slick fax paper. Curtis said he thought Tolya Sverdloff was a clown but useful, that he could make introductions.

At some point Curtis told his contact, his control, whatever the fuck you call them, that Val was hard to control, she had a big mouth. About six months earlier, Val stopped answering his e-mails. He wrote. She didn't answer. He said he had to see her, he was coming to New York.

It took hours to work out the dates until I found a receipt for some book. Curtis had bought books from Dubi Petrovsky. I looked at the stuff I'd taken off the shelf in his office. Russian history, mostly, nationalist crap. When I put in a call to Dubi, I was hoping he was in his shop, and I got lucky. As soon as he checked his records, he found Curtis' name.

"You were right. This guy, Grisha Curtis was here, July 5." Two days before Val was murdered. "He buys some Russian novels, you want the names?"

"Take me through it," I said, and Dubi told me a young guy had come in, said he wanted books for a lady, a distant relative of his mother.

"I said, is she Russian? He said yes, and I asked her name because I sell to so many Russians."

"What did he say?"

"It was for Olga Dimitriovna."

When Dubi described him, I knew for sure it was Grisha Curtis.

"I said, I just sent novels to Olga, and he asked which ones and who bought them, and he was very nice and made like he knew Olga and her friends, so I told him. I said Tolya Sverdloff ordered them, or perhaps it was his daughter, and that a friend had delivered them, and he said, oh, Mr Sverdloff must be a nice man, and I said yes, and he asked for different books so he would not give to Olga the same books. He used his credit card."

Grisha had used his own card. Like I thought, he was a novice, a zealot with an obsession, not a pro. But somebody else had been involved, somebody who did his dirty work on Masha, I was guessing, but I didn't think it was Grisha, not that first killing. It was the work of a professional thug.

"Artie?"

"Yes?"

"He came back."

"What?"

"He came back. He bought history books," said Dubi, "the kind Olga never read, including Solzynitsin's most recent essays, the attacks on the West, the Russian nationlist crap. Nobody reads this shit," added Dubi succinctly.

"What dates?"

"He came back on July 7, end of the day, he buys this stuff and also some photographic materials, brushes to clean old-fashioned lenses, this sort of thing, I don't ask why."

"You're sure of the date?"

"Yes."

"Anything else?"

"I had one or two photographs by Valentina Sverdloff on the wall and he couldn't stop staring at them."

I tried not to fall asleep, I drank a warm beer, I called Bobo Leven and when I finally got through I told him about the books, and that through all Curtis' notes written in English—which many were—there were references to somebody called T, and amounts of money next to the name. At first I thought it was for Tolya. I went and put my whole head under the cold-water tap. T. Who was T?

Dripping, cold as ice, shaking from fatigue, I went back into the room and called Sonny Lippert.

"Come home," said Sonny Lippert. "You heard from Sverdloff?"

258

"He calls. He doesn't say much."

"You got anything over there, Art? On the Sverdloff girl?"

"Maybe. I don't know."

"Listen to me, Artie, forget this, just come home. Your friend Tolya is running his own private investigation into his daughter's death, man. He's got that kid, Leven, moonlighting for him. He's everywhere, he's on TV, in the papers, yelling and screaming about the Russkis, man, about how they got state terrorism all over again."

"Go on."

"Shit is what is hitting the fan," said Sonny. "Shit is what he's going to be up to his waist in. He's making a lot of noise, he talks crazy stuff about radiation poisoning, about people at the top stealing money, he doesn't give a flying fuck who he talks to, man. The TV talk shows are eating it up between election news. He makes a great show, man, but he's crazy, the thing with his kid, talks about how she's a martyr, he's nuts and I don't blame him, and I know he's your friend, but you have to stop him."

Somebody had used the word saint for Val. Mrs Curtis, her mother-in-law had said it: she was a saint, she'd said. Maybe it wasn't just a turn of phrase for her, maybe it meant more. Who would have posed her like that, like a saint, or a martyr?

"Sonny?"

"Yeah?"

"Do me a favor, will you?"

"Sure, man."

"Call me back in an hour, okay? Call me. If you don't get an answer, call this number," I said, and gave him Fiona's cellphone.

"You're not coming."

"I'll be there soon."

"I'll call you," said Lippert. "You think somebody is enjoying our conversation? You think that funny little click is our other conversationalist?"

"I don't know, Sonny. I don't know how to do this. I'm a New York homicide cop. There's nothing here I understand."

"Maybe you should have listened to your father, he could have taught you the spy thing, right? Yeah, sorry about that, man, forget the fucking joke."

I hung up.

I went to the window. It was getting light. Nobody outside. I waited. Nobody in the hall. I put my clothes back on, and waited, and went back to the paper trail.

Most of what Curtis fed his control, if that was what you called it, was titbits of information, gossip about the London scene. Only when Val began making a fuss about officials, when she began talking to Russian journalists, did the exchanges between Curtis and the guy in Russia heat up.

My face burned with fatigue. Legs buckled. No sleep. I washed my face. Fiona Colquhoun would be looking for me at Tolya's by now. I had to get back. I put on my jacket, and stuffed the papers as best I could inside the pockets.

Had I been wrong to talk to Fiona?

Was I wrong to trust anybody? Even Larry? Or Tolya? Were they all Russian spies at heart, secrets buried so deep you could never separate the truth from the paranoia that made you distrust them and made them unreliable?

I went downstairs. The clerk was asleep behind the desk. I now knew that Tolya Sverdloff had not been the target. Valentina was not killed as a warning to him. She felt herself to be an American girl with the right to say whatever she wanted, to do whatever she wanted. And she was murdered for that, for what she said.

Footsteps rang out louder and louder on the hard sidewalk behind me. If I showed my gun in London, I'd be in trouble. I wanted to get the stuff I had on Grisha home, or at least to

Fiona. She was my best gamble here.

But Grisha was behind me, like he had been, barely visible, almost never showing his face; and in the early morning rain, sidewalk slick as marble, I ran like a crazy person.

The footsteps came after me, and so fast I couldn't think, a pair of arms like tree trunks locked around my shoulders and somebody dragged me up a short stretch of street and into a narrow mews, an alley, behind a row of cars.

It wasn't Curtis. I got a glimpse of the face, it was only muscle, a thug. But Curtis had sent him, Curtis, who knew I had been in the building, and the hotel, who knew what I was doing. He had the means. He knew the right people. He would know who to call to summon the creep who was ripping at my eyelid with his fingernails.

There was a wound over my eye, and old wound that had healed badly, and it was as if he knew, as if he had studied a picture of me to see where I was vulnerable. He pulled at the skin. I was on the ground, wet, almost too tired to move. Again he peeled the skin from the wound, digging his nail in. The pain was unbearable.

In Russian, I swore at him, his mother, the country, everything I could think of, and he pulled back, looking for his gun, maybe. In that second, I managed to reach for my weapon, grabbed it, swung at him and hit hard with the butt. Again. I hit him until he let go and fell back on the sidewalk. Next to him was a pair of wire-rim glasses, the lenses shattered.

I didn't wait to see if he was alive or not.

By the time I got back to Tolya's, it was light. Upstairs I looked at my eye. The raw skin was bleeding and I patched it up with Band-Aids.

I took a hot shower. I got out and wrapped myself in a towel, and poured myself a drink, and knocked it all back, and then it came to me. I got it.

My God, I thought. The m on Masha, the letter carved in her flesh, wasn't an m. It was a Russian t, the version of the lower case t. I got out of the shower and called Sonny Lippert.

"It wasn't an m."

"What?"

"The creep who carved an initial on Masha, the girl in the playground, it wasn't an 'm' for 'Masha' like we thought: it was a Russian 't'. There was a T in Grisha's notebook, ask around, Sonny, okay? Look for a guy with a T."

"Jesus," he said.

"Do it."

He had already hung up.

"You were onto something, man," said Sonny when he called back. "Earlier you said T, you said the letter T was in the note-book, look for a guy with a T? Turns out your Bobo Leven been looking very hard at a thug named Terry. Terenti is his Russian name. I got onto Leven to tell him what you said. Terenti looks very good for the girl in the playground, for Masha. They picked him up already. I'm betting he killed her. We're checking evidence. You feeling okay?"

"Yeah, fine. Doesn't matter. Leven's doing his job?"

"I don't like him, Artie, man, he's a hustler for sure, he has a foul mouth and he's a fucking racist little shit, but he's smart, and he worked this case like a crazy person."

"What else?"

"Terenti's other jobs have all the same earmarks," said Sonny. "The duct tape. The setting up the bodies like statues, like the girl, Masha, on the swing. He moves easy between New York, London, Moscow, Mexico, Havana, wherever he wants. He travels legal, we found entry dates into New York that would match up."

"He wear glasses?"

"Jesus, man, how did you know? Yeah, he looks like a guy who reads books, little wire-rim glasses, maybe he thinks he's Trotsky, or some other revolutionary fool."

"Yeah, well, reading books doesn't make you nice," I said. "What kind of books?"

"I'll ignore that," said Sonny. "We think he killed Masha, but Valentina Sverdloff, it doesn't look like the same guy. We're checking everything, all the forensics, top priority."

"Just call when you make the case," I said.

"We won't let this one go, Art," he said. "You know what I hate about this global thing, Artie, man, I used to run my investigations in New York for New York, and now everybody is running around the planet, and nobody knows who works for anybody. It's porous like it's never been and we whore ourselves to anyone with a buck, so the intel is just out there, all of it," he said. "The more we do business with asshole countries like Russia and China, the more loopholes there are. Also, the creeps that got the money can just disappear. Plus you got a jackass running Homeland Security who forgets to put air marshals on planes. We're in a whole new place, man, we're in a lateral thing, which means no place."

"Listen, you said this Terenti reads books, you mean literally?" It popped into my head like a jack out of a box.

"Yeah, man. They picked him up, he had a pile of them in the motel room."

"In Brighton Beach? The motel?"

"Yeah."

"The books were in Russian?"

"I heard yes."

"Who's keeping you in the loop on all this?" I said.

"Listen, you know Dubi Petrovsky?"

"Yeah, the guy where you got me that first edition Conrad, right? Big guy, shop out near the beach?"

"Right. Find out if he sold the books they found with this Terenti creep, okay?"

"Sure, man. You think this could turn on books?"

"With Russians, yeah, sure, they love to think of themselves as intellectuals, right?"

"One more thing."

"Yeah, Sonny?"

"Terenti, turns out he's done it before, he signed his work on another girl. The letter m in Masha's flesh, his signature, like he was the author of the job."

"My God."

"Come home soon as you can, man."

CHAPTER FORTY-ONE

"Please come," he said. "My car is waiting," he added, calling me *MooDllo*, the name no one except Tolya ever uses. "Asshole, I need you to meet me."

"Where?"

"My car is waiting downstairs. Ivan is there," he said.

I went to the window of Tolya's Notting Hill house and looked out and saw the car, the driver.

"I have to go," I said to Fiona, who had been waiting for me when I stumbled in. The guy who'd beaten me up had left me looking bad, but she didn't ask, just washed off the blood, using some antibiotics she found in Tolya's bathroom.

"I have to go," I said to her again, and gave her most of the papers I'd found in Grisha's office on Moscow Road. Not all. Not the notebook.

"Don't ask me where, okay?"

"Yes," she said.

"Just come," said Tolya into the phone. "I need you Artyom," he said. His voice was low and hesitant, like a sick man's.

"What's wrong with you?" I said when I found Tolya waiting for me in Larry Sverdloff's house. From the outside, the house resembled a fortress. A dozen guys were planted in the garden, sitting in deckchairs, speaking into their earpieces, and sipping water. More stood outside the front gate.

"It doesn't matter," said Tolya from the chair where he sat in Larry's study. His skin was gray. He worked hard to catch his breath. I got a chair and pulled it up beside him.

"Where's your cousin?"

"Upstairs."

"Let me get him."

"No," said Tolya. "He's fixing things. Let him do it." He reached for a plastic tube of pills on the table next to him, swallowed a few capsules and washed them down with a glass of vodka he poured himself.

"What is it?"

"Nothing," he said. "I can't find my shoes."

"They're next to the couch," I said.

"Can you get them for me, Artyom? Please?"

"Sure."

I got a pair of his Gucci loafers, bright yellow skins, gold buckles, and brought them to him.

"Sorry to ask, man," he said, slipping his feet into the shoes. "I'm just a little tired," added Tolya speaking half in English, half in Russian. "I need to get going."

In all the years we'd been friends, I had never known Tolya like this. He looked lousy. There was a moment when he clutched his left arm as if in pain, and I reached out, but he gently pushed me away. He spoke to me like a supplicant, like a guy who needed help even with his shoes. I tried not to show what I was feeling, but I think he knew.

"When did you get here?"

"An hour ago," he said, glancing at his watch. The band was loose on his wrist.

He leaned forward, elbows on his knees. He wore a rumpled black suit.

"Listen to me, I came to see you, and Styopa, too," he said, referring to his cousin Larry's patronymic. "Only you two, okay, nothing else, nobody else, no one. Is anyone with you?"

"No. Tell me."

"I came, you see, because I can't tell you anything on the phone, not anymore, and because I have to go soon."

"When?"

"An hour. Two."

"Where?" I said.

"It doesn't matter."

I reached in my pocket for cigarettes.

"You're smoking? Give me one, please?" Tolya said, trying to conceal a rasping cough. "No lecture."

I lit my cigarette and tossed him the lighter.

"So, Artyom. So. You use my nice lighter?" He tried to joke.

I waited.

"Put on some music, please, Artyom," said Tolya. " Something nice."

There was a CD player in the bookshelf and I went over and found a CD I knew he liked. I held it up.

"Sinatra okay?"

"Always," said Tolya. "Sure. But classical now, Verdi," he said. "Larry has this recording, *Simon Boccanegra*, the Covent Garden version, Tito Gobbi, Victoria de los Angeles, Boris Christoff, please Artyom, it's on the table," he added, as if choosing his last record. When I put it on the turntable, Tolya closed his eyes and listened for a few seconds.

"You should listen sometime, Artyom." He smiled. "It's about a poisoned drink and reconciliation. Turn it louder, please."

"You don't want your cousin to hear?"

"He already knows most of it."

"Most?"

"I left out certain things."

"You don't trust him?"

"Of course I trust him, it's for his sake," said Tolya. "My cousin thinks he is leading the loyal opposition, he thinks he and his people and their money can bring down Putin and the

Kremlin. He has made tremendous fortune, billions, so now he hears there is trouble in Ukraine, he supports Orange Revolution, he hears there will be trouble in Georgia this summer, he sends money to what he calls the democratic forces. It makes him a target." Tolya sat up. "It's not about him, it's about you. This is why I came to see you, Artyom. Your fingerprints were all over Val's place. Excuse me." He said, hauled himself to his feet like an old man, and slowly made his way out of the room to the bathroom.

"Why did they look for your fingerprints, Artie?" said Tolya when he returned. "Was there a reason?"

"They probably run everything through the computer."

"Yes, perhaps," he said, "but people ask questions."

"Which people?"

"It doesn't matter. I just wanted to warn you."

I was pretty stunned. I kept my mouth shut.

"By the time I got to New York, they had taken Valentina away," said Tolya.

"I'm sorry."

"You tried. Your Mr Roy Pettus is asking about you."

"I needed his help."

"You're naive," said Tolya softly.

"Just tell me."

He picked up his glass and sipped the vodka.

"I got to the loft and my Val was gone. Leven, you call him Bobo? He was waiting as if he knew I was coming. It took balls. He sees me, he gets up and doesn't know what to say, just stands there, this skinny tall boy, long arms hanging down, showing respect, and I think to myself, I should offer my hand. So I put out my hand, and I think he is going to kiss it. 'I'm sorry, Anatoly Anatolyevich. Please forgive me,' Leven says in Russian."

She wasn't there, of course. They had taken her away. Together they went to the morgue but he couldn't look at her body.

"I love all my kids, Artie. Val's sister, of course, and my boy who I almost never see, but she is special. Valentina is like me. She never took shit from anybody. She wanted to do things how she wanted. Even as a little girl when I bring them to Florida from Moscow to be safe, she is a rebel."

I didn't say anything, just waited for him to catch his breath and take another slug of the vodka.

It was the hot dog that got to Tolya, he said. Before he and Bobo got to the morgue, he saw the lunchtime crowd, and in it, a man eating a hot dog with yellow mustard and listening to his iPod. He saw the mustard, the white strings of the iPod, the man's red shirt very clearly. Then they went inside.

"I can't look," said Tolya. "I just went back outside. You love her, Artie? I know that. I know you loved her also not just as my daughter. I know that you did and that you never touched her. You said to yourself, this is not right, and you left it."

"What else?"

"In the official world, it's hard to get information."

"You bought some?"

"Yes."

"What was it?"

"They tried to poison her, Artyom." he said. "Turn off the music, please."

"With what?"

"Polonium-210."

"The autopsy?"

"They said they were still testing. They didn't know how to look. You have to know how to look for the symptoms. In another week, or perhaps two, she would have lost her hair, her skin, everything. She would have died very fast, very ugly. But Leven gave me the pictures he took of her at home, after she was dead, she looked very pretty in her summer dress Artyom, everything was in place. How was that possible I asked myself? I asked myself over and over, and I don't know. Maybe I was wrong about the poison, maybe I went crazy, or maybe the poison had not yet started its work on her body."

"But you came here to see me."

"I think, I must tell Artie about the fingerprints. I must tell him before anything happens to him."

"You think it was me?"

"I only know your fingerprints were everywhere in her apartment, even on the desk, the pictures, the bed, everywhere, even things in the wastepaper basket, old boxes of film, on brushes she uses to clean her negatives. I tell everybody, Artie Cohen had nothing at all to do with this. He was often here, he is our friend, of course his fingerprints are in the apartment. And I don't ask you anything at all," he said. "This second killing was not murder. Whoever did this, it was a blessing," he said. "It kept her from dying like Sasha Litvinenko. It kept her from being eaten from inside. It was from mercy, I understand," said Tolya who got up, kissed me on the cheek and went to his room.

CHAPTER FORTY-TWO

"It wasn't me."

"Then who?"

"Do you believe me?" I said.

"If you tell me, of course," said Tolya, but I could see he didn't believe me, not completely.

"Will they believe me at home?"

"I don't know."

"Who, Artyom?"

"Grisha Curtis. You were right, it began in London, you can get anything here, buy anyone."

The housekeeper came in with a tray of drinks, but Tolya shook his head.

"I must go," said Tolya, barely reacting to the information about Grisha. "We all travel too much now," he said. "Russians feel they have to keep moving or somebody might take this right away again," he added. "Don't worry, I'm okay," he added, but it was hard for him to talk and he caught his breath constantly the way you might catch your clothing on a thorn.

"You should eat."

"It's all right. I've had everything," said Tolya. "I've had my share," he added. "I've had all the good things." He left the room again, and I listened to the music until he came back, carrying a black raincoat and a small bag.

I asked him again where he was going.

"Where is Curtis? Is he in Moscow?"

"I don't know. You're going after him?"

"What do you think, Artyom? To Moscow?"

"Probably, yes," I said, and regretted it as soon as I did. In that instant I knew Tolya would go after, him and in Moscow Tolya would be in bad trouble.

"What else?"

"Curtis knows I have stuff on him, he knows I got it from his office, that I can make the connection that he hired this Terenti creep to kill Val, and Terenti got it wrong and killed Masha by mistake, and then Grisha took over. He knows I can make the connection to Valentina. I think he was furious when this Terenti shit got the wrong girl and killed Val himself. If he went to Moscow it's because the Russians won't let the Brits extradite, he probably thinks he's safe there."

"I see."

"Do you?"

"Then he killed her twice, once with the Polonium, the second time because he suddenly thought about her suffering horribly, and so he suffocated her and laid her nicely on the bed. And I believed it was you. Oh God," said Tolya. "I want you to stay here for a little while, please. To be safe. I'll call you as soon as it's safe."

"Where are you going?"

"I'll call you."

I ran out of the house and caught him near the car. He was bent over, trying to catch some air, to get a breath. I took his hand.

"What's the matter with you, what's wrong?" I put my hand on his shoulder.

"It's nothing," he said. "I'm just tired."

"Where's he going?"

"He didn't tell me," Larry said. "He asked me to go to New York to look after things there for him."

"I thought Fiona said you were in danger, that you should have already left England, wasn't that it, what happened?"

"I didn't go," said Larry. "I had to be where Tolya could find me if he needed me. I'm not such a coward as you might think, Artie. But now I'll go to New York for him. And you must stay here. He said if you went to New York now, there would be questions about Val's death."

"Is he going to Moscow? He shouldn't go to Moscow, it will be bad for him. He'll act crazy."

"I can't stop him. Look, I'm going to have to leave myself," said Larry. "Do you need any money?"

"I don't know. Yes."

"Then just take it." He held out a wad of cash. "Anything else I should know? I might be able to help."

I told him I beat up a creep near Moscow Road with a gun.

"God, Artie. That means your prints are in Valentina's room in New York, and also on some creep in London. Did you kill him?"

"I don't know."

"I'll make some calls. Chances are it was just a hood nobody will give a fuck about. Was he black?"

"No."

"Islamic?"

"I don't know. Why?"

"If he was Islamic, you'd be in better shape. The cops here personally feel one less is a better thing. It doesn't matter. But they're not crazy about guns here, at least not officially, and there's only so much I can do, so just stay put, right? Just a few days. Don't make calls. Don't take any."

"What about Fiona Colquhoun?"

"What about her?"

"She'll wonder where I am."

"I'll let her know as much as I can."

"How well do you know her?" I asked Larry.

"We're friends," he said.

"How good?"

"Good enough. It's fine. You don't need to know anything else about it, just stay here, Artie, okay? Just stay until we know it's okay for you to go home to New York."

"Until when?"

"Until I call you. I'm on your side, you know."

I stayed overnight at Larry's. I swam in his pool. I tried to sleep. I knew that Tolya had followed Grisha Curtis to Moscow. But I had seen the look on his face when I told him I thought Curtis had killed Valentina and had then gone to Moscow. Tolya had nothing else to lose, I knew if he found Grisha, he would hurt him, or kill him.

In spite of what Larry said, I had to know. I tried Tolya on half a dozen numbers. For two days, I worked the phone. But he had vanished.

It was true, I was in bad fucking trouble, my prints on a gun I had used in London. My prints all over Valentina's room. My pictures were in her room, or had been.

I thought about calling Fiona. I knew I was on the edge, dancing at the very edge of an open manhole cover and I could fall into the sewer. Fiona Colquhoun had access and I trusted her, more or less. I gave it one more day. For one day, I'd go quiet. Maybe two.

I stopped answering e-mails. I turned off my cellphone. I bought a pay-as-you-go phone and gave Fiona the number but nobody else.

Stay out of London, she said. I felt crazy from waiting. I swam in Larry's pool, I swam so much, my skin wrinkled. In a shop in the little village near Larry Sverdloff's house, I picked up a couple of books, one or two spy novels, and sat in the pub reading, drinking a little beer, keeping to myself.

In spy novels, in the Bourne movies, that kind of stuff, guys always leave false traces; they use different names; they have extra passports and money in Swiss banks.

I thought about moving into some remote hotel, but they'd ask for my passport. At night I went through the papers I had taken from Grisha's office, following the dates, the e-mails, working out when he had been in America.

By Wednesday, two days after I'd seen Tolya, I was going nuts. The weather had turned hot and outside the pub, a couple of boys kicked a football around. I walked back to Larry's, and on the way I called Fiona Colquhoun from a public payphone. From inside the red box I watched an old lady bicycle past.

Fiona told me to wait for her near the village post office, and half an hour later, her green Mini pulled up.

"Grisha Curtis is gone, we think he's in Russia, as you probably guessed" she said. "The last we have on him is his buying a ticket. We don't know if he boarded the plane, but we have to assume it. We have our people in Moscow on it. You always believed he killed Valentina Sverdloff?"

"Yes."

"But now you're sure."

"Yes. He hired a thug to do it who messed up and killed another girl, Masha, and when Grisha saw how he butchered her, he had to kill Valentina himself. He couldn't stand the idea of Val ending up like Masha, wrapped in duct tape, left in a playground."

"I got you a visa."

"Thank you."

"I assumed you'd want to go."

"Thanks. I know that Tolya Sverdloff thinks he was poisoned, like Litvinenko, he thinks his daughter was also poisoned. Something is wrong with him, but not this. I need to convince him. This is your subject," I said. "Help me."

"Yes," she said.

"Thank you," I said, and I told her about the thug Terenti they'd picked up in New York for Masha Panchuk's murder. "I'm guessing he beat me up the other night, too."

"We can't find him," she said. "It's a bloody can of worms."

"Yes."

Handing me an envelope, she said, "Your visa. This should get you out of here and into Moscow."

"You knew?"

"I knew you'd try to go, and if you have to go to Moscow, and I know you will, do at least pretend you're an American tourist with an interest in Russian culture. When you get there, use a different name, at least for a bit, try to stay safe," said Fiona, putting her hand on my shoulder. "These days I can't help you over there, Artie. We Brits are not in good odor. If there's trouble in Georgia, which is what I'm hearing from the chatter, they won't be in love with Americans, either," she said. "I wish to God you wouldn't go at all, but you will, and this is the best I can do for you this end."

"You'll let me know what you find out?"

"If I can."

"In that case, lunch when I get back," I said. "I'll bring the wine. I like your hat."

"I got it in Israel," she said. "Did you know there are an awful lot of Russians there now, Tel Aviv's a bit like a Russian colony by the sea. No matter, I'm glad you like my hat. And, Artie?"

"What's that?"

"Don't for God's sake take the bloody gun with you. And don't try buying one in Moscow."

"You have me pegged as some kind of gunslinger, or what? You think I'm Dirty Harry?"

"I don't know. Are you?"

I thought about it. I had never liked guns, but all the years I'd been a cop, they had become a kind of body part.

"I hear you," I said. "And I don't love guns."

Her mouth turned up in a smile.

"I wouldn't blame you, considering the scum we're dealing with, but it's about your safety. If you're caught with a weapon in Moscow, they won't be nearly as nice as I am," said Fiona. "You were wondering, I imagine, what my relationship is with Larry Sverdloff?"

"It's none of my business."

"Good," she said. "Don't think about it. He's helped me, leave it at that," she said, and suddenly I felt just a flicker of jealousy.

"What else?" I said, getting up from the bench. As Fiona got up, too, I realized she was as tall as me.

"Don't pick your toes in Pushkin Square," she added, and we both laughed and exchanged banter about our favorite old movies, especially comedies.

"God, don't you wish life was like that?"

"Yeah, of course," I said. "More comedy would be great."

For a few more minutes we chatted about movies, and the weather, and her daughter, unwilling to part, sensing it could be our last conversation.

Fiona adjusted her straw hat so it shaded the gray eyes, pushed her thick dark hair away from her face, and said, "I can get you to Russia, but please try to make yourself invisible, they'll be watching you."

"Who?"

"In Moscow? Everyone."

PART FIVE
MOSCOW

CHAPTER FORTY-THREE

As soon as I'd put my bag in the overhead luggage rack and sat down on the airport bus into Moscow, a gang of teenagers in pink t-shirts crowded around me, like something out of *Lord of the Flies*, except that they were pretty girls, nice girls, who wanted only to recount the great time they'd had at camp near Sochi on the Black Sea.

The little girls swarmed me. Giggling, chattering, clutching their backpacks and books and fashion magazines, they flopped onto the remaining free seats near me in the back. The little ones, who looked about eight or nine, had sticky faces from the candy they were cramming into their mouths, and it was smeared on their dolls and stuffed animals, including an immense white plush bear. I helped its owner stash it in the overhead rack.

The older girls, thirteen, fourteen, kept track of the younger children; acting as chaperones they made sure the little ones were in their seats, then the teenagers sat and began to gossip to each other. At first a few complained about taking the regular airport bus. The plane had been late. The private bus intended for them had not appeared.

All of them wore the candy pink t-shirts that read I ♥ Putin, except for one whose logo read IF NOT HIM, WHO? Medvedev had been president for two months, one girl said, but everyone knew that Putin was the man who mattered.

The girl closest to me—she was about fourteen—looked at

me with interest and asked me in Russian where I was from, In English, I said that I didn't speak the language.

"You are from where, sir?" she said in English, and told me her name was Kim. I said New York City, and she grinned and looked excited and tapped her pal on the shoulder and told her that New York was wonderful and not at all like the rest of America, and the shopping downtown, Broadway, the things you can get, the designer bags, the shoes at Steve Madden, and the cute boys! She had been with her aunt twice, and, oh, New York, she said again, gabbling, running her words together, excited, practically jumping up and down.

Kim, the leader, the spokeswoman for the gang of girls, took charge. Camp had been fun, they said, with Kim as a translator. She explained that at camp they swam in the sea and camped under the stars, they had athletics, games, dramatics—she had been the star of an entire play they'd written and produced by themselves.

So many kids were going to camp these days, she noted, and the girls giggled when she described the Love Tents at a place on Lake Seliger. More for poor young people, of course, said Kim. At the Love Tents, she said again, older teenagers were encouraged to make babies for the fatherland.

The girls giggled some more.

I want four children, said one girl.

Suddenly, all the girls were talking at the same time. I pretended not to understand anything, waiting until Kim translated. The talk was of boys.

I would marry Vladimir Vladimirovich, said one of the girls, I would like this type of man we have for our leader. I would like one similar to him for a husband.

"You admire Mr Putin, sir?" said Kim, the English-speaker. "It is right word, admire?"

I didn't answer right away, and another girl said in Russian, "He is American. He does not understand." Nobody translated this. "Americans think they run the world, they think we are just a dumb old-fashioned country."

I ignored her, pretending I couldn't understand, and said I was a tourist and a travel writer. I was in Moscow to see the sights, the Kremlin, the museums, the churches.

I asked for their advice; they told me about Novodevichy, the convent and the cemetery, they mentioned Gorky Park, the museums, too, and the metro. The subway, said Kim, translating, was the most beautiful in the world. And the best ice cream, of course.

I listened. I thought about Grisha Curtis. I had come to Moscow to hunt him down. I knew Tolya would already be on his trail, and I had to get there first.

I didn't want Tolya killing Grisha. I didn't want Tolya in harm's way. He hadn't left me any messages, I didn't know where he was, I figured he was here, someplace, in this vast sprawl of a city where I grew up and where once I knew my way around every back alley. I looked through the glass, the flat countryside, the suburbs, the endless billboards passed. We got closer to Moscow. The bus slowed. The traffic slowed up, roads clogged, then gridlock.

I was glad to be out of London. Mrs Curtis was dead, maybe because she had talked to me. Would her own son kill her for that? The rich cousin who lived on Eaton Square? I had left a trail of death spreading behind me like an infection.

"Tell him about St Saviour," said another girl on the bus, and Kim told me about the beautiful cathedral, most beautiful in the world, she said, that had been a swimming pool, and which had been restored so beautifully, so much gold, she said.

I said, to make them talk more, fill me in on this new Moscow—it was seventeen years since I'd been back—and that I admired Russian culture very much. They asked me what I did exactly. I said I was doing research for my new book and also on vacation, and hoped my answer would be good enough, but they were observant kids.

"But you are doing what? In your real life?" asked Kim.

My real life?

Again, I said I was a travel writer, and I wrote books and an online blog about foreign places. They told me the best writers were in Russia, and then one of them offered me a candy bar, explaining Red October produced delicious chocolates, Russian chocolates.

She held out an Alionka bar. On the wrapper was the familiar picture of a rosy-cheeked little girl in a baby babushka, the tiny headscarf tied under her chin.

I unwrapped it slowly. The smell rose up. The same smell of the same chocolate my father had brought home for me every week in his leather briefcase, and now the girls on the bus said: taste it.

Breaking off a piece, I ate it, pretended it was a delightful new treat, something I'd never tasted, and the girls all said, eat some more, eat it all, we have enough, come on, as if it were a competition, a way to rate me, and I bit into the chocolate again, nodding and smiling for their benefit. When I looked out of the window, I saw my father.

I pushed my face against the window. Traffic bumper to bumper. Crowds on the street. Neon. Billboards. Shops. A city I hardly knew, and then I saw him just near Lubyanka Square, the KGB headquarters where he had his office when I was a kid.

The huge yellow stone building, where the statue of the founder of the Russian secret police was "hanged" when communism collapsed, hanged, hauled away. I always loved meeting my dad there because the KGB was next to Detsky Mir, Kids' World, the greatest toy shop on earth, it had seemed then. I remembered. Lubyanka, with its terrifying jail, was sometimes joked about and in private called "Adults' World".

I saw my dad, walking along, perhaps heading to his office, swinging his good American leather briefcase in which he brought home my chocolates.

Alionka had been my favorite of all the sweets he brought home—cranberries in sugar, a chocolate rabbit for New Year's, Stolichnaya with the same label as the vodka and vodka inside the candies.

Outside the window, the evening sun lit him up, as he dodged traffic, and jogged gracefully across the street, carrying the briefcase he had brought home from America, which he polished every night at the kitchen table.

You think it smells of America, my mother always said a little dismissively, but he was proud of it because other officers carried satchels made out of East German leather, or even cardboard. On my father's fine leather case was a label that read Mark Cross.

In the 1950s and 1960s, when my father was a young hero of the KGB, times were good, he always said. Khrushchev times, when you could honorably defend your country, and people felt good about doing it, or some of them did. Things were changing. Sputnik went up in 1957 and we were full of ourselves, we Soviets, and then Yuri Gagarin. They had believed, some of them, we would see the great days of real socialism, that we would rule the world in a just way.

When I was a baby, my father went to America, he was in New York during the Cuban Missile Crisis. My mother told me that during the crisis she had gone to bed some nights expecting not to wake up in the morning. My father was away from home. She was alone with me in the apartment in Moscow, and she kept me in her bed.

How I had adored him, my father who brought home chocolate candies wrapped in gold foil paper from a special store, and who took me fishing. He talked to me in English. We had a nice place to live, or that's how it seemed to me back then, until things started going sour for us, my mother talking too loud, saying too much, telling people how pissed off she was at the failures of the USSR, especially after Brezhnev.

My father lost his job. We lost our apartment. We left Moscow for Israel.

My mother was still there, in a nursing home in Haifa. Alzheimer's meant she didn't know my name. But she still smoked secretly.

In our apartment in Moscow, I had once come into the living room to find the desk she used on fire. I poured water over it, and when she came home, my mother said, "What happened?" She admitted to me when she had a cigarette, she blew the smoke into the drawer. This last time, she had dropped the butt into the drawer, too. Some paper caught fire. After that we laughed and laughed about it. My mother's "smoking drawer", we called it.

Why did I think about it now? I thought about them both, her, my father. In Israel, he had been blown up on a bus by a bomb, a mistake, intended for another location.

Is it good? Do you like it? The girls twittered like high-pitched birds gathered at feeding time.

It's good, I said. Very nice chocolate for sure, I said. Thank you. Yes, wonderful chocolate.

It is better than American? asked Kim who confided to me that her real name was Svetlana but everybody called her Kim after her grandmother whose name stood for Kommunistichesky International Molodezhny. It meant Communist Youth International, she explained and added that her great-grandmother had been called Vladlena, for Vladimir Ilych Lenin.

"First for the while we love Mars Bars, Snickers, my older sister who is now already thirty, she tells me everything is good if it comes from West. She loves this West. She wants everything West. But now we prefer our own candies," said Kim. "It is much better. Higher percentage chocolate," she explained, and mentioned that her grandmother had worked in the Red October factory, and had explained all of these things. Her grandmother, she added, had actually seen Comrade Stalin. The other girls sighed slightly.

Shut up! I wanted to shout at these hectic children: shut up. But I smiled and said, okay, you win, better than American candy bars. I like this chocolate very much, I said, speaking in the slow loud deliberate way Americans do when they're in foreign countries, as if everybody around them is stupid or deaf. This seemed to make them happy and the girls smiled at each other knowingly. I was an okay kind of American.

Being in Moscow, looking out that window, seeing my father in the street, knowing it was a hallucination, it made me feel a little nuts. He was dead.

Maybe I had seen his ghost. In Moscow, you could believe in ghosts if you let go of your own present and let the past flood you.

Tall, tan, athletic, braces on her teeth, Kim, who was now chattering with the other girls, could have been European, American, Australian, except that she was in love with her president. And her expression, when she mentioned him, was a little bit crazy. Shining with devotion. She reminded me of a little girl I had been in the Komsomol with. I had been a young Pioneer, like everyone else, white shirt, red neckerchief.

My father had imposed it on me, and anyhow it was what everybody I knew did. In our group was one girl, very pale, blue eyes, hair the color and texture of corn-silk, braided and wound around her head, and when we sang patriotic songs, she was the one who always announced the concert by sounding out "Vladimir Ilych Lenin" in a piercing, shrill, high, zealous voice. She believed. She was a believer because she came from a working-class family, the father a drunk, the mother a factory cleaner, who had only their belief, and the bundles of dripping meat allocated to the mother at work.

A world long gone, replaced by one with easy access to food and chocolate, but admired by these girls, sentimentalized by them, and sometimes even their parents. In my time, at least when we went home, we took off our public faces. We made fun of the crappy culture and preferred the Beatles.

We hung out like young hoods in Pushkin Square, near the statue of the great Russian poet-hero, exchanging titbits of information about John, Paul, George and Ringo and wondering, as we examined forbidden pictures, which one was which. Tolya always said to me it was the Beatles who brought down communism.

"It caused us to defect internally from the system, Artyom," he always said. "It made us flee from everything around us inside our souls."

Where are you? I thought. Tolya, where are you for God's sake?

"Say cheese!" Suddenly, Kim, picked up her phone and snapped my picture. The other girls followed. There was something about Kim of the little spy, taking pictures, hoarding them, as she chattered about the fatherland, the need to resettle internal immigrants back where they came from, especially if they came from the Caucasus.

One of the little girls—she was about nine—let off a stream of invective about the foreigners, as she called them, the Caucasians and the others who came to Moscow to work at the markets and clean the streets, and how dirty they were and how frightened her mother was of them.

Don't talk to these dirty animals, her mother had told her. Don't let them touch you.

I waited for the translation, but Kim told the girl she must not use nasty language, especially in front of foreigners, even if they didn't understand, it wasn't nice, and suddenly I got the feeling Kim knew I spoke Russian, that I understood. But she only smiled and we all smiled some more and I finished the chocolate bar to the amusement of all the little girls.

At the bus terminal, the girls said goodbye to me, and the tiny one with the big stuffed bear kissed my cheek. Kim handed me a second chocolate bar from her bag, and asked me to write down my name and my phone number and the hotel where I was staying. She planned on asking her mom if she could invite me to their house for tea. I said thanks and gave her a phony name—I became Max Fielding—and jotted down the National Hotel because it was all I could think of, and we all smiled some more, and then the girl who hated Caucasians turned around and snapped my photograph with her silver digital camera.

Snap snap. Suddenly all the girls got out their phones and little digital cameras and took more pictures of each other, and of me, each one posing with me, then posing in groups. Snap snap.

Come on, please, said Kim, one more, one more picture, so I can keep you. Okay, now with my mom, and she beckoned her mother, a good-looking woman with pale platinum hair who posed with me, and shook my hand and said I was welcome.

They tumbled into each other's arms to say goodbye and waved at parents who were waiting and then they began to slip away; and I was alone, except for Kim who called out, "One more, please?" and held up her phone and with serious determination took a final picture as if to capture me for once and for all. I was now the official prisoner of little Russian girls in pink t-shirts. I ♥ Putin.

CHAPTER FORTY-FOUR

Moscow was hot and dusty. The National Hotel was full. I couldn't remember any other hotels, only the National and the old Intourist, which had been replaced by a Ritz Carlton where they wanted twelve hundred bucks a night.

I didn't have that kind of dough. I didn't really want to stay in a hotel anyhow. It would make me too visible. I glanced around the lobby at the Ritz Carlton, and left.

I needed a place to stay.

As soon as I hit the streets, a fog of paranoia descended and clung to me like the humidity. I went towards Red Square. Everything in this place led to Red Square. I went on instinct, God knows why. I had to think of a place to stay, so I walked, trying to lose myself among the tourists.

There was a replica of Resurrection Gate that had gone up since I'd been here. I had heard about it as a kid. The sixteenth-century gate which had formed an entrance to Red Square was torn down by Stalin in 1931 to make it easier for tanks to get through to the square. And just in front of the gate—it looked like cardboard—was a guy with some monkeys.

"Picture, picture, you want a picture?" shouted the monkey man.

He had two monkeys working the crowd for him, in fact. One of the monkeys looked like a little old man in a child's outfit, little blue shorts, a jacket, a cap. The other was smaller, and had a skirt on.

"Fuck off," I said.

Before I knew it, the man had tossed the monkeys at me, one into my arms, the big one on my back. He snapped my picture.

"Get them off of me," I said, beginning to panic. "Get them fucking off me."

The wall of noise from traffic was incredible, a million cars in gridlock. Hummers, Range Rovers, Mercs, Moscow money liked its cars big and loud. On the street a guy sidled up to me to offer me police kit for twenty grand, complete with flashing blue light, siren, special plates, which would get me out of traffic and into the VIP lane.

Was this Tolya's alternative universe, this place where we had both grown up? Was this Tolya's other planet, the place where he had disappeared? I barely recognized Moscow, the traffic, the stores, the signs, the neon, the crowds. I'd only been back once in the early 1990s. I looked around for a taxi.

Parched, I went into a grocery store to buy a bottle of water. It felt like a stage set, stocked like a fancy New York deli with salad, bread, meats, cheeses, imported canned goods, flowers, fresh fruit, cookies, wine, cake.

I walked some more. It was getting late now, sun going down, the Moscow night coming on. The whole city seemed about to explode, as if somebody had tossed a lighted match onto a sea of oil.

In the street, I held out my hand for a cab. A shabby beige Lada pulled up. The driver in jeans and a red t-shirt asked where I was going. I gave him the address of Tolya's club. As he drove, he bent over the wheel in a weird contorted way. After a few minutes, I realized he was a hunchback.

The driver asked if I was a foreigner. He said did I need anything?

What was he offering? Girls? Drugs? I didn't know. I didn't know anything about this place.

When the driver finally pulled up at the curb and turned around, I saw he had a soft young face, and I gave him extra cash.

For a few seconds, standing on the street, I fantasized that I'd find Tolya at Pravda222, find him behind the bar, cradling some thousand-dollar bottle of wine the way I had that morning in New York. But I knew he would be lying low, looking for Grisha Curtis. I had already called his apartment, his ex-wife's dacha. I didn't want to try anybody else. I was afraid my calling would get him into bad trouble.

If Tolya was hiding, I'd try for anonymity here. Nobody else at the club would know me. As I went in, and dropped my bag at the coat-check, I became Max Fielding, a travel writer, always making notes in my little notebook.

Pravda222 was pretty much exactly like Tolya's other clubs.

"Branding, Artyom," I could hear Tolya say. "This is how it works. Rich people like security, they like a name they know, you must have a brand."

How excited he had been when he opened his club in Moscow, his third club, and now he was on his way to a global brand. But Moscow, this is special, Artyom, he had said. This is like coming home.

Mahogany paneling, old chandeliers, long bar, de-silvered mirrors that Tolya told me he picked up at the flea market in Paris, and which caught the light. On the walls were the Soviet posters he had collected: Mayakovsky, the Stenberg Brothers, Rodchenko, a painting by Malevich that must have cost millions. Waiters in white bistro aprons checked the tables, the linen, glass.

People were filtering in quietly, the early part of the evening, most coming for dinner.

A handsome guy in a beautiful black suit, the cut so perfect I knew it was custom-made, approached me and asked if he could help.

I needed help. I told him I knew Sverdloff through a friend. It worked like a charm. The guy offered me a table, I said I'd sit at the bar. He offered me a drink, I said Scotch, please.

Konstantin was the suit's name, and I told him I was Max Fielding and gave him the information I'd given the kids on the bus. I didn't know if he believed me or not, but he welcomed me to Moscow and said did I need anything, and excused himself to greet somebody who had arrived and had perched on a barstool four down from where I sat.

While I drank I read an English-language paper I'd picked up at the airport. Fifty-four per cent of Russians, according to a poll, consider money the most important thing as compared to eleven per cent of Americans, the piece said. Things were going to fall into an abyss, another columnist had written. Give it two months, give it until October, he said, and the price of oil would plunge, and everybody would be left high and dry, stranded, screwed. Putin announced, meanwhile, that everything would be wonderful for a hundred years.

A couple of men who had planted themselves at the bar began telling jokes. They were well dressed, nice clothes, good accents. I made out that they were a pair of Moscow architects.

After a couple of drinks, they started talking about people from the former Sov republics. Then one cracked a joke about Obama. They laughed. What a joke, one said to the other in Russian.

"I say to myself, hope?" he said. "I say, change? I see a black guy, and I say, okay, how much?"

I was slipping between planets. I didn't bother telling them Obama was probably the only candidate who could help us out, and we needed help. I didn't bother. They wouldn't get it.

I sat and drank for a while until the suit—Konstantin—came over, and asked if I needed anything else, and I mentioned I was looking for a place to stay. An apartment, maybe, instead of a hotel, I said. I wanted to get the real feel of being in Moscow.

I was pretty surprised—maybe it was too good to be true and I should have known it—Konstantin said he might have a solution. He asked if I wanted to eat, a waiter brought me some smoked fish and another drink, and about half an hour later, the American appeared.

Konstantin made the introductions and the guy got up on the stool next to me, asked for a beer, shook my hand. He had a Midwestern accent, and asked where I was from.

"New York," I said.

"I love New York. I'm from Minnesota," he said, and grinned. "Small town you've never heard of. You just got here? Max, right?"

I nodded.

"Willie Moffat," he said. "Konstantin over there told me you were looking for a place to stay?"

In the background, Sinatra sang "Moonlight In Vermont".

"I have to go back to the States, I fixed my flight," said Moffat. "I was trying to set up to rent my apartment. My Russian sucks. So I asked Konstantin who knows everyone in Moscow, if he could help. I want to do it off the books, so I get it back, it's for a few weeks."

I ordered another drink and listened to Moffat, wondering who he really was, this tall balding American with square shoulders who had appeared suddenly with an apartment for rent. I looked in the mirror at the people behind me. Half expected to see Grisha Curtis shadowing me the way he had in London.

"How long for? The apartment?"

"Like I said, few weeks, a month tops. Listen, I'm sorry to make it kind of urgent, but I have to leave tonight, and it would be great if you wanted it," said Moffat, fumbling for a pack of cigarettes. "Great thing about Moscow is you can still smoke," he said. "The thing is, my mom is sick, and I don't want to leave the apartment empty, you know? I just got it, and if you leave it empty, even after you pay off the realtors and do the bribes and shit, you can lose it. I don't exactly have all the paperwork signed and sealed yet. But you'd be fine for a few weeks, honest." His words spilled out in a rush, he was a guy in a hurry, but best I could tell he really was in a hurry to see his sick mother.

"Go on."

Moffat looked reassured.

"I just started a new job here," he said. "I'm on a private water project, and everybody is desperate about housing, it's insane, you want to rent a decent place in a good area, it's like the competition is completely nuts. I found this place. I mean, this girl found it for me, and it's in a building that's not really finished, look I could show you." He was repeating himself. He was eager. Too eager?

"Yeah, I'll take a look, why not," I said casually as I could. If it worked out, I'd have a place to stay and nobody would know, I wouldn't have to deal with a hotel, and the paperwork. As best I could, I was trying not to leave a trail, trying to keep to myself.

"My car's outside," he said. "If you want, I can leave you my car with the apartment," added Moffat, who found Konstantin in the middle of the laughing drinking crowd, pressed some money into his hand, thanked him.

"I'll tell Mr Sverdloff I saw you if he comes by. Mr Fielding, isn't that right?" said Konstantin.

"Is he in Moscow? You didn't say."

"I heard so," he said, his face bland and unrevealing. "But he has not been into the club yet."

"Doesn't he always come here?"

"I don't ask these questions."

"Sure, tell him Max said hi. And thanks," I said, slipped a few large bills into his perfect suit jacket, and went to get my bag and look at Moffat's apartment.

In Moffat's new blue BMW, he asked me what I did. I told him I was planning to write a travel guide to the new Moscow.

"Who's the girl?" I said, making conversation as he drove us to the building.

"You knew? You had to figure I didn't care so much about the apartment just for myself, right?" He grinned and said his girl was really something, but he knew she wanted that apartment, and he had taken it on a six-month basis with an option to buy.

He was an engineer, he said, and told me about his life in Red Wing, Minnesota in so much detail, by the time we got to the apartment, I knew that his father was a doctor, an internist, and his brother liked golf, and more or less everything else about the Moffat family.

I made some conversation about the baseball season to prove I was a good American.

Moffat was a diehard Twins fan, but he commiserated with me over the Yankees and over Torre leaving and I admitted only a dumb fan like me could stay loyal to such a fuck-up of a team.

We talked politics a little. It was all Americans talked about, that and the baseball season. He liked Obama, he said. Had shaken his hand at a rally. I fell in with the conversation.

"You sound homesick already," Moffat said.

"Yeah. For sure."

"I don't know your last name," he added amiably.

"Fielding," I said.

At Moffat's building, a caretaker was half asleep on a chair in the lobby. He looked at me suspiciously. Moffat stuffed some money in his hand.

"I call him Igor, he reminds me of *Young Frankenstein*," said Moffat, chuckling. Igor also worked with the construction crews, said Moffat in English. Igor didn't speak English. He didn't speak much at all.

I followed Moffat up six flights of stairs—the new elevator wasn't installed yet, and I was panting by the time we got there. He showed me around the two-room apartment with high ceilings and tall windows, peeling mint green paint in the bathrooms and olive green tiles, a big sofa and flatscreen TV in the living room, a brand-new king-size bed in the bedroom. In the kitchen a Soviet-era Elektra stove that was six feet tall, and emitted a strange smell I couldn't pin down. Gas? Sewage?

Moffat apologized for the stove and said the new appliances would arrive any day. In the meantime, he had put in a microwave and a fancy silver espresso machine.

I didn't plan on cooking.

I said I'd take it.

He gave me the keys. He gave me his phone numbers. I had picked up a local pay-as-you-go cellphone as soon as I got off the plane, and I gave Moffat the number. I used Fiona Colquhoun for a reference. Said she was my British book publisher. My own phone, I had turned off and put in my pocket. I didn't want anybody using it to track me down.

Fiona already knew where I was; she'd made it happen, I had to trust her, she was all I had. There was nobody, nobody, I could trust anymore, except for Tolya Sverdloff and he had disappeared, slipped away, evaporated. I began to wonder if he had died. I remembered the gray pallor, the way he clutched his arm. Where was he?

Two weeks, Moffat said, until he was back. Three tops. I tried to give him some money for rent. He said he was fine with me just staying, water the plants, make sure the place is occupied, put on the lights when you go out. He didn't want any break-ins, not by real-estate creeps or any other creeps. What kind of creeps?

Before I could ask, Moffat was gone, dragging a suitcase back down the stairs, and I sent Fiona Colquhoun a message to tell her a guy called Moffat might call for a reference on somebody name of Max Fielding, and that this Max—me—was writing a travel guide. If Moffat didn't check my reference, I'd know it was a set-up.

If I hadn't lived in America for almost thirty years, I would not have quite believed in Willie Moffat from Red Wing. But I'd met plenty like him, this good, nice American. And I'd spun him enough of a story about myself to keep him happy.

A picture of the Russian girlfriend—Moffat's girlfriend—was on the table near his bed. In a bikini on a beach someplace, she had a fantastic body, the legs, a feral face with cheekbones sharp as glass.

Oh, Willie, man, I thought, this is a big mistake. But he was gone, and he was in love, so what could I do?

I was stashing my stuff in a couple of drawers in the bedroom when Igor knocked on the door to see if anything was leaking. He had heard water. He asked if I spoke Russian. I shook my head and put out my hands, palms up, and shrugged to indicate I didn't know what the hell he was talking about. I knew he just wanted a good look at me.

Later that night, early into the morning, unable to sleep, I went up on the roof of Moffat's building to read through Grisha Curtis' notes again, looking for clues about where he would go in Moscow. Find Grisha, I'd find Tolya, and the other way around. In my mind they were cuffed together.

I sat on a low plastic beach chair somebody had left out on the roof and I could see all of Moscow spread out: the blaze of neon, the river of red made by the tail lights on the endless stream of cars, the smear of gold and purple as the sun came up on another boiling humid Moscow day, when the smog hung in thick curtains of pearly gray until the sun burned some of it away.

Below me was the area of Patriarchy Prudi, Metro Mayakovskaya, late nineteenth, early twentieth century building, referred to in real-estate ads as "pre-revolutionary" the way somebody might list a Park Avenue apartment as "pre-war". Some featured "Western renovation". Some mentioned "Stalin-era" buildings.

From my roof, I looked down over M. Kozikhinsky Lane. I had walked enough earlier to see the shops, the girls in their Manolos and Louboutin shoes, I had seen Nikitskaya Street.

For hours I gazed down from the roof at the area, where Bulgakov made his Master and Margarita do their business, and where as teenagers who read this forbidden book, the real thing, not the censored version—we were the children of privilege and there was always somebody who could get a copy—we had all come and loitered and smoked and discussed the novel in pretentious terms, unless we were at somebody's flat examining the lyrics of "Sympathy For The Devil" which we knew had been inspired by the novel.

Once, in New York, I had dated a girl who thought *The Master and Margarita* was about cocktails. It didn't last.

I replayed the conversation I'd had with Tolya at his cousin Larry's place in England.

Tolya had been sick when I'd seen him in England. Had someone given him polonium to eat? Was it Grisha, who had already killed his daughter?

Tolya didn't answer my calls. He must be dead. Tolya Sverdloff, who had saved my ass over and over, and I couldn't do anything for him. I couldn't even find him. If he was alive, he would have answered my calls.

Grisha was gone. They had disappeared, both of them, Tolya slipping like a man on a stellar banana peel. During his interplanetary trip had he missed the connection, the spaceship home? I was tired. In Moscow I knew if I let on what I was doing, I'd disappear, too.

So I was here, pretending to be an American, not my American self, not a New York cop, just a tourist who could speak a little bit of basic Russian and who understood less.

I would be an irritating travel writer I decided, the kind who thinks an interrogation is a conversation, who always wants the facts and figures and dates, the kind who keeps a little notebook in which he arduously inscribes all this, who discusses the hospitality industry with a kind of smug know-it-all attitude.

I went down the stairs from the roof onto the sixth floor and into the apartment. The air conditioner was broken. I took a tepid shower, changed, stuffed money into my pocket. I picked up the phone, tried dialing a local number, heard what I was listening for: somebody was on the line. Somebody was sharing my phone.

Or was I paranoid? Had the Russian disease, along with the booze and heat, made me crazy? It was time for me to get moving.

I headed out into the city. I wanted a gun.

CHAPTER FORTY-FIVE

The bear at the entrance to Ismailova Park was chained up. People stood around waiting for the hourly performance, when, according to the sign, the bear would perform. WE WORK WITHOUT MUZZLES, said the sign.

This was a different city from the Moscow of fancy shops, it was a place where, on the outskirts of town, people went for cheap clothes, and, on weekends, to sell souvenirs to foreigners.

At dawn I had left the apartment. On the Moscow streets everywhere I looked, I saw Grisha Curtis, saw him walking in the opposite direction, turning a corner, waiting for me, leaning against a wall.

Even in the morning, the air was so thick and sticky, it coated my skin like grease. I studied the map in my hand. I was looking for a train station. I was a tourist in the city where I grew up. I was a ghost, the son of a ghost.

The area around Kazansky Station was jammed, people leaving, coming in, hanging out, sleeping on the ground. On a boom box, somebody was playing Metallica. Hordes of people with Asian faces milled around. The women were wrapped in shawls, and they came and want, dragging big bags of stuff to sell. A couple of girls, couldn't have been more than fifteen, loitered on one corner, looking for men in cars.

I waited for the light to turn green before I crossed the street. People glanced at me, half amused. In Moscow, like New York, nobody waited for the lights. A girl with long skinny legs in high-heeled boots darted across the street like a large insect.

This station, crammed with people sleeping on the floor, with beggars, with children in filthy clothes screaming and running, with people selling fruit, caviar, vodka, wooden dolls, under-pants, home-made brooms, sticky candy, was a good bet. I figured it for the kind of place a low-level hood might have something for sale. A .22, a little piece of shit, the kind of thing that would make me feel secure, nothing more. I didn't want a high-end weapon.

In Moscow looking for a gun, I was a hick. It took me the best part of an hour to find out you could get one at Ismailova Park, the flea market at the edge of Moscow.

The stalls were jammed with matrioshka, the wooden Russian dolls, some of them the traditional girls with cheeks painted red, others political figures, sports figures. A row of the dolls depicted beaky-nosed men with ringlets, and I said, in Russian "What are those? Who are they supposed to be?"

"The Jews," said the woman behind the stall.

Fur hats, hand-knitted scarves, more dolls, painted plates, table lines, the usual Russian stuff. I asked careful questions. I climbed some wooden steps, three women in peasant outfits were singing some old Russian songs, and I put change in the basket for them, and went on.

Up here were the antiques, the porcelain figures, the Soviet army gear, the bad oil paintings, the rugs, and a man selling posters.

I stopped for a minute. Piles of old posters were on his stall, posters depicting Soviet space, Soviet agriculture, politics, heroic figures. I moved on, I looked into the faces of guys sitting by their stalls playing chess. I searched for somebody who might sell me a gun.

Then I saw the postcards, and the period photographs; jumbled on one stall were pictures of men and women in high-collared blouses and turn-of-the-century suits—sepia photographs from the beginning of the twentieth century. Something drew me to one picture. I picked it up. It looked familiar, this family photograph, and I saw the resemblance. It was a picture of my father's grandfather, who had fought in the revolution. Next to him was a young man with a baby, a little boy, my father. I would never get away from this place, this country. I bought the picture.

I went back down. I went to the edge of the market where there were people selling canned food and old shoes. A guy in rap pants saw me, and sidled up to me, and offered me meds, a handful of pills he probably swiped from a hospital. I told him in Russian to fuck off. Another had some weed, and I blew him off, and turned my back. But they had made me for a guy who wanted something and if it wasn't drugs, it was probably weapons.

The gun I got was a .22, like a toy pistol. It wasn't new. It looked like something for shooting rabbits. The guy sold me a box of ammo to go with it.

It was a piece of crap, and after I paid him cash, and put it in my pocket, I felt like a fool. What good was it except to give me some kind of solace, I thought as I left the market.

I got the subway. I looked at my notebook for the address I wanted. Changed trains. Got lost. I was looking for the shelter where Valentina had worked, the shelter she supported.

When I emerged from the subway someplace near the center of town, I realized I'd made a mistake again. I stopped to ask directions. A plump woman in a hot pink dress smiled and told me how to go. And then I saw him.

If I hadn't screwed up, if I hadn't lost my way, maybe I would never have seen him on that corner. But, of course, he would have found me, one way or the other, this guy in a Brooks

Brothers jacket, blue and white seersucker, who stood on the opposite side of the street, staring at me. He removed his Ray-Bans and peered hard. He looked like an American tourist—the jacket, the khakis, the dark blue polo shirt, the Timberlands.

Head cocked, stare quizzical—it was like a performance, a man asking himself: do I recognize that guy in jeans?

Once more he looked, raised a hand as if in greeting, got his cellphone out.

Who was he? Was he somebody from home I didn't remember? How else would he know me? The intensity of his interest bothered me. He didn't call out. He didn't approach me, and I backed off into the subway station.

I wasn't officially on the job in Moscow. I wasn't a cop here. As a Russian kid, I had never thought about being a policeman. All I ever wanted was to listen to jazz and find an easy life. If we'd stayed, I would have ended up teaching English. I would have been just another cog in the system, an unhappy guy who drank too much and secretly listened to music at home late at night.

Tolya Sverdloff thought I had a moral code, that I became a cop to help people. He didn't understand. I'd become a cop because it seemed the best way to fit into New York, to belong.

It was for the sense of belonging that I loved being on the job, because of the other guys, the noises in the station house, the late-night drinking sessions, the weddings and funerals, people like my friend, Hank Provone over on Staten Island who had made me part of his family. No matter how brutal things got, no matter what shit I saw or stepped into—and this included the criminals and the cops—I wanted in.

The subway train shunted into the station I was looking for, I got out and found my way to Valentina's shelter, her orphanage. When I saw it, saw the little cross that had been hung on the wall in the vestibule, something in my gut told me this was where it had all started.

CHAPTER FORTY-SIX

"She was like a saint," said the tiny woman at the shelter when I asked about Valentina. "She gave us money, clothes, food, diapers for the babies. She found jobs for the young women we rescued from train stations, and the girls whose parents pimped them out for small change, girls of twelve and thirteen, would you like some coffee, please?" added the woman who introduced herself as Elisabetta Anton.

Her small smooth face was surrounded by fine white hair. Her age was hard to tell. Her English was exquisite. On her office desk was an iPod with small speakers. From it came the Beatles. "Norwegian Wood" was on, turned very low.

"A present from Valentina," she said. "She knew when I was a girl, long ago, the Beatles meant everything to me and they were banned for so long. I'm sorry, I was thinking about her. I like to think about her. The news was so devastating it was hard to believe, but I was not surprised."

Orphanage Number Six, as it had been in Soviet times, was a free-standing building with a ramshackle playground next to it. The concrete walls outside were stained with water. It still served children, Elisabetta told me, but some rooms had been converted to house older girls who needed shelter. In them, she showed me the desks, a pair of beds with blue spreads, posters of pop stars.

The building had been scrubbed endlessly, there were colorful pictures on the walls done by the kids, but there was a dank sour smell was there, as if it literally came out of the walls.

In Elisabetta's office was a framed photograph of a little girl. It was Luda, the child Val had tried once to adopt.

Elisabetta offered coffee again and I refused, and sat down opposite her at her pine desk. She put a pack of Russian cigarettes on the desk followed by a small box of chocolates.

"Please," she said.

"Not surprised, you said?"

"When I heard, I thought to myself, he did this to her. They did this."

"Who?"

"One moment," said Elisabetta. She closed the door and lowered her voice. "I know what happened," she said. "I know. I said to her, my darling girl, please be careful, please go slowly. But Valentina was an innocent, you see. She didn't understand about greed. Or money. She simply didn't get it," Elisabetta added. "We had begun taking in girls of ten, eleven, twelve, who were working in the train stations as prostitutes, there is a lot of money in Moscow now, and while the girls used to go to Western Europe and America, there is more money here. It had become big business and there are big, how would you say it? Big players. In business. In the government. I said to her, Valentina, you must not talk about certain people. But she didn't hear me. She was, after all, an American girl. Is somebody there?" she called out, and half rose from her seat. Nobody answered.

"Who were you expecting?"

She turned up the volume. "Eleanor Rigby" played.

"I don't know," Elisabetta said. "Since Valentina's death, there have been people dropping by for no reason in particular, you see. She took everyone on. She criticized everyone and everything she didn't like, she picked up the phone and called government officials. Worst, she spoke to journalists. This can get you killed. She made friends with a woman who wrote about the abuse of children and girls, and the money and the connections with the government. Let me show you some of the girls, her girls," said Elisabetta, taking a binder and opening it, turning the pages, showing me the pictures.

I stopped her. From my pocket, I took the picture of Masha Panchuk.

"Yes," said Elisabetta, "she was one of ours. Her name was Maria. She was a Ukrainian girl who ran away from home and was found by her uncle who put her to work. Valentina got her out of the country and to London. I don't think she was sixteen years old." Turning pages in the binder, Elisabetta found the girl's picture, a sad beautiful girl, photographed by Val.

"What did they call Maria?"

"We called her Masha."

It had started here. In this shelter, on a crummy backstreet in Moscow.

"Masha's last name, it was Panchuk?"

"Not then. Only after she married a fellow named Zim Panchuk. You knew her?"

I told Elisabetta about Masha's death.

"My God," she said.

"I think she was killed in Val's place, she had a purse Val had given her with her name in it, and when they realized it was the wrong girl, they went after Valentina."

Elisabetta put her small chin on one hand and smoked with the other.

"Who did it?"

"You knew her father?"

"Of course. Anatoly Anatolyevich, he gave us money. He came here a few times, he was so jolly with the little children, and he sang for them, and brought them presents, usually food so exotic they had never seen it. They thought he was Father Christmas," she said. "He did whatever Valentina asked. In the last few months, I believe, she spent most of her time working on our behalf. I felt she had become obsessed."

"You said she made friends with a journalist?"

"I'm not sure."

"Please, tell me."

"It's dangerous," she said. "They kill journalists."

"They killed Valentina," I said. "I need help."

"I'll see," she said. "But now there are babies who need feeding. I must go."

"I'm a policeman. In the United States. Valentina's father is my best friend, she was my friend." I leaned over the desk.

From a drawer, Elisabetta took a photograph and sat gazing at it. "She was such a special girl," she said. "She was pure."

"Valentina?"

"Yes, her soul was pure," she said, and handed it to me. In the picture were Val and Grisha, his arm around her.

"You knew him?"

She nodded.

"What did you think?"

"I met him quite a while ago, not long after Val started helping us. She wanted everybody to love him, the way it always is when you first fall in love. Recently she had stopped talking about him. I didn't pry. Once, she said just that he didn't believe in the things she believed in anymore."

"I see," I said. I had heard it before. Valentina had fallen hard for Grisha at first. Later, she backed away, then broke it off. For this, I thought, most of all for this, he killed her.

Elisabetta got up to leave.

"Have you seen him?" I said.

She turned from the door.

"Yes."

"When?"

"He came in a few days ago," said Elisabetta. "He asked about Mr Sverdloff. My assistant talked to him, he wanted Valentina's files, she said there were none, that she had taken them to America with her."

"How was he?"

"Angry," she said.

"Enough to kill?"

"My assistant was frightened, it's all I know."

Elisabetta went to the back of the building where I could hear the babble of babies, and returned with a short fat woman. "This is Marina," she said, introducing the woman. "She is a journalist, but she helps us here at the shelter. I have to go."

"Marina Fetushova," said the woman, and lit up a stinky Russian cigarette.

I introduced myself to Fetushova. She didn't move, just kept smoking.

"You help out here?" I said in Russian.

"None of your business."

"I need information."

"We can't talk here," she said, and without another word, she walked through the front door, blowing smoke into the open air. I followed her.

We were at the edge of a playground where a gang of eight-year-olds were climbing a jungle gym and skipping rope. Fetushova watched them.

Head set between beefy shoulders, she wore a sloppy green sweater and a gray skirt. In spite of the booming voice, and the fact that she swore like crazy, she had a cultivated accent.

"You're a cop?" she said.

"Yes. From New York."

"What is it you need?"

Her tone was brusque, almost hostile.

"I want to find somebody."

"Who's that?"

"Grigory Curtis."

Fetushova swore, calling Curtis a prick and much worse, and then turned away.

I grabbed her arm.

"Don't do that," she said, shaking loose. "Don't fucking touch me."

"I'm sorry."

"I can't talk to you here," she said.

"What's wrong with here?"

"Don't be an ass."

The sun beat down on the playground. The kids kept playing.

"So somebody knew about Val's involvement here?"

"Yes." She nodded.

"People watch this place?"

"My God, you're naive. What do you think?"

Leaning forward, as close to her as I could without her slugging me, I said, without thinking about it, "I'm desperate."

Her expression changed slightly, a mixture of sarcasm and sympathy.

"You don't sound like a fucking pig cop," she said.

"I'm a friend."

"You're from where?"

"Here."

"Moscow?"

"Yes."

"Where did you grow up?"

"You're interested?"

"I'm only talking to you while I finish my smoke," she said.

"Give me one."

She offered me the pack, and her lighter. I told her the street where I grew up, the street where we moved after my father lost his job, the school I went to.

"Yeah, me too, same time," she said.

There was a flash of recognition. Now she understood, it seemed to say, she knew all about me. But I looked at her and saw an old Russian woman, not somebody my age. Maybe that was what her work had done to her.

"You remember the music teacher?" I said. "At our school?"

"Okay, forget the fucking small talk," said Fetushova, drawing back, throwing her cigarette on the sidewalk, crushing it with her foot, walking closer to the playground.

"What happened here?"

"Fuck you," she said. "I don't talk about it," she added, but she didn't leave, just stood and watched as women came and went, bringing packages to the shelter. The kids played. The older girls watched them. In this shabby district, everybody was poor, shabbily dressed. But you could hear the traffic, the rumble, the scream of it.

In the middle of town, you saw a Moscow afloat on Russia's supplies of oil and natural gas, heard the world bellowing for fuel, prices skyrocketing. In the center of the city, you could feel it, as if the resources, oil and gas, aluminum, nickel, diamonds, gold, and the revenues poured down a chute into the city from the Far East and the former republics. Money, money, money.

It was the biggest city in Europe now, ten, twelve, sixteen million, depending if you counted the floating immigrant population and dozens of billionaires. I could feel it flexing its muscles, bragging rights claimed like a prizefighter who had taken the title. But at the shelter, there were only the kids and the stained building and old women in headscarves who looked like Russian women had looked for centuries. They brought home-made dumplings, and black bread, whatever they could afford for the children.

The little girls in tiny blue shorts and striped t-shirts ran around, laughing. They clambered up the jungle gym. I thought of the children in the green square in London, hanging upside down. An older girl sat on one of the swings, swinging higher and higher. I watched her. I couldn't take my eyes off her.

I saw it all over again. I saw the girl in the Brooklyn playground, I saw Masha Panchuk. Fetushova had picked up her bag, lit up another smoke, was getting ready to go.

"Was somebody hurt here?" I said. "In this playground?"

"What the fuck does that mean?"

I told her about Masha Panchuk, the way she died, I told her all the details.

She dropped her cigarette, hand trembling.

"My God," she said.

"What?"

"Wait." She hurried into the shelter where I tried to follow. "I said wait."

"About a year ago, Valentina took this picture," said Fetushova, returning with a print in a plastic sleeve.

Stomach turning, I looked at the picture. A girl on a bench, the jungle gym visible behind her.

"Here?"

"Yes," Fetushova said.

The girl was wrapped like a mummy in duct tape. A doll was on her lap.

"Jesus Christ."

"This playground," she said. "The girl was thirteen. She belonged to a bastard very high up, close to the Kremlin."

"Belonged?"

"He owned her. You can as good as buy these girls," said Fetushova. "Somehow she got away. Somebody found her on the street and got her here. The son of a bitch thought the girl might talk. He hired a thug to do this. Shut her up. Tape her up. She was found like this."

"Dead?"

"Of course."

"They murdered the kid?"

"Yes."

"Why all the duct tape?"

"It's an old gangster punishment. You make it look like the old mob, the officials can deny it. They distance themselves. The fuckers look clean as a whistle, they give the shelter money, they go on TV, official TV, we only have official TV now, of course, and say how dreadful this is."

"Valentina?"

"She had started working with us when it happened. We asked her to take pictures. The girl in Brooklyn, she looked like this one, the duct tape?"

"Yes. I think they were after Valentina and got the wrong girl."

"Fuck," said Fetushova. "Somebody hired a creep who knew about this?"

"I think it was Grigory Curtis."

"Piece of shit, piece of mother-fucking donkey turd," she said. "You know him?"

"I want him," I said. "He's here. Elisabetta told me he had been here to the shelter."

"He wouldn't have the stomach to do this kind of job, if it was him, he hired somebody who fucked it up, right?"

"Yes."

"And when it came to Val, all he could manage was a pillow over her face. Fucking bastard. I have to go." She looked around.

A couple of guys lounged at the edge of the playground. They looked like low-level hoods, or street creeps from the FSB.

"Who are they?"

"Garbage men," she said, laughing. "We call them garbage men, I just don't know what kind of garbage."

"Where can we talk?"

"I can't talk."

"I'll be at your office. I'll wait for you," I said.

"Just don't get me killed," said Fetushova.

CHAPTER FORTY-SEVEN

I left the shelter. I had already checked every place that was mentioned in Grisha Curtis' files; in the stuff I had stolen from the office on Moscow Road. I had checked, quietly as I could: an apartment where he'd lived; a bank he had worked at; a gym where he did weights.

I couldn't exactly call up the FSB and ask for his contact. I couldn't say, who ran him, if somebody did. Maybe a real spy would know how.

So I worked the obvious places. Nothing. He wasn't good at keeping secret files, but he was good at hiding.

I felt him on my back all the time. At every corner, I looked over my shoulder, and put my hand on the little gun in my pocket.

Paranoia took over in Moscow. I walked as fast as I could, heading for the subway, always feeling somebody behind me, turning sharply, thinking I'd see Curtis, when there was nobody at all.

I stopped near an old Moscow housing project, twelve tall buildings, most in an even worse state than when I'd been here in the 1990s. I put my head into the hallway of one of the buildings; it stank of piss, like it always had, the elevator was still broken.

A few elderly women sat on rickety chairs on a patch of grass outside, and I scanned the faces, thinking I might recognize somebody, but they stared back, blank, and went on fanning themselves against the heat with newspapers. Living on meager pensions, they seemed completely unconnected with the new Moscow.

I asked the oldest of the women if she had known Birdie Golden. My mother's best friend who had taught me English lived and died in the building with the broken elevator.

"Yes," she said in Russian. "You are?"

I told her who I was. She beckoned me to lean down so she could kiss my cheek.

"Birdie loved you very much," she said. "She talked about you all the time, you were like her own son," said the woman, who invited me to take an empty chair and offered me a bottle of water from her bag.

I wanted to stay. I wanted to sit in the sun like the old women and talk. I realized Olga Dimitriovna had reminded me of Birdie a little.

"There is a man looking in this direction," said Birdie's friend, and I glanced over my shoulder and saw one of the garbage men from the playground.

"I should go," I said.

"Please come back," said the woman, and I said I'd try, even while sweat was running down my back and my hands were cold. I had to get Marina Fetushova to tell me what she knew. Whatever it took. Now, I thought.

I found her at the radio station where she worked.

"Fetushova, Marina," she said, sticking out a hand as if she had never met me before, and I saw this was for show, for the other people at the small radio station where I found her.

The radio station was in a couple of rooms in a concrete building near the Arbat, a dingy place with stale air thick with the rank smell of old cigarettes, no air conditioning.

Fetushova half pushed me out of the room where four people pored over scripts and fiddled with equipment. From another room, door shut, came the sound of American Blues. Buddy Guy, Mick Jagger covering a raucous Muddy Waters number about champagne and reefers.

A guy stood on the landing, leaning against the wall. Security for Fetushova and the others, I guessed. I started for the office.

"Not in there. I don't like to compromise anyone else," she said, pushing me back out into the hallway.

"Let's go outside," I said. "A cafe."

"I told you what I know. You're a cop, you're Sverdloff's friend, you were Valentina's friend. She mentioned you to me once," she said, and sat on the bottom stair, elbows on knees.

"What did she say?"

"Said you were okay. I have to get back to work soon."

I leaned against the railing near her. "I want to know why Valentina Sverdloff was killed."

She gave a short tough laugh. "You know what I was before?" she said.

Russians always told you what they were before, before, before the Soviet Union crumbled, before everything changed. Physicists who now sold fur coats. Linguists who drove cabs. Guys who once ran market stalls were billionaires. You went up the scale or you went down, but everything had changed. It was as if they had all migrated to a different planet. Except for old people, like my Aunt Birdie's friends. Old people stayed where they had always been; so did the poor in the country-side.

"What were you?"

She grunted a laugh.

"For a while, I was a scientist, I was educated as a scientist, and I was in forensics, and then I thought, fuck it, I'll be a cop. It doesn't matter, nothing changes, we're master and slave, the elite and the mass, the hierarchy remains," said Fetushova, "You know what it is, it's fucking Orthodox Christianity whose aim is to enslave people, Maybe my grandchildren's grandchildren will see some kind of civil society. I have three of them. You're surprised?" She reached in her brown leather bag and took out a folder, opened it, showed me her children. Two girls and a boy, good-looking young people. In the boy's arms was a baby.

"What are their names? Are they here in Moscow with you?"

No, thank God," she said, and then seemed sorry she had revealed this and stuffed the pictures back in her bag.

"You said you were a cop."

"You don't believe me? I'm not fucking kidding you, Mr Cohen. I was. So I saw everything. I see everything. It's all façade, the FSB is about money, the gangsters of the 1990s have moved sideways into it." She sucked at her cigarette. "Literally. I mean literally. I saw how the corruption worked, small, bigger, I see it now and I can't keep my mouth shut. My friends say I'm like a woman with Tourette's syndrome, you know?" She blew a harsh puff of smoke in my face. "I still have friends in the police, I have friends in the FSB, retired KGB officers. You think the spook world was a place of endlessly reflecting mirrors and no moral spine, everybody and everything up for grabs during the Cold War? Now there is only money. Everything is money."

"I believe you."

"Most of all, as a cop, I saw how they treated women. Whatever the crime, the women were culpable. Rape was a joke at the police station most of the time. I imagine it still is. It was my beat. When I got here," she gestured at the radio station, "I was still ranting, people thought I was nuts, and I was nuts, I am nuts. Valentina came to me, and I said, go the fuck away, it will get us all killed, and I'm a dead dog anyhow." From inside the studio I could hear voices, and music.

"What about this radio station?"

"They keep us on the air to show what a free society we are, we say what we want, and they let us alone partly because it's the only way the Kremlin assholes can get real information. They have a need to know, especially the big shots at the FSB.

Funny, right? They need our little station because they need a source of fact, they need us because we report things as they are. On the other hand, we could go off the air any minute, poof, but for now, we're all there is." She sucked in more smoke.

"Money? You were talking money."

"I told Valentina, she had to be careful, but it made her crazy when she discovered how many girls were being prostituted and how many officials were pocketing the cash, and the one thing you don't talk about here is their money, especially where our leader is concerned." She sneered as she said it. "I told her, but she didn't listen. She talked and talked, she thought she was impregnable, an American girl with rights. Free speech, Marina, she says, I can say what I want. We don't have free speech. Putin said so. He said Russians never had free speech."

"What happened?"

"Finally, Valentina got me to go on the air with it, to tell about deputies who keep girls at home, who offer them to foreign diplomats, one had a book of pictures, so friends could choose the beauties they liked, some of them were little, twelve, thirteen. I told only facts."

I felt bands tightened around my head.

"Valentina felt she should put herself on the line if I did. She called in to the show, gave her real name and supported me with more cases."

"My God."

"Also, Valentina had a video."

"Fuck. What did she do with it?"

"I made her give it to me, but I don't know if she made copies or put it on the Internet or sent it to somebody. A couple of top FSB guys are in it, a little girl."

"Fuck."

"Yup. Fuck is right." She smiled. Her teeth were discolored. "So you want me to give you Grisha Curtis? You plan to kill him, you want to avenge your friend, like in the novels?" She cracked another smile. "I'll put out some calls. But don't tell me what you plan to do."

I agreed.

"You don't care anymore about what happens to you, as long as you get him, isn't that right? Artie? That's what Valentina always called you."

"Yes." I took hold of her dry hand, the skin peeling. "Get me the video. Please," I said.

"You were in love with Valentina, weren't you?"

"Yes."

"She was a good girl. If I can get the bastards, it would be fine, we have nothing, no laws, no courts, no free speech. Whoever thought it would have been Yeltsin, that old fatso sot, who left the press alone? He had something. But this one." Her eyes glistened. "What the fuck, the economy is probably going down the tubes in a few months and we can all wallow in the shit together."

I started for the door.

"Take it easy," she said, her voice down a few decibels. "Your pal Sverdloff might still be alive." She shook her head. "But do this quietly. Find Curtis. You don't want somebody killing Sverdloff before you get there, if he is alive."

"Be careful," I said. "You be careful."

She snorted, rolling her eyes, pulling at her shabby green sweater that barely covered her fat belly. "Careful? You want me to find this tape for you, you want me to find this Curtis for you, and you say be careful?"

"I'll give you my numbers," I said.

"I have your number," she said, and hoisted herself off the step, went back into the radio station and closed the door.

CHAPTER FORTY-EIGHT

"Artemy Maximovich Ostalsky? Artie Cohen?"

That night, I saw the man in the blue and white jacket again. Near Pushkinskaya, he suddenly appeared. He said my name, I turned.

Compact man, medium build, with short elegantly cut white hair and light brown eyes like milk chocolate, he wore a pair of pressed khakis, a white Oxford shirt, the sleeves neatly rolled to his forearms, which were tan.

Only the loose skin around his neck and the deep lines in his face made me think he could be seventy or even more. On his feet were the Timberlands, he had the blue and white seersucker jacket over one arm—it was a hot, heavy night—and he could have passed for a well-heeled tourist strolling Moscow's main street in the early evening.

I didn't answer. I didn't know him, or want to, and before I ran into the subway, the man smiled lightly, shrugged and then walked away as if he'd made a mistake about knowing me. But he knew my Russian name.

He saw that I had heard him, that he was right, that it was my name, and then he ducked into a car waiting at the curb. I felt I was going crazy, but it's what happens to you in Russia, and after that, I saw a horse.

*

"It really was a horse," said a hooker standing in the doorway of McDonald's. "You aren't crazy," she added, munching her Big Mac. "Every night, they bring horses in from the country. People come out of bars and clubs late and they ride across the city. The gypsies bring them, and people ride, and sometimes girls wait until their men are drunk enough to buy them diamonds at all-night shopping malls, and then they put the boyfriends on the horses and watch them ride away." She looked at me and burst out laughing. "You think I'm telling you the truth?" she said. "You want to come someplace with me?"

I shook my head, and she was gone. All that was left of her was the wrapper from the burger tossed into the gutter.

I looked at my watch. It was pushing eleven. I found a cab. Heading back to the apartment, I realized where I had seen the man in the blue and white jacket who called out my name. I had seen him at the bus station when I arrrived from the airport. He had been waiting for one of the children on the airport bus. I didn't understand. I didn't have time for it, either.

At the apartment, I climbed the stairs, changed my sweat-soaked clothes, and took the rest of Larry Sverdloff's cash out of my bag. Then I packed. I put Grisha Curtis' files and my clothes in the suitcase. While I was checking my phones, messages, texts, e-mails, I heard somebody pounding at the door.

When I opened the door, I saw Igor, the caretaker, with a package in his arms.

"Yes?"

He hesitated as if working out what to say to me.

"Look."

I took the package and peeled back some of the newspaper. It was a tangle of old bones.

Taking my arm, Igor made me follow him down the stairs into the ground-floor apartment. Half of the walls were covered with marble slabs, the rest was empty and unfinished. Empty cups stained with tea littered the floor.

In the bathroom floor was a hole. It had been covered up with linoleum, and worn, turd-colored Soviet carpet, both now pushed aside in a heap. Igor pointed to the hole in the ground.

"Somebody died here," he said. "This is interesting for a historian like yourself?"

"Travel writer," I said, and turned to go back up to the apartment. But Igor wasn't finished and he followed me doggedly. He pointed to the bones.

Maybe it was the tension that made me start to laugh. I couldn't stop. Sitting on a toilet floor in Moscow beside a Russian named Igor who had produced some old bones like an offering. What else could I do except laugh? He looked at me like I was crazy.

"You think this is funny, the bones of the dead?" and crossed himself three or four times, and I pretended not to understand.

"No, not funny, never mind. What do you want?" I knew this Igor had an agenda.

Did he want some money? Did he think the bones valuable? Did he plan to call the cops and accuse me of – what? Tell somebody a weird American was occupying the top floor flat? He told me he was afraid of the bones; he said that old bones could bring terrible curses on people who did not bury them properly and asked if I would wrap them up again and find suitable burial ground.

I pushed some bills into his hand because I wanted to get rid of him. He smiled a lot now and offered me a smoke. He didn't leave though.

"Right, what else?" I said, and gave him more money.

"Somebody comes to see you!" he said. "Young guy, black hair, you know this guy?"

"What was his name?"

Igor was silent, but I knew it was Grisha Curtis. I told Igor to get lost, and he went back down the stairs. The bones, which

I saw were from a butcher shop, I put in a closet. It didn't mean anything. It was just Igor wanting money, wanting to stall and bargain before he told me about Grisha coming by.

Grisha Curtis had been here. He knew the apartment where I was staying. I started figuring how to bait Grisha Curtis, how to get him to visit me again.

He knew I was in Moscow. He knew where I was living.

Had it been a set-up? Was it the manager at Tolya's club? Willie Moffat?

I didn't care. I wanted Grisha here. I wanted him at the door. I wanted him to hunt me down in Moscow, in a bar, a restaurant, on the street. No more disguises, I thought. I'd show myself everywhere, I wanted him to see me, find me, get in my face.

When I saw Curtis, when I looked at him, I'd know if he had killed Valentina.

I couldn't wait. I figured the best way was to show myself around, try to flush him out, draw attention, get him to come for me. Come on, I thought. Come get me!

I put on my best clean shirt and the expensive shoes from London. Gun in my pocket, I went over again to Pravda222, this time as Artie Cohen.

Come on, I thought again. I'm waiting.

CHAPTER FORTY-NINE

At the front door of Pravda222, I asked if Konstantin was on. He wasn't. I asked if Sverdloff was in, and made sure the girl at the front desk knew he was my pal. Over the sound system, Frank Sinatra was singing "Come Fly With Me", in that voice that crackled with so much sexual vanity.

I knew that nearby, in the shadows of the fancy apartment buildings, there would be plenty of security. Moscow was full of big men with weapons under their jackets, who knew how to make themselves invisible, at least to tourists.

The girl at the desk, long legs, polished skin, pearly teeth, picked up the phone, smiled at me, considered the condition of her long fingernails and rings, and then smiled again, more fulsomely this time, and led me inside.

Late at night, Pravda222 was a different scene. The girls and boys who served drinks were dressed up in skinny suits by some local designer, tight jackets, narrow pants. The new Russians understood style, they had been told this endlessly by Western fashion writers. It made them preen.

"What's your name?" said a girl at the bar in perfect New York English. "Where are you from?"

"Can I buy you a drink?" I said.

"Sure."

We exchanged bullshit conversation about stuff, movies, food. The girl next to me showed me her red crocodile Hermès bag, a Birkin, she said, stroking it lightly.

"These are the little gods of Moscow," she said, and told me she had waited five years for it. She made me look at it as if it were a rare work of art. Together we inspected the skin.

She was a talkative girl. I thought she might have more to say, something I could use. I bought her a drink, I asked if I could buy her another drink and let her know I knew Tolya Sverdloff.

"Do you know this place well?" I said.

"Of course," she said.

"Do you know the owner?"

"Tolya Sverdloff? I wish," she said.

She stroked her bag like a pet. The club filled up. The girl with the bag spotted a good-looking man in a good-looking suit and lost interest in me and tripped away in his direction.

Rich Russians read all the magazines—I'd seen them in the bookstores—and they knew what to do. They looked good, even if they seemed to be in costume. The men wore linen shirts, sleeves rolled up casually, jeans, pale leather Prada loafers, no socks.

I moved to a table in the corner, back to the wall, ordered ginger ale and a salad. The couple next to me on the dark soft leather banquette were Brits and they wanted attention, they wanted to get in on things, they had heard me speak Russian to the waiter, they had seen the girl with the pearly fingernails treat me like a big shot, they wanted a piece.

"That looks rather good, actually," said the woman, peering at my salad.

"Smoked eel," I said politely.

"Yum," she said, and went on chattering, telling me an oligarch, a friend, a Russian friend, very dear, such a lovely man, not at all just about money, always helping people, had rung ahead to say they would be made welcome at the club, at Pravda222, which was the only place worth going in Moscow

he had said, their own private oligarch. Just really philan-
thropic, they had seen him at the White Nights Ball the other
week. They had seen him in St Tropez.

Nice, I said, and continued eating.

"You are?" said the woman, who was wearing tight white
jeans and a strapless top.

I told them my name was Art.

"From the States?" she said.

"New York."

"Oh, great, brilliant," she said. "We absolutely adore New
York, don't we, darling? I'm Dee, everyone calls me Dee, of
course, and this grumpy old man is Martin, my husband." She
put out her hand and touched his shirt.

The husband, Martin, who was not interested, nodded. He
was drinking cognac steadily, glancing at me, looking pissed
off while I talked to Dee.

The noise rose. The music played. The crowds swirled around
as if it were a party at somebody's house, nobody staying in
one seat at one table, but moving around, greeting, kissing,
joking.

"Let's order some fizz, darling, shall we?" said Dee and the
husband snapped his fingers for a waiter, and one of the girls
in a tight pants suit, striped, like a clown's, appeared. He ordered
a bottle of Cristal.

"Oh, darling, nobody drinks Cristal anymore. Let's have a
nice Pol Roger Rosé, make it a magnum, shall we? A nice year.
What's a nice year, darling? So there's enough for Art, here. We
love New York," she said. "We always stay at the Mercer. We
just adore it. Last month we ordered two chairs by the Campana
Brothers from Moss, for the children's room, of course, it's the
most divine shop, you must must know it, and Murray—he
owns it, of course, you know that—is the most extraordinary
man with such brilliant taste. We see him every year at Art
Basel in Miami," she said, then turned to the husband. "Can

we have some caviar, darling, the lovely stuff I like so much, darling?"

The husband grunted. The woman said to me, "Our friend Tolya who owns this club is the only one who can still get the great Beluga, you know."

She rattled on. Her braying English voice penetrated even the noise of the bar. She was very tall and very blonde and looked like a horse. I was startled when she said "Our friend Tolya".

"Tolya?" I said.

"Oh, yes, you know, that marvelous Russian chap who owns this place, and the others, New York, London, such a genius, the food and wine, the people."

"You know him well?" I said.

"Enough," she said. "Yes, of course, we've been to his wonderful house in Notting Hill, a book launch, wasn't it? Yes, for someone we know a bit. "

"You've been to his club in London?"

"She couldn't get in," said the husband. "That's how connected she is, that's how much she knows. She was like a little puppy at the entrance, oh, we know everybody, please can I come in," he added in a mocking voice.

"Fuck you," she said. "I got us in here, didn't I? It was only because darling Tolya wasn't there. He'd be so incredibly upset to know we hadn't got in. I mean, here we are. I wonder if Tolya will be here tonight? I think he's actually rather a late-night person."

My head hurt. Too many bars, too much to drink, here, New York, London.

The champagne arrived, and the husband refused it and continued drinking cognac, so I shared it with the wife. We drank. Dee moved closer to me. Wiggled around in her jeans and the little strapless top.

I tried not to laugh, but it didn't matter. She didn't notice. The husband looked furious and gloomy and he was drinking more seriously. Sinatra sang. Dee sang along. I watched the crowd, looking for Grisha Curtis, looking for Tolya.

Suddenly, a stream of invective came out of Martin's mouth and I looked over and saw he'd spilled his drink down the front of his white linen shirt. He got up, leaned down and grabbed his wife's arm.

"We're going," he said. "We're fucking getting out of here, that is if you're finished with your American." He said the word American as if it were a curse.

She pulled away.

He held tight on to her wrist. Her long horsey face pinched up in pain.

"Let go," I said.

"Fuck off," he said.

All around I could hear people talking about us in Russian. Americans, Brits, they said, terrible manners, didn't know how to behave. Through a fog, I could hear them speaking Russian, I could hear somebody talk about calling the cops. I was pretty drunk myself, but then I saw Dee's face.

She was in pain. Her bastard of a husband was holding her wrist so tight, I thought he might break it. So I socked him. Hard.

I had held in too much, I didn't know if I wanted to draw attention to myself, maybe flush out Grisha, or if it was pent-up rage, but I punched him again. He teetered backwards, grabbed hold of a small table, pulled it down and crashed to the floor. He didn't move.

"Thanks," said Dee. "I was sick to bloody death of his carry-on. He thinks he owns the planet because he's in business with a few bloody Russians, and he can behave like the pig he is." She went over and crouched beside him, and shook him.

I didn't wait to find out how he was, I made for the door, but I was shaking, and before I got outside, somebody had grabbed me.

"We've called the police," said the doorman. He held on to my arm. "Sit," he said. Already I could hear the sirens in the distance. I tried to get away and the doorman punched me, and that was it. It was over. The cops were coming for me, and I'd given my real name, I had wanted to attract attention, to get Grisha Curtis to come after me. I got it.

Now I was a sitting duck. Sitting bird, Tolya always said, one of his rare goofs in English, and I had never known if it was on purpose or not. Somewhere I heard Tony Bennett singing "The Best Is Yet To Come", and I was hurting enough I couldn't even get it up for some irony.

The doorman yanked my arm so hard, I winced and wanted to cry, but I kept it back. I hit back. I was in Moscow, I had punched out a tourist and a local, I was fucked.

CHAPTER FIFTY

"You look like shit."

When I came to, my head felt like it was cracking, like it was inside a nutcracker, and somebody was talking at me.

I squinted through my bruised eyes and saw I was in a small apartment, lying on a couch, a mattress on the floor was made up neatly with a striped Indian bedspread, the shelves full of CDs and DVDs, a table, two chairs. I sat up. Sitting cross-legged on the mattress was a guy in gray sweatpants, a white shirt and socks. Hanging from a hook in a plastic dry-cleaning bag was a police uniform.

"Who the hell are you?" I said to the man. "Arkady Renko? Where am I?" I got up. "Fuck, my head hurts."

"Drink your tea," the man said, and I saw there was a mug of green tea on a little table next to the couch. "Drink," he said in Russian. "You need the doctor."

"Are you a policeman?"

"Sure. Sometimes," he said. "I do many things."

He crossed the room to the table, sat on a chair, opened his cellphone. He was short and big, chest like a weightlifter, waist whittled down, and he moved as if he understood his body and was aware other people would understand it.

His shirtsleeves were folded up high on his arms, which were sculpted, veins standing up on them, and while he talked, he flexed one, watching it as if it were alive. His face, though, was an intellectual's, he had thoughtful eyes, and he was going bald. On a leather thong around his neck he wore a pendant the shape of a peace symbol.

"Artie Cohen?" he said to me as if to confirm, not to question. Without waiting for an answer, he said, "I am Leven, Viktor. The cousin of Boris, whom you call Bobo."

"Bobo told you I was in Moscow?"

"He says to please keep my eye peeled out for you," said Viktor, who was about forty. He handed me a glass of apple juice and some aspirin and told me his father and Bobo's were brothers, his father the elder. "My cousin asks if you need help," he said.

He produced a picture of the two cousins. "I am Viktor, and you are in very deep shit," he added, in Russian now, "You understand?"

I nodded. "You have coffee?"

"I'll make coffee," he said, got up with one agile bounce and went into a tiny kitchen and came back with a mug of black coffee, instant, barely hot, in his hand. He'd made it under the tap.

"Drink it," he said.

"What happened?"

"You went to the club Pravda222, twice at least, and using two different names, the name of Max Fielding and your own name of Artie Cohen, which is the name by which I know you."

He spoke very precise English as if he had learned it from a language study tape or from a BBC radio program. He took pains to use the definite article which, of course, doesn't exist in Russian and he used it so often it was stilted, comic even. I answered him in English so that he would not be insulted.

Viktor sat down on the mattress again, and crossed his legs in some crazy yoga position. He leaned back and switched on a CD player. George Harrison. "Here Comes The Sun" played.

"It calms me down," said Viktor. "Never the fuck mind. Listen to me, it is not a good idea to try killing people here. You understand me?"

"I wasn't trying to kill anyone."

"So now everybody knows you're here, everyone, they know you came in without a proper visa, and that you called yourself Max Fielding, and pretended to be some kind of travel fucking writer," he said. "They know who you are."

"I want them to know, and who the fuck are *they* anyhow?"

"I think you need a doctor," said Viktor. "The cut on your mouth looks like shit."

"How did you know where to find me?"

"Artemy, excuse me, but if you spend three years in the fucking Russian army it's not so hard to find one American like you in Moscow. Anyhow, my cousin Boris told me to watch out for you. He says to me, watch out for this guy who can be one fucking asshole, but he's a good cop, okay? He says he works this terrible case of Valentina Sverdloff, daughter of Anatoly, and he stays with it, and he knows you'll come here, so I watch for you. I watch you, I see you go to Marina Fetushova, who I also know, and I think: he's a crazy fucker. This is really dangerous. Naturally, I figure you will show at Pravda222, so I hang there, though it costs me a fucking arm and two legs. So I say to my cousin Boris, Borya, you owe me a lot. "

My mouth hurt. Somebody had punched me plenty hard. I could taste dried blood.

"What happened to me?"

"Before the cops came to the club, you had a little fight with the doorman who is aided by some of his pals. They told you you should fuck off out of Russia."

"Jesus."

"You shouldn't carry a gun in Moscow, you know, not a crappy illegal, how did they call them, six-shooter? Makes you look like a tourist," said Viktor. "Carry a knife if you have to put something in your holster," he added, laughing at his joke.

"What do you need, Artemy Maximovich?" he said, finally. "How can I help you?"

I drank the sludge in the coffee mug. I didn't know if I could trust him, either. No firm ground. Like Tolya had said, no traction anywhere. But he looked okay, and he was related to Bobo.

While I drank the coffee, he told me he had been a soldier, fought in Chechnya, which meant he got beat up plenty, being a Jew in the Russian army. Full of shrapnel, he had returned to Moscow. He could make decent money doing security, he said. One of his three daughters attended school in England, in Brighton by the sea. I knew there was more he didn't tell me.

"What else?" I said.

"You've been all the fuck over Moscow," said Viktor in Russian. "Cafes, restaurants, every place, and then you show up at Pravda222 last night and then you punch out a guy who, thank God, was only an Englishman, and currently we Russians formally fucking speaking, applaud people who mess up on the English, but we have to keep a fucking façade, man, and he's an Englishman with connections, an Englishman who was invited by certain kinds of people including one tiny oligarch, not a big one, I grant you, but big enough, and is also rich and connected himself, if an asshole. You think London stops at the border? This British guy is a lawyer, he works for Russians."

I liked him. For one thing, he could laugh, a deep belly laugh that rose up from his middle, and made him cry from laughing. Jokes, the only thing that saves us, said Viktor, and then we tossed around a few jokes, and laughed about the really bad Russian gangster films that were coming out. I wanted Viktor for a friend.

"I have to find Tolya Sverdloff," I said.

"Mr Anatoly Sverdloff has made too much noise," said Viktor. "I think the death of his daughter has made him crazy, which I understand. I would be the same," he added.

"What kind of noise?"

"He will now do anything to get back at people who killed his daughter. He says she was poisoned with polonium-210. This makes people paranoid."

"Who?"

"Everybody. The FSB says the British killed Litvinenko, others that it was Russian friends of Litvinenko in London. There is also talk of provocation, nothing has any reality anymore, just like Soviet times, you know? No firm ground. None," said Viktor.

"Listen, man, I'm a New York cop, I just want the creep who killed my friend's daughter, and I want to know where the fuck he is. No politics, okay? I'm grateful to you, but let's just skip the political discussion."

"Everything is politics," said Viktor, who tossed the butt of his cigarette into a yellow cup where it sizzled in the dregs of the coffee. "Once upon a time, I would have saved the remains of this cigarette."

"Do you know where Sverdloff is?"

"Nothing is sure."

"There's somebody else," I said, and described Grisha Curtis and saw a flicker of fear scurry across Viktor's round face, like a mouse looking for food where there wasn't any.

"You're in big trouble," he said. "You're playing with guys who are very, very connected. Get a little rest and I'll make some calls."

"No."

"Listen to me, they got hold of you at the club, they beat you up, next time they'll cut your tongue out, or kill you, okay? Or if it isn't the creeps, you'll disappear into the official pit where nobody climbs out, they know about you, they know the New York police have been looking at you for Valentina's murder, that your prints were everywhere in her apartment, they know everything about you, that you came to Moscow before, you're fully recorded in the files, you're on the list."

"What?"

"You grew up here, they know this, they know you came back to Moscow in the early 1990s."

I put my hand in my pocket.

"The cash is here," said Viktor, and handed me the pile of money. "You're lucky as a girl with big tits that nobody took it off you," he added. "But, then, we're not all just about the money, hard as it may be for you to believe."

"You sound like Bobo," I said. "I have to get up."

"Sleep," said Viktor, and gestured to the mattress and brought a blanket and said he'd be back before it was light.

I couldn't keep my eyes open. Before I crashed, I wondered if there had been anything in the coffee.

George Harrison seeped into my sleep. I opened my eyes.

"What time is it?"

Viktor, sitting on one of the chairs, was watching me while I tried to wake up. He looked at his watch.

"Five past eleven."

"In the morning?"

"Yes."

"The guy's dead? The British dick?"

"No, sadly, the fool is fine. His wife liked you, he took a poke at you, and you socked him. Nobody is bringing charges, but nobody wants you hanging around Moscow either, so tell me what you need and let's get it done and let's get you out of here."

"Why are you doing this?"

"For Bobo, for our family, or as you say, whatever."

"You knew about Valentina?"

"This poor girl found out too late she had a boyfriend who was a little bit of a fascist."

"Grisha Curtis?"

"You met him?"

"Only at a party in London. For a minute. You know where he is?"

"I've heard rumors."

"I need your help," I said finally. "I think if we can find Sverdloff, we can find Curtis. Or the other way around."

"Sverdloff is most important, yes?"

"Yes."

"Take a shower. I made soup. There's a clinic we could try, I made some phone calls while you were sleeping. We have to go fast, people are asking about you," he said, and sent me into what passed for his bathroom where I took a shower under a tepid drizzle of water, and borrowed a clean t-shirt from him.

He made me eat the whole bowl of borscht and some bread and cheese, and then he drove us in his second-hand blue VW to a fancy clinic near the river.

All the way, he played Indian music. It drove me out of my skull, but I kept quiet. Viktor knew what he was doing.

The clinic was all glass and steel. Gorgeous women in starched white dresses and little caps on their hair were the nurses, though they looked more like Playboy models. In a sunroom with a huge flatscreen TV on the wall, patients looked well fed. The doctor, wearing Zegna from head to toe, was impatient.

"Look again," said Viktor, showing him Tolya's picture.

"Yes," he said.

"Yes, what?"

"I think he was here. I'm not sure," said the doctor, who was eager to get away.

"What did he have?"

The doctor called out to one of the costumed nurses and handed her the picture, told her to look up the records, made a gesture that indicated she was not to tell us too much. Said he was busy, gave us an engraved business card, mentioned we could make an appointment. He shook our hands, looked at his Rolex, and disappeared with that self-important stride only doctors and lawyers have, the kind that lets you know they are busier than you can imagine, and important and have great big balls.

After the nurse pretended to look through some files on her new Mac, she took Tolya's picture in her hand.

"I don't have anything on him," she said. "I remember him. He told jokes, but he was very ill. I have a feeling it was his heart. He didn't stay long enough." She inspected a calendar. "Monday night. The 14th. I told him he must stay in the hospital, but he just wanted pills. He said he would come back. He never came."

"You gave him the pills?"

"I'm not sure," she said. "Perhaps you'll wait until the doctor is free again?"

"Sverdloff didn't leave an address, a contact?"

"Nothing."

"Ravi Shankar. A genius," said Viktor, nodding at his iPod that was plugged into the car. "I love the sitar."

"I have to find Sverdloff."

"Listen to me, you have to pay attention, you have to be careful, you think like an American, but this place is not normal anymore, this is a police state, this is only one guy who is running things, and you have to pay attention." Viktor said it so quietly I could hardly hear him.

"Why do you tell me all this?"

"My cousin Bobo tells me I should say these things to you. I should help you. You help him, you help the family."

"I want the boy," I said. "I want Grisha. I think Tolya Sverdloff came here to look for him. I think maybe Tolya already found him. He followed me to the place I was staying, maybe to the club, on the street, and then he went away."

"You think Mr Grisha has gone to be with Marx as we used to say? You don't think he's already dead?"

"Who do you really work for?"

"This one, that one. I was a soldier, I told you. For a while I was a detective also, like Bobo. I'm freelance. Some of the time I help with joint terrorist things, even your friend from Wyoming. Bodyguard, too, for money. This and that. I keep telling you. You have some idea, yes?"

"Roy Pettus?"

"He's okay," said Viktor.

"Yeah."

"What's your idea?"

"I need to go somewhere by myself. One hour. Look, there are some bodies I heard about, dumped out by a place you don't need to see. One might be Grisha Curtis. I have a friend who's a homicide cop."

"One hour."

"I'll take you to my place. You can wait there. Don't go back to your apartment. Don't go out. Please, this is serious, you'll get in trouble, you'll get me in trouble, you'll get people killed if you don't listen. I'll get your stuff from the apartment, if you want."

"You know where I'm staying?"

"Sure."

"You knew as soon as I got here?"

"Stay here," he said as he pulled up in front of his building. "Pray one of our bodies is Curtis. You have contacts with anyone here?"

"Who would I have contacts with?"

"Cops? Journalists other than Fetushova? Friends? Old friends?"

"Not anymore," I said.

"Family?"

"Dead."

"Friends of family?"

"Also dead. What the fuck are you asking for?"

"Children of friends of family, parents?"

"I don't know. Maybe."

"Okay, so think."

"Just fucking tell me what you want to know."

"FSB," he said in a low voice.

"I don't know these bastards."

"KGB."

I said I knew what the fucking FSB was, and that it used to be the KGB, and how the fuck would I know anybody in it?

"Your father."

"He's been dead a long time."

"They like the families, the children, you have heritage, they'll talk to you. Sooner or later somebody will remember your father and say, what about him, what about the son, he's one of us."

"Jesus Christ."

"In this country, even according to my pious Christian friends, Christ is dead," said Viktor, picking up his car keys.

CHAPTER FIFTY-ONE

I didn't wait for Viktor Leven. I had an idea I had to get going. Maybe I was already too late.

At Moffat's place, I looked for Igor the caretaker. He was out. I went into his hutch and then into the half-built apartment. Upstairs I looked for the bones. They were gone. So were Willie Moffat's golf clubs. Maybe Igor had gone to sell them both.

I had come back to the apartment to get a few of my things, and lock the place up so Moffat didn't come home and find everything gone. As soon as I got inside I knew somebody had been there, looking for me, searching through my stuff, papers, a notebook, but nothing else. Everything else was in place: TV, desktop computer, espresso machine. It wasn't a thief. It wasn't Igor.

I locked up, left a note for Moffat, pushed the keys under the door, went out to look for a taxi. I could have taken Moffat's car, but it was too risky. Traffic cops were on the make all over Moscow. They stopped you. They asked for money. I was guessing it was the reason nothing had been done about the traffic. Maybe the traffic cops' union put up a fight. Maybe it was the only way they could feed their kids. I didn't want to drive another guy's car, not now.

My phone rang. A familiar voice was on the other end, but the line was blurry. I couldn't make out who it was, and then the line went dead. I had my clothes and papers in my carry-on, I didn't know where the hell I was going, but I wasn't coming back here. I had cash, and I had the gun. Viktor Leven never took it off me.

I flagged down a cab. I made a deal with the driver for the trip out to the country, twenty kilometers, give or take, and he was willing, glad of the work, a chubby little cheerful Georgian with two teeth missing, who told me he loved Americans and for me he would make a deal. We did it in sign language, and the couple of words of Russian I admitted I knew.

I kept up the idea that I didn't speak Russian much and that I was just a tourist, at least for a while, and then I gave it up.

From the rear-view mirror hung a little Georgian flag. I felt okay in his car. Georgians disliked the Russians plenty. There was going to be trouble, he said. South Ossieta, Russian army, the whole thing was going to blow up, and soon.

"What were you?"

"I was a history teacher," he said. "I need the money," he added, half turning to look at me.

I asked him to take me to Nikolina Gora, a village out in the Moscow countryside. He asked where exactly. I said I was looking for someone, I'd let him know.

His name was Eduard, and he was a shrewd guy. He said, if I was looking for information around Barvika, the town you came to before you got to Nikolina Gora, he would call his sister who cleaned houses nearby and heard all the gossip. It was all a Georgian girl with a dark complexion could get around Moscow. She cleans their fucking toilets, he said. I said, call her. He put his foot on the gas.

He got on his cell, he called his sister and they gabbled away for twenty minutes while we sat in traffic. I understood the sister had agreed to meet us. Eduard turned the radio up.

It was a hot windy day, sky sludge-colored, dust swirling across the windows of the crummy taxi, no air conditioning. From behind I could see the sweat streaming down my Georgian's neck. He wiped it with a paper towel.

You think of Moscow as a winter city, its ugliness and sprawl disguised. In summer, you see it as it is. I remembered the summers now, dusty, everyone jamming into cars or on a train or a bus to get out of town.

I rolled down the window as we headed out of town on the highway, and Eduard chattered away, mostly in Russian, trying out his English and sign language, half turned towards me and grinning like a fool. I figured we were going to crash.

It was a long time since I'd come out here, the last time to Sverdloff's parents' dacha in Nikolina Gora.

The Rublevo-Uspenskoye highway was always the best road in the entire country, all eleven time zones of it. Big-time creeps had their official country houses out this way, right back to Stalin. Even now, where once the ZiL sirens blared, there were big Mercs and Range Rovers.

At the end of the turnoff to Putin's place were two cop cars.

The driver mentioned Putin as if spitting and showed me his rough hand, thumb down.

He talked on and on, pointing out the building sites at the side of the road. He pulled over and invited me to join him in the front seat.

Under the seat, he had a bottle of Georgian wine, which was illegal in Moscow, more or less, the bastards have put a levy on it, he said. No love lost. Hates the fucking Russkis. Ed, he said I should call him, Ed, you say in West.

He passed me the bottle. I drank some of the thick heavy red. He drank. We toasted Georgia.

Out here, ten, fifteen miles from the center of Moscow where I remembered only countryside, huge stands of trees had been replaced by billboards and gated communities and shopping malls and ugly McMansions. You could hear the birds twitter and smell the exhaust as big cars slammed down the country road.

"Pricks," said Ed. "Bastards. All. All same."

We passed the billboards: German dental centers, Meissen china, Princess cruises, real estate, spas, all the billboards pushing capitalist pleasures.

Ed, who had worked as a tour guide for Georgians up to see Moscow, was in full flow, holding forth on the origins of the dacha, knocking back gulps of red wine.

Everybody has a dacha, said Ed, even workers and poor slobs, everybody has a little patch of land. The dacha meant escape.

My own parents had had a dacha for a while when my father was in the KGB, a cottage a few miles further out in the countryside. My father took me fishing, I swam in the river, friends came to eat.

Best of all, there was a huge Grundig radio my father had somehow managed to acquire. In those days there were only official radios and radio stations, nothing you wanted to listen to.

A foreign radio on which you could listen to foreign stations was an immense prize, only available to the privileged. Antennae sprouted from cottages all over the countryside.

My mother listened for news from Europe, my father, and his best friend, Gennadi—the man I called Uncle Gennadi—to jazz. Teenagers fiddled with the knobs on their parents' radios, trying to get the BBC and the Beatles.

I knew all about the life in dachas outside Moscow, and it came back to me so powerfully I had to shake myself out of the memories.

"Luxury mall," said Ed, and points out the window, then pulls up. "Come with me. Look, see what the new world has brought to us, here we are, a capitalist country with a peasant's soul." He looked around. "It's to keep the wives busy shopping and away from Moscow, so men can be with their mistresses."

The mall was exquisite, all sleek wood and glass, more Milan than Moscow. Every label in this label-mad country was here: Gucci, Bulgari, Graf, Bentley, Prada, Zegna, Armani, Ralph Lauren. But it was like Alphaville, empty, devoid of life, dystopic. Ed understood this.

"Everything is façade now," he said, leading me to the far end of the mall where, in a Lada, a woman was waiting.

Ed's sister was a small pretty women, about fifty, who got out of the battered car, embraced her brother, and said to me, "How can I help you?"

I asked her if she knew the way to a certain dacha in Nikolina Gora, and she got on her cellphone, made a few calls, and told me her husband's cousin had worked nearby and would call Eduard with directions. She climbed in her car, and, waving, drove away.

Then, without warning, Eddie hustled me back in the car, and pulled back on the road, going at the legal speed. The police car he said he had seen didn't stop us. I never noticed it. I was losing my focus.

"Russian cops," Ed said, and spat.

When Ed got the call from his brother-in-law's cousin, he found the right road to the dacha I was looking for. He gave me his cell number. I offered him extra money. He refused.

Georgians loved America, he told me sincerely, and he hoped we would remain eternal friends. We shook hands, and then he left me at the junction where the main road joined a dirt path to the Sverdloff place.

It was getting dark now, the sky purple with rain clouds. I started up the path. I could see the house clearly.

The garden sloped down to a stream that fed the river, but it was overgrown, weeds had pushed up through the grass. The hydrangea bushes, neon blue in the evening light, were in bloom. Fireflies glittered everywhere.

I had been here once before in the summer, a long time ago. Under an immense tree in the garden was an old trestle table where we had eaten dinner, me, Tolya, his parents, his cousin, Svetlana.

The dinner table had been surrounded by friends of the Sverdloffs, writers, artists.

Tolya's father, almost as big as his son, sang songs from *Oklahoma!* I remembered the physicist who told me the truth about red mercury. Most of all, I remembered Svetlana in her white skirt and blouse and a bright red shawl. I loved her. The next day, because of me, she was dead. A car bomb went off in her car. Meant for me.

Svetlana had been the beginning, it was Svetlana I saw in Valentina, at least a little. I realized that now.

From the woods behind the house I could hear cicadas. Could hear the stream. At first I didn't hear anything else. Then I heard the flick of a lighter, the sound of somebody lighting a cigarette. Soft footsteps fell on the path. I walked a few more yards, and I saw her.

Near the front gate was a silver bike, a girl leaning against it, looking at the house. It was all I could do to keep from crying. Valentina? Valentina! My God!

She was there, wearing her skinny white jeans and a little black top, her hair was short, dark red, and she was walking slowly, smoking a cigarette on her way to her grandparents' house.

PART SIX

CHAPTER FIFTY-TWO

I watched as Valentina Sverdloff strolled to the gate of her grandparents' house. Half in a trance, I followed her. I had seen her in New York on her own bed, had felt for her pulse.

That day, I had sat beside her, held her cold hand, absorbed, after a while—I never knew how long—that she was dead.

She was dead, and after they took her away, the ME had cut her up and stitched her back together on a metal slab. Bobo Leven had told me. Tolya had told me. I had read the report.

Russia, this fucking country, I thought. A country that makes you see things, makes you believe in shit that doesn't exist, in ghosts. It was all I could think. I'd left it the first time when I was a kid, only sixteen. I'd come back once, got sucked in, gone away, swore I'd never come back. Never again. It did weird things to you, every part of you.

I knew that Val was dead. Again I pictured her on her bed, saw myself lean down and put my mouth in front of hers. No breath had come out. No breath, no pulse, nothing. In New York she had been dead.

But she was here in this strange evening light, in front of me, tall, lanky, hair ruffled by the breeze, wearing the white jeans, swinging her arms, back to me, smoking a cigarette and almost at the gates of the old Sverdloff dacha. I put down my bag and started to run.

"Val?" I shouted, stumbling on a tangle of uncut grass. Valentina?

Even saying it made gooseflesh run up my arms. I pulled on my jacket. I'd been carrying it, and I put it on and zipped it up and fumbled in the pocket for cigarettes. Val, darling?

"Artie, right?"

"Yes."

She had turned around and was coming towards me, still smoking. Now she tossed her cigarette on the stone path and crushed it under her red sneaker.

"You don't recognize me, do you? I met you a while back. I'm Valentina's sister. Her twin. You remember? Maria. Everybody calls me Molly."

They were identical twins, but only in looks. Different voices.

"You know he's dead, don't you?" she said.

Tolya was dead.

I wasn't sure I could stand this. For a second, I was so dizzy I had to lean against the garden wall. What would I do without him?

"Ask me, I'm glad Grisha is dead, you know," said Molly. "I never liked him. He was bad, every which way, he was a shit."

"Grisha Curtis?"

"Who did you think I meant?"

"It doesn't matter. How?"

"I don't know. Somebody said he was drugged, somebody said a knife, other people thought he was strangled. This is Russia, Artie. Somebody will find out, I don't care, I'm glad!"

"When did you hear?"

"Yesterday. They all gossip, like crazy," Molly said. "I'm staying over at my mom's dacha about a mile away. Over in Barvika. Grisha's uncle has a place. Somebody found him in the woods, it's all I know. And everybody was excited because there were police around, that kind of shit."

"You're sure?"

"Sure. You need a cigarette or something?"

"Yeah," I said, taking the pack Molly offered. "Thank you. Of course I remember you."

"Val probably told you I was the good girl, the one who fit in, even in Florida, I dated boys who played football, I liked to shop, I was student president. You know my best friend in junior high was a little Russian tennis player from Almaty. When she lost some junior tournament, she killed herself. I decided I hated Russians right then." Molly lit up, offered me her lighter.

Her hair was reddish brown, bangs over her forehead. A canvas bag was thrown over her shoulder. There was a wooden bench outside the dacha gates, and she sat on it. I sat next to her.

"He killed her, you know?" said Molly. "The bastard killed my lovely sister, he murdered her."

"Grisha? You know that?"

"Yes."

"How do you know?"

"I saw him," she said. "I saw him in Moscow a few days ago and he looked at me, and I could see he was terrified, as if he thought I was Val. I tried to find him again, but I couldn't. He's only met me a few times. I felt it. Twins feel things about each other. Did he?"

"I think so. Tell me what you know about him."

"I met him a couple times."

"What?"

"I met him in London last summer. He was very good-looking in a sort of spooky sci-fi way, you know? Very, very handsome, carved features, always smiling, great smile, good low voice, and funny, well, sort of funny," said Molly. "I met Grisha's mother at that sad little wedding in London. Val was all lit up. I think for the first time, just plain in love. Regular old-fashioned love and sex and somebody your own age, a nice good boy you were going to be with forever. She was a different kind of girl, but she had that in common with all of us."

"Go on."

"Val always liked older guys, rougher, smarter, remember Jack Santiago? She liked interesting people, which got her into trouble, she didn't have real good pitch for emotional stuff. So at first I thought, wow, about fucking time Val met a regular guy, a nice guy, her age. But she was coy about Greg, or Grisha, or whatever the fuck he was called, I think she was shy, she told me to keep it to myself. My poor mom, Christ, she didn't even know Val got married. I had to tell her after Val died."

"What else?"

"Something went wrong between Grisha and Valentina the last few months, and then she was dead. My father went off his rocker. I went to her place and looked for all her diaries and stuff, but most of it was gone."

"I was there."

"Where?'

"In her apartment. Her stuff was all there, everything, her pictures, clothes, everything."

"After she was murdered?" Molly said.

"Yes. So somebody was in there not long afterwards."

"It was him."

"Why did you come to Russia?"

"Like I said, our mom has a place not far away. She said she had to come here, she said she had to come to Russia, to her dacha, she's half out of her skull because of Val, and because Dad went to New York to get her and bring her body back, apparently Val told him once she wanted to be with her grandparents in the cemetery, and I'm thinking, he's out of his mind," Molly added. "But I could imagine Val wanting it, for a while she became obsessed with Russia. We kind of stopped talking a lot, we were in different places," she said. "Oh, shit, Artie, why did I make her feel bad?"

"No, she also loved New York. You didn't make her feel bad."

"I told her the Russian stuff was bullshit. Maybe it was because I always knew our dad preferred her. He never said or showed it, I just knew, they were connected in a different way."

"I understand."

"Thanks. Listen, I have to take my mom to New York. We don't know if Daddy is ever coming. We're leaving in the morning. But I wanted to see this place. I rode my bike over," she said, pointing to the bicycle parked against the fence. "I don't care about any of this Russian crap, you know, and the old house, our grandparents? It gives me the creeps. Daddy gave us the house, I told Val she could have my half. She said okay, but first we had to visit together, so we planned it for this summer." She tossed her cigarette on the ground. "I miss her so bad, Artie."

"Was she going to live here?"

"I think Val wanted to make it a country retreat for her kids."

"Kids?"

"The girls she took care of. I don't know what to do with it now."

"Where's your father?"

"I don't know that either. We've only been here a few days. We were waiting for him. I think all that happens in this country is you get sucked in like quicksand and you can never get out. I hate it. It killed Val, and maybe it killed my dad. Fuck Russia, you know?" Her tone was defiant but her eyes were full of tears.

"When did you talk to him, to Tolya?"

"Over a week? Sunday? Maybe Monday. He was in London. He promised to come. He said, I'll meet you. Wait for me. I'm still waiting. I called somebody in New York. Val's body is still there."

"You knew about Val when?"

"From my mom."

I thought of something, "Do you ride a red Vespa?" I asked.

"Yes, why?"

"Somebody saw you on it not long before Val was murdered."

"I brought it to the city, to New York. I was intending to give it to Val for a present, because I needed a car in Boston. I didn't go right over to her place, I just rode around and saw friends, and I went out that night. My God, she was still alive while I was riding that fucking scooter, and I was too late after that. Somebody thought I was Val, is that right?"

"Yes."

"I could have saved her."

"No. Grisha killed her."

"I'm glad the bastard is dead. Over in Barvika, they're all talking about it, boo hoo. I bet he fucked every one of those stupid girls. All they want is to marry an oligarch," said Molly. "I'm glad he's dead." I'm really glad you're here. My dad always talks about you, like all the time. Like you would know how to deal with this kind of shit. He said if I was ever in trouble, and he was away, I should call you."

I took a cigarette from her and we lit up and smoked for a few seconds in silence.

"We need to go inside the house," I said finally.

"You think he's here?" She glanced at the house where the windows were dark. "Maybe he's hiding from somebody," she said. "I need him to be here now," she said. "I'm scared to go in."

"Why?"

"I think I'll find him in there. You know, not alive."

"Why would he be hiding, who from?"

"It's the elephant in the room, isn't it Artie?"

"Yeah."

"If Daddy knew Grisha killed my sister, what would he do?"

said Molly. "He's not like other people's dads, you know? This is what we're not saying, that if he found Grisha, that would be it. And then they'd get my dad, too, they'd put him away for murder."

The light was fading, Russia closing in on us. I moved towards the house.

"Molly, look, I should tell you, just in case, I have a gun. I just don't want to freak you out. Okay?"

She smiled.

"Oh, Artie, honey, I grew up in Florida, I'm like from America, from real America, from Florida where they fuck with the elections and everybody has guns," she said. "It's the American religion, you know that. My mother has a gun, for Pete's sake, honey." Molly had a slight Southern accent, and the sweet look of somebody who had been happy most of her life. She was a nice girl.

One hand in Molly's, we went through the high gates, which were unlocked, then we stumbled through the weeds to the house.

The front door was locked. It had glass panes in the top half, and one was broken. I pushed it, and it fell in. I managed to push another one of the panes in too, and I heard it shatter lightly on wide planks inside the house.

It was very quiet. I listened to the house through the broken window. I couldn't hear anything except a faint creaking noise, maybe a breeze, or a rat. Mice. Nobody was here. Sverdloff wasn't here. Was he? It was a big house, two storeys. I listened some more.

"Let's go," said Molly. "Come on."

I reached through the broken glass and found the doorknob, and turned it. The door opened and together we went inside the house.

CHAPTER FIFTY-THREE

Like a dog uncertain of what it was hearing, I stood in the doorway. Molly tried to go ahead. I tried to stop her, I put my arm out, but she went in anyway. She had a little flashlight in her purse. She turned it on and it made a narrow cone of light in the dark house. The old wide oak planks creaked under her feet.

"Molly?"

"Just wait, Artie," she said, and I lost sight of her as she moved through the square hallway into the living room. "Wait," she said, her voice echoing back at me. "Wait."

I could hear her walking away after that, into the house. Her cell phone went off. She talked to it in a whisper and I couldn't hear the words. I stood still and smelled the dust.

In the distance I saw a fluttering light, then I saw two. There are no ghosts, I told myself, except in the minds of Russians. But not in the real world.

I was beginning to hallucinate. Things swayed with the unreality of this candlelit world. Voices talked into my ear. My hand was ice cold on the metal of my gun. I held it in front of me. I watched the lights.

"You look like you saw something," said Molly, reappearing. "Like you saw a spook," she added, holding a couple of candles she had lit. "You okay?" In this light I saw how young she looked, much younger than Valentina had ever seemed.

"Come on," I said, and we went through the house, one room at a time, looking for something. Anything. I thought I could smell Sverdloff's aftershave, his cologne, the special scent he had made up for him in Florence in a medieval building on the Arno, he always said. It smelled of grapefruit. It arrived in New York in elaborate packages which contained the cologne in crystal bottles with carved gold stoppers. He had given me a bottle of it for a birthday.

"You smell him, don't you?" said Molly.

"Yeah."

"Me too. He always wore that stuff his friend Lorenzo made for him. He tried to get me to wear it. He was here, wasn't he, Artie? He was in this house." She spoke calmly, like a young doctor discussing the possibilities of a fatal disease.

"Yes."

We moved through the rooms together, Molly with her candles.

Most of the furniture had been covered with dustsheets. One of the windows in the main room with its old beamed ceilings was broken, and a bird had left its nest in a corner of the room, high up, under the sloping roof.

In the kitchen, Molly put the candles on the long trestle table, a film of summer dust covering it, a huge tureen in the middle, the old copper samovar on a side table.

Everything the way I remembered it, but suspended in another time, unused now, empty, dusty. Except for the Grape Nuts. At one end of the table was a box of Grape Nuts, and an espresso pot, and a little empty blue tin that had contained caviar.

Molly picked up the pot, and made a face.

"There's still coffee in here."

The table looked as if somebody had left in the middle of breakfast. A cup was overturned, a napkin dropped on the floor.

"Only my dad eats Grape Nuts. He's crazy for them. He always takes them with him. And caviar." She picked up the little blue tin. "He's so weird, he buys wine for a grand a bottle and drinks it like Coke, but he won't travel without a box of Grape Nuts for breakfast, then he'll have eggs with caviar, you know? Crazy asshole," said Molly, smiling and then bursting into tears. "Where *is* he?"

"You okay here for a minute? I want to look around," I said, after a while, and she nodded.

I left her one of the candles, took the other, and she looked at me and giggled.

"What?"

"You look like some kind of weird phantom, the gun in one hand, the candle in the other. God, Artie, where is he?" She lit a cigarette, and tossed the match in the empty cereal bowl.

"Don't," I said.

"Evidence?" she asked, taking it out of the bowl.

"I guess."

"I was thinking of doing forensics anyhow," she said. "Med school. I'm not going to be any good with people that are alive, you know," said Molly.

"Yell if you need me," I said, and went towards the study and music room that had been Tolya's father's domain.

All the time I could smell Tolya. He had been here. He had been here, but he was gone, unless there was something upstairs. I was hallucinating. From the kitchen I heard Molly singing an old Beatles tune.

"Hey Jude", she sang to herself off key.

In the study, the walls were still jammed with books, books to the ceiling, new and old, in four languages. Records, old LPs were on other shelves.

There was a broken leather sofa under the windows. A big old-fashioned desk was on the other side of the room and above it was a portrait of Tolya's mother.

I sat at the desk. There must be a caretaker or the house

would have been stripped clean. Theft in the countryside had turned into big business. And Russians, like the Brits, once they had the dough, wanted a country life where they could pretend they were gentry. Or intellectuals. Or aristocrats. Or something they had never been and never would be. They could get the trappings. Books and furniture like Sverdloff's could be cleaned up and sold for a bundle.

The leather-topped desk was scarred but there was no dust. Somebody had been cleaning up for sure. Somebody had been watching the house.

I left the study and climbed the stairs to the bedrooms. I checked all four.

The last room I went into had been Tolya's when he was a boy. I sat on the lumpy bed with the sagging springs. I looked at the pictures on the wall, pictures of rock bands Tolya had played with and bands he had loved.

I went to the window and pulled up the shade, then pulled it down again. I looked in the closet. I could smell him here. I knew he had been here recently, but where was he? What had happened?

I lay on the bed and stared at the ceiling.

I got on my hands and knees, and looked under the bed.

I lay flat on the floor now, and stretched myself so I could reach all the way under the bed where I saw something yellow on the floor. I reached out and grabbed it, and sat up and leaned against the wall.

It was a huge yellow silk sock, dust balls hanging off it. It was one of Tolya's socks. It was dusty, but it looked new. It smelled of some fancy talc Tolya used. There were still grains of the powder on the sock.

I knew now Tolya had left the house in a hurry, leaving the cereal and the socks. Nothing to tell me where he had gone, no clues. All I had was the sock, and, in the closet, a shoebox that had contained sneakers. I looked inside.

My God, I thought. He left without this. He left in a hurry, or maybe he left it for me.

"Molly?"

"Yes?"

"I found this stuff in Tolya's old room."

On the table I placed a couple of boxes of Staticmaster brushes, the kind I'd seen in Valentina's darkroom. "Read this," I said, pushing over the instructions I found in the box of brushes.

"What is it?"

"I think Tolya left this. I think he left it as a message, I think he was trying to tell us something. I saw these brushes in Val's darkroom in New York. There were always a lot of them. I know that Grisha bought some from a guy in Brooklyn, too," I said.

From outside came the distant sound of a car.

"What's that?" said Molly.

"Read this thing with the brushes," I said.

"Give me a minute," said Molly, picking up the piece of paper, looking at the instructions, hands shaking. "I used to see these at Val's place," she said. "She used them for cleaning her negatives. She wouldn't use a regular camera, only that fucking antique Leica that supposedly Bertolt Brecht gave our grandfather if you can believe it. I'm such a philistine I wasn't sure who this Brecht guy was. Literature wasn't my thing. Val was very finicky about her photos, I'd say, Jesus, Val, why don't you just use like a make-up brush, I'll get you some, and she'd throw me out. I don't get what you're saying, Artie."

"How did she die?"

"Somebody smothered her. Put a pillow over her face."

"Go on."

"I thought about that. She was strong as an ox, right? So it was somebody she knew. She wasn't letting just any creep into her place, right? But there was something else. My dad was rambling one time, when I saw him in New York, something about her being killed twice, something I figured for crazy because he was out of his brain. He was right. He kept talking about this guy, Livitsky, or someone that died in London. I thought he was paranoid."

"Litvinenko. What if he was right?"

"The autopsy didn't show anything," she said. "It would have shown. Shit."

"What?"

"It would only show if you knew what you were looking for."

"I think that's what Tolya said, or maybe the poison hadn't started working."

"I think my dad was just out of his mind about Val," she said. "Even if they knew to look for Polonium, it's very febrile stuff." She crushed out her cigarette in an ashtray and put the butt in her cut-off jeans pocket.

"Molly?"

"What?"

"There were wrappers from Antistatic brushes on the floor of her bedroom when I found her there," I said.

"Christ, she once told me Grisha was so nice about her photographs, always offering to help. My God, he did it Artie. He would have known how, or could have found out. You think that could be it? He did that to her, and then felt bad?"

"Tolya said something like that."

Molly re-read the instructions on the box of brushes. "You would really need to know how to get them bulk," she said. "You would need to grind this shit up and make sure she ingested it. You'd have to know where the Polonium was coming from to be sure it was still potent."

"Grisha had connections," I said. "Is your Dad sick?"

"I don't know. He keeps that stuff to himself, why?"

"I saw him in London, he looked bad."

"You think?" She gestured to the box of brushes. "Is that a car? Outside?"

"We need to go. Now."

CHAPTER FIFTY-FOUR

The car was coming closer. We were still sitting in the kitchen. I still had Tolya's sock in my hand along with the box of lens brushes.

I got up and looked out the window. I could barely see the car, its lights out. Somebody was coming. Somebody who didn't want to make a lot of noise, and I thought: it's Tolya. It has to be. Who else could it be at this time of night, the weird purple sky heavy with rain, the humidity rising from the grass and coming down from the sky, so my skin was slick with sweat.

I blew out the candle.

"What's happening, Artie?"

"Somebody just drove up to the gate."

She rubbed her eyes. "You think it's my dad?"

"I don't know. Why don't we go out of the back door, and through the back gate just in case it's not him. How far is it to your mother's place?"

"A mile, not far."

"We can walk. I don't want you riding your bike at night, there's too many crazy drunk drivers out there. Stay on the side of the road."

"Who do you think it is?" she said, taking the box of brushes from me and shoving them into the bag.

I thought about the man in the seersucker jacket. I thought

about Grisha, or maybe it was just Ed, the Georgian taxi driver. Maybe Ed, the good Georgian, had come for me.

"It might be the taxi driver," I said.

I had to take care of Molly. I had promised Tolya I'd look after Val, and I didn't and he never blamed me. All that was left was her twin sister.

I pushed on the metal gate in back of the house, and it clattered with a rusty iron noise. We went through and stood together on the empty road that ran behind the Sverdloff dacha, and Molly pointed to the left. Her mother's place was down the road. And then she stopped dead still.

"What?"

"I left my bike out front. They'll see it."

"Leave it," I said. "We need to go."

"What if it's my dad?"

"We'll walk a little, and then we'll wait. Okay? You can go to your mother's place, I'll walk you most of the way and then and I'll go back and see who it is."

"I want to go, too."

"No," I said, "I can't do that. I can't let you. Just go back to New York, tell Bobo Leven. Take the brushes back to New York. First you go see my friend, Sonny Lippert. Right away, give him the brushes. Put them in something safe, wrap them up good, okay?"

She nodded.

"If you get stuck in Moscow, go see this guy, Viktor," I said.

She held out her arm. "Write it here, so I don't forget," said Molly, and I scribbled the numbers with her red pen.

"Come on, we have to go," I said, but she hesitated.

"Listen, I have to tell you something. In case I don't get another chance, or whatever."

"Of course."

"Val told me she liked you for real. She told me that if you weren't our dad's best friend, she would have . . . never mind."

"Thank you."

"She called me the day before she died, said she had spent the night with you. She sounded really happy.

"I'm glad you told me." I took her hand and we started down the road together, listening for the noise of a car, or footsteps.

I walked with Molly until we were within sight of her mother's dacha, and she kissed me on the cheek, and I watched her run up the path until she got to the front gate.

I watched her go, swinging her arms, looking like Valentina from behind, only turning to give a jaunty wave, before she disappeared behind the gate and the stands of white birch trees.

I turned around and walked back to Sverdloff's dacha. It took me fifteen minutes, maybe more. From the road, I could see a small light on the porch that might be somebody lighting a match.

CHAPTER FIFTY-FIVE

"Hello, Artie."

I saw him as soon as I got through the gate. He was sitting on the steps, smoking. I didn't turn away, there wasn't any point, I just kept going until I had climbed the same steps to the porch, and was sitting next to him. It wasn't a cigar in his mouth. It was a cigarette and he offered me one.

The man I'd seen all week in the seersucker jacket held his Zippo lighter up for me.

In the flame I could see his face a little better, a pleasant round face, short white hair, a snappy haircut, calm milk chocolate brown eyes, big ears which, if he'd grown up in the West, somebody would have fixed.

In that strange purple light, I could see he was older than I'd thought, maybe seventy-five. He wore a black polo shirt and khaki pants and loafers instead of the Timberlands I'd seen him in before.

"Where is he?" I said.

"Sverdloff, you mean? Your friend, Tolya?"

"Yes."

"I'm going to take you to him."

"You have a name?" I said, wondering if I could get my gun out of my pocket, and if I did what I would do with it.

"Bounine," he said. "Fyodor Samuelovich." His English was perfect. I figured him for some kind of creep, somebody who was in business with Sverdloff. Or maybe he was a cop. In this fucking country, they were the same thing.

He didn't talk after that, and he didn't threaten me, he just got up off the steps and brushed his pants.

"Are you coming with me?" he said, though I knew there wasn't any choice.

"I have to do something first," I said, thinking about Molly down the road with her grieving mother.

"Not right now," he said. "Have you got a weapon with you?"

"Why?"

"It would be better to leave it before we go."

"Where are we going?" I took the gun out of my pocket and placed it on the porch, then I picked it up, emptied it, and tossed it into the bushes. "Okay?"

He shrugged and I knew one of his guys—because he would have guys all around the house—would retrieve it.

"How did you find me?"

He smiled slightly. "It wasn't that hard," he said. "You stayed in a flat, I believe, where the caretaker was quite eager to make a little money. He said you disrespected the bones of the dead."

"God."

"I know. He called in at the local police station and was told the bones were from a butcher, and he then mentioned a foreigner staying in an empty flat."

"I see." I'd been an idiot to talk to Igor. I'd been stupid. Out of my head.

"Please get in the car with me? I'd be grateful," he said. His cigarette was still held between his thumb and forefinger the way my father always held them.

I got in. He turned the key. Turned the car around. He put a CD into the slot, and "Fontessa", the exquisite MJQ track, played.

"You like this music?" he said.

CHAPTER FIFTY-SIX

"I'm so happy to see you, Artyom, my friend, I'm happy." Tolya took my hand like it was a life raft.

In his pajamas and a bathrobe, he was propped up on a hospital bed. Oxygen tubes ran into his mouth. Machines around him monitored his vital signs. He breathed heavily, gasping a little.

It was the same clinic where I had been with Viktor Leven, the fancy medical facility. Viktor had heard right about it in the first place, but the staff had stonewalled us.

A light blanket lay across Tolya's legs, but his feet were bare.

"Get me those slippers, can you?" he said softly, and I kneeled down and found some slippers and put them on his feet. "I wish I could smoke," he said.

I sat on a straight chair close to the bed.

The room was large with two windows that looked out on to a courtyard. On the walls were prints, Monet's flowers. A half-open door led to a bathroom.

On one side of the hospital bed was an easy chair. In the corner farthest from Tolya sat a middle-aged nurse, glasses on her nose, looking at a TV with the sound off. She rose, asked if I'd like to be alone with Tolya, told me she would sit outside the room in case he needed anything. I thanked her.

"How are you?" I said because I couldn't think of anything else.

"Better because you're here, Artyom." He pushed himself up on the pillows.

What was it, a little more than a couple of weeks since he had asked me to take books to Olga Dimitriovna in Brooklyn? It felt like a lifetime.

"You have something to tell me, Artyom? You have that look." He tried to smile.

"Yes. It wasn't you. They didn't kill Valentina because of something you did, it wasn't you," I said, and he began to weep. "They murdered her because of what she was doing at the shelter in Moscow, because she talked about it, because she got in their faces and accused them of stealing money and using little girls."

"My God," he said, and put his head in his hands.

"It wasn't you."

He looked up at me, an expression of terminal sadness on his face.

"What difference does it make?" he said. "She's gone. And it was me, Artyom, it was me because I got close to evil, and it killed Val, and it killed poor Masha Panchuk, who also was somebody's daughter." He closed his eyes. I thought for a moment he was sleeping. Then he looked at me. "This is my prison, a very nice one, of course, but I can't leave."

"What?"

"They arrested me, asshole, tuft of mouse turd, my great dear friend."

"What for?"

"They came to my parents' house, in Nikolina Gora, and they brought me here. You realized I had been there? At the dacha?"

"Yes."

"How?"

"I could smell you. Listen, I know what happened. To Val, I know."

"You never liked the scent, you figured me for queer because

I like the perfume Lorenzo made me. I'd like to see Florence again."

"Shut up."

"How can I, when it's such a pleasure to have you here to torture this way?" said Tolya, joking around like he always did, though I could see it was an effort, the speaking was an effort, the simple act of it.

"What are they saying you did?"

"Sit closer to me, asshole," said Tolya. "Move your chair over." He looked at the ceiling.

"You think they're sharing our conversation?"

"Just like the old days," he said. "You remember? Were you ever arrested?"

"Only with my mother. In her refusenik period," I said. "Only then. You?"

"Yes, spooky KGB guys in bad raincoats said I was of interest, as they say, in my rock and roll period, when I was on stage with my Fender Stratocaster, which nobody had seen, which I had arranged to get by not exactly kosher means. But I told you all this a million times, asshole, all about how much fun we had back in the day, Artyom. They let me go after they scared the shit out of me for twenty-four hours. Back in the day, Artie," he said, switching to English. "It feels like a million years ago. How did I become like this?" he said. "How did I become an asshole of capitalism? I was a rock and roll hero. People wrote my name on walls, like Eric Clapton. 'Sverdloff is God', it said, or something like that, I don't know if we had God back then. 'Sverdloff is God'," he said again wistfully.

"Things changed," I said.

"I wanted to go to the West in a hot-air balloon, I wanted to sail over the Berlin Wall. Instead I went with a business-class ticket. Return."

"Talk to me, Tolya. What's going on here?" I pulled my chair close to where he sat, and he leaned down and I could feel his breath, could smell the sickness.

"A man in a nice jacket from Brooks Brothers brought me. Off the rack," he said, trying to smile. "The jacket. Old for the job."

"What is he?"

"He told you his name?"

"Yes."

"Fyodor Bounine. Fyodor Samuelovich Bounine. You get the joke, right? FSB, maybe he has these initials embroidered on his underpants. It's his real name, of course, but he thinks he's a wit. Very good English. Very good Chinese. And Arabic. And very pleasant to me. Asks me a lot about you."

"Nobody hurt you?"

"It's not like that. They arrested me on money-laundering charges, they say." He snorted, trying to laugh. "Then they add murder. It happens. They just take you away, nobody knows. You can't call, nothing."

"We can get you a lawyer."

"It doesn't work like that."

"I saw Molly," I said, not knowing if I should tell him.

He leaned forward. "Where? She's okay?"

"I saw her at the dacha. She's fine. She's with her mother. I told her to go back to New York, or Boston."

"I want her out of this fucking country. Get her out. Will you do this for me, Artyom? Please. Whatever it takes."

"I already started on that," I said. "I'll do anything."

"You don't owe me."

"You mean Billy," said Tolya. "We never spoke of this."

"Yes."

"You want to speak about it," said Tolya. "You want me to confess? You want to confess?" He laughed to diffuse it, and I didn't answer. "I did for you what a friend does," he says. "You couldn't let them put your nephew, Billy, back into an institution. You told me that day on Staten Island, near Fresh Kills, the garbage dump. You knew he had killed and you couldn't let him run away, or be free by himself. But you didn't want him locked up again. There wasn't any other way," he said. "It was okay. You think I'm somehow immoral, don't you Artemy?" he said softly without any anger. "You think because I am able to kill, I'm a killer."

"No."

"Sometimes you have to do what is right, even if it's not moral. Sometimes it's kinder. Revolutionaries never thought about that, they thought about their ideologies, they thought if only they had the right words, people would stop suffering. It's ideology that kills people."

It was this about Sverdloff I never came to terms with. I never understood how he operated in a world where he dealt with crooks and creeps and still remained himself. Remained a man full of life, happy with life, a guy who could eat and drink and laugh, who loved his kids and his friends.

Or had been. Had been that man before Valentina died. A guy who would do anything for me because we were friends. When he took Billy away a few years earlier, when he made a decision I couldn't make, it was everything. I should have kept Val safe for him.

Say it, I thought to myself. Killed Billy. Tolya killed Billy to save him. He did it for you.

"I wish I could see Molly one more time," said Tolya.

"What's the 'one more time' thing?" I said, jaunty as I could.

"I'm dying, Artyom."

The nurse came into the room, held out a little paper cup with some pills, Tolya took them and she offered him water. Tolya thanked her, and in a little while some color flowed back into his face.

"You're in pain?"

"It's not so bad."

"Is this the polonium?"

"No," he said.

"And Val?"

"There was never any polonium, Artie. The autopsy would have showed it. I let them believe this for a while because people paid attention. I had leverage with the press because of it, it was much more exciting for them. Everybody loves a story about crazy radioactive shit."

"What do you need?" I said.

"Everything is finished."

"Grisha Curtis killed Valentina."

"Yes."

"But not with polonium?"

"No," said Tolya. "I made him talk to me when I found him in the woods, in the grounds of his uncle's dacha. He made it look that way, he put the empty packages of Staticmaster around, so it would look as if somebody had poisoned her. But he just killed her, he stuffed a pillow over her face."

"Did he mention a girl in London, Elena Gagarin?"

"Yes, he beat her up. He was afraid she was talking to you, that somehow she knew something. She was a sad girl, she didn't know anything, but she liked to retail gossip."

I looked at him. "You said they added murder charges to your arrest."

"What do you think I did when I found this bastard who killed my Valentina?"

"I understand," I said.

"That's good."

"What is it, if it's not polonium?"

"My heart," he said.

After he caught his breath—it was unbearable to watch him try to speak—he said, "I asked them to let me see you."

"I'm happy."

"They said what do you want, and I said, I want to see my friend. Fyodor Samuelovich said fine, where is he, and I said I didn't know. But I knew you'd follow me to Moscow. And he said what is your friend's name, but I could see he already knew, and when I said it, when I said your name, he smiled. But he already somehow knew it was you."

"How?"

"Maybe they have people in New York, or London. I think maybe Fyodor Samuelovich, call me Sammy, no kidding, wants something from you. As soon as I said your name, I could see it. He's an old guy, but he gets it, he learned from the best, he's a hustler like the rest of us. He wants something from you," said Tolya for the second time. "Whatever it is, don't do it. Can you help me?" he added, trying to get out of bed and into the easy chair.

I put my arm under his. He leaned on me, and I could feel the weight and the fatigue and the sorrow. He sat down heavily.

"Tell me how to help you." I looked at the ceiling as he had done.

"What difference does it really make? They know everything. I always wondered why people made such a fuss about bugs, when they knew it all. They didn't hurt people to find out. They hurt them to make a point to other assholes, warn them, make sure they were afraid."

"Go on."

"You understand what I did? About this guy, this guy who killed Valentina? He was a monster. He killed her and he hired a thug who killed Masha Panchuk, but you knew that. The thug, this Terenti, saw Masha leave my club and thought it was Val, and he followed her to Brooklyn to the playground where you found her," said Tolya, speaking his mix of English and Russian. "You have any cigarettes?"

"Don't be ridiculous."

"Asshole, if I am dying, I want to die smoking. I wish I had some cigars," he said. "You know at first, I thought they arrested me because I told jokes."

"What?"

"I did what I wanted in London, New York, I did bad deals, when I was mad at officials in Moscow, I made jokes, I talked too much, I said what I wanted. I laughed at them."

"Of course."

"I'm glad I told them what I think of all of them. I'm glad," he said.

"You always tell great jokes," I said, putting my hand on his. "There must be something you want. Tell me what to get you, tell me how I can help?"

"They take good care of me here, Artyom, but I think there's a little catch."

"What is it?"

"I think at some point, they will move me from this lovely hospital to someplace not quite so nice, you understand, to a different sort of hospital. The Russians are quite good at this, stashing people away in hospitals far from Moscow. I want to get out, but not if it costs you too much. I'd like to see Molly," he said. "But I want you to remain this moral man I admire."

"What else?" I pulled my chair close to him, and leaned over to touch his arm.

"You understand what I had to do? But they can call it murder. Cases last a long, long time here. They can last your whole life. Listen, don't be so sad."

"I'll get you out," I said, thinking suddenly of Roy Pettus, who had asked me to do favors for him. Pettus would come in handy. Maybe Fiona Colquhoun, too. Maybe they would help.

"What would it take?" I asked again.

"I can't tell you, I don't know," said Tolya, closing his eyes. "They'll tell you. Bounine, he'll be waiting when we're finished here. I mean for you, Artyom. Not if it costs you too much," he said again. "Okay? Do not sell your soul to that devil, I'm not worth it anymore," he said, and closed his eyes.

By the time I got up to leave, Tolya was back in the bed, asleep. I looked at him, lying on his back, his big feet sticking out of the blanket, and I realized I had seen him like this before, in a dream, in a terrible nightmare where I couldn't save him.

I felt bereft. Here was the one person, the single human being I could always count on, who would show up when I needed him, who was a pain in the ass, but was there, big, solid as a mountain, on my side, available. My friend. It wasn't in my plan for him to disappear, to die, to simply not be there. Somewhere deep down I had expected us to get old together. That wouldn't happen. He needed a new heart. I couldn't give it to him.

CHAPTER FIFTY-SEVEN

"Coffee?" said Bounine when we reached his office in Moscow.

We didn't speak much on the short ride from the clinic, but now he chatted, made polite small talk while I sat down across from his desk. A secretary brought coffee and a tray of snacks.

Bounine told me he had spent time at the UN in New York, and he had also lived in London. He sipped some coffee and, as if it were a casual thing, assured me that Sverdloff would be well treated.

"When are you letting Tolya out?"

"Please," he said, gesturing at the snacks on the table, cake, and cheese and cold meats.

"I'm not hungry," I said, wanting to punch him. I tried to stay cool. I tried not to think about Tolya in the hospital bed.

"I'm sorry we had to pick you up at the Sverdloff dacha like that. I really should have phoned you instead." He handed me an envelope. Inside was a video.

"What is it?"

"Marina Fetushova said she would send this to you."

"You know her?"

"Everybody knows everybody here," he said.

"You've looked at it?"

"Yes. It's just a few low-level officers, all retired now, and some girls, not very nice to watch, but the girls are all over eighteen, we've checked. It's not important, not anymore."

"And Grisha Curtis? He's in it?"

"Sadly, yes. But he's dead, so it doesn't matter either. You can keep it if you'd like."

I took the package.

"But you were following me, weren't you, you followed me all over Moscow, right? How did you spot me?"

"We like to know where our visitors are," he said.

"You knew I was here almost as soon as I arrived."

"Yes."

"How?"

He laughed. "It was accidental. It was my granddaughter."

"What?"

"Would you like a drink?"

"Sure."

He got up and went to a table on the other side of his office. He picked up a bottle of Black Label, held it up and I nodded. He poured some in two glasses.

"There's no ice, I'm sorry."

"You already knew I drink Scotch?"

"You're a New York cop. I assumed you might like Scotch. How I miss it."

"The Scotch?"

"The city."

"Yeah, well, let's move on to the subject, I'm not here for nostalgia, am I?"

"My granddaughter's friend met you on a bus from the airport. I took the girls to the ballet the next night, and young Kim was excited about her trip and the nice American she had met on the bus, and she showed me your picture, the one she took with her cellphone. It was just chance. I saw you, I recognized you."

"Christ. You breed them young."

He laughed. "It wasn't like that. You were from New York.

I had told my granddaughter and her best friend so many stories about New York."

"You have stuff on me? Why? Because I left this miserable country when I was sixteen? Because my mother didn't like losing her job because she was a Jew? It was in another century."

"We don't have stuff on you, Mr Cohen," he said, using my American name. "All we knew was that you didn't register at a hotel, but it was your picture on Kim's phone. After that, I had a few colleagues ask around. And there was the crazy caretaker, Igor, of course. Otherwise, you'd be hard to find in this huge city."

I drank the Scotch in two gulps, he offered more, I refused. "What are you going to do with Sverdloff?" I looked at the door, an old padded green leather door, the kind the apparatchiks used to have. On the desk was a red plastic phone. My father had a red phone.

"You're looking at my old phone," he said, smiling. "I keep it as a souvenir."

"I see you keep Putin's picture on the wall, is it a souvenir?"

Putin's chilly face looked down from over the table with the Scotch. Beside it was a picture of Medvedev, the new president who was only Putin's puppet. Also very short. You saw him on TV, he looked like a dwarf.

"Yes, but Mr Putin does more good than not," Bounine said. "People feel safe and they have food to eat."

"I want my friend out of that place," I said. "I want him out, and I'll do what it takes. State department. Anything. He's a US citizen."

"He isn't, in fact," said Bounine. "He has a Russian passport. He has a UK passport. Nothing from the US. Maybe the Brits will help you. Or maybe there is somebody in the US."

"Thanks."

"I think you're friendly with Agent Roy Pettus, isn't that right? I met him a couple of times when there was quite a lot of Russian-American friendship after 9/11, when we did some work together. Look, Artie, I could help you, if you like," he said. He leaned back and stretched out his legs to look at his dark brown loafers.

"I've been wearing these for almost forty years," he said. "I got my first pair of Bass Weejun penny loafers at B. Altmans on 34th Street. I thought it was so stylish, this putting of a shining penny in your shoes. So American."

I was missing something, and I said, "So you see this picture in your granddaughter's friend's phone, how come you were so interested in it, how come you recognized me, how the fuck did you know who I was?"

"I knew your father," he said. "He was my boss."

Usually I figured life was mostly random. Unless you were religious and believed in some kind of cosmic pixies, it was random. On the job, you sometimes got lucky, you tripped over something useful, there was an accident; mostly you solved a case this way.

Bounine's story about the little girl's phone was the kind of thing that happened. It happened. When he mentioned my father, though, something in me resisted. I tried not to believe him. Not at first.

"It's true," he said softly. "I worked for Maksim Stepanovich for several years in New York City. I was a kid. I was just out of language school, my first year in the KGB," he said. "I was twenty-four and I got lucky. I had good connections. It's true. Later, in Moscow, we continued to work together, though he was promoted faster then me. He was a brilliant agent, Artemy. I remember your mother, too. She wasn't in New York. But I met her here in Moscow. She loved France. Isn't that right?"

I fumbled in my pocket for some cigarettes. Bounine threw me a pack, and I lit one, and sucked in the smoke like a drug.

"And you saw me on the street."

"Yes. I saw you in the phone, and I thought, my God it's Max, my old friend, but he's been dead so long. I ran a few things through the system and I discovered you were calling yourself Max Fielding. It seemed to connect. Max, you see, you used your father's name."

I had never thought about it when I picked the name out of the blue, never once thought about the fact that it had been my father's name. He had been Maksim. Max to his friends. To me he was my father. My dad. The only good thing about this miserable country where I grew up, my father, and my mother, of course. But most of all, him.

"What system?" I said.

"Ours. Yours, too. Why not? We throw bombast at one another, but we're allies, more or less, your Mr Bush was just here with Mr Putin in Sochi, and from the time he invited his good friend Vladimir at the Texas ranch, we began setting up systems to share certain things."

"So you shared me? Pettus shared me with you?"

"It's never that simple."

"I want Sverdloff out."

"I understand."

For a few minutes, Bounine sat, silent, sipping his whisky, as if weighing his thoughts.

The photograph showed my father and Bounine, both very young, both in hipster suits and narrow ties. My father's arm was around Bounine's shoulder and they were standing near the arch in Washington Square Park. In the corner of the photograph, my father had written his name and a fond message to his friend, Sam. July, 1962.

"Jesus."

"Yup. We were Max and Sam in New York," he said. "And when I discovered that you were Sverdloff's friend, I thought to myself, Artemy will want to help his friend. And I will help him because his father helped me. I have something else for you," he said, and removed a large envelope from his desk. "Will you have dinner with me? I don't want to talk about any of this here."

I nodded.

"Good. We'll make a plan, you and me. We'll make a plan to get your friend out."

CHAPTER FIFTY-EIGHT

GUM, the great department store on Red Square, was outlined in little white lights. It glittered like Christmas on the soft summer night.

The manager of the small Italian restaurant just to the left of the entrance to GUM appeared as soon as we arrived. He smiled and shook Bounine's hand, and mine, and showed us to a table on the terrace just outside. All Red Square was spread out in front of us, St Basil's, the Kremlin, GUM, with its lights. Bounine ordered a bottle of red wine. I asked for Scotch.

"It's fine, nobody will bother us here," said Bounine. "It's mostly tourists. You seem edgy. I'm not going to arrest you or put some idiotic muscle on you, you don't believe these myths about us anymore. Do you? The FSB is different. We don't do those things. We did, once, of course, the KGB had idiots just like the CIA. Well, slightly better educated idiots, but we're a different country."

"Yeah?"

"It's true." He sipped the wine. "Let's order. The rabbit lasagna is delicious."

I ordered steak. He ordered the pasta. I wasn't hungry.

"What do you care about in this new kind of country, as you call it?" I said.

"We care about our own. We value our people. We encourage

people to keep in touch, to act like a family. In our business we often go on vacations together, quite a lot of us have married into each other's families. We respect the children of the great agents who taught us. Like you."

I kept my mouth shut. I was too wrecked to eat much. I lit a cigarette. I didn't want him to see my hands shake. I had been up against killers and creeps, jerks who beat me up, people who murdered children. This was worse. I wanted Tolya out of the rathole he was in. I'd do anything. Just ask, I thought. Just tell me what it is.

"It's okay, Artie, I like that name, I remember your dad saying he was going to call your Artemy and would make your Western name Artie because he adored the way Artie Shaw played clarinet."

"So?" I tried for nonchalance.

"Is your dish okay?" he said, as if it were a social occasion.

"I'm not hungry."

"Would you like another drink?"

"Sure."

Bounine ordered it for me.

"We didn't poison Valentina Sverdloff. Nobody poisoned her, but I think you already know that," said Bounine. "We don't do that kind of thing anymore. Not for decades," he chortled slightly. "Did you know your dad and I were young guys together in New York City, in the early 1960s? Yes, I told you, I'm sorry, I repeat myself a bit. We loved it, but he loved it most because of the music. Did you know?"

"And Sverdloff? The polonium?"

"My dear boy, of course not," he said, sounding surprised. "Oh, no, it's become an explosive urban myth, ever since poor Litvinenko died, but that was a single terrible event. Some idiot had the idea of using polonium-210 on the assumption nobody would trace it. It was, thank God, a one-time blunder." He smiled and when he smiled it lit up his face and made it charming, like a TV anchor, all sincere intelligence and warmth, and all invented for the moment.

"So you understand, we had nothing to do with Miss Sverdloff. I promise you," Bounine added.

I drank.

"Unfortunately the young man she married turned out to be a bad egg, as we used to say. He found out he had married a passionate young woman, who spoke her mind, perhaps too much, and he didn't agree with her, and I think, personally, he went off the rails."

"Or one of your creeps told Grisha Curtis to kill her. Or he was yours, this Curtis creep."

"You could be right. Grigory Curtis was eager to help us, perhaps too eager. I don't like zealots. There are, in any system, always one or two loose cannons," said Bounine, who had a taste in English for clichés.

"But not you."

"No."

"What about Larry Sverdloff?"

"He's one of those Russians who live in London and think they can make another revolution, it's almost touching, that they think they can overthrow Putin, using their money to back various dissident groups. It reminds me of the days when Lenin and Trotsky and the rest of them sat around Europe plotting. It won't come to anything."

"What's wrong with Tolya Sverdloff?"

"Didn't he tell you?"

"Yes, but I want you to tell me."

"Sverdloff, of course, has heart disease. He had it when this all began. Didn't you know that in New York? Our doctors say he's been ill for quite some time."

Did I know? Had I seen something in Sverdloff's face that night in New York on the roof at his club?

"I'll give you the number of his doctors in New York, or in

London," Bounine added. "He may need a transplant. We can help. Perhaps it would be good for him to have a strong Russian heart?"

"Why would I believe you?"

"Why would you? For Sverdloff's sake." He put down his knife and fork and picked up his wine glass and glanced at the crowd in the square. "Things are much better now. People live well, they travel, they read books they like to read, listen to rock music, of course. I saw Paul McCartney play Red Square. Can you imagine? Of course, things are better."

"I want him out now. Tolya Sverdloff. I want him to come home with me, to New York."

"I understand. And we take care of our family, Artie. We like doing business with people we know. So many of our recruits can trace their lineage all the way back. You're our family."

"You think the FSB or the fucking KGB is some kind of aristocracy? You think the pricks who do your work have lineage?" I was sorry I said it. I was sorry in case in made it worse for Tolya. I bit my lip. I drank the Scotch.

"You are more like your mother," he said. "Dessert?"

"Tell me how I can get Sverdloff out of here?"

"I have an idea," said Bounine. "How lovely it is tonight," he added.

It was a soft beautiful summer night. The red star on the Kremlin glittered. All around Red Square, ice-cream sellers fixed cones for tourists. A soldier leaned casually against the red granite of Lenin's tomb and shared a joke with some tourists while a little boy had his picture taken against the mausoleum.

Bounine followed my gaze.

"You see things do change for the better," he said. "I'm going to have an armagnac, perhaps a really nice one. Will you join me?" He gave a little shrug. "I hope all this lasts," he added.

"All what?"

"All the good things we have now. Who knows? In a year, two years from now it might all disappear, the whole enterprise might just go bust," he said. "Maybe capitalism wasn't such a good idea, after all," he added, chuckling. "If the economy goes belly up, well, let's hope for the best, shall we?"

Did he order the armagnac at the cafe overlooking Red Square because it was Sverdloff's drink? Bounine reached into his brief-case, and said, "I nearly forgot."

He pulled out the envelope he had taken fom his office and opened it. Inside was an old-fashioned black and white school notebook. Bounine opened it at random. It was covered with my father's elegant handwriting. Bounine offered it to me.

"Your father's diary from his years in America," he said. "When you left Moscow, he was asked to leave his notes behind, of course, but I kept it. 'One day' I said to myself, 'I'll give this to Max's son.' To you. I saved it for you." He handed it to me.

"What do you want from me in return for the notebook? What's the price?"

He shook his head.

"It's for you. I've kept it too many years. It's yours, Artemy, it belongs to you. I was so sorry when I heard your father had died in Israel. I wanted to write, I wanted to send you the diary. I couldn't, but I mourned for him."

"It was a long time ago."

"He was a brilliant agent, he could listen all day and all night. He could get people to tell him anything, usually in the easiest way. But he was also a patriot. He did what he had to do," said Bounine. "I envied him. I could see that, even when I was a young man. He could have gone all the way. To the top, I mean."

"Except for my mother."

"Except that."

I got up and walked a few yards into the square and away from Bounine. All my life I had kept my father as I had remembered him. I kept the handsome blue-eyed young man who brought me candy and took me fishing and introduced me to jazz and told me, secretly, quietly, about New York City as if it were a paradise just over the horizon.

In those days, we imagined the KGB was a force for good, part of the future of the wonderful socialist state that had sent a man into space first. And even after that, even after I knew it was all lies, I kept my father as I remembered him, the one good thing about this miserable country where I grew up.

In some way I'd built everything on the notion that he was a good man. But Bounine had made me listen to the other truth. "He was a brilliant agent, he could get people to tell him anything. He did what he had to do." I knew what it meant. Under my feet as I walked back to the table, I felt the cracks between the bricks. The ground seemed uneven.

"What do you want from me?" I said to Bounine. "For Tolya Sverdloff. What do you want?"

"I just thought it would be nice to keep the family contact with you, and I could drop in on you when I'm in New York," said Bounine. "Nothing much. Sometimes we just need someone who can talk to people in their own language. I don't mean English, of course, I mean their own lingo, idiom, on their own terms."

Don't sell your soul to that devil, Tolya had said. Don't do that.

"And for that you'll let Tolya out? You'll let me take him home?"

He nodded.

"And these things you want help with?"

"There are always people we like knowing about, here and there, in New York, possibly next week or next year," Bounine said, drinking his armagnac slowly.

I knew what Bounine wanted. He wanted me for an errand

boy when he needed one. He wanted a line to me when he needed it. He wanted me to join the family business.

"You want to know how ill Sverdloff is?"

"I can see."

"He's tough, you know. He could be treated. I talked to the doctors. He could have some time left."

"What about his businesses?"

"I don't know about business, Artie, I never became a good capitalist."

"Bullshit."

"He could have time left. He might get well. His businesses are, well, how shall I say it? His own business." He smiled at the small joke.

"You're all bastards," I said, and finished my Scotch, watching him light up a cigar. It was one of Sverdloff's Cuban brands. The smoke swirled up around us.

"You really look like your dad," he said. "So what do you think? Do we have a deal?"

I didn't want to think. I wanted to go home to my other life. But my other life included Tolya who had done something nobody else would have done for me. I owed him.

From the restaurant's sound system, a lilting Brazilian tune played, something by Joao Gilberto. I looked across Red Square, the last streak of light in the sky above the red star, above St Basil's and the Kremlin.

And then I saw the horse. A girl rode the animal bareback, pressing her heels against its side, leaning forward to cling to its neck, stroking its mane, galloping across the square, laughing, hair streaming out behind her, skirt billowing in the evening breeze, as she headed for Resurrection Gate. And people looking began to laugh and cheer and blow her kisses. Somebody started an old Russian song and the others joined in. Even a couple of cops laughed before they chased her away.

Smiling, Bounine tossed his American Express card on the table, to pay for dinner, and the drinks. It was a Platinum card. And it was as if the gesture, the tossing it on the table, included me as if he could charge me on his Amex card.

It occurred to me in the pleasant cafe, surrounded by civilized people, savoring good wine, enjoying dinner, laughing merrily at the girl on the horse, that maybe this was how they did it now, maybe now everything was only about money, even spooks charged their thugs and hands-for-hire to American Express.

Bounine followed my gaze. "You're not imagining it," he said kindly. "It really is a horse. You see that at night in Moscow."

I put my coffee cup down.

He took a little sip of the armagnac, held it to the light with satisfaction and said softly, "You'll help us, then, won't you, Artie?"